Orders flashed through the multiple layers of the Charon city, radiating from the vast, central tower to thousands upon thousands of processing vats throughout the labyrinth. Within seconds, openings had appeared throughout the city and sleek black shapes began rising into Charon's eternal night. They hovered in the sky, eclipsing stars, their ebony surfaces drinking the feeble light of the sun, as other shapes joined them . . . and more . . . and more. The city's vats were growing them by the thousands, transforming the very rock and ice of Charon into the prime operational cluster.

Slowly and in utter silence, one of the great black shapes hanging in Charon's sky began to move. Another followed . . . then, seconds later, a third . . . and a fourth. Within moments the entire armada was on the move, locking onto the faint strands of magnetic force emanating from the distant Sun and drifting into space. Once clear of Charon, the armada began to accelerate, traveling sunward, toward the home of Buck Rogers, faster and faster, until it crowded the speed of light. . . .

ARRIVAL

THE MARTIAN WARS TRILOGY

THE INNER PLANETS TRILOGY

INVADERS OF CHARON

THE 25TH CENTURY

Invaders of Charon, Book Three

WARLORDS OF JUPITER

William H. Keith, Jr.

TSR Inc.

WARLORDS OF JUPITER

First Printing: February 1993
Printed in the United States of America
Library of Congress Catalog Card Number: 92-61082

9 8 7 6 5 4 3 2 1

ISBN: 1-56076-576-3

TSR, Inc.
P.O. Box 756
Lake Geneva, WI
53147
U.S.A.

TSR Ltd.
120 Church End
Cherry Hinton
Cambridge CB1 3LB
United Kingdom

For Heather

SOLAR SYSTEM

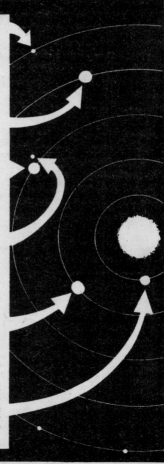

The Asteroid Belt

A scattered anarchy of tumbling planetoids and rough rock miners, where every sentient has the right to vote, and the majority rules among five hundred miniature worlds.

Mars

A terraformed paradise, Mars was reborn through the most sophisticated technology. Yet, the ruthless Martian corporate state of RAM spreads its evil tentacles throughout human space from this paradise.

Earth

A twisted wreckage despoiled by interplanetary looters, Earth is a declining civilization. Its people are divided and trapped in urban sprawls and mutant-infested reservations.

Luna

An iron-willed confederation of isolationist states, the highly advanced Lunars are the bankers of the Solar System, "peaceful" merchants willing to knock invading ships from the skies with mighty massdriver weapons.

Venus

A partially terraformed hellworld, where only the highest peaks can support human life. As the Uplanders build their great ceramic towers, the nomads of the vast, baloonlike Aerostates cruise the acidic skies. Far below, in the steaming swamps of the lowlands, reptilian hu.manoids struggle to make the world to their liking.

Mercury

Home to an underground civilization of miners, its surface is paved with huge solar collectors, massive mobile cities, and gaping strip mines. Far overhead, the mighty orbital palaces of the energy-rick Sun Kings spin in silent majesty.

PROLOGUE

It was lonely here in the deeps of the Outer System, fourteen hundred million miles from the terraformed life and warmth of Mars. Saturn was a golden star against the frosted glory of the Milky Way, the worlds of the Inner System sparks set to either side of a wan and shrunken sun. Capt. Grigor Kleist was a long way from home.

He hated it, the emptiness, the isolation that had cocooned the RAM light cruiser *Sharonov* and the twenty men and women aboard for the three months they'd been searching this sector half a billion miles beyond Saturn's orbit. With a suppressed shudder, Kleist turned from the observation blister and floated himself across the ship's bridge to the holographic display. The 3-D graphics describing the sphere of space through which *Sharonov* drifted reduced the emptiness to something he could grasp, a measurable quantity he could dismiss as a part of his duty to RAM.

Best of all, it confirmed for him that *Sharonov* was not entirely alone in the star-illuminated void.

"Let's have the breakdown," he snapped. He could have called up the figures on the display, but at the moment he needed to feel a part of the human activity on the bridge. "How's it read?"

"Ice and frozen rock, Captain," the sensor officer

reported. She looked up from her board and met his eye. "And not much of that. Range now 180 thousand."

Lieutenant DuBois was a tall, attractive woman, a long-legged farm girl from the Chryse Steppes of Mars. Absently, Kleist wondered if she felt the loneliness out here the way he did. It might be worthwhile to find out, he mused, despite the breach in discipline that might entail.

"I want a detailed spectroscopy," he said, pushing thoughts of warmth and companionship aside for later. "Weapons, arm the pulse laser."

"Aye, sir," *Sharonov*'s weapons officer said. "Powering up now."

Kleist glanced at the forward screen, where a slate-gray sphere pocked with craters turned slowly, the irregularities in its surface casting black and shifting shadows. A red cross hair appeared on the screen, centered on the object. A low-powered laser burst would vaporize enough of the crust for a spectrographic analysis.

The thing was called Chiron, and it had been a mystery since its discovery in 1977. With a diameter of just over a hundred miles and a crust of ice and rock enclosing an icy core, it ranged across the gulf between Saturn and Uranus, neither planet nor comet. Most astronomers lumped Chiron with a growing family of oddball objects—ice asteroids, noneccentric comets, and the like—occupying the outer reaches of the Solar System.

Scanning a short text entry in *Sharonov*'s computer, Kleist noted that men had touched down on Chiron once—during the Russo-American-Japanese expedition of 2090—but that the ice-bound little worldlet was too distant and too metal poor to warrant either colonization or commercial exploitation. It certainly held no interest for Kleist. The only reason he was here at all was the chance that another RAM ship, the *Delta Crucis*, had visited Chiron eight years earlier.

That meant it was at least remotely possible that the Device had been found there.

Kleist knew nothing about the Device save the inevitable rumors—that it was an alien artifact of unknown powers picked up by the *Crucis* shortly before that ill-fated ship had been lost. He had a description of the thing, of course: a silver, metallic sphere eighteen inches in diameter, though it reportedly could change form as though made of some material at once solid and liquid. According to the *Delta Crucis*'s final radio transmission, the three-man RAM scout had found the Device adrift in space less than two million miles from Chiron.

In the depths of so much emptiness, the proximity of the two could not possibly be coincidence. *Sharonov* had been ordered to investigate Chiron on the theory that where one Device had been discovered, another might be found as well.

"Fire."

Two seconds later, a pinpoint of light winked briefly against black shadow. "Analysis coming through, Captain," DuBois announced. "Carbonaceous chondritic material . . . water . . . ammonia . . ." She stopped, her brow wrinkling in puzzlement as she studied the data coming up on her computer screen.

"What is it?"

"Sir . . . I'm not sure. We're picking up traces of pure metals. Titanium. Cadmium. And metallic alloys that—" She shook her head. "I've never seen anything like this. Neither has the computer. All it'll tell me is 'unidentified.'"

Kleist frowned. "Debris left by the 2090 expedition," he said. "We hit a garbage dump."

"We'd be able to identify the metals. This doesn't look man-made."

Kleist felt his pulse quickening. Not man-made! Perhaps what they were looking for was on Chiron's icy surface. . . .

A warning claxon added its harsh, repetitive bray to the sudden commotion on the bridge. "Captain!" the ship's tactical officer called from his station. "Threat warning! Multiple objects, incoming, range five-zero-thousand, bearing—"

"I see them!" The 3-D display showed a dozen traces

sweeping out from Chiron with *Sharonov* as their target. "Battle stations! Helm! Evasive maneuvering! Weapons! Antimissile defenses on automatic! Launch countermeasures!"

The weapons officer looked up from his console. "Sir, I don't think they're missiles. They're—"

Something struck the *Sharonov* with a deep-throated clang that reverberated through the hull . . . and then the ship was ringing with multiple impacts too quick to count.

"Alert, alert," the ship's computer announced in precise and unhurried tones. "Hull integrity has been breached. Alert—"

Kleist heard the *hiss-thump* of pressure doors automatically sealing off the bridge, the sudden babble of voices over the intercom as crewmen throughout the ship reported pressure loss, power failure, malfunction. . . .

The tactical officer screamed, pointing toward the starboard bulkhead. *Something* was eating through, dissolving steel and plastic in a circular patch six inches wide. The bright silver patch was ballooning inward, growing to a shimmering sphere two feet across before it broke free from the bulkhead and floated into the bridge.

As he groped for the M-50 laser holstered at his hip, one part of Kleist's mind noted with fascination that the . . . the *thing* had sealed the breach in the hull behind it, leaving some of its quicksilver self behind as a kind of plug. Another silver balloon was growing from the port bulkhead, and a third from the overhead. He aimed his pistol at the first globe, hesitating because its mirrored surface was certain to reflect any laser energy; the ricochet could kill his own bridge crew.

The silver globe was changing shape, unfolding like some incredibly complicated metallic origami construct. Silver tentacles whiplashed through the air. Cables as thick as his little finger encircled his wrists and arms and legs. The laser was snatched from his hand and *eaten*—he saw it dissolve in the monster's grip—and then metallic threads were tearing at his clothes as thicker strands dragged his limbs apart, spread-eagling him. He heard DuBois shriek in terror and helpless fury and knew the rest of the bridge crew was getting the same treatment.

More of the silver invaders had broken in. They were everywhere, some huge and complex and menacing, some small and quick. As he was held, pinioned by a dozen tentacles, a silver sphere the size of a soccer ball touched the bare skin of his chest.

Kleist's numbed shock, his astonishment at the suddenness of the attack, melted into a searing black terror as the alien sphere began shrinking, dwindling away to nothing six inches from his horrified eyes. He could feel the thing oozing through his skin and into his chest, the sensation at once ice and fire and an indescribable, white-hot pain spreading to his gut and arms and head. He screamed then, his tortured voice blending in a shrill chorus of agony with the rest of his bridge crew. Pain blazed like an exploding sun, searing nerves raw, devouring them.

Then the thing flowed into his brain, and he drowned in a merciful blackness.

CHAPTER ONE

A liner, the *Golden Argosy*, Ceres registry, fell
toward the king of worlds. From 112 thousand
miles out, Jupiter was a titanic, color-banded
sphere spanning better than forty degrees of sky. The
Jovian rings, not as majestic as Saturn's, were thread-
thin scratches of light ruled against the night to each
side of the planet's disk. The rust-colored oval of the
Great Red Spot, a centuries-old hurricane wide enough
to engulf the Earth, glared out at the approaching ship
like a baleful eye.

Maj. Vince Pirelli stood in the *Argosy*'s small and
sparsely furnished passenger lounge staring at the planetary disk now filling most of the forward viewscreen.
Orange, brown, and ivory swirls streaked the gargan-
tuan world ahead, flooding the lounge with red-golden
light. During twenty-one years of service with the New
Earth Organization's military arm, he'd been in Jupiter
space perhaps a dozen times.

The beauty, the sheer glory of the sight, never ceased
to move him.

Golden Argosy had already passed the major Jovian
satellites—cratered Callisto, icy Ganymede and Europa,
and the sulphur hell of volcanic Io. Balanced on the star-
hot plasma storm of its drive flare as it decelerated at
one G, the ship was dropping tail-first now toward the

tiny moon called Amalthea. The image on the lounge viewscreen was being relayed by a camera mounted on one of *Argosy*'s aft fins.

"I can never quite get over how big Jupiter is," he remarked to the slim, dark-haired woman at his side. Like Vince, she wore civilian clothing, a stylishly practical smartsuit coverall.

Like Vince, too, she was a member of NEO Intelligence, though she held no military rank. "It's too big," Jovanna Trask said. "The mind just can't grasp the scale."

"Big enough to swallow thirteen hundred Earths," Vince agreed. "I wonder what it's like, living there." He nodded toward a dark, tiny lump of rock silhouetted against the sweeping, cloud-banded grandeur. "In Amalthea."

Jovanna laughed, a little nervously, Vince thought. "Maybe they stay underground and never come up to look," she said. "Otherwise they'd never get any work done."

"That sounds like a perfectly idyllic existence," a childlike voice said behind them. Vince turned and saw a small, silken-furred creature entering the lounge.

"Hello, Galen," Jovanna said. "We're almost there."

"So I see." Less than four feet tall, Galen was a Tinker, a member of a genetically engineered species that preferred small, enclosed spaces and was perfectly at home in the labyrinthine warrens of underground Lunar cities or planetoid colonies. The little gennie blinked at Vince with eyes remarkably human in a face betraying his mostly simian ancestry. "You realize, of course, that your body hasn't had time enough to acclimate. Speaking professionally, I still think this is a bad idea."

"Actually, Doc," Vince said, "so do I. But it's not like we have a choice."

Galen was an anomaly among Tinkers, a gennie species originally designed as engineers and technicians. He possessed the Tinker's innate cleverness with tools and things mechanical, but somehow he'd found his niche studying the engineering marvels of the human body.

Galen—as with many Tinkers, his self-chosen public name reflected the area of his expertise—was a medical technician, and a good one. For the past month he'd been supervising Vince's preparations for a stay in high G.

Jovanna looked questioningly at Galen, touching her ear with one slim forefinger.

"The lounge is safe," Galen said in reply to her silent question. He slipped a small, electronic device from one of the pouches attached to his body harness and showed it to her. "I scanned it before I came in. No listening devices, and the intercom is off."

"Good," Jovanna said. "Maybe we'll find what we're looking for in Amalthea," she offered, turning to Vince. "It's been six weeks, after all. Dr. Kowalski is probably back at Solar Geographic by now, assuming she really left in the first place."

"Maybe," Vince conceded. "But I wouldn't count on it." He sighed. "And until we know for sure, it's gravitol and daily spins in the carousel for Kaiten and me, just in case."

Dr. Marlene Kowalski was quite a popular person just now, Vince mused. A senior research biologist at the Solar Geographic research lab in Amalthea, she was the person first approached by Ciudestreyan traders six weeks earlier, the very first scientist to actually see the enigma that NEO called the Artifact, and RAM called Far Star and the Device.

The Ciudestreyan Nomads, deep-space traders occupying a strange, gene-engineered tree-city in cometary orbit around the Sun, had reportedly found the Artifact aboard a derelict RAM spacecraft in the deeps of the Outer System, somewhere beyond the orbit of Saturn. Eight years later, as their city passed near Jupiter, they'd visited the Solar Geographic labs with their find, hoping to find a buyer or at least an assessment of its value, and Dr. Kowalski was the scientist who'd actually had a chance to study the thing.

Unfortunately, Solar Geographic didn't have the kind of budget that would support the purchase of mysterious and presumably alien artifacts from Nomad traders, and, in any case, the Ciudestreyans seemed to favor putting it up for auction at their next *Tempomercad*, or market time, when their city looped through the Inner System at its orbital perihelion.

But someone else had taken notice. Evidently, RAM agents had seen the Artifact in Amalthea and reported it, and a RAM heavy cruiser had been dispatched to Amalthea with orders to recover the Artifact at all costs.

RAM—the name was the acronym of the old Russo-American Mercantile Corporation, though that term was long obsolete—was already the single most powerful entity in the politically fragmented System. What RAM didn't own outright it controlled, and what it couldn't control it dominated through threat of sheer, naked aggression. Headquartered on Mars, RAM enforced its political will across the breadth of the Solar System through an immense battlefleet that at least equaled in numbers the minor fleets and space squadrons of all of the other worlds put together. Two powers alone actively battled RAM's political, economic, and military control: the pirates of the so-called Rogues' Guild, operating out of the loose confederation of asteroids known as the Belter Anarchy; and the rebel fleet of NEO, struggling to throw off the RAM domination of Earth.

Chance—and a minor skirmish in the ongoing RAM-NEO war—had marooned Vince on Ciudestreya shortly after its emissaries had returned from Amalthea with their treasure. He'd seen the Artifact, realized at once it could never have been made by humans, and alerted the NEO squadron that was already approaching Ciudestreya to rescue him. In a short, sharp battle in nearby space and within the Nomad city itself, rebel forces had savaged a much larger RAM force.

In gratitude, the Ciudestreyans had given the Artifact to NEO.

Ciudestreya was now an expanding cloud of radioactive debris, target of a RAM vengeance raid scant hours after the last of the city's population had been evacuated to new homes in the Asteroid Belt. But the Artifact survived. At last report it had been smuggled to a NEO lab facility somewhere in the Belt—even Vince didn't know the location—where a team of scientists from Earth was trying to crack its secrets.

The Artifact, a silvery, shape-shifting object that somehow recorded visual images and planted them in an observer's mind, was the product of a technology far beyond anything man had yet mastered. In all the history of human exploration of the Solar System, this was the first hint that man was not alone in the universe, that other minds than his quested after knowledge. What secrets might be learned from a detailed study of its high-tech magic?

Vince didn't know. The benefits, the unleashed power of a major technological breakthrough, were impossible to forecast. What he did know was that it was essential that the Artifact and its secrets be kept out of RAM's hands. If their scientists managed to get a handle on the technology behind the Artifact's secrets, RAM would become unbeatable, unstoppable, possessing a science-based black magic that could enslave the entire Solar System in a high-tech Dark Age lasting for ten thousand years.

And that, ultimately, was why Vince's small intelligence team had been dispatched to Amalthea by NEO Command. If RAM couldn't grab the Artifact for itself, it would certainly try to get the next best thing—Dr. Marlene Kowalski.

RAM had already tried once, and NEO agents on Mars had reported that they were going to try again. RAM had identified Kowalski as a scientist who had actually seen, handled, and studied the Artifact, and they would spare no cost or effort to pick her up for a leisurely and RAM-thorough interrogation.

NEO wanted Kowalski to help in their own investigation of the Artifact and, at the same time, to deny RAM a similar opportunity. RAM was almost certainly searching for a second Artifact now that NEO had control of the first. Kowalski's notes and observations could conceivably help that search. At the very least they would be of tremendous value in any probe of the Artifact's mysteries, by NEO or RAM.

They were only three, but it was thought that their small number would let them succeed where RAM's heavy-handed investigations a month earlier had failed. The two humans and the Tinker were traveling undercover aboard the *Golden Argosy*.

Secrecy was imperative. Vince and Jovanna were posing as RAM executives, while Galen carried electronic documents identifying him as a physician with an interest in the biological experiments being carried out at Amalthea's Genetics Foundation labs. They were well aware that there was at least one RAM agent in place somewhere in Amalthea, the individual who'd alerted RAM to the Artifact's existence in the first place.

"I still don't know how NEO expects us to get Dr. Kowalski to trust us," Jovanna said. "She has no reason to love RAM. If we introduce ourselves as a couple of RAM big shots—"

"Actually, we don't know what Kowalski's politics are," Vince reminded her. "She's not Terran, you know. She's an Aerostater, though her bio claims she hasn't been back to Venus for ten years." He grimaced. "As far as enlisting her for NEO, we're just going to have to play it by ear."

"We may have to, ah, play it by ear, as you say, just to find the lady," Galen pointed out. "I gather no one's even seen her since RAM sent the *Amazonis* to pick her up. If she did, indeed, flee Amalthea and go into hiding in one of the Jovian cities . . ."

"No one said the assignment was going to be an easy one," Vince said.

Galen, still holding the detector, held up a warning finger. "Watch it," he said. "Someone's coming."

Moments later, two more of *Argosy*'s fourteen passengers, a computer tech and a red-headed skimmer pilot, wandered into the lounge, forcing Vince and the other NEO agents to restrict their conversation to comments typical of tourists and business travelers.

Amalthea was swelling rapidly in the viewscreen, growing from a tiny pebble silhouetted against the ivory-and-scarlet glory of the Jovian clouds to a world in its own right. Potato-shaped, perpetually aligned with Jupiter by tidal forces, Amalthea was less than 170 miles through its long axis and measured perhaps 100 miles from pole to pole.

"There," Jovanna said, pointing at a tiny circle of lights on the end of Amalthea opposite Jupiter. "I think I can see our ship lock."

As *Argosy* closed on the moon, other structures—domes, communications masts, and the gaping maw of a surface-lock access—became easily visible. The moon's surface was brick red, startlingly so. The color came from sulphur blasted into space by the continuous volcanic eruptions on neighboring Io, then swept up by Amalthea in its twice-daily orbits of Jupiter. The constant rain of sulphur had long ago buried Amalthea's craters and other surface features, giving it a smooth and dusty look.

From several hundred miles out Vince could just make out the barely discernible blue glow of Amalthea Station's electromagnetic shielding. This close to Jupiter, ships and port facilities alike huddled within powerful EM cocoons that sheltered them from the giant planet's intense radiation belts. The interplay of force field and charged particle generated shifting patterns of luminous red, green, and blue, like a terrestrial aurora. A brief play of pale sparks marked the passage of the *Argosy*'s EM shields through the larger field protecting Amalthea.

"May I have your attention, please," an official-sounding voice called over the lounge intercom speaker. "We are now docking at Amalthea. For their comfort, all passengers will please be seated and fasten their safety harnesses."

The five of them took seats and strapped themselves in. Moments later, gravity vanished as *Argosy*'s drive fell silent for the first time since their midcourse turnover two days earlier. For several moments they were in freefall as Amalthea grew large enough to finally block giant Jupiter from view. The ship lock swelled huge on the viewscreen, framed by strobing guide beacons projected holographically in space. Gravity returned briefly—one-half a G for two minutes—followed by several thumps as maneuvering rockets fired. Tail-first, *Golden Argosy* fell through the gaping lock, which slowly closed shut above it. There was a final nudge of deceleration, then magnetic grapples locked home with metallic clangs.

They'd stopped moving, surrounded now by a cavern lined with windows, immense power conduits, and the web-work traceries of ship gantries. The blunt snout of a pressurized boarding tunnel was snaking its way out toward the newly arrived ship.

Vince unbuckled his harness, then stood carefully, testing the familiar, faint tug of microgravity. Amalthea's surface gravity measured five-thousandths of a G, which meant that Vince's lean, five-foot nine-inch frame now weighed less than a pound. A careless misstep, and he could find himself on the ceiling, and with a gravitational acceleration of less than two inches per second squared, it would take him several seconds to fall gently to the deck again.

"Ladies and gentlemen," the speaker voice said, apparently ignoring the presence of nonhuman passengers like Galen. "Welcome to Amalthea Station. Please watch your step."

Good advice, Vince thought as he watched Jovanna and Galen unstrap and carefully stand. But it wasn't the problem of walking in microgravity he had in mind.

RAM was here, and possibly the dangers and intrigues of other, less obvious political threats. A NEO squadron, he knew, was being assembled at that very moment, in case armed intervention was necessary to secure Kowalski's safety, but that squadron couldn't move until his team had found the doctor and convinced her to join NEO's cause. Until then, Vince and his team were entirely on their own.

They would indeed have to watch their step.

CHAPTER TWO

Amalthea Station was small as interplanetary terminals went, and not very busy. All of the large interplanetary liners called at Ganymede, and most of the traffic around Amalthea consisted of small Belter packets like the *Argosy* and short-haul local shuttles from other Jovian satellites.

As they emerged from the boarding tube, the rock-hewn chamber of the arrival area felt sterile to Vince, cold and cheerless. At the customs gate they handed their identity disks to a bored customs agent and his rather decrepit-looking robot assistant.

Traveling under forged documents always carried a certain element of risk in a computer-monitored culture, but the customs agent scarcely glanced at the data that appeared on his screen when he inserted the disks in his reader, and the robot was only concerned with monitoring the 3-D security scan of their bodies.

"Welcome to Amalthea," the man said. In the time-honored fashion of bureaucrats everywhere, he didn't sound as though he meant it. "Business or pleasure?"

"Business," Vince replied and the NEO agents were ushered through to the main concourse.

"Traveling as RAM Security has its benefits," Jovanna said. "He scarcely looked at us. I could have brought RW along after all."

RW was a digital personality, an electronic creature of cyberspace, and Jovanna's friend. Although she was a valued member of the covert team, they'd elected to leave her at NEO's secret Trinity base in the asteroids. An overly zealous customs agent who checked the wrist computer where RW was normally carried would wonder why they were bringing a terabyte-sized program into Amalthea, and Vince wanted to keep a low profile.

"Amalthea's about as apolitical as you can get," Vince said. "As long as we're not smuggling in weapons, they don't care much who we are. But they still might have pulled a program dump if they'd spotted RW. We couldn't chance that."

"I know," Jovanna said. "I just wish she were here, that's all."

Following glowing, holographic arrows, the new arrivals were led through an access way and into the Amalthean Strip, a broad, high-walled cavern lined with shops, bars, and the inevitable funhouses of a typical spaceport strip. Dozens of people moved along criss-crossing travel lines like spiders navigating complex webs. The main dock was behind them; a transplex window fifty feet long and carved from solid rock separated the strip from the docking bay. Opposite was a vid display fifty feet across. Jupiter, vast and overpowering, given scale by the red-brown slash of the Amalthean horizon across the bottom, filled its electronic screen.

The other passengers off the *Golden Argosy* streamed past the three NEO agents, making their way hand-over-hand along travel lines strung from poles set into the terminal's floor. Some gawked at the giant screen; most, old hands at microgravity and breathtaking view alike, moved with practiced efficiency into the Strip and toward the tubecar platforms.

Vince paused to admire the banded swirls and streaks of colors, continent-sized storms that crawled and twisted as he watched. "That view," he said, "must be Amalthea's principal export."

"See Amalthea and die," Galen quipped, "of terminal gosh-gee-whiz. Well, I'm off, humans."

"Be careful, Galen," Jovanna warned. "We'll see you at the hotel when we're done."

"No problem," the Tinker said wryly. "Who better to investigate a gennie farm than a gennie?" He reached out with long arms to grasp a nearby travel line and began following the other new arrivals toward the tube-cars.

Amalthea had a permanent population of perhaps three thousand, most of them employees of one of several corporations that had settled the world in a cooperative venture. The NEO agents had agreed to split up to investigate Marlene Kowalski's disappearance. Galen had an appointment to talk to someone at the Genetics Foundation as soon as they arrived, while Vince and Jovanna were to meet with a representative from Solar Geographic. Their contact was supposed to have met them at customs, but evidently there'd been a delay. Vince and Jovanna stood near the access way for a moment, uncertain about where to go.

"Mr. Peron?"

Vince turned at the voice, careful to keep hold of the travel line. A man, ponderously overweight but stylishly dressed in an ornate gold-and-scarlet bodysuit, was making his way toward them. "I'm Vince Peron," Vince said, using his NEO-designed alias. "This is my assistant."

"Joanna Travis," Jovanna said, introducing herself.

"Delighted. I am Dr. Heller of the Amalthean Council. Forgive me for not meeting you as soon as you arrived, but I got held up in a conference."

"The council?" Vince asked, one eyebrow rising. "Our visit here was supposed to be low-key."

"Our distinguished visitors from RAM always rate the very best," Heller said, beaming with what looked to Vince's practiced eye like hearty insincerity. "And your message said only that you wished to question someone at Solar Geographic about the disappearance of Dr. Kowalski. As it happens, I'm vice president of Solar Geographic's Amalthean lab and . . . ah, you're familiar with the way our government works?"

"A council made up of representatives from each of the founding Amalthean corporations?"

"Precisely." He spread pudgy hands, still beaming. "So I can assist you as a representative for Solar Geographic alone, or for the Amalthean government, whichever is called for."

"That's most kind of you, Doctor," Vince said. "Still, we'd rather not attract attention to our presence here." He gave Heller a conspiratorial wink. "You know how it is."

"But of course. Sir, madam, rooms have been reserved for you at the Amalthean Hilton. Your luggage has already been forwarded to the hotel directly from your ship. If you would care to follow me? . . ."

They traveled to the offices of Solar Geographic aboard a private tubecar, plunging through the maglev tunnels that connected the vast chambers hollowed out of Amalthea's core.

Amalthea had been colonized as a joint venture between several corporations. Largest of these was Skimmertech, a private corporation that mined hydrogen from the upper fringes of Jupiter's atmosphere for shipment to the Inner System. Next was the Genetics Foundation, a Mars-based corporation that was pioneering the biological seeding of Jupiter with man-made life.

Solar Geographic was a consortium of businesses and government-sponsored research-and-development corporations that operated science facilities scattered throughout the inhabited Solar System. Their lab at Amalthea was large and well-equipped, devoted to the study of magnetic and radiation effects in near-Jupiter space as well as the biology of newly created gennie life-forms within the depths of the Jovian atmosphere.

Half an hour after their arrival, Vince and Jovanna stood in Heller's lavishly furnished office in the suite of caverns reserved for Solar Geographic's Amalthean labs. Their host had offered them their choice from a superbly stocked private bar, and both had chosen iced drinking bulbs claiming to be genuine Terran orange juice.

"You're sure you'll have nothing mixed with those?"

Heller asked. "I stock those as one component of a very old drink called a 'screwdriver.' Strange name, that. Always wondered what it means."

"This is fine, thanks," Vince replied. He took a swallow from his bulb, then grimaced at the sour tang. Somehow he doubted that these particular oranges had ever been within twenty million miles of Earth. "So, Doctor," he said, setting the bulb aside. "What can you tell us about Marlene Kowalski?"

Heller looked apologetic. "There's really nothing more I can tell you that I didn't tell the other RAM people who came here looking for her. Captain, Captain . . ." He snapped his fingers.

"Zotov," Jovanna said, supplying the name.

"Zotov! Precisely! His ship called here some five weeks ago. The *Amazonis*, her name was. Captain Zotov was most interested in, ah, talking with Dr. Kowalski when he learned that it was she who had actually examined this so-called alien artifact."

Vince's eyebrows climbed his forehead. "You don't believe the Nomad discovery was genuine?"

"You must be joking." Heller made a face. "How could it be real? I mean, look at the facts, Mr. Peron. Never in the history of space exploration has any trace of extrasolar intelligence been discovered. And the, ah, Nomads are not exactly the sort you can trust, are they? Criminal scum, the lot of them."

Vince allowed himself a small, tight smile. A month ago, the Nomads of Ciudestreya had rescued him from certain death. He no longer shared the anti-Nomad prejudice common to many people throughout the system. "I suppose not. What can you tell me about the . . . Device?"

"I never saw it. Three representatives of the Ciudestreyan government arrived here at Amalthea in a patched-together refugee from a junkyard and asked to see someone with expertise in biology. Dr. Kowalski was our senior biologist, so she met with them in Lab Twenty. As far as I know, no one else was present."

"What happened then?"

Heller shrugged. "Dr. Kowalski was with the Nomads

for several hours. Afterward, she came and told me that
they were requesting a hundred million credits for, ah,
something she claimed was 'most unusual.' Well, the
whole thing was perfectly ridiculous, of course. A hundred million, why, that's Solar Geographic's entire operating budget for a year! Imagine wasting my time with
such nonsense! I ordered her to have nothing more to do
with those charlatans and gave orders for them to be
escorted back to their, er, shuttle. And that was the last
we saw of them." Heller suddenly looked alarmed.
"There's not going to be any problem over this matter
with RAM, is there? I mean, what else was I to do? . . ."

"Oh, there's no problem at all, Mr. Heller," Vince said
with a reassuring heartiness. "No problem whatsoever."

Privately he was astonished at Heller's short-sighted
stupidity. Obviously, the man was guided by precon-
ceived ideas of what was and was not possible, a most
unscientific attitude. Hell, Vince had seen—no, experienced—the Artifact while he'd been with the Nomads.
One glance had convinced him that the shimmering, silvery sphere could never have been manufactured by
human technology . . . or conceived by human minds.
One hundred million credits? What price could be placed
on a genuine artifact of an extrasolar technology? The
thing was literally priceless, if only because it would
ultimately change completely the way man looked at his
place in the universe.

"I agree that the Nomad find was almost certainly a
forgery," Vince continued smoothly. "But, you know how
department supervisors can be. RAM wishes to make
absolutely certain that the Device is, in fact, a fake.
Since Dr. Kowalski was the only one on your staff who
actually saw the thing, you can understand why it is
important that we talk with her."

"We'd like to stress that Dr. Kowalski is in no trouble
with RAM," Jovanna added. "We're certainly not here to
arrest her, or anything like that. We'd like only to ask
her a few questions."

"I understand perfectly, Miss, ah, Travis. And if I
knew where she was at this moment, I would most cer-

tainly tell you. Solar Geographic enjoys excellent relations with RAM, and we wish to keep it that way. Unfortunately, she disappeared at just about the same time
that the *Amazonis* docked here."

"Any idea where she might have gone?"

He shrugged expansively. "There are really only three
possibilities, Mr. Peron. One, she could still be here in
Amalthea, someplace. In hiding, perhaps, with friends. I
find it difficult to credit that, however. Ours is a small
community, and she would have been seen by now. If she
were still here, I would know it.

"Two—the most likely possibility, in my opinion—she
was able to obtain passage aboard a ship and flee Amalthea entirely." He paused while consulting his wrist
computer. "Yes. There were three ships at Amalthea at
about that time: the *Canada*, a small free trader that
departed for Earth the day before *Amazonis* arrived; the
Gavilan, a Mercurian ore freighter that left a week
later; and the *Oberon*, a Jovian system shuttle that
makes a regular run between Amalthea and Ganymede
once a week. She would have left the day *Amazonis*
arrived. "Ah!" He looked up and nodded happily. "You
know, Marlene might very well have bought passage on
the *Magnificus Triplanetary*."

"The luxury liner?"

"Exactly. The *Magnificus* was berthed at Ganymede at
the time. In fact, she was supposed to leave for Mars the
day *Amazonis* arrived, but there was some delay, as I
recall. Have you thought of checking the *Triplanetary*'s
passenger list?"

"We've checked," Vince replied evenly. In fact, NEO
Intelligence had already investigated all three ships at
Amalthea, plus the *Triplanetary* at Ganymede, and had
turned up nothing. "You mentioned three possibilities.
She's not here and she didn't take a ship. What else is
there?"

"Why, Jupiter itself," Heller said. "One of the cloud
cities with facilities for human guests. I wouldn't credit
that very much at all, however."

"Why not?"

"Because she would have been down there now for over five weeks." He spread his hands. "Can you imagine living that long in two and a half Gs? I can't."

○ ○ ○ ○ ○

So far, Galen had found the staff at the Genetics Foundation less than enthusiastically cooperative. He suspected that it was because he himself was a gennie, however, rather than the fact that they had anything to hide. Antigennie prejudice was common throughout the Solar System, but it was Galen's experience that the humans who actually worked with gene-engineered life-forms were the worst. They maintained a usually unspoken—but sometimes outspoken—attitude suggesting that, since gennies were manufactured in genetics laboratories, their naturally evolved makers were somehow inherently superior.

In fact, the genes in Galen's DNA were as much the product of almost four billion years of evolution as any full human's. They'd simply been assembled in new and imaginative ways, blending in Tinkers the genes of gibbon, chimpanzee, and human to create an artificial species with traits of all three.

As thinking and as rational as any full human—more so than some people he knew—Galen had broken the genetically imposed conditioning on his kind toward mechanical aptitude and engineering skill. In medicine, "tinkering with biological systems," as he liked to put it, he'd found the perfect expression of his own sentient independence.

But that didn't help him when he was confronted by antigennie prejudice, especially when it was the cool and calculating professional superiority of a human genetics engineer.

"I really don't understand your interest in this matter, ah, Mendel," Hubert Shelton said. He was a high-ranking executive with the Genetics Foundation, and his manner suggested that men such as he shouldn't be forced to waste their time with such trivialities as visiting gennies. "Why did RAM send you?"

"Because," Galen replied, "RAM Internal Security thought that I might bring some special insight into a case involving a genetically engineered species. Or don't you believe my credentials?"

At the mention of RAM's security service, Shelton's eyes widened and his voice lost some of its superiority. "Oh, not at all, ah, Mr. Mendel—"

"That's Dr. Mendel," Galen said, savoring the flavor of his cover name and title. "If you please."

It would have been better, he thought, if a human could have handled this part of the assignment. It was fun watching Shelton's discomfort, but Galen was beginning to think that he was simply not going to get any useful information out of the man. The forged electronic documents naming him as a member of RAM's Internal Security could carry him some distance by playing on raw fear, but people like Shelton were incapable of understanding that gennies could reason as well as they.

Or, in this case, better.

"Of course." Shelton still seemed unable to bring himself to use the Tinker's honorific title. "But maybe if you could tell me why RAM Security is interested in the Stormrider cities . . ."

"It is enough," Galen replied haughtily, "that we are. Tell me about them, please."

Galen already knew something about the Stormriders, a gennie species designed specifically to colonize that most hostile of all of worlds, Jupiter. They lived in enormous, floating cities, few of which had ever been seen by outsiders. Their atmosphere—eighty percent hydrogen, nineteen percent helium, with traces of methane, ammonia, and other poisons—was deadly to non-Jovians. The gravity, two and a half times Earth normal, would cripple a Terran or a Venusian and crush anyone raised on a lesser world like Mars or Luna. Though they carried on trade with the rest of the system, specializing in new and exotic products of gene engineering, the Stormriders themselves were rarely seen off Jupiter.

Galen had always wished he could see a Stormrider in the flesh but knew that he probably never would. Secretive and mysterious, they rarely ventured beyond the boundaries of their world at all.

And, like Jovanna, he could never visit Jupiter himself. The huge planet's gravity would crush his frail Tinker's form designed for smaller, more forgiving worlds.

"I understand that there are several Stormrider cities that have accommodations for human visitors," Galen observed.

Shelton nodded, but his already sour features twisted with disapproval. "There are. Twenty-four of them, in fact, out of several hundred. But you'd never be able to visit them. No Tinker ever could."

"I'm well aware of that, Mr. Shelton," Galen replied evenly. "Actually, RAM is particularly interested in one human who may have ventured to one of those cities: a Dr. Kowalski, of Solar Geographic."

Shelton spat a word foul enough to startle even Galen, who thought he knew most of the more colorful human idioms.

"I take it you know the lady?"

"Know her? Yeah, but she's no lady. A damned Aerostater spy's more like it. The rumor is that she fled Amalthea to avoid getting picked up by your owners."

Galen diplomatically ignored the human's use of the word "owners" to describe his presumed superiors in RAM. Shelton seemed to think that all gennies were property, a generalization that was manifestly untrue. "I take it from your tone you don't believe that, however."

"Hell, Kowalski fled Amalthea to get away from the Genetics Foundation. She's been working against our interests on Jupiter for years."

"Indeed? Do you know where she went?"

"Not for sure, but I can make a pretty damned good guess. She's often gone down to Jupiter before, and when she does, it's always to the same city. Vrahk' dreleschaah."

The explosion of sound made Galen blink. For a moment, he thought the human had sneezed. "Excuse me?"

Shelton smiled, tight lipped. "A Stormrider name. Means 'thunder city,' or something like that. Up here, we just call it Vrahk." He pronounced the final consonant as a harsh, rasping sound, a bit sharper than the German "ch" in the name Bach.

"How do you know that? RAM has been looking for her for some time."

Shelton gave Galen a peculiar look. "I passed that information on to Mars two weeks ago. I assumed you were here following up on my report."

The news jolted Galen. Shelton had as much as admitted that he was RAM's agent in Amalthea. It must have been he who first reported the Artifact's arrival, his message that had brought the *Amazonis* from Mars to retrieve it.

"Actually, I'm not," Galen said carefully. A wrong word now and Shelton might begin questioning his RAM Internal Security identification. "They didn't tell me much of anything, actually."

The man nodded, and Galen realized he'd just confirmed Shelton's belief that gennies, however bright they might seem, were still little better than animated tools. Property . . .

"We had Kowalski followed a few times," Shelton said, "back when we first suspected she was working against us. Until the man following her had an 'accident.' "

"What kind of accident?"

"Slipped and went over one of Vrahk's guardrails." Shelton grimaced. "Not a nice way to go. Down there it's even money whether you fry first or get crushed by the air pressure. But dead is dead. We've been monitoring Kowalski in other ways since then."

"You're sure she's in Vrahk, then?"

"I told you, that's just a guess. But it's a good one."

"I'd heard she might have gotten off Amalthea some other way."

"Yeah. One of my people managed to plant a tiny transmitter on her, back before the flap with the alien Device. Uh, you know about that?"

Galen nodded.

"Well, somehow she discovered the transmitter. Placed it aboard a local shuttle, the *Oberon*, the day the RAM cruiser called here looking for her. For a while, everyone, including the *Amazonis*'s officers when they came looking, assumed she'd either made it to Ganymede and boarded a passenger liner there, or that she caught a tramp freighter called the *Canada* and headed for Earth. But when she didn't turn up on either ship, I wondered if she might not have headed down to Jupiter instead. Makes sense, you see. She has . . . friends there." The way he stressed the word told Galen he didn't approve.

Galen felt the thrill of accomplishment, though. Just after the Ciudestreyan affair he, Vince, and Jovanna had discussed the possibility that Dr. Kowalski, a biologist known to be interested in Jovian life-forms, had escaped RAM by hiding with the Stormriders. That was why Vince had been spending all of his time lately working out in high-G carousels and dosing himself with gravitol. He'd seen the possibility from the very beginning that he might have to visit the Jovian cloud cities.

But until this moment they hadn't known which of two dozen Stormrider cities outfitted for human habitation Kowalski might have gone to. Shelton might be a RAM agent, but he'd just helped NEO locate the elusive Marlene Kowalski.

There was just one problem.

"Tell me, Mr. Shelton," Galen said. "Have you reported your suspicions to RAM? After your original report, I mean."

Again, Shelton gave him that peculiar look. "Of course. Weren't you told anything by your owners?"

Galen gave him his best disarming smile. "You know how it is. The word never gets to the people who need it the most. I was sent to find out which Stormrider cities Kowalski might have gone to. I imagine headquarters is sending another, better equipped force to actually apprehend her."

Shelton visibly relaxed, and Galen ended his interview with the man as quickly as he could without fur-

ther arousing his suspicions. He had to get back to Vince
and Jovanna with this news. If Marlene Kowalski was
anywhere, she was in the Stormrider city of Vrahk.

The only problem was that RAM, the real RAM, now
had the same information and was almost certainly on
its way back to Jupiter at that very moment.

How long did they have? Galen had no way of knowing, but two weeks was plenty of time for a RAM task
force to be assembled at Mars and make the passage to
Jupiter. The NEO team would have to hurry, or Marlene
Kowalski would fall into RAM's hands no matter what.

And he, Vince, and Jovanna would all be dead or, far
worse, prisoners of RAM.

It was not a pleasant thought.

CHAPTER THREE

They met in the Jovelight, a carousel restaurant attached to the Amalthean Hilton complex. An enormous wheel revolving on its side, with access through the hub and tables and chairs around the inside rim, the Jovelight was one of a number of places visitors and natives could go to enjoy the amenities of gravity—such as liquids that poured instead of being squeezed from a drinking bulb. The management kept the Jovelight's spin gravity set at four-tenths of a G.

Jovanna enjoyed the sensation. Four-tenths G was Mars normal, and she could close her eyes and almost imagine she was back home. When she opened them, of course, the illusion was dispelled. The restaurant's floor curved up and away in opposite directions, though the area was divided into intimately small and secluded rooms so that hotel guests halfway around the circle could not be seen enjoying their meals upside down. The floor was set at a slight angle to the walls to compensate for Amalthea's native five-thousandths of a G, and one entire wall electronically displayed the view outside, Jupiter huge above a broken red horizon, its soft glow flooding the restaurant with pastel reds and orange-brown light.

They'd not come to the Jovelight for the view, however. The restaurant was a prearranged rendezvous where Vince and Jovanna could "accidentally" bump into one of their fellow passengers from the *Golden Argosy* and invite him to sit at their table for a chat. Despite the antigennie prejudice common in Amalthea, there was no rule against a Tinker eating with humans, though a few of the restaurant's other guests gave the trio dark and disapproving looks.

Still, Galen's tiny scanner indicated that their conversation was not being electronically monitored, and the restaurant, moodily lit by only the glow of Jupiter from the wallscreen, was dark enough that any watchers would have needed infrared goggles to read their lips. Though they had to assume that others—possibly Heller and the Amalthean government, possibly Shelton or other RAM agents—would be spying on them, the Jovelight offered a reasonably safe place for the NEO team to meet and talk.

"Vrahk," Jovanna said after Galen had filled them in on the results of his meeting with Shelton. She looked up from the remnants of her meal. The menu had called it veal, though it almost certainly was the product of a tissue culture vat somewhere here in Amalthea. "Could Kowalski have been there all this time? I mean, five weeks is a long time to take two and a half gravities."

"I suppose its possible," Vince said around a mouthful of gene-tailored lobster. "If she's a Venusian, like Shelton said, she's used to nine-tenths of a G, and there are plenty of carousels in Amalthea that simulate Jovian gravity. Solar Geographic, the Genetics Foundation, Skimmertech, even our own hotel, all have them. I doubt that anyone from Mars or one of the asteroids could handle it, though."

"Maybe she thinks no one from RAM would come after her," Jovanna suggested.

Vince shrugged. "Terrines are gene-tailored for heavy gravity work. No, she's relying on something other than Jupiter's gravity to protect her."

"Speaking of Terrines," Galen said, fingering the tall glass of distilled water he'd ordered. "Has anybody heard from the fourth member of our team yet?"

Jovanna nodded. "*Dread Reprisal* arrived at Cargo Lock Five about an hour ago. I accessed Amalthea's approach control records through the computer in my room. She's in her *Industrious* guise and was wearing the tail number 514."

Vince placed his fork on his empty plate. "I feel a lot better knowing Kaiten made it okay," he said with feeling.

Kaiten was a Terrine, a renegade Terrine, which theoretically put him on NEO's side in the war against RAM. A genetically tailored race of warriors, Terrines combined the genes of sharks, cats, and humans in heavily muscled, roughly humanoid packages designed for killing and indoctrinated with an absolute devotion to RAM Martians.

Somehow, and for reasons the Terrine himself had never fully explained, Kaiten had broken his RAM conditioning and become one of the most feared pirates of the Belter Anarchy. Since the Ciudestreyan affair, when he'd been recruited by the notorious Black Barney, he'd been working for NEO, carrying on a one-gennie war of his own against his former masters.

Dread Reprisal was Kaiten's raider, a cruiser-sized ship manned by sixty of the most vicious space-faring cutthroats Jovanna had ever known, pirates apparently kept in line solely by Kaiten's rather forceful personality. Outwardly, *Reprisal* resembled an ungainly freighter, and, with the name *Industrious* painted on its corrosion-streaked prow, it often passed itself off as a slow and harmless cargo vessel. The number 514 was a prearranged code to the NEO agents already in Amalthea. It meant that the special cargo they'd requested was on board, and that all was ready for the next part of the operation.

"I'm not sure I'm going to enjoy staying here with *Reprisal*'s crew on the loose while Kaiten is down there in Vrahk with you," Galen said. "Who's going to control them while he's away?"

"You're supposed to be a RAM official," Vince said with a smile. "If they get rowdy, arrest them."

"I think I'll leave that to the stabbers," Galen replied, using a common slang term referring to the local police.

"How will they react when RAM, the real RAM, I mean, shows up?" Jovanna asked. The news that an enemy flotilla might be arriving at any time had spiced their meal with a sharp urgency.

"We'll worry about that when it happens," Vince said. "I think by then we'll have other things to worry about." He glanced at his fingerwatch. "I'd say we'd better get moving. The sooner we get this over with, the sooner we can be out of here and on our way back to the Belt."

Galen left them then, to return to his quarters, while Vince walked Jovanna back to the rooms that Dr. Heller had reserved for them. Like every other habitation in Amalthea, the hotel was buried deep beneath the moon's surface. The VIP suite at the Amalthean Hilton, however, was a showcase of the latest in full-sensory electronics, the rooms large and luxurious, the walls, ceilings, and floors designed to project a long list of scenes from an impressive menu accessed through the hotel's computer.

The display could have reproduced anything from a Roman orgy to the acid-dripping swamps of the Venusian lowlands. At the moment, though, Jovanna had her room configured for a late evening somewhere on Earth. Three walls and the ceiling looked out over a forest at night. A soft breeze scented with lilacs caressed her cheek and ruffled her short hair. Beyond the veranda's railing, the landscape was cloaked in night, the airless hostility of Amalthea's surface electronically replaced by the illusion of air and warmth and the rustle of trees in the dark. A silvery, crescent moon hung low above the horizon.

She'd selected the scene from a library of Earth backgrounds. Even the gravity was correct. The hotel's VIP suites were each set within independently spinning carousels, designed to imitate any gravity desired.

At one G, Jovanna weighed two and a half times what she would have on Mars. One reason she'd set the room's spin gravity so high, besides wanting to make it earthlike for Vince, was that she wanted to experience for herself a little of what Vince was going to experience on Jupiter. She felt heavy, dull, and tired. After a few moments her back and the bottoms of her feet ached, and her rather small breasts felt like twin sandbags hanging beneath the fabric of her smartsuit. Each movement was unpleasant, and she dreaded what might happen if she fell. She felt a bit dizzy, too, though she didn't know if that was from the effects of high gravity or from the spin-induced Coriolis effect of a small, quickly rotating system. She had to be careful where she placed her foot with each cautious step.

"Nice," Vince said, walking easily to the railing. He leaned against it a moment, listening to the night sounds. "I take it you like exotic settings."

Jovanna cocked her head, puzzled. "Exotic? No, I thought it would remind you of home. Of Earth."

He turned, then, and for just an instant the indirect lighting from the bedroom at her back highlighted pain. Then the expression was gone and he laughed. "I don't know what it is, but it isn't Earth."

"But the menu said—"

"I think Earth might have been like this once, a few centuries ago, when there were still forests."

"Oh—"

Jovanna closed her eyes, mentally kicking herself for her stupidity. Born and raised on a terraformed Mars, she'd never been to Earth, a planet still struggling to recover from centuries of mismanagement, war, and ecological disaster. She knew that large parts of man's homeworld were barren and uninhabitable, that most of the population still lived in self-contained arcologies as artificial as any habitat in Amalthea, but when she'd seen the listing for "Earth scene, the forest at night" in the computer library, she'd not even stopped to think that it might be pure fantasy, a simulation of things as they had been once, not as they were now.

"I feel so damned clumsy sometimes," Jovanna said, her voice small. "I guess I'm so used to Mars, I didn't even stop to think—"

"Hey, it's okay," Vince said, seeing her distress. "Really. I always wondered what it was like. And . . . what it's going to be like again." He gestured at the dimly seen forest. "That's what it's all about, you know."

She knew that by "it" Vince meant NEO and the rebellion against RAM; they had to assume that the room's complex electronics could be used to spy on them, and they had to be careful about what they said.

"It's a little hard for a Martian girl to understand." Jovanna knew that much of Earth's devastation was the direct result of over a century and a half of RAM's exploitation, a savage, ongoing rape of minerals and resources that threatened one day to render the entire planet uninhabitable. NEO's rebellion was, as much as anything else, a desperate, last-ditch attempt to snatch Earth's fate back from the hands of its RAM masters. Most Terrans involved with NEO were in it because they looked forward to the day when Earth's seas and forests would live again.

Vince looked up toward the unseen ceiling of the hotel room. "Room computer," he said. "I want to see Jupiter."

Forests and night remained, but the sky changed dramatically. Stars shifted in their positions, and a circle stretching from the horizon half-way to the zenith went black, edged by a scarlet-hued sliver of light. The sun, dazzlingly bright even at three and a half times its distance from Mars, touched the Jovian horizon with living flame, a fiery diamond set on a golden band.

"Just in time for sunset," Vince said.

"I can see it moving, Vince."

Amalthea's orbit carried it around Jupiter once in almost exactly twelve hours, quickly enough that the eye could just detect the sun's apparent motion as it set behind the vast bulk of Jupiter at the beginning of the six-hour night. As she watched, the dayside terminator crawled beyond the horizon, and the sliver of daylight beneath the setting sun dwindled, suffusing into a rosy glow of atmosphere-scattered light.

The stars brightened, though the circle of night overhead looked at first like a jet-black hole outlined by dia-

mond dust. Then as her eyes became accustomed to the
darkness, Jovanna could see new details within the
depths of Jupiter's night side. Aurorae, electrically
charged flickers of green and red, played and twisted at
the poles, dimly illuminating the familiar bands of cloud
in an alien light. Deep, deep within the clouds, thunder-
less lightning flared and pulsed like silent, rapid-fire
bomb blasts, pinpricks of light against the darkness,
each bolt carrying the raw power of dozens of thermonu-
clear warheads.

The view was at once awe-inspiring and terrible.

"You know," Vince said, staring up into the lightning-
touched depths of the Jovian night, "someone once said
that you could describe the whole Solar System as the Sun
and Jupiter, plus some scattered debris. Take every other
planet and moon and asteroid in the system, including the
other three gas giants, lump them all together into a new,
giant planet, and Jupiter would still have better than
twice its mass. Did you know that that planet gives off
more than twice as much heat as it gets from the sun?
That's the only reason life can exist there at all."

She tried to read his expression. "You're not getting
nervous about going down there, are you?"

Even if there were electronic eavesdroppers, it
wouldn't hurt if they knew about Vince's upcoming visit
to Jupiter.

Vince turned, a shy smile tugging at the corner of his
mouth. "A little, I guess. I don't know what to expect.
And, like you said earlier, Jupiter's just too big to grasp
its scale. A planet of giants . . ."

"You'll manage, Vince," she said quietly. "You always
do, somehow, no matter what the odds. I don't think I've
ever known anyone so . . . so capable."

"As a pilot, maybe," Vince said. His eyes were drawn
back to the looming world above them. "But this is going
to take something more than a rocketjock attitude. You
know, Jo, I wish you were coming too."

"Good God, why?"

"It's going to be damned lonely down there without
you."

The admission startled her. Ever since she'd met Vince, twenty-one years earlier, she'd had the gnawing feeling that he didn't think much of her abilities, that he didn't think much of her. Only very recently, since the Ciudestreyan affair, in fact, had their strictly business relationship become modified by professional respect and, more recently still, by some feeling deeper than friendship.

"Vince, I—"

She was in his arms, and she heard her own pulse roaring in her ears. His face was very close to hers.

It wasn't as though she'd actually known Vince for twenty-one years. For nearly all of that time she'd been on Mars, working undercover for NEO, and it wasn't until Vince had arrived and pulled her out just a few months ago that she'd really started to get to know the man. This was the first time Vince Pirelli had ever responded to her in any way other than as a friend or as a NEO team leader.

Well, there had been that rather startling kiss and embrace after they were reunited on Ciudestreya, but she'd just been glad to see him after thinking he was dead, and she'd assumed he'd felt the same way. Almost . . . almost she dared wonder if the two of them might already be more than friends and teammates.

He looked as though he were about to kiss her. His closeness, his scent, the fierce light behind his dark eyes, were overpowering. She parted her lips, an invitation . . .

And suddenly he'd released her, had turned away and left her swaying, the strength draining from her knees. The unaccustomed gravity nearly dragged her down, and she had to catch hold of the veranda railing to keep from falling.

"Vince? What's wrong? What did I do?"

"Huh? Oh . . . God, Jo, I'm sorry. Nothing. You didn't do anything. It's me. I . . . I'd better go now."

At first she'd been afraid she'd done something to offend him. Now, fear was replaced by anger. "Damn it, Vince, what the hell's going on?"

He turned, spreading his hands and smiling apologetically. "Bad manners on my part, Jo. Forgive me. Maybe we can talk later, when I get back."

Vince seemed to be saying that he didn't want to talk about it in front of their presumed audience, but Jovanna had the feeling that something else was bothering him. She watched as he walked toward the door of the suite.

"Vince?"

He stopped. "Yeah?"

"Be careful. Good luck down there."

He threw her a crooked grin. "Hey, you know me, Jo. Always careful, always ready. But thanks."

"I wish I could come with you too." She walked toward him slowly, feeling with each step the agonized protest of muscles unused to a full Earth gravity. Her feet hurt, her back hurt, and this was only one G! How long, she wondered, could she tolerate Jupiter, weighing six and a quarter times what she was used to on Mars?

"I don't think you'd like it, Jo. But I'll be back as fast as I can. We'll pick up where we left off. Date?"

"It's a date." And then he was gone.

"Room computer," she called as soon as an indicator showed that the elevator access to the suite was clear. "Gravity at four-tenths of a G." Slowly, the spin gravity decreased until it was again Mars normal. "And kill the simulation," she added.

At her back, the lightning-flecked glory of the Jovian night faded, leaving the walls of her room bare and unadorned.

She didn't want to see Jupiter anymore.

CHAPTER FOUR

An hour later, a bored traffic controller received a routine request for small craft deployment and launch within Amalthea's Docking Bay Five, a small facility used primarily by freighters and provisioning vessels. There was only one ship in the bay at the moment, an aging, corrosion-streaked cargo tramp that had berthed only a short time before.

"*Industrious*, you are clear to deploy small craft," the controller said. He set aside his drinking bulb and glanced up at the large wallscreen above his console, keying in a request for a camera close-up. The freighter hung suspended in the cavern of the docking bay, nakedly exposed by the glare of a dozen spotlights, anchored in place by the skeletal tangle of its berthing gantry. "Your deployment call sign will be Victor Three-One."

"Victor Three-One, copy," an anonymous voice replied over his headset. "Beginning deployment."

Ships in port frequently used shuttles or gigs for short hops to other satellites and bases within the Jovian system. A freighter captain, for instance, might send his cargo officer in the ship's boat out to Ganymede or Europa to check prices or make final arrangements for special cargo handling. The traffic controller assumed that Victor Three-One's mission was something of that sort. The dorsal cargo hatch of the relic in Dock Five was slowly swinging open.

"Victor Three-One, Control," he said. "What is your destination?"

"Control, Three-One. Jupiter."

Again, nothing unusual there. Amalthea was the orbital port-of-call for all supply runs to the Jovian cities. There was burgeoning trade between them and the Aerostaters of Venus, for instance, and Inner System merchants sometimes ventured into the giant planet's atmosphere to arrange for the purchase of bloat meat or other Jupiter-grown biologicals.

Something was extending from the freighter's cargo deck . . . no, two somethings, pencil-slim shapes with sleek, back-swept tail fins, their twenty-foot hulls parallel to *Industrious* and anchored by bulky magnetic grapples. Shark-lean and deadly, the clean and streamlined hulls of the small rockets contrasted with the rustbucket bulk of the mother ship.

"Hey, Gary!" the controller said, calling to the duty senior controller. "Lookit this!"

"What the hell are those?" the other man said, staring closely at the screen. "Fighters?"

The controller already had a computer search going, cycling through the small craft files. A window opened in the lower left corner of the main screen, showing plan and elevation schematics matching the streamlined shapes now suspended outside the freighter's cargo bay.

"Kraits!" the senior controller said. "My God, Kraits! Now what are—?"

Both men had heard of the X-23A Krait and knew its reputation, though neither had ever seen one this close before. The RAM cruiser that had visited Amalthea a few weeks earlier had carried Kraits piggy-backed to its hull, but the warship had parked itself in orbit, too far out for either man to get a good look.

"Ah, Victor Three-One," the senior controller said, keying his throat mike. "Are those things X-23s?"

The visual display's picture broke up in a burst of static, then congealed into a close-up from a cockpit camera. A head stared down at them, far bigger than life on

the wallscreen, helmeted but with the visor open. Both
traffic controllers gaped at the fanged muzzle, flat nose,
and golden cat's eyes that met their astonishment with
the cold and humorless calculation of a predator con-
fronting its prey.

Neither man had ever seen a Terrine face-to-face,
either, but both knew very well what they looked like.
"No," the face said, showing triangular white teeth.
"They are not. You have not seen us. You have not seen
me. Is it understood?"

Kraits were the latest in RAM fighter technology, Terrines the most savage and dedicated of RAM's soldiers.
Industrious, obviously, was some kind of disguised
fighter transport. It could only be here on some clandes-
tine mission, and the Amalthean traffic controllers were
well aware that their own government sought to maintain friendly relations with RAM at almost any cost.

"Ah . . . we copy, Three-One," the senior controller
said, his voice unsteady. "Y-you are cleared for immediate departure."

"Thank you, Amalthea Control," the nightmare face
said, its grin unpleasant. "You are most efficient."

First one, then the other Krait slipped free from the
grapples. Falling slowly in Amalthea's microgravity, the
fighters almost appeared to be hanging motionless, tail-
down. Then their maneuvering thrusters fired, spewing
invisible streams of plasma, edging them toward the
docking bay doors overhead.

"Kraits and Terrines!" the first controller said to his
boss. "My God, what should we do?"

"Open the bay doors, of course," the supervisor replied.
"And keep this quiet! I'm logging Victor Three-One as a
supply shuttle."

Balanced on their secondary thrusters, the Kraits
accelerated out of the lock and into free space.

○ ○ ○ ○ ○

Vince checked again the array of panel lights and
computer displays on his console and hoped that his

crash course in X-23 avionics three weeks before had prepared him for this. The Krait was the most technologically advanced fighter in existence, with computer controls so sophisticated some NEO pilots joked that the things flew themselves.

Unfortunately, the Krait was so new that, so far, only a handful had fallen into NEO hands. These particular X-23s had been captured in a NEO-pirate raid on the RAM military facilities on Phobos less than a month before, and Vince was still unfamiliar enough with the controls that he couldn't give full rein to his rocketjock's instincts as the craft responded to his touch. Turning his helmet to look out the starboard side of his canopy, he could see Kaiten's X-23 maintaining close formation as Amalthea dwindled astern.

"Not much like booting an old Starfire, is it?" he asked his Terrine wingman over the ship-to-ship lasercom channel.

"Negative," was the curt reply. "Engage magnetic screens."

Good advice. Jupiter's radiation belts would fry any unscreened life-form or electronics in seconds. Vince studied his displays for a moment, then pressed three numbered touchpads. The words "MAGNETIC SCREENS ENGAGED" wrote themselves across the top of his main display. Moments later, the two Kraits plunged through the blue haze of Amalthea's screens. Ahead, Jupiter's night hemisphere, the bands and swirls of pastel color dimly illuminated by aurorae and the silent flare of cloud-buried lightning, hung ominous and huge. Meteors flashed and sparked in silence, the steady infall of debris spiraling into Jove's atmosphere. To each side, the Jovian rings were twin thread-thin streaks of sunlight sharply divided by the planet's shadow.

"Entry program downloaded," Kaiten's voice said over Vince's helmet phones. The Terrine's voice was harsh, his words as sparsely offered as ever. "Target beacon identified and locked. Go to autosequence Alpha."

"Autosequence Alpha," Vince replied, touching another series of numbered panels on his console to

begin the maneuvers already programmed into the
Krait's computer.

"AUTOSEQUENCE INITIATED: FULL COMPUTER
CONTROL" appeared on the display. Vince felt a thump
transmitted through the hull as maneuvering jets fired.
Jupiter began drifting past his canopy; the Krait was
aligning itself on a new heading. "RETROFIRE SE-
QUENCE ENGAGED," the screen read now. "IGNITION
IN 10." As he watched, the "10" changed to a "9," then
the "9" to an "8." He kept his hands off the controls, and
instead snuggled back against the Krait's acceleration
couch and braced himself for what he knew was coming.

The countdown reached zero and a massive, unseen
hand slammed Vince back against his couch as the
Krait's engines fired with a bone-crushing acceleration
of five Gs. The pressure dragged on, minute after
minute, until drawing each breath became a struggle,
and his ears were ringing with the effort.

His thoughts strayed back to Jovanna, despite the
savage pounding. He'd been thinking of her a lot lately.
Ever since his rescue from Ciudestreya, in fact.

When he'd first met her, twenty-one years before,
she'd been shy and awkward, a whizz with computers
but as clumsy with people as anyone he'd ever known.
She'd proven herself, though, time after time. For
twenty years she'd worked secretly for NEO on Mars,
hidden within the heart of the RAM beast. When NEO
Intelligence decided to form a new special operations
team based in the Asteroid Belt, she'd been chosen both
for her knowledge of computers and for her detailed
understanding of RAM and RAM's methods.

Vince had never approached Jovanna with the typical
fighter jock's come-on. He liked her, but somehow he'd
never thought of her as a potential conquest. Why? He
himself wasn't sure. Twenty-one years ago she'd been so
plain and mousy he'd scarcely noticed her. He was, after
all, a pilot, able to take his pick of any number of good-
looking and available girls who happened to catch his
eye, and the shy little computer tech simply didn't rate
his attention.

But later . . . well, she looked a lot better now than she had, especially when she fixed herself up. The first time he'd seen her in makeup and a skinsuit he'd nearly dropped his teeth. Still, there'd always been a distance between them, as though they already knew each other too well to ever become close.

What, then, had changed?

Vince was attracted to Jovanna, very much so. He'd begun to realize that when he'd been marooned in the Nomad city a few weeks before. When they'd met afterward, they'd embraced like long-separated lovers. Their relationship had deepened since then, but he still wasn't sure where it was going.

The acceleration cut off, leaving Vince suspended in his harness in a blessedly silent weightlessness. Jupiter appeared much larger now, and he could see a streak of day-bright glory outlining the curve of the eastern horizon as the two Kraits hurtled toward dawn.

Some thirty-two thousand miles above Jupiter's cloud tops now, the Krait was drifting over the sweep of the planet's ring, and the fighter's sensors had detected the thin plane of dust, rock, and ice, invisibly shadowed a thousand miles beneath the fighter's belly. He glanced to starboard and saw Kaiten's X-23 still there, its outline difficult to make out in the darkness.

The trouble was, he realized with new insight, he couldn't afford to get involved with anyone now. There was so much to do, and a war that made a mockery of long-term plans.

His thoughts about both Jovanna and the war were a confusing tumble of memories, emotions, and doubt, thoroughly mingled with a deep-seated doubt in himself. For a long time Vince had felt that the events of the struggle with RAM had managed to pass him by, that the high-profile heroes of NEO's propaganda machines, like Buck Rogers and Wilma Deering, were fighting and winning the war while he'd spent the past twenty years running minor and routine intelligence operations and training baby-faced kids to fly combat missions. He'd had to face the bitter reality before; he was getting old, too old to play the hotshot rocketjock or the dashing secret agent. It was time to settle down . . . maybe with Jovanna. . . .

But he couldn't quit. Not now, not yet. Vince Pirelli desperately wanted to accomplish something worthwhile in the war. It wasn't that he had to be a hero like Buck Rogers. He just needed to feel that he'd done something, that he'd made some small difference in the battle to wrest Mother Earth back from the avaricious grasp of RAM.

A few weeks before, he'd thought that, just possibly, his discovery of the mysterious Artifact, his recovery of the Artifact for NEO, might have been the difference he'd been looking for. He had helped keep it from falling into RAM's hands, after all, and if RAM had managed to keep the thing for itself, God alone knew what the Martians would have been able to do with it.

But NEO had spirited the Artifact away and there was no evidence that it could be used as a weapon, no indication that it might lead to contact with aliens or a final victory over RAM. Like most events in war, it had not been a turning point or even an important victory.

Vince very much wanted a victory, something he could call his own contribution to the war. Until he found it, until he knew that he'd made his mark and the war was not passing him by, he couldn't afford to explore his deepening relationship with Jovanna, could not consider self or comfort or even the promise of a family of his own.

But time was passing all too quickly. Damn it, he was getting old, with nothing to show for it but twenty-some years of routine reports, training schedules, and a growing dissatisfaction with a lifestyle that simply no longer suited him.

Sunlight exploded over Jupiter's eastern limb as Vince's Krait felt the first shivering buffets of the uppermost traces of the planet's atmosphere. He was still thousands of miles above the cloud tops, but Jupiter's atmosphere, predominantly hydrogen at this altitude and still far too thin to provide lift, was beginning to heat the hull with reentry friction. Lightning exploded far beneath him, illuminating a swirling maelstrom in the clouds wide enough to have swallowed all of Asia whole.

Side by side, the two Kraits plunged through thickening air toward their destination, visible now only as a point of light electronically projected on their cockpit displays.

His ship's computer chuckled to itself, then projected a scattering of stars across Vince's heads-up display. They were Jovian cloud cities, still too distant to see with the naked eye but pinpointed by the Krait's electronic senses. One of those stars was encased in red brackets—their destination.

They would be arriving at Vrahk'dreleschaah within two hours.

○ ○ ○ ○ ○

It no longer thought of itself as Capt. Grigor Kleist.

If it thought of itself at all, it was as the cluster controller, since it directed the activities of the other remotes of its cluster. During the past few tens of thousands of seconds, however, it had learned a great deal about the shell it was occupying. Each specific datum acquired, however, led to more questions. The remote units that called themselves humans were alien beyond anything the controller had expected. More specimens would be needed beyond the twenty found infesting the *Sharonov*.

By chance, the controller had taken over the human that functioned—in a limited and inefficient way—as *Sharonov*'s controller. For thousands of seconds, the controller had studied the human's structure, chemistry, and operational parameters, but the Kleist human had malfunctioned seconds after the controller had begun downloading its data stores, and little of use had been recovered.

The controller understood the computer running *Sharonov* quite well, far better than it understood the humans. It was possible that humans were remote computers of some kind for a larger system, but if so, their operation was still a complete mystery. Humans were apparently autonomous, programmed systems functioning through interlocking chains of weak, multiple, and frequently contradictory algorithms. The data won from close study of captured humans were conflicting and unsatisfactory. A far larger sampling of specimens would be needed to classify their patterns of data processing and the variations in their hardware patterns. Why, from the preliminary examination of the twenty units infesting the *Sharonov*, it appeared that no two were exactly alike on a microscopic level, an alien concept to the network. Stranger still, they were locked into those differences, with no ability to shape-shift!

Fascinating!

There were now more than one hundred remote units composing the peripheral node aboard *Sharonov*. Twenty occupied the humans, while the rest had branch-merged through *Sharonov*'s body. Though no two of the node's units shared the same exact outward shape, all of them, on a microscopic and submicroscopic level, were precisely identical. Among the humans, their microstructures were similar, but the arrangement varied enough that no two units were the same. Even on a large scale, they were similar, but disturbingly different from one another. The patterns in their fingertips, for example . . . why were those all different, from one finger to another, from one human to another? And there were physical differences—those between Capt. Grigor Kleist and the one that called itself Lt. Karen DuBois, for example—for which there was simply no explanation.

More data were needed. With it, perhaps, the supervisor nucleus would be able to make sense out of this confusion.

It was fortunate that the memories of *Sharonov*'s computer were relatively easy to access and read. Though much touching on the humans was difficult to comprehend, all of the data were recorded in the universal language of binary mathematics and easily translated. It had not been hard to glean references to something the humans referred to as "the Device" or "the Artifact," and, from its description, to deduce its nature.

Apparently, megaseconds ago, an isolated system remote, a seeker, had made contact with human units. *Sharonov*'s data indicated that the seeker had been taken—at least for a time—to the satellite of the largest gas giant in the system—the one the humans called Jupiter.

Sharonov's computer had all of the navigational data necessary for the controller to set course for that satellite as soon as it had assimilated the raw figures. The seeker might still be there, and it would have vital data on human activities and programming.

The controller would join with the seeker, acquire its data, and transmit it to the supervisor nucleus.

Linking with the branch-merged cluster units infiltrating *Sharonov*'s systems, the controller studied the planetary system-in-miniature spreading before the ship's sensors. Central was Jupiter, a vast and bloated gas giant banded by swirling vapor streams and given color by strange chemical compounds. Circling Jupiter were innumerable smaller objects, some natural satellites, others artificial and under power.

One satellite, brick-red and showing the pale-blue halo of magnetic shielding, grew steadily larger in the controller's sensory apparatus.

Sharonov was less than an hour out from Amalthea. Very soon, now, the controller could begin answering some of the questions the network's supervisor nucleus had about humans.

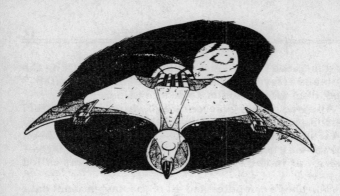

CHAPTER FIVE

The Kraits dropped through strangeness, wending their way into the depths of Jupiter's atmosphere through a fairyland of cloud formations, eldritch mountains, cliffs, spires, and walls sculpted by alien winds. It was early morning now, and the ramparts towering above the fighters ahead and to either side sent shafts of golden sunlight slanting above the shadowed deeps and topped each rounded cloud-mountain peak with glory.

High overhead, ammonia-crystal cirrus clouds stretched feathery plumes across an achingly blue zenith. Below, the highest peaks of cumulus mountains were glacier white and touched with fire where the sunlight turned them golden. The cloud walls dropped to either side of the tiny Krait fighters, plunging through layer after layer into the abyss below, canyons carved from shadow, light, and vapor. The colors were intense and vibrant, an artist's palette of hues, reds and browns, ochers and golds, burnt sienna, violet and scarlet, the stains of strange organic compounds forged within the deeps of Jupiter's atmosphere and lofted skyward by upwelling currents of air. The colors grew darker with depth, until the eye lost the shape of the clouds entirely in the black gulf of the Jovian Deep.

His autopilot off now, Vince gripped the Krait's control stick tightly, holding the craft steady on the course indi-

cated by his computer. The hull had cooled after its
meteoric descent through the upper atmosphere. To save
fuel, he'd switched his engines to ramjet mode. The
Krait was gulping huge quantities of hydrogen through
the intakes, heating it to star-hot plasma in its reactor,
and blasting it astern in an incandescent jet. Gravity
dragged at Vince, wearing at him despite his exercise
and drug regimen over the past weeks. It was worse
than he'd expected. He wasn't looking forward to leaving
the embrace of his fighter's cockpit.

Deep within the black chasm far below, lightning
flared and forked with eye-searing intensity. Vince
hunched forward, bracing himself against what he was
sure would be an ear-shattering blast of thunder, but all
he heard transmitted through the transplex of the cockpit was a thin, tinny crackle. Shock waves, it seemed,
lost much of their violence in an atmosphere that was
mostly hydrogen and helium.

There was plenty of buffeting, though. Wind speeds at
this altitude exceeded three hundred miles per hour, and
it took all of Vince's pilot skill to hold the ship steady,
even with the aid of computer-directed control surfaces.
The air outside his cockpit was wonderfully clear. The
nearest wall of cloud, clearly delineated on his radar
screen, lay a hundred miles to starboard, but each detail
of its windswept, richly textured surface was as crisp
and as clear as if it had been carved from stone a few
yards off his wingtip.

Everywhere he looked, clouds piled upon clouds in a
bewildering profusion of form, texture, and hue. Unlike
the Inner Worlds, Jupiter had no solid surface. Every
feature, every band, spot, and swirl visible from space
on this king of planets lay within the upper three hundred miles of an atmosphere that grew ever denser and
hotter as depth increased. Usually thought of as a cold
world, Jupiter in fact gave off more heat from its own
collapsing core than it received from the distant sun. At
the cloud tops, the air pressure hovered close to that at
sea level on Earth and the temperature was minus 190
degrees. Six hundred miles deeper, the pressure was so

intense that gas gave way to a boiling ocean of hydrogen, liquid despite the furnacelike temperature. Some thousands of miles below that, beneath an ocean deep enough to drown most other worlds, liquid hydrogen compressed into semisolid sludge, ultimately compacting to a metallic mantle around an Earth-sized core of rock and iron.

Lightning exploded again in the depths, a raw display of voltage that would have powered a terrestrial city for years.

"Three-One Alpha, this is Bravo," a rough voice called over Vince's ship-to-ship lasercom link. "Do you read, over?"

"I read you, Bravo," Vince replied. "How's it going?"

"All systems nominal," Kaiten said. "I am reading organics, bearing one-eight-five, range thirty miles. Visitors."

Vince looked in the indicated direction but saw nothing. Clouds banked and swirled in colors ranging from red and purple to dark brown. A vast oval spiral of rust and scarlet, surrounded by a crinkled sea of brown, fluffy-looking cumulus caught his eye. The Terrine's eyes were sharper than his. Maybe . . .

Yes! He saw them now! Motionless above the red spiral were what looked like gnats or motes of dust caught in a single shaft of sunlight. There must have been hundreds of them, thousands, perhaps, and he realized that their lack of movement was an illusion of distance. They were rising in the hot-air thermals above the storm, but at thirty miles they seemed motionless. To be visible at all at that range they must be enormous. Vince keyed a command into his console, then studied the magnified image that appeared on one of his monitor screens. Each speck was the size and shape of a dirigible and trailed diaphanous streamers, like sheets of gauze hanging from a body that looked tiny only in proportion to the enormous gasbag that held it aloft.

Bloats, the gene-engineered cattle of the Jovian clouds. Vince had read about these creatures, which blended the heavily altered genes of terrestrial cows and

whales in creatures that more closely resembled a cross
between a blimp and a Portuguese man-of-war. The
gauze sheets were their feeding mechanisms, organic
nets that trapped and absorbed organic compounds
adrift in the Jovian winds. With such an abundant food
supply, bloats grew to incredible size.

"Three-One Alpha, this is Bravo," Kaiten said. "I'm
losing definition on my radar sweeps."

"Same here." Static sparked and sizzled across the
console displays showing radar images. He could make
out the cloud walls, like sheer rock cliffs, but the bloats
were lost in the clutter. "It's almost like jamming."

Thanks to its internal heat and powerful magnetic
fields, Jupiter was the source of tremendous radio
"noise," a constant waterfall of static that made ordinary
radio communication all but impossible and radar unre-
liable. Fortunately, laser light was not subject to radio
interference.

"Perhaps it is," Kaiten pointed out. "The city is visible
now. At the same altitude as the bloats, and five degrees
to the right."

Vince shifted his gaze and got his first glimpse of a
Jovian cloud city, the drifting sky-island called Vrahk.

Life on Jupiter depended on the fact, known since the
twentieth century, that there was a thin layer within the
gas giant's atmosphere where the air pressure was five
times that of Earth at sea level and the temperatures
hovered between thirty and one hundred degrees
Fahrenheit. Liquid water could exist there, though the
air was still a poisonous brew of hydrogen, helium,
methane, and ammonia.

There the genetic engineers had first seeded the clouds
with their living experiments. Here their greatest tri-
umph had been realized, and the Stormriders of Jupiter
stretched wing against an alien sky. Here, too, the Jovian
cloud cities had been created, first of metal and plastic
imported from worlds where such materials were accessi-
ble, later from genetically sculpted, living creatures. All
cloud cities now were living, gene-tailored animals supported by enormous bladders filled with the one gas that

rises in a hydrogen atmosphere—hot hydrogen.

Bloats stayed aloft because their metabolism heated vast quantities of hydrogen, filling the vast, sausage-shaped dorsal gasbags that kept them aloft despite the planet's gravity. The Jovian cities were actually derived from bloats, huge living organisms so intricately reworked that they no longer bore the slightest resemblance to living creatures. On Vince's screen, the city looked like a neat stack of three or four dishes topped by an enormous, translucent dome. Within the dome were dimly seen buildings, spires, and smaller domes, but the entire structure was at least a mile across, and anything as small as an individual building was nearly invisible.

The city, Vince noted, appeared almost motionless, though it was adrift on winds that made an Earthly hurricane seem calm by comparison. The nearest cloud wall was a sulfur-and-ocher mountain ten miles beyond. Cloud cities, Vince had read, usually rode with the air currents, but they could also be guided through the sky using hydrogen jets set around their perimeters. For them, course control was a daily matter of life and death, the only way to avoid deadly up- or downdrafts. The towering cloud masses were updraft regions, the canyon gulfs areas of cooling, sinking air; a city caught in either extreme would rapidly be carried into levels where it was either too cold or too hot for life. Too, the turbulence within the smallest of storm clouds would shred the largest city. During his briefings for this mission Vince had been warned to stay well clear of the smooth, wind-sculpted sweep of the cloud walls.

A chimed warning tone sounded from his console, startling him. The ship's computer was alerting him that someone was trying to reach them at a frequency of 301.5 MHz. The radio had been switched off—there was nothing to hear, after all, but the crash and roar of Jupiter itself—but he turned it on now, punching up the indicated frequency and directing the computer to clean up the random noise as much as possible.

Static hissed and spat despite the computer processing, and at first Vince could make out nothing. Then he realized that he was hearing another series of sounds behind the static, an eerie, shrill, barking rasp that somehow seemed to carry the force and shape of words.

"Is language," Kaiten said over the lasercom channel. "I think."

"I think so, too," Vince said. "Better answer them, I guess. I hope they can hear us."

Back in the Belt, no one had been quite certain how Vince and Kaiten would be able to communicate with the Stormriders, or even whether the Kraits' radios could be heard against Jupiter's thunderous roar. They'd assumed, though, that the Stormriders themselves would take care of that. There was trade between Jupiter and other worlds, after all, so there must be some protocol of approach.

"Cloud city, cloud city," he called. "This is Flight Victor Three-One. Do you copy me, over?"

Static shrilled and roared for a long moment. Vince was about to try again when a voice answered, high-pitched, almost girlish in timbre, but with the measured cadence of someone speaking with authority. "Victor Three-One, this is Vrahk'dreleschaah Airspace Control. Who are you and what is your purpose here?"

"Ah, Vrahk Airspace Control," Vince replied, not even trying to pronounce the full, ponderous Stormrider name. "My name is Vince Pirelli and I'm here to see Dr. Marlene Kowalski. She is in great danger, but I believe we can help. Over."

There was a long pause. "Vince Pirelli," the voice said at last. "Our records indicate that your real name is Peron and that you are with RAM. What is your unit and the purpose for your trespass within our domain?"

Vince hesitated. A wrong step now could wreck any chance of meeting Kowalski. The Stormriders evidently had electronic access to the computers governing Amalthea's spaceport and docking facilities and in any case would certainly suspect that two Krait fighters carried RAM personnel. If the Stormriders thought they were RAM, they would never see Dr. Kowalski even if she was in Vrahk as Hubert Shelton had suggested. It was a big city, and there were only the two of them.

But no one back at NEO headquarters had been sure how the Stormriders would react to an announcement that Vince and Kaiten were NEO. The Jovian gennies had no involvement in the war against RAM, no reason to side with either Earth or Mars. In any case, Stormriders were not known for their open and trusting natures.

Still, there was no point in continuing the fiction that they were RAM, and Vince didn't want to try some other lie—such as their being scientists or traders—which could be checked electronically. He'd long before elected to tell the truth.

He just hoped that at longer ranges his Krait's transmissions were being drowned by the far vaster radio noise of the planet itself. It would be embarrassing if eavesdroppers on Amalthea could hear what he was about to say.

"Vrahk Airspace Control, we belong to the New Earth Organization. RAM is our enemy, though we were forced to pose as RAM at Amalthea to avoid suspicion. We need to talk to Dr. Kowalski, and quickly."

Silence, torn by static. A lightning bolt flared in the blackness of the gulf below, and the roar of its static shrilled above the faint hydrogen crackle of its thunder. "Why should she want to see you?" the voice said at last.

"NEO has recovered an unusual artifact first studied by Dr. Kowalski on Amalthea. We have reason to believe that RAM is now here to find out what she knows, and they won't be gentle with her. We're here to offer her a way to escape RAM."

"You could easily be RAM spies."

"There are only two of us. Surely the great Stormriders of Jupiter are capable of protecting one human woman against the two of us while you check out our story. Or are you afraid?"

There was another hesitation, even longer this time. Vince's final challenge was risky, but calculated. Those humans who'd dealt face-to-face with Stormriders reported them to be haughty, proud, and a bit arrogant.

The implied charge of cowardice might open a chink in their armor.

"We are not afraid," the voice responded after still another pause. Vince had the feeling that they were conferring with one another after each exchange. "But we see no purpose in allowing potential enemies to enter our city."

"Why don't you let Dr. Kowalski decide whether or not she wants to see us?" Vince suggested. "Tell her . . . tell her we're also offering her the chance to continue her studies of the Artifact." Surely the scientist in Kowalski would jump at such a chance.

Pause . . . the seconds dragging on and on as Jupiter roared and hissed and shrieked its ongoing chorus.

"Prove that you are not RAM," the voice said.

"If I were a RAM spy," Vince said reasonably, "I assure you I would not arrive in a RAM fighter posing as a RAM agent and accompanied by a Terrine. The deception was necessary to fool RAM agents on Amalthea, but we can prove that we are NEO if you let us land." He wondered how the Stormriders were at logic.

"You could be a deranged RAM spy," the voice said. Was there a trace of humor behind the words? The voice was too harsh, too inhuman, for Vince to judge. "Permission is granted to land in Bay One. Follow us in."

" 'Follow—' " He'd assumed the speaker was inside the city. The command to follow made it sound as though he was in a ship or aircraft.

A shadow swept across Vince's Krait, startling him and making him look up. What he saw made him gasp with surprise.

He'd seen holos of Stormriders, of course, but never had he seen one in its natural element . . . on the wing. Its body was nearly as long as the Krait. Its wingspan was incredible.

Sunlight touched translucent, outstretched membranes, turning them to luminous gold. *Megaureoptera jovis* was the Stormrider's scientific name, the great goldenwing of Jupiter. The name did not begin to describe the creature's size, beauty, and sheer majesty.

Those vast wings were often described as batlike, but they were much more like the wings of the extinct pterodactyl. The hands had become part of the wings, each located a third of the way from the body to the wingtip and supporting the featherless, translucent membrane from a curved, elongated fifth finger. The wing's base was held taut by the Stormrider's legs, which splayed to either side and seemed to serve as dual stabilizers. The thickly knotted arm muscles were anchored by a sternum that jutted from the creature's chest like the keel of a boat.

Vince could just make out the humanoid outline of the body—Stormriders were derived from human genes, with the genes of rays and sharks added—but the arms and legs were almost lost against the spread of those magnificent wings. The head was elongated and streamlined, dominated by enormous, pupilless eyes and extended into a slender crest that must have aided the creature in steering. Its skin was naked and leathery, a mottling of reds and purples on its dorsal surface shading to pale oranges and golds below.

The Stormrider passed his Krait less than ten feet above the cockpit. The turbulence of its passing jolted the Krait and made Vince tighten his grip on the stick. Another passed, more distant than the first, sunlight flashing from outstretched, golden wings. Others followed. Vince and Kaiten were in the midst of a great host of Jovian Stormriders surrounding them, herding them as they must herd the far larger and clumsier bloats. Some, Vince saw, had devices of some sort clasped in the bare, prehensile toes of their feet. Weapons? Communicators? He couldn't tell.

"Follow us," the voice on the radio ordered once again. There was no threat, but the authority behind that voice convinced Vince that disobedience was not a good idea.

"We're following," Vince replied. He shifted to the lasercom channel. "Kaiten?"

"I heard. I am with you."

Banking the Krait slightly, Vince swung the fighter's prow to align with the city, now plainly visible to the naked eye. Stormriders filled the sky ahead. What a sight!

Vince very much hoped he would live long enough to describe it to someone else.

CHAPTER SIX

As minutes passed, the Jovian city grew until it filled
the forward windscreen of Vince's Krait. Even less than
a mile away it still looked like something manufactured,
a thing, not an animal.

A gaping maw a hundred yards tall opened like a cavern on one side of the stacked-plates body. Stormriders,
their wings golden slivers astride the rising thermals,
gracefully circled a slow and clumsy bloat, guiding it
toward the opening.

Though enormous, the bloat was tiny compared to the
city, the gliding Stormriders tinier still, like flies swarming about a cow. There was a flurry of activity at the
bloat's underside, and the trailing membranes dropped
away, exposing the four spindly, dangling legs that
spread the creature's nets as it grazed the Jovian skies.
The bloat's gasbag and body, urged along by the aerial
herdsmen, continued drifting forward, vanishing into
the opening.

Bloats were the city's food supply, the cavern the city's
mouth. The size difference between living city and bloat
was not quite as extreme as that, say, between extinct
Terran whales and the krill upon which they fed, but
hundreds of the floating Jovian cattle must have been
herded into that gaping maw each day just to power its
metabolism. Like the bloat, the city-creature drew

hydrogen from the air, heated it, and circulated it into the gasbag that held the mile-wide island afloat at the five-atmosphere level. The process required a great deal of heat, and bloat carcasses were the fuel that generated it. Leftovers fed the city's population, while multiton scraps were processed and frozen for shipment offworld. Bloat meat, Vince knew, was popular elsewhere, especially among the Aerostaters of Venus.

Their escort seemed to be leading them around the side of the city, away from the maw. Now Vince could see the nozzles of maneuvering jets, huge, knotted openings clamped shut by massive sphincters. Much smaller openings, like balconies arrayed along the side of a city-sized arcology, appeared to be entrances to the city. Vince held the Krait steady as the opening toward which their escort was guiding them grew steadily larger.

Landing gear down, he cut back on the power until the Krait's handling felt slow and mushy in the thick air, pulled the nose up, then held his breath as the opening blurred around him. There was a sharp jolt that hurled him forward against the restraining straps of his seat . . . and then he was stopped, the Krait motionless on a broad, flat floor within a cavern with softly glowing walls and a high vaulted ceiling. Kaiten's fighter lurched to a stop to his right, its undercarriage entangled at the last moment, he saw, in strands of membranous filament stretched across the opening.

He was down in the city of Vrahk'dreleschaah. He began shutting down the Krait's systems, bracing himself as he did so for what was to come. Stormriders had a reputation of proud arrogance, a disdain for the lesser creatures who visited their world. If his next conversation failed to convince them of who he was—or if they believed but simply didn't care—he and Kaiten would in all probability die here.

As he unfastened his harness, Vince remembered Galen repeating Shelton's story about the RAM agent who had followed Kowalski to Vrahk, and shuddered. Much of the city was open, and it was a long way down.

Carefully, he checked his cockpit's gas mix, verifying

that it was pure nitrogen. Releasing a standard oxygen-nitrogen gas mix into the mostly hydrogen atmosphere outside was a bad idea; one spark could cause a nasty explosion. After equalizing pressures, he cracked the fighter's canopy, then unhooked himself from the cockpit life support. A backpack unit stored behind his seat would provide him with air for ten hours. As he settled the life-support pack into place and began fastening its straps, his knees nearly buckled with the savage gravity. Massing 180 in one G, Vince weighed in at a hefty 450 on Jupiter, and the backpack and helmet added at least another 60 pounds. He extended the Krait's ladder and carefully clambered down to the floor. Together with all of his equipment, he now massed over a quarter of a ton, and a wrong step could break bones.

Kaiten appeared at his side as he turned away from the Krait. The Terrine, a fearsome figure in his red-and-black battle armor, topped Vince by a foot. He, too, seemed to be moving slowly, careful with the placement of each step.

"Our reception committee waits," Kaiten said. His voice, normally a rumbling bass, sounded metallic, high-pitched, and thin, like that of an out-of-breath child. They were using their external suit speakers and microphones, knowing that radio would be next to useless against Jupiter's electromagnetic roar. Even at five atmospheres, though, hydrogen did not carry sound well. Vince hoped he could make himself understood.

Turning, looking up, he got his first close look at a Stormrider.

Outside, against the sky and cloud and sunlight, they'd seemed large. Here, within the confines of the city walls, they were true giants. There were dozens of them, each standing at least fifteen feet tall, many as much as twenty, and, when they stood upright, Vince's head reached only a little above their knees. On Earth, an adult Stormrider would have weighed half a ton. Here they weighed a ton and a quarter, though they moved with a strange and alien grace that belied their enormous mass.

Wings rustled, a leathery hiss of dry membranes. The creatures rarely stood upright. Usually a Stormrider crouched, his hands flat on the floor, his arms bracing the upper part of his muscular torso. The wings, so broad when riding the open sky, folded into a surprisingly compact package; their little fingers, each more than twice as long as Vince was tall, swept up from the floor and back up over their heads, holding most of the wing membrane arched well above their heads. The ceilings in this place, Vince realized, were high and vaulted for good reason.

How could such creatures fly in this gravity? Vince knew the physics involved: those wings were designed more for soaring, for riding hot columns of rising air, than for true flight, and the air pressure of five atmospheres at this altitude compensated for their weight. Still, with their wings folded and their tremendous bulks supported on all fours, they did not look like creatures of the air. Vince found himself thinking of the bumblebee, a Terran insect that managed to fly despite aerodynamic studies proving that it could not.

One of the Stormriders was grasping an electronic device of some sort in one hand and seemed to be scanning the two NEO agents with it. Vince imagined they were being checked for weapons or explosives . . . a sensible precaution in a city held aloft by a giant balloon. Satisfied, apparently, the being switched the scanner off and chirped at the others.

Another Stormrider, one of the largest, shuffled forward, its head six feet above Vince's even when it crouched on all fours. Raising itself then, hands held at chest height, it flicked its wing fingers to each side. Golden wings spread halfway open, framing the giant's body, but whether in formal greeting or in threat display, Vince couldn't tell.

"*Throvidronvinav*, Tenth Speaker for the Warlords of the Violet Lightnings," the being said, the voice shrill and high-pitched, but carrying the same measured authority Vince had heard before. "Prove now the truth of your spirits."

The Stormrider spoke Anglic, though the words were strangely shaped by his wide, lipless mouth, and Vince wasn't sure what the being meant by proving their spirits. Carefully, Vince reached into his suit's pouch and produced his military ID, a card encoded with his service record and NEO authorization. Though most of the data could only be accessed through a computer reader, its surface included Vince's holograph and the NEO globe emblem.

"Meaningless," the giant said. He didn't even take the card, and for the first time Vince realized that the beings' hands, heavy and thick-fingered, were ill-suited for delicate tasks. "Tell us why the Warlords of Vrahk' dreleschaah should not now feed you to God."

"The major has given you ample reason already," Kaiten said sharply. "If we were RAM, there'd be a lot more than two of us here right now!"

The Terrine obviously meant to sound defiant, but his little-girl voice sounded comical. Despite the danger, Vince nearly laughed out loud.

"Look, ah . . . Throv," Vince said. He hoped he wasn't committing some gross impropriety by shortening the huge being's name. "We must seem pretty strange to you, as strange as you are to us. How could you possibly tell whether we were telling the truth about anything? Why don't you let Dr. Kowalski decide? She's human. She'll know whether or not we're lying." He desperately hoped that that was true.

"Search us for weapons," Kaiten said. "Guard us. Only let us talk to her."

Vince nodded, then stopped, suddenly aware that the gesture might mean nothing to these strange giants. "That's right. If Dr. Kowalski's not convinced we're who we say we are, then *phht*!" He jerked his thumb over his shoulder, pointing toward the opening at his back. "Over the side. Maybe we can learn how to fly without spacecraft, like you."

A thin, gurgling rasp sounded from the creature's throat. It took Vince a moment to recognize it as laughter. "You show courage, wingless one. And good logic."

One hand moved, rustling a folded wing and indicating Kaiten. "That one will remain here, hostage to your spirit. You will come with me."

"Kaiten?"

"Is okay," the Terrine said. He looked up at the winged creatures closing in around him. "But hurry back before I decide to test how fragile these monsters' wings are."

"Stay out of trouble and for God's sake don't make them mad. I'll be back as soon as I can."

Vince followed the huge being through seemingly endless corridors. The Stormrider city seen from within felt more alien, more organic, than it had looked from outside. Floors were smooth and flat, but the walls had an odd, pebbly texture and glowed with a pale luminescence. There were no right angles or squared corners anywhere, and the air was heavy and wet, shrouding the floor in a carpet of fog and condensing on the walls and on his pressure suit as droplets of clear liquid.

They reached a door, like every other doorway in the place stretching at least thirty feet above the floor, and Vince was ushered through. In the room beyond, obviously an air lock, his escort paused to don a transparent mask that fit snugly over his head, and an environmental-support pack that hung from his neck and over his chest, riding on either side of the jutting, muscle-bound keel of his breastbone. Vince heard the shrill hiss of venting gas. His suit began to balloon as the outside pressure dwindled, and he punched at the buttons on his left arm, ordering the suit to compensate.

"The atmosphere is now suitable for your kind," the Stormrider said, his voice muffled slightly by the mask. In an oxygen-nitrogen atmosphere, the tones were bass-deep and rich.

Cautiously, Vince cracked his helmet's seal, then removed it. The air tasted flat and metallic and was still quite wet. He hoped that the Stormrider technology was up to the task of removing every trace of the Jovian air from the lock, because any mixture of hydrogen and oxygen would be dangerously explosive. Vince could not smell the sharp pungency of ammonia, however; the city's filters and circulators must be highly efficient.

The lock's inner door opened, and Vince stepped into a startlingly earthlike office with richly carpeted floors and walls hung with brightly colored tapestries. The sole concession to Stormrider anatomy was the ceiling, which was more than thirty feet high. One entire wall was transparent, looking out into the violet-and-red glory of a Jovian cloud wall, and there were banks of electronic communication gear, computer consoles, and display screens that must have been imported from elsewhere. In one corner was a shiny complexity of tubes, dials, and cylinders that, to Vince's untrained eyes, looked like some sort of research equipment, an electron microscope, possibly, or a powerful lepton imager. The center of the room was dominated by a heavy desk of black Venusian stonewood. Two other masked Stormriders besides his escort were already in the room, one to either side of the desk and dwarfing the woman behind it.

Anywhere else in the Solar System the woman would have seemed big. She was not fat, but her build was aggressively stout and muscular. Her unflatteringly utilitarian smartsuit revealed a waist as thick as her hips and arms as massive as any man's, but she seemed petite between the golden giants crouching silently to each side.

"You're Vince Peron, and you're from RAM," she said without preamble. Her face was square with heavy features, but her hair was shiny, long, and black. "I'm Doc Kowalski. My friends here are all for tossing you over the side, but I thought I'd hear what you have to say first."

In answer, Vince reached toward his suit's pouch. The woman's huge guards stiffened at the movement, both raising long, knob-headed batons in clawed fingers and aiming them at the Earthman. They looked like electrical weapons of some kind.

"Gently, friend," Kowalski said. "Those charge guns of theirs'll fry you to a crisp if you even twitch funny."

Very, very slowly, Vince completed the motion, pulling a computer disk from the pouch and gently placing it on Kowalski's desk. She chirped something at the Stormriders, the harsh notes rasping in her throat, and they lowered their weapons. They remained watchful, however, the forward-leaning crouch of their bodies revealing an alertness that the huge, pupilless eyes could not.

Kowalski took the disk, examined it briefly, then dropped it into a reader on her desk. After a moment, one of her computer display screens lit up, showing 2-D video images recorded weeks before. Men and women worked together around a lab bench, Vince, Jovanna, and Galen among them. Resting on the bench was a basketball-sized sphere as brilliantly silver and as polished as pure liquid mercury.

"I'm not RAM," Vince said, "and my real name is Pirelli. I work for NEO. The scenes you're looking at were recorded at a NEO lab in the Asteroid Belt. Do you recognize the silver globe?"

"I should say so," she said. On the screen, one of the researchers touched the silver sphere with outstretched fingers. As though in response, the sphere quivered, then seemed to turn itself inside out, writhing into a four-sided pyramid shape.

"And do you recognize that man?" he asked, pointing to a tall and powerfully built man with red hair and a bushy, walrus mustache. "The one standing next to me?"

"I've seen him," she admitted. "On Terran newscasts. Colonel MacGregor, isn't it?"

"One of NEO's top military commanders, and a member of the NEO council. He came all the way out from Earth to see the Artifact," Vince said. "That woman over there is Francine Garrison. She's also on the council. The guy touching the Artifact now is Dr. Karl Gunther of the Berlin Academy of Science. No friend of RAM, I'm sure you'll admit if you follow the news."

"So what's your point?"

"That NEO has the Artifact now. We managed to grab it before RAM could get their claws on it, and this tape is proof. I had something to do with that affair, and they had me in to describe what I'd seen."

Kowalski's eyes narrowed. "You handled the sphere yourself? You touched it?"

He nodded. "Yep."

"What did you . . . see?"

"Another world. Icy, frigid, barren, with a moon or planet hanging enormous in a black sky. There was a . . . a city. Not like any city I've ever seen. Enormous, sprawling, cold, sterile, with towers and blue lights and weirdly shaped buildings that didn't look like anything made by man." Vince shivered. "I'll never forget it as long as I live."

Kowalski was nodding. "Yeah. You've seen it. So did I, when it was here."

"We found out that some traders brought it here, that you were the one who first saw the Artifact."

"That's right. They were Nomads, from a deep-space city called Ciudestreya. They claimed they'd found this thing when their city was way out beyond Saturn's orbit. Somewhere near Chiron, in fact. That scene wasn't Chiron, though."

"You're sure of that?"

"I know enough astronomy to know the difference between a planet and an asteroid, yeah. That . . . that memory in the sphere was of a larger place, someplace a lot farther away. Chiron never had something in its sky, that moon or planet or whatever it was. And the technology that made the sphere was not human."

"Which is why both NEO and RAM are interested in it, Doctor. That's why we want you to help us."

"Help you? Why should I?"

"Because, quite frankly, RAM wants you for the same reason. You've seen the Artifact, studied it, and they know that we have it. They're going to want to pick your brain, Doctor, and, knowing RAM, they're not going to be polite about it."

Kowalski snorted. "Why do you think I'm down here? They came looking for me and the . . . what'd you call it? The Artifact. They came after me and the Artifact with a goddamned heavy cruiser. The Artifact was gone already. Solar Geographic didn't have the credits to meet the Nomads' price. When the cruiser showed up at Amalthea, though, I thought I'd better make myself scarce." Her eyes narrowed suspiciously. "You know, sonny, you still haven't convinced me you're not RAM."

Vince gestured at the computer screen. "I'm in that video. If that doesn't convince you, what will?"

"With computer technology what it is today, you could show me a tape with you talking to Buck Rogers and it wouldn't prove you were with NEO. Things like that can be faked just by scrambling some zeros and ones in the tape's digital code."

"Then what—"

"Aw, hell, I believe you," Kowalski said. "RAM wouldn't go to this much trouble to convince me. Like you told the Tenth Speaker, there, they'd just send in an army and drag me away." She grinned maliciously. "And that'd take some dragging, let me tell you!"

"Will you come with us?" Vince asked. "I can promise that—"

"Come with you? Hell, no!"

"But you said—"

"I said I believed you, sonny, not that I'd come with you. Why should I go traipsing off across the gukin' Solar System when I have all I need right here? When I have friends right here?"

"I, ah, assumed you'd welcome the opportunity to have another crack at the Artifact. We're convinced that it represents an alien technology, that it's something built by an extrasolar intelligence. It could be the most important discovery in the history of man and . . . why are you laughing?"

Kowalski was leaning back in her chair, her head and shoulders bobbing up and down as she suppressed a deep, soundless chuckle. Splaying her hand on a palm reader on her desk, she unlocked a drawer and removed something which she held cupped in her hands. Gently, she dropped it on the black wood in front of Vince.

He sucked in a sharp breath. It was a tiny globe, a bright silver sphere the size of a ping-pong ball. "Is that what I think it is?" He extended a finger to touch the shiny surface. It was slick, cool, and hard. Though he listened hard with his mind, however, he sensed nothing else.

"It's inert," Kowalski said. "Dead. My guess is that below a certain critical mass it doesn't work."

"How did you get it?" Vince remembered how difficult it was to handle the Artifact. Normally solid, it was as amorphous as a thick liquid when it was changing shape, and attempts to pull a piece off for closer examination always failed.

"Wasn't easy. That stuff is real resistant to temperature change, let me tell you. Even at thirty degrees above zero absolute it was just as liquid, if that's the right word, as it was at room temperature. But when I used liquid helium to cool part of it to four degrees absolute, it turned to something like putty and I was able to pinch off this chunk." She grinned. "Didn't hurt the big one any, and I didn't think those Nomads'd miss this itty-bitty piece."

"So you're studying this sample here?"

"Damned right. And I can do a better job without those . . . memories of some place I've never been to getting in the way. Hell, I've already learned stuff that'd knock your socks off!"

"The science team working on the Artifact would welcome your input, I'm sure."

"Yeah, I just bet they would. Well, you can tell 'em, if they haven't thought of it already, about the trick with liquid helium. But I don't want any part of it." She patted the sample on her desk. "When I'm ready, I'll publish a paper describing my conclusions. Believe me, sonny, your NEO scientists are gonna be in for a shock!"

"If you have some special insight, don't you think you should share it? That's what science is all about, isn't it? Free inquiry, sharing observations—"

"Ha! Why don't you share your input with RAM? Your scientists get together with their scientists for the benefit of mankind!" When Vince didn't answer immediately, she scooped up the tiny sphere and put it back in the desk drawer. "I'll tell you the truth, Pirelli. I don't give two milligrams of sodium chloride for RAM or NEO. They can both go blow themselves up for all I care. Only reason either one wants this thing is they figure it'll give them some sort of advantage in their war. War, ha! A lot they know about it. My friends here could tell·'em a thing or two about war."

"It's not just that," Vince said. "NEO can't let RAM have the advantage in technology the Artifact might give them, true, but ultimately, what we learn will be for the benefit of everyone."

"If there's any benefit to be had." She laughed again, and Vince had the feeling that she knew a secret, something vastly amusing.

"You would be safer with us," Vince said, a little desperately. Kowalski seemed determined to stay in Vrahk, and he was running out of arguments. "Sooner or later RAM is going to find you here."

"If they do, they're liable to be sorry." One of her bodyguards stirred, ominous and huge within the leathery rasp of wings. "Those damned fools in the Genetics Foundation imagine that these people belong to them. Imagine! Well, a little longer and the system'll see just who owns who!"

"Dr. Kowalski—"

She cut him off with a sharp chirp. The one who'd accompanied Vince to the room, the Tenth Speaker, touched him lightly on the shoulder.

"Come," the Speaker said. "You will return to your companion."

"Dr. Kowalski, please listen," Vince tried again. "RAM knows you're here. You won't be safe unless you let us help you. I don't care how many of these giant canaries you have around you!"

"Good-bye, Pirelli," she said firmly. "I don't think we'll meet again."

The Stormrider, gently but with a veiled strength Vince could never hope to match, guided him from the room.

The mission, Vince thought glumly, had failed.

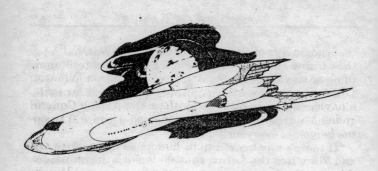

CHAPTER SEVEN

The chime sounded at Jovanna's door, and she ordered the room's computer to identify her caller. It was Galen, his disturbingly human eyes betraying his worry. At her command, the computer opened the door.

"Jovanna!" the Tinker said urgently as he entered. "They're here!"

"Who?"

"RAM, who else? They have a warship at the main dock right now! The *Dread Reprisal*'s already taken off, just in case RAM IDed it during the Phobos raid."

Jovanna wondered who might be listening in, then decided it didn't matter. If a RAM military vessel had just docked at Amalthea, it didn't matter much whether Shelton or other RAM agents in the satellite knew that she and Galen were NEO, not now. Their best hope lay in losing themselves in the Amalthean population, and worrying about Shelton later.

Leaving the hotel room, she followed Galen into the elevator to the carousel room's hub, then out into a passageway that took them deeper into Amalthea. They moved quickly, pulling themselves along hand-over-hand in the almost nonexistent gravity. It reminded her vividly of the last time she and Galen had fled RAM pursuers, in the heart of a military base in Phobos.

"How many are there?" she called after Galen.

"Only one ship," he called back. "A light cruiser, crew of about twenty. But there's a bigger squadron following them, RAM's Jovian squadron, a couple hours out. They're already on the Amalthean Approach Control radar. This moon's going to be crawling with RAM troopers before we know it!"

The passageway opened, moments later, onto the Amalthean Strip. Galen pointed toward the transplex window overlooking the docking bay, where a RAM light cruiser was suspended in the tangled steel complexity of a port gantry close alongside the liner *Golden Argosy*. Jovanna could read the name printed on the vessel's prow: *Sharonov*.

"It's Plan A, then?" They'd been worried about what might happen if RAM showed up before the mission was complete, and had worked out several alternate plans. "Plan A" called for Jovanna and Galen to hide somewhere already picked out by Galen where there were no cameras or eavesdropping devices, assume disguises, and then emerge to mingle with Amalthea's population. Not even a RAM invasion armada could screen three thousand civilians for a couple of NEO agents.

"That's it. I've found a place for you in the engineering spaces. It'll be a tight fit, I'm afraid, but you'll be safe enough until you can change your clothes and face."

"What about you?"

"I'll be safer staying in the ventilator ducts," Galen replied. "There aren't many Tinkers in Amalthea and I'd stand out among you human types like an octopede on your dinner plate. But there must be a hundred thousand miles of passageways through the rock. They'll never track me in there."

"We should have some time, yet," Jovanna said. "In a ship that small, they'll spend some time first shutting down systems and—"

"And what?"

"My mistake," she said. "Look there, to the left."

A RAM naval officer was emerging from the access door that connected the customs gate area with the strip. He was a tall, gaunt man in an unkempt gray uniform. He hesitated at the mouth of the access tube, his head moving jerkily back and forth as though he was looking for something. As they watched, a second RAM officer came through the tube, a woman with long, stringy blond hair. Her uniform tunic had been torn down the front and was hanging open, attracting more-than-curious glances from male passers-by.

"Odd," Galen said. Another man emerged. He wore no uniform tunic at all, and there was a smear of something dark across his face. "The way they're standing around with their mouths open, they look like tourists, country hicks in to see the bright lights of the big city."

"Something else strange," Jovanna said softly. "Look at their uniforms . . . and the woman's hair."

"What about them?"

"Torn and dirty uniforms. Dirty faces. Tunics not tucked in or hanging open or missing entirely. Uncombed hair. Remember, Galen, I spent twenty years working on Mars. In the RAM I know, that woman would be gigged for having her hair down like that. In zero G it could get caught in machinery or drift into the captain's face. Not to mention having her uniform tunic open that way. People don't dress that informally anywhere but in the Belt!"

"They do look like a scurvy lot," Galen agreed, "not the sort to pass a military inspection."

"That's just it," Jovanna said. "RAM's particular about how its military people look. They hold inspections before letting them go on liberty. Any ship's captain who let his crew leave the ship looking like that would be shot."

"Maybe they're only pretending to be RAM," Galen ventured.

"Who are they, then? Pirates?"

"Maybe."

"I suppose, though even pirates know enough to clean themselves up if they want to impersonate military personnel. This is really weird."

The first RAM officer began pulling himself along a

travel line, followed a second later by the woman and
another man. There was an information kiosk nearby,
and the three gathered around it, apparently interrogating the computer. Other men and women continued to
emerge from the access way, some going off in small
groups, others alone. None looked in the slightest like a
typical RAM crewman with spotless uniform and military bearing. It looked, rather, as though they'd just
been through the fight of their lives. Several showed visible wounds on face or neck or hands, and all had a
glassy-eyed, vacant air about them as though they were
dazed or in shock.

One man with open tunic and raggedly torn trousers
made his way toward them, pulling his way mechani-
cally along a travel line and passing them without a second glance. Jovanna caught a whiff of an unpleasant,
sharply sweet odor as he passed.

"That one could use a bath," she whispered after he'd
gone.

"I count twenty of them," Galen said, still watching
the access way. "I think that's the lot. God, we could
walk aboard that cruiser now and take it without a
shot!"

"I'm more interested in the crew," Jovanna said.
"There's something very wrong."

"I know. Did you see the wound on the one that went
by?"

Jovanna nodded. There'd been an open sore on the
man's neck like a broken boil. "What about it?"

"Gangrene would be my guess. Did you catch that
smell as he passed? That guy shouldn't even have been
moving."

"Maybe the crew is sick." She felt an unpleasant
crawling sensation. The man had been so close. She suppressed a cold shudder. "Maybe they've been infected by
some sort of plague."

"Maybe. That might explain the sores. Why weren't
they stopped at the customs gate?"

Jovanna's eyes widened, and she pointed at the access
way. "Look!"

Two more figures were emerging. One was human and was wearing the blue-and-white uniform of an Amalthean customs officer. The uniform tunic was torn, as though he'd been in a fight. Just behind him was the robot Jovanna had seen at the customs gate, a humanoid shape in black and grey metal and duraplas.

"No disease would affect robots," Galen said. "And here come some more people. Look at them, stumbling like zombies! They must have been at the customs counter when that RAM crowd came through."

"They must be taking them over somehow." The thought was horrifying. Alien.

"What do you want to do?"

She nodded toward the lone RAM crewman who'd passed them. "That guy. He's alone. Let's have a closer look."

But, she thought, not too much closer. Despite the evidence of the robot, it was impossible not to think of some sort of deadly plague, a disease that destroyed the victim's mind.

"Sounds good." Galen reached into his harness pouch, extracting three separate items of metal and plastic. Two plugged together with an audible click. Something like a pen with a glass point screwed tightly into one end. "Insurance," Galen said in response to Jovanna's unspoken question. "Something I tinkered up that the customs people couldn't spot. Let's go."

Grabbing a travel line, they pulled their way after the lone RAM crewman.

O O O O O

The former Grigor Kleist had little trouble drawing information from a simpleminded computer built into a kiosk at the spaceport. The cluster controller, still occupying the Kleist human's body, together with the entities occupying Lieutenant DuBois and Sergeant Meyer, was able immediately to identify the transport net within Amalthea and locate the nearest terminal. The controller knew, however, that understanding the humans inhabiting Amalthea, understanding their strange behavior, was almost certainly a task far beyond its parameters.

Tentatively, the controller had begun cataloguing humans as Type 1 or Type 2, based on the outward anatomical differences between individuals such as Kleist—a Type 1—or DuBois—a Type 2—but the lack of identity between different humans on a smaller scale was still bewildering. On every human the controller had examined so far, the patterns of ridges on the tips of their fingers, the patterns of blood vessels on the backs of their eyes, the shapes and patterns of ridges on their brains were different. Different!

And then there were the outer skins. Every human wore them, multiple layers of fabric that covered all but hands and heads. The outer skins of the human found aboard *Sharonov* were outwardly similar, but here, within the Amalthean caverns, the humans were clad in a bewildering variety of outer skins, each different in texture, in color, in pattern, and in how much of the human it covered.

No two humans, it seemed, had exactly the same outer coverings, just as none had the same fingertip patterns, the same facial features, the same ordering of cells or hair or anything beyond the gross arrangement of body, limbs, and organs. The reasoning behind those differences was completely beyond the controller's understanding. Simply communicating with such a strange system was going to be difficult in the extreme, and understanding its behavior already seemed impossible.

Why, for example, did each human they passed stare openly at the little group? Why did so many of the Type-1 humans exhibit so intense an interest in the areas of skin exposed by the DuBois human's torn outer coverings? Why, when the remote team entered the crude tubecar conveyance after punching the buttons to select their destination, did the humans already in the car suddenly crowd their way out, leaving the remotes alone in the vehicle? Puzzling behavior indeed from puzzling devices. The cluster controller wondered if the supervisor nucleus and its universal mapping program could even begin to unravel its complexities.

First and foremost, the remote team had to locate the seeker. According to *Sharonov*'s computer, that probe had been here in Amalthea only a few hundred thousand seconds ago. One human, designated by *Sharonov* as "Dr. Marlene Kowalski," appeared to have actually seen the seeker and might well know where it was now. The seeker, designed to periodically transmit bursts of data back to the supervisor nucleus, had fallen silent after its brief encounter with the Kowalski human. If the remote team could track the seeker through the Kowalski human, if it could then make direct physical contact with the seeker, data stored by the seeker since then could be acquired and transmitted.

Perhaps that data would hold the key to human behavior.

Unfortunately, *Sharonov*'s records also indicated that Kowalski was no longer in Amalthea. However, they did include the name of another human, one involved with the organization called RAM, who might know where Marlene Kowalski could now be found.

So the remote team's target was now Hubert Shelton of the Genetics Foundation.

It was a short tubecar trip from the spaceship dock to the main office of the Genetics Foundation. A lone human, a Type 2, rose from behind a desk as the controller entered the foundation's front office and uttered a piercing but uncommunicative shriek.

"Cease making that noise," the controller said. Its speech was thick and slurred, the words difficult to shape. What a ponderous and slow method of communication! "We require immediate access to Hubert Shelton or Marlene Kowalski."

The human screamed again, backing away from the desk until it bumped against the wall. Obviously, communication was going to present very special difficulties.

Action was required, immediate and direct. The controller raised one arm, willing the remote cells manipulating it to flow toward the end. Hand and fingers swelled, then dissolved in a blob of lustrous silver. The human's eyes widened and the pitch of its vocalizations rose sharply, the sound waves hitting a frequency of nearly eleven hundred hertz. The blob at the end of the Kleist-controller's arm flicked out in a dozen slender threads, lashing across the human's face, body, and wildly thrashing arms.

If the remote could not gain coherent information one way, it would get it another. As the human struggled, the remote's thread-thin extremities penetrated the human's skin and muscles, slipping in between the cells, avoiding the larger tubules carrying a salty, organic fluid and seeking out the many-branched fibers of nerves that the controller had noted in the specimens aboard *Sharonov*. Nearly a quarter of the remote's mass seeped into the struggling human, extruding itself into microscopic fibers, racing along nerve trunks toward the organic computer governing the entire central nervous system—the brain.

The controller had already learned from the Kleist human how to interpret the raw data flooding the human's nervous system—searing pain, denial that this could possibly be happening, and a stark, nightmare terror that was threatening to overload the human's physiological responses and deactivate it completely.

A door opened, and a second human entered. "My God!" it yelled. "What are you doing to her? What the hell are you?"

The remote occupying the DuBois shell speared the newcomer in a hurtling mass of writhing tendrils. The human shrieked, staggering back against the wall, as silver threads pierced the skin of face and neck and torso, slicing effortlessly through flesh and clothing alike.

This is the human called Hubert Shelton, the DuBois remote said, radiating the data through low-frequency radio waves. Instantly, the Kleist-controller withdrew its tendrils from the pinioned Type 2 and turned its full attention to the Type 1. As the Type 2 slid slowly to the floor, visual organs wide and staring, the Kleist-controller added its tendril-probes to those of the DuBois unit.

Where is the Dr. Marlene Kowalski human? Communication with the human, even by feeding coded impulses directly into its nervous system and reading the response from its brain, was a ponderously slow and inefficient means of communication. The subject's pain and terror were genuine barriers to understanding; the controller was not even certain the human understood the question.

Then one of its questing probes entered the subject's brain, slipping easily between two cervical vertebrae and sliding up the spinal cord and into the brain stem. Pausing to orient itself, it quickly located the subject's hypothalamus, and the region within that seemed to control the human's sensations of pain and pleasure. Electrical current flowed.

As the Shelton human's pain faded in a haze of ecstasy, the answers to the Kleist-controller's questions became easier to read.

○ ○ ○ ○ ○

Jovanna and Galen cornered the *Sharonov* crewman in a blind-end alley between a cheap restaurant and a Strip joyhouse. He'd gone in as though looking for a through street or business entrance, found himself blocked by the cavern's rock wall, and turned to leave again. The two NEO agents stood at the entrance to the alley, their quarry cornered within.

"Okay, you," Galen said. He held the covert weapon tightly gripped in one small, hairy fist, the glass-tipped barrel aimed at the crewman's chest. "We don't want to hurt you. Just give us some answers."

Jovanna stared at the *Sharonov* crewman as fear prickled the hairs at the back of her neck. The sweetish smell was stronger than ever within the narrow confines of the alley, and the blank stare from unblinking eyes was cold and utterly empty of human feeling. The sore in the man's neck looked weeks old, a swelling of mottled black and red, but at the center she glimpsed something that looked like . . . metal? The rest of his skin was as pale as death.

"Hurt . . . you . . ." the man said, his jaw slack, the words slurred and almost unintelligible. A string of saliva dribbled unnoticed from the corner of his mouth. Was he repeating Galen's words, or uttering a threat? Raising his left arm, he extended it toward Jovanna, fingers clenched tightly in a white-knuckled fist.

Suddenly, the fist shimmered, swelled, and . . . melted, separate fingers dissolving into a glob of liquid metal that rapidly ballooned until it was as big as her own head. Jovanna gaped, not believing her eyes, not able to react as silver tendrils exploded from the mass with lightning speed and arced through the air toward her face.

She screamed. . . .

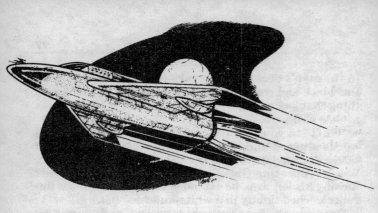

CHAPTER EIGHT

Jovanna stumbled as she took a backward step, her legs swinging out from beneath her as she lost her balance in Amalthea's low gravity. Galen, his Tinker's reactions far quicker than hers, slammed his body against her hip, knocking her aside as the net of squirming tendrils hissed through the air where her head had been half a second before.

With neither hands nor feet touching the ground, Jovanna could only flounder helplessly as she drifted toward the pavement with the agonizing slow motion of a nightmare. The *Sharonov* crewman, momentarily thrown off balance by his missed shot, groped for a travel line with his right hand while withdrawing the tangled snake's nest of tentacles sprouting from his left wrist for another shot. Horrified, Jovanna saw the crewman's hand reforming itself, as fragments of tan flesh drifting on the surface of the liquid metal began to join together, shaping fingers, palm, even the network of veins on the back of the monster's hand.

Galen, standing alongside Jovanna as she fell, triggered the device in his hand. A dazzlingly bright star of light appeared on the *Sharonov* crewman's left arm, high up near the shoulder, then slashed down across his chest. Oily black smoke boiled from the man's flesh; his uniform tunic shriveled and blackened beneath the touch of Galen's laser. Skin, muscle, and bone opened in a broad furrow, revealing something that reminded Jovanna of highly polished chain mail underneath.

That single laser bolt should have killed a human, would at least have crippled him with pain and shock, but the crewman was still moving, darting toward the mouth of the alley, toward her.

It wasn't a man. It was a monster, a thing, the human features of its face softening and blurring as though the monster was having trouble keeping its mask in place. Jovanna had an instant's blurred impression of the thing's left arm, burned off above the elbow, dropping to the ground like a wrinkled, empty shell, of a silver net of tendrils sprouting from the stump, lashing wildly above his head as they seemed to dwindle back into the still-human part of its body.

Jovanna hit the ground as the thing raced past. Almost without thinking, so quickly did it happen, she shoved her leg into the thing's path. Its legs hit hers with a dull shock, and the creature went sprawling headfirst into the street, its face smacking into the pavement and tearing as it slid. Galen stood above Jovanna, the laser clutched in both hands as the thing pushed itself into the air with all fours, then spun, momentarily hovering in Amalthea's microgravity.

Most of the face had been torn away; what stared back at Jovanna was a skull still shrouded in tatters of flesh, with a writhing, silver something like a metallic net or web crisscrossing the bone just beneath the torn skin and muscle. The flesh rippled and twitched, as though it had a life of its own, as though it were trying somehow to reform itself and repair the hideous damage. Skin and muscle melted as she watched, flowing together, blending with liquid-flowing silver.

Then Galen fired again, the shot striking the thing between its shoulder blades, burning through its spine. Its body crumpled, folding in the middle, then collapsed slowly in a heap of jumbled limbs on the street.

But it wasn't dead, not yet. Flesh split in a dozen places, the skull cracked open with an audible pop, and

silver-bright liquid poured from the openings, collecting
into a heaving, basketball-sized mass perched atop the
ruined, steaming corpse.

"The Artifact!" Jovanna yelled. As bright and as
quick-changing as liquid mercury, as reflective as a pol-
ished-steel mirror, the shimmering object was a twin to
the alien device Vince had found on Ciudestreya.

Galen fired a third time, this time directing the laser's
energy against the sphere. Light dazzled from its curved
surface, blindingly intense. The silver monster scarcely
seemed to notice but extruded four slender, jointed limbs
and a stalked cluster of what might have been some sort
of sensory apparatus, gripped the nearest travel line in
clawed appendages, then skittered away in the low gravity like a giant, metallic spider hauling its way along a
web, its motions too fast to follow.

Jovanna heard a woman's scream from the street outside the alley mouth, then a man's shouted curse. Galen
vaulted across Jovanna's body in pursuit. Grabbing a
travel line at last, Jovanna pulled herself to the street.
Galen floated there, one hand on the line, the other still
clutching his laser, as several civilian passers-by stared
at the two of them.

"Where is it?" she snapped at the Tinker, her voice low
and urgent. "Where did it go?"

"That way . . . somewhere." Galen gestured vaguely
toward a three-dimensional mob of panicked civilians
along the Strip that was still swirling apart, like water
disturbed by the wake of a passing boat. "I lost it. It was
just too fast."

Jovanna tightened her grip on the line. She was shaking, her heart pounding in her chest at a terror-driven
pace. "My . . . God!" she gasped when she could speak at
all. "Galen, what . . . what was that thing?"

Galen stooped above the torn and ruptured body lying
in the mouth of the alley and prodded it with a foot.
Flesh crumbled, dust-dry and literally falling to pieces
at a touch. The corpse was scarcely recognizable as
human. With one hand, Galen pulled a rib from the
hollow wreckage of the chest, squeezed his tiny fingers,

and the bone splintered into four or five fragments. Dust swirled in the air.

"I think," the Tinker said slowly, dropping the shards, "that it was using a body as a kind of disguise. Or like a puppet. It was pulling this guy's strings from inside."

The sweet smell was overpowering, and Jovanna recognized it now as the stench of decay.

Jovanna was having trouble taking in Galen's words. "The man we followed in here was . . . dead?" she asked. "A corpse?"

"What's the old Terran folk myth? Zombies? The living dead?" Galen continued to probe the body with inquisitive fingers as he spoke. Pieces crumbled away like bits of rotten wood. "The body cavity is almost empty. Except for the lungs, the internal organs are missing."

Jovanna felt as if she was going to be sick. She fought back the gorge rising in her throat. "We've got to contact NEO," Jovanna said, her voice barely under control. "We've got to . . . tell them. Warn them."

"Warn them?" Even Galen seemed shaken. He looked up from the grisly remains, his expression blank.

"What . . . what we just saw, in there," she said, pointing at the crumbling corpse. "It must have been related somehow to the Artifact, the silver sphere Vince found in Ciudestreya."

"The Artifact never did anything like this."

"It looks the same, and it can change shape. We've seen that much." She shuddered. She was certain that her first impression was right, that the Artifact and the thing they'd just encountered were products of the same technology. Or was it something more than mere technology?

Outwardly, the two might have been twins, identical spheres of silver-gray metal that could ripple and flow like liquid to assume a different shape. Possibly the Artifact wasn't as versatile as this new shape-shifter, or as intelligent. Whatever it was, the Artifact seemed to possess no intelligence or volition of its own, while the horror occupying the RAM crewman's body had been possessed of a terrible awareness, a malevolence staring back at her through a dead man's eyes.

But the two must have the same source. The NEO scientists studying the Artifact now at their secret lab in the Belt could be in terrible danger.

"Galen, we've got to warn them!"

"I think," Galen said, "that we'd better tell the local authorities what we saw here. And NEO. And maybe RAM as well."

"RAM? Are you completely nuts?"

The Tinker stared at her, human eyes in a furry, simian face. She could see the fear there. "You don't understand, do you? We just saw twenty of these things get off a RAM ship. Twenty human zombies controlled by . . . by something I can't even begin to understand. These things are pretending to be human."

"Maybe they're just looking for the Artifact. Maybe the Artifact . . . maybe it's one of them."

"Maybe. And maybe we're facing an invasion." He shook his head. "Jo, this is way too big for us alone. It may be too big for NEO. Go find someone, a stabber, someone with the government. I'll stay here and watch . . . this."

Oh, God, please, no, she thought as she left the alley, the simple, desperate prayer running through her mind over and over and over. God, please, no. On the main thoroughfare of the Strip, there was no sign that anything strange had happened. People continued to move along the micro-G handlines, going about their business, and the panic stirred by the escaping monster seemed to have melted away.

Gone, too, were the oddly dressed zombies. Please, God, no . . .

The thought that a number of those silver horrors clad in human bodies were moving now within the population of Amalthea was terrifying.

What kind of a nightmare had just been unleashed on the Solar System?

O O O O O

The cluster controller had known, of course, the instant one of its units had been cornered and attacked. Although it needed to be in direct contact with another remote to exchange more than limited and superficial data, it was aware in a general way of impressions, thoughts, and sensory input from all of the remotes in its own cluster.

Clearly, the disguises the remotes had assumed would not long fool the human network. The controller was beginning to realize that there was a great deal about the humans, from the inflections of the crude sonic transmissions that served them as a means of communication, to details in the way they wore their strange, multiple outer coverings, that the network did not yet fully understand.

Rising, the controller withdrew its probing tendrils, allowing the Shelton human to collapse lifeless to the floor. The controller now possessed the information it sought. The Kowalski human was almost certainly somewhere in an artificial construct floating in the atmosphere of Jupiter. Precise coordinates of the city had resided within the Shelton human's long-term data storage. The controller had them now, together with much else.

It was tempting to reenter the Shelton human, to add the water, carbon, and other materials of its hardware to the controller's own mass, to use the Shelton human and the Type 2 lying next to the wall as external hardware to house newly extruded remotes.

But the part of the cluster controller sensitive to electromagnetic frequencies was aware of electrical power flowing through conduits hidden in the walls around it. Possibly, some kind of alarm had been sent. Other humans would be arriving soon. There simply wasn't time to assimilate these two.

Carefully, it composed itself, settling the shell of the Kleist human into place, making certain that none of its own body showed. Tuning itself to a high-frequency radio wavelength, it began transmitting instructions to the DuBois remote.

<<SUBORDINATE LINK ESTABLISHED WITH CLUSTER UNIT
FIVE>>

<<ATTENTION: PRIORITY INTERRUPT>>

<<SPECIFIC TASK/NEW TASK DIRECTIVE>>

Cluster Unit Five, inhabiting the DuBois Type-2
human, replied.

<TASK INTERRUPT ACCEPTED>

<CLUSTER UNIT FIVE STANDING BY>

Streams of data flowed from the cluster controller,
reprogramming the subordinate unit.

<<HUMAN MAPPING TO BEGIN AMALTHEA>>

<<CLUSTER UNIT FIVE TO ACCESS KOWALSKI HUMAN/
JUPITER>>

<<MISSION PARAMETERS/SUBTASK SPECIFICATIONS FOLLOW
. . .>>

It was imperative that the cluster find the Kowalski
human and, from it, learn the current location of the
seeker. Obviously, the human network had deduced the
presence of a rival network—the cluster—and would
soon marshal its own forces in defense. The cluster
would have to act swiftly.

The controller had already discarded the notion of
sending one of its remotes to Jupiter aboard the *Sharonov*. The captured RAM cruiser was not designed for
operations within a gas giant's atmosphere and would
almost certainly be destroyed in the attempt. There
were alternatives, however, and, as the controller continued to outline the parameters of the mission to Unit
Five, it was accessing other units of the cluster by radio,
directing them to secure the necessary transport.

Cluster Unit Five, meanwhile, began carrying out its
new programming. Its first subtask was to discard the
DuBois hardware in favor of the shell of the Shelton
human, lying now on the floor at their feet. The Type 2's
shell shuddered, split, then collapsed as the gleaming
mass of Unit Five oozed from a dozen openings, flowed
across the floor, and began seeping into the Shelton
human's body. The change of hardware was logical. The
Shelton human's outward form was familiar to the
Kowalski human and should be granted access.

Besides, these human hardware shells became increasingly unstable with time, making it difficult to maintain an effective illusion. How did humans function with such flimsy and inefficient hardware? Very soon, now, the controller would have to find another, fresher shell and discard the Kleist human form for good.

Of far greater priority, however, was the need to communicate with the supervisor nucleus. That task the controller had reserved for itself, and it would commence as soon as a secure place for the cluster was found here within Amalthea. The cluster units scattered through the moon's artificial environs were already beginning to carry out this new set of subtasks.

○ ○ ○ ○ ○

Jovanna watched as Galen probed at the hollow shell of a body lying on the autopsy table before him. The stench of decay was strong here, despite the whirr of ventilator fans overhead. How much of the smell, of the closeness of the room, was in her mind, she wondered, and how much was real? She wanted to leave, wanted to at least turn away from the horror that had once been a person lying on the dissection table, but could not.

It had not taken long for Jovanna and Galen to present their case to the Amalthean Corporate Council. The body of the *Sharonov*'s crewman spoke for itself, and it hadn't been long before word was received of new horrors, of the crumbling body of another *Sharonov* crewman—crewwoman, rather—found in the office of Hubert Shelton of the Genetics Foundation. They'd also found Shelton's office secretary, still alive, but reduced to screaming, terror-stricken incoherence.

Jovanna had been there in the hospital emergency room when the secretary had been brought in, strapped into a basket stretcher. Before they'd sedated her, she'd shrieked over and over that "they" had taken Shelton, that "they" had gotten into his body and walked him away.

Unfortunately, Hubert Shelton himself was missing.

All they had to work with was the sedated office worker and the dry-as-dust corpse of what once had been a young woman.

They'd identified her through ID data in her uniform's smart circuits: Lt. Karen DuBois, sensor officer of RMS *Sharonov*. Her body had been brought here, to Solar Geographic's medical labs, where Galen had been showing several Amalthean doctors what he'd discovered about the first corpse, lying now on another table nearby. Now, it seemed, there were two corpses off the *Sharonov*, and the mystery of what had happened to them was deepening. Everyone was reluctant to accept Jovanna's and Galen's tale of a silvery, shape-shifting parasite, an alien; but neither could they dismiss the story out of hand. The mute testimony of two bodies wouldn't permit it.

So a half dozen of Amalthea's rulers gathered there in the autopsy theater, Kenneth Heller and five other senior personnel from the Amalthean Corporate Council. Most looked as ill as Jovanna felt, their faces paste white and beaded with sweat.

"It's almost as though all of the moisture has been leached from the body," the green-gowned doctor standing across the table from Galen said, his voice muffled slightly by his mask. Dr. Morgan Caldwell was Amalthea's leading pathologist. Assigned to Solar Geographic's medical department, he doubled as the colony's chief coroner and autopsy specialist when necessary. "And, just as in the other body, the internal organs are missing, save for lungs and stomach. I wonder why those organs were left?"

"Speech," Galen replied. "If the . . . ah . . . puppet master was to make its puppet speak, it needed functional lungs, larynx, tongue, and palate. The lungs were left, obviously, as a reservoir for air even though the victim was no longer breathing."

"The stomach seems to have been used as a reservoir for water," another doctor said.

"I thought," Jovanna said, licking her lips, "that the water was gone."

"Most of it is," Galen replied. "But if the mouth and lungs aren't kept moist, they get too dry to work. Same with the eyeballs."

"Incredible," Caldwell said. "These . . . these things invaded the body, used it as a kind of disguise? What happened to the internal organs?"

"I don't know," Galen admitted, placing a medical probe on the magnetic tray at his side. "Either the invaders use them for food, for energy, or . . ."

"Or what?" Heller demanded from the sidelines.

"Or they're able to use material from a human body to replicate themselves."

"My God!" one of Heller's aides said. "You can't mean that these monsters are . . . are reproducing!"

"They appear to be living organisms," Galen replied blandly. "One characteristic of all life-forms is the ability to reproduce."

"What I don't understand," Caldwell said, "is how they get these bodies to function at all." He snapped off a finger-sized piece of tissue, so dry it crumbled in his fingers. "What's left here is so desiccated, so empty."

"It was like the invader was actually holding the body together," Jovanna said. She closed her eyes, recalling the pieces of skin and flesh floating on the monster's silvery hand. "For a moment, it looked as if it was pulling the pieces together, sort of like a giant jigsaw puzzle."

"I can't really imagine that," Heller said. "It doesn't sound like the illusion could be . . . realistic."

"It was realistic enough," Jovanna said. "Believe me."

A door at the end of the room opened, and an aide entered, keeping his eyes averted from the autopsy table. He handed a slip of paper to Heller.

"This is from Airspace Control," he said, reading quickly. "A RAM battle squadron is now on final approach to Amalthea. The flagship *Syrtis Major* will be docking within one hour."

Jovanna darted a sharp glance at Galen, who met her eyes with a worried look of his own. So far, in all of the confusion, they'd been able to maintain their cover as RAM agents investigating Kowalski's disappearance.

The arrival of a RAM fleet would change everything. Either they would have to go into hiding, or they would have to reveal themselves as NEO to the RAM commander, hoping that he would join forces with them against a greater threat, a common enemy. Their forged, electronic identification would never fool the computer records aboard a RAM battler.

"There's, ah, more," Heller said slowly. "Dr. Mendel," he said, using Galen's cover name. "You believe these monsters are reproducing?"

"We can't afford to ignore the possibility," Galen replied. "Why?"

Heller gestured with the paper. "Fifteen minutes ago, Airspace Control challenged a Skimmertech shuttle leaving Bay Five without clearance. There was no answer. A few minutes later, the bodies of five Skimmertech personnel were found at the shuttle's docking gantry, all dead."

"Like this one?" Galen asked.

"Not as far as we know. They were apparently killed when the area was opened to vacuum. Security's bringing the bodies in now for examination."

"I'd like to see them," Caldwell said, laying aside his instruments and straightening above the table. "And you should probably have your security people looking for other bodies like these two. It's possible that the invaders are getting rid of the old bodies as they, um, wear out, or decay. If Shelton's secretary can be believed, they've already hijacked his body. They may be killing other Amaltheans, too."

Heller nodded, his expression glum. "Could these invaders be interested in the Jovian cities? Is that why a shuttle was stolen?"

"How can we even guess?" Galen replied. "We don't know enough about these things even to know what they're after. Maybe you should warn Jupiter, though, just in case."

"We will," Heller replied, "but it'll take a while. Most of the cities are on the far side of the planet right now. Because of the radio interference, we have to use laser

communications, and that requires direct line-of-sight.
It'll be thirty hours before they're in communication
range again."

"Thirty hours!" Jovanna flared. "Why the hell don't
you have lasercom satellites?"

Heller shrugged. "Satellites are expensive. And we
never really needed them. The Stormriders have always
preferred their . . . isolation."

"We might set up a lasercom relay," one of the coun-
cilors suggested. "Send the signal to Callisto and bounce
it to Ganymede. I think Ganymede will be in the proper
alignment soon."

"Maybe," Heller said. "Maybe. But we're still dealing
with Stormriders. They're just not rational."

"They'd better learn how to be rational, then,"
Jovanna said, "because if they don't, they're going to be
dead!"

She swallowed her anger, but her feeling of helplessness left her weak and trembling. Vince was in one of
those cities, and she knew with a horrible premonition
that the stolen shuttle was on its way to that same city.
The similarity of Artifact and invaders, the fact that
Shelton knew where Marlene Kowalski was hiding, the
fact that he'd vanished after the invaders had appeared
in his office, all suggested that they were after Kowalski, and for the same reason that both NEO and RAM
wanted her. She'd examined the Artifact, handled it,
experienced it. Now the invaders—some of them, anyway—were on the way to Vrahk.

Vince and Kaiten were in terrible danger, and there
was no way she knew to warn them.

CHAPTER NINE

Beyond the parapets of the city, shafts of sunlight slanted across the ramparts of the cloud canyons at the approach of the Jovian sunset. Vince and Kaiten had been waiting in a large, Terran-acclimated room for nearly two hours. A pair of Stormriders, huge, masked, and bearing the electric-rod weapons Vince had seen earlier, waited with them in gloomy silence.

They were not under arrest . . . not quite. They still had their weapons and were free to go anywhere they wanted . . . except back to the office suite where Marlene Kowalski stubbornly refused to see them a second time.

But they couldn't leave. A RAM fleet of at least fifteen ships had just arrived at Amalthea.

Vrahk had been out of communication with Amalthea for several hours, and it hadn't been until just after Vince's unproductive meeting with Kowalski that the alignment of three of Jupiter's moons had changed enough to allow tight-beamed laser communications to reach the city from Amalthea.

Vince and Kaiten sat in liquid-filled, high-G recliner chairs in their quarters, watching 2-D images transmitted by the Amalthean news service. The arrival of part of RAM's Jupiter fleet, it seemed, had taken everyone in Amalthea by surprise, and the news commentators were venting endless speculation on RAM's interest in the tiny Jovian satellite. RAM troops had already disembarked in the moon's main docking bay from a dozen assault deployment vehicles, while the battler *Syrtis Major* orbited at a distance.

Cameras in Amalthea gave repeated close-ups of the battlefleet. The *Syrtis Major* was a roughly streamlined cylinder half a mile long, with a crew of five hundred and a full squadron of X-23 Krait fighters carried on board. The battler formed the heart of an entire battlefleet consisting of two heavy cruisers, four medium cruisers, and nine smaller vessels, including a couple of long-range transports serving as troopships. RAM had arrived in force, ready for anything from a space battle to all-out invasion.

And until the fleet left the vicinity of Amalthea, there wasn't a way in hell Vince and Kaiten were going to be able to rejoin Jovanna and Galen. They'd be spotted by the RAM picket ships before they got within fifty thousand miles of Amalthea, and snapped up by cruisers or a squadron of Kraits within minutes.

"Damned lucky for us our hosts aren't that eager for us to leave," Vince said, staring glumly at the screen. "I'd hate to have to try to run that blockade."

"Stormriders know that RAM is our enemy," Kaiten observed. The Terrine shrugged huge shoulders. "They let us stay short time, anyway. Perhaps Kowalski put in good word for us."

"I doubt it." Vince glanced uncertainly at their enormous chaperones. Did either of them speak Anglic? It probably made little difference. Vince was certain that the quarters were wired, and anything they said was probably being relayed to Kowalski. "I don't think she cares either. Her first concern is for her Stormriders, not system politics."

Vince had spent much of the past hours wondering about Kowalski's relationship with the Stormriders. It was almost as though she were their leader; certainly she enjoyed a special relationship with them, guarded by their warriors, deferred to by their representatives. Of all the peoples of the Solar System, Vince knew, the Aerostaters of Venus enjoyed the closest relationship with the enigmatic Jovian Stormriders; possibly that was due to the similarity in their respective ways of life, inhabiting floating dirigible cities. It was a relationship that was largely covert, since the Genetics Foundation still considered the Stormriders to be its exclusive property. It was possible that Kowalski's distance was more an unwillingness to jeopardize her position on Jupiter than any lack of interest in RAM-NEO affairs.

The arrival of the RAM battlefleet could change all of that. RAM might well come down to Vrahk to capture her, and there were people at the Genetics Foundation in Amalthea who would be more than willing to help do it.

A video image of the RAM battler, a huge and menacing silhouette against the glowing, cloud-swirled backdrop of Jupiter, was replaced by the features of a blond woman in a fashionable, business smartsuit, a reporter for the Amalthean News Service.

"Speculation continues," the woman said, squarely facing the camera, "as to the true reason for the arrival of the RAM battlefleet. Adm. Mohar Singh, the battlefleet's commander, insists that the visit is a courtesy call only, one occasioned by the need for Martian scientists to consult with members of the Genetics Foundation and Solar Geographic on technical matters. Why these scientists should have been escorted to Amalthea aboard a RAM battler, of course, is a matter—"

The reporter's face was gone, replaced by a snowstorm of static. Vince tapped at the controls inset in the arm of his chair. "Strange," he said. "Shouldn't get static like that through a lasercom transmission."

"Perhaps laser link broken," Kaiten said.

"Maybe, but—" He stopped. The two Stormrider guards were acting strangely, their crested heads thrown back as though listening, their arms raised, the wings partly extended. "That's damned peculiar."

"Listen . . ."

Vince could hear it now, a faint, rapidly fluctuating twitter barely audible above the hiss of static from the vidscreen speakers. It sounded almost like a jamming transmission used in combat, except that there was a regularity to the pulses that sounded intelligent, almost like a high-speed data transmission.

Abruptly, the static on the screen was wiped away, replaced by a message reading "Transmission difficulties. Please stand by." The electronic signal was gone, and both Stormriders relaxed, their hands dropping again to the floor as their great wings folded tightly against their flanks.

"What the hell was that?" Vince wondered.

"We apologize for the technical difficulties," the woman on the vid display said, her earnest features again filling the screen. "As we were saying, Amalthean government authorities have as yet been unable to ascertain why—"

Vince cut the sound. A green light was winking at the bottom left corner of the screen, a warning that someone wanted to talk to them. He touched another button on the arm of his chair. "Vince Pirelli."

Marlene Kowalski's face replaced that of the reporter. She looked concerned. "Major," she said. "What do you make of the communications interrupt we just experienced?"

That confirmed that they were being spied on, Vince thought. They'd known the two NEO agents were watching the vidscreen.

"Could have been almost anything, Doctor," he replied evenly. "Though electronic interference isn't likely on a line-of-sight laser feed."

"Agreed," the heavyset woman said. "Both the Stormriders and instruments here confirm that a powerful radio broadcast has just emanated from Amalthea."

"From Amalthea?" Vince shook his head. "That doesn't make sense. How could a radio signal interrupt a laser-com transmission?"

"As yet we don't know. Some of my 'riders are working on that now."

"Stormriders are sensitive to radio, aren't they?" Vince had heard that the huge gennies could "hear" radio waves, though how they used the talent to communicate against the hiss and crackle of Jupiter's natural radio interference he didn't know. Certainly, the two in the room had heard something. They were still agitated, speaking now to one another in low, urgent chirps.

"That's right. As you say, it doesn't make sense."

While both radio waves and lasers could be used for communications, the two had absolutely nothing to do with each other. The one depended on modulated radio waves, the other on modulations within beams of coherent light. The fact that radio could not jam a laser communications net was precisely the reason lasers were used in near-Jupiter space; where Jupiter drowned out ordinary radio with its background roar, lasers provided clear and static-free communication, at least along direct lines of sight.

"I've got another problem right now," Kowalski continued. "What do you make of this?"

The image on the screen shifted to a view from a camera mounted somewhere outside, probably on the outer wall of the city. Vince saw the scarlet glory of the Jovian sunset, banks and cliff walls of color-banded clouds.

In the center of the picture was an odd craft of some kind, dark-hulled, flat, with a gaping intake visible beneath the bluntly streamlined nose. The vessel was angled just enough that Vince could make out the lettering on its port side: "SKIMMERTECH S-08."

"That's a shuttle of some kind, isn't it?" Vince asked.

"Right," Kowalski's voice replied. "Skimmertech is one of the big Amalthean corporations. Make their living skimming gas, hydrogen, mostly, from our upper atmosphere. Usually we don't have anything to do with 'em. Notice anything strange?"

Vince studied the vehicle for a moment longer, unsure what to look for. The Jovian sky was growing rapidly darker as he watched, and details on the darkened ship were increasingly hard to make out. It was difficult to see where the little ship's wingtips were.

"Running lights!" Vince said abruptly. "He's not showing running or acquisition lights!"

"Yes." Kowalski's voice was dry. "We thought that was curious."

Vince watched the shuttle for a moment. He could see the ghostly forms of several Stormriders about the shuttle, winged shapes that gave scale to the small vessel. "Have you talked to the pilot?"

"Briefly. The pilot called our Airspace Control a few moments before that blast of, ah, interference. Identified himself as Hubert Shelton and announced that he would be docking here in twenty minutes. He's refused all subsequent communications."

"Did you say Shelton?"

"That's right, Major. Know him?"

"Yes." Vince had not met the Genetics Foundation bureaucrat, but Galen's description had been succinct and he'd seen recorded images of the man. What puzzled him most was the man's presence aboard the shuttle. It was decidedly odd that the bureaucrat had come in person. No Genetics Foundation executive would run errands to Jupiter himself, not if he could send a corporate underling to endure the Jovian gravity instead. That suggested that Shelton had come in his capacity as a RAM agent. Vince could imagine several reasons why a RAM spy might choose to visit Vrahk just ahead of the battlefleet's arrival, none of them pleasant.

"Airspace Control warned him off," Kowalski continued, "but he's ignored every warning. I suppose we could shoot him down, but I'd like to know what's so all-fired important that a corporate bigwig decided to come here in person."

So Kowalski had been thinking along the same lines as he. Did she know that Shelton also worked for RAM? "I'm curious about that myself," Vince said thoughtfully. Shelton was probably coming to threaten Kowalski with the RAM battlefleet behind him, but that still didn't explain his personal involvement.

"I've given permission to let him land in Bay Two so that he won't see your fighters. I thought you should know, though, just in case he came here looking for you."

"Thank you, Doctor." It seemed more likely that he

was here for Kowalski. How far, he wondered, did her neutrality extend? "If he's here to see you, I wonder if my friend and I could listen in?"

There was a moment's pause. "Very well," Kowalski said. "I would be interested in your reactions."

Minutes later, Vince and Kaiten watched with rapt attention as the Skimmertech shuttle swept in through the bay opening, snagging the filmy strands of netting that served as arresting gear and lurching to a heavy-bodied halt. The picture, transmitted from a camera high up on the docking bay's wall, gave an unobstructed view of the shuttle's side hatch as it cycled open. Several Stormriders gathered on the deck outside, waiting to escort the human passengers and crew. A man appeared at the air lock door. He waited as a ramp unfolded from the hull, then walked with heavy, carefully placed steps.

"My God," Vince said.

"That man," Kaiten said. "He . . ."

"I see it. Good Lord, I see it! What in God's name? . . ."

On the deck, the Stormriders, too, were reacting with surprise, even consternation. Several humans were striding off the ramp and onto the docking bay deck, accompanied by a single robot. The robot was of no interest—a Ceres Model XXIV-L humanoid utility model—but the others!

There were five of them, three men, two women. Four wore RAM military dress; the fifth, in ornate civilian attire, was Hubert Shelton. All were armed. Vince saw at least one rocket rifle and several hand lasers. Tunics were torn and sloppy, one man wore no shirt or uniform tunic at all, and all bore wounds or strangely puckered sores on exposed parts of their bodies, but Vince scarcely noticed these details. All of his attention was focused on one fact.

Of those five people, not one was wearing helmet or life-support pack!

What he was seeing was starkly and absolutely impossible. Jupiter's atmosphere was sheer poison to humans. They should all be dead . . . and yet they were walking about as though nothing in the least was wrong

Two of them were already walking away from the shuttle while the others, three humans and the robot, argued something with the Stormriders. Vince couldn't hear. One of the Stormriders appeared angry, though, and seemed to be trying to call the two back. He raised the charge gun in one hand, gesturing with it.

The shuttle exploded.

One moment it was resting quietly on its landing gear, the next it was lying on its side, wings smashed, its hull wreathed in flame as the shrill echoes of the blast rang from the docking bay walls and falling chunks of debris clattered across the deck. All of the Stormriders were down on the deck, those magnificent wings of theirs twisted and torn. The humans were down, too, three of them, anyway. Vince caught a glimpse of the two who had already been clear of the shuttle when it blew racing into an open corridor, one lugging a heavy rocket rifle.

The others, still by the wreckage of the shuttle, were burning. Horribly they were moving as they burned, flesh cracking and shriveling away from silver-bright bones even as the flames, starved for oxygen, dwindled and flickered out. . . .

No, not bones! Damn, what were those things? Vince was still trying to get a good look when there was a second explosion. Another spacecraft parked in the bay just beyond the shuttle vanished in a billowing cloud of orange flame, and instantly, the camera image flickered once and died.

"Dr. Kowalski!" Vince yelled. His hand slapped the communicator switch on his chair. "Dr. Kowalski, please reply!" There was no answer. "Come on, Kaiten! We've got to get the hell to Kowalski's office!"

The big Terrine already had his sidearm out, a big-bored Arean Arms M-44 slug thrower with fifteen explosive-tipped rounds in its grip magazine, an old-fashioned weapon but a devastatingly effective one. Vince drew his own Starflash laser pistol as the two made their way to the door, checking the power feed and battery pack. He hoped the two of them had firepower enough to stop those . . . those things.

What kind of monster looked human but breathed hydrogen-helium?

More to the point, he wondered as he hurriedly donned his environmental suit and sealed the helmet shut, what kind of monster forgot that hydrogen and oxygen were a dangerously explosive mixture that could be touched off by the slightest spark? That, he was certain, was what had destroyed the shuttle. The "human" crew had emerged without even bothering to cycle through the air lock. The hydrogen-helium air at five atmospheres had flooded aboard, mixing with the oxygen-nitrogen atmosphere in the shuttle. There must have been turbulence enough to spill some of the deadly mix back into the docking bay. A Stormrider's charge gun had provided the spark—*bang*!

The second explosion had probably gone off when another human ship had been damaged, its hull cracked enough to admit hydrogen to its sealed interior. It was a good thing there'd been no more human ships in Bay Two; every one of them could have gone up in a chain reaction that could have destroyed half the city.

Vince could only guess at what the invaders were, but he'd already leapt to some pretty wild conclusions. Obviously they weren't humans. They could be gennies—Spacers, for instance, could survive in any atmosphere or in hard vacuum—but Vince was already thinking alien as he lurched down the cavernous city corridor. Alien . . . as in nonhuman extraterrestrials, the builders, perhaps, of the Artifact. The fact that they seemed to be somehow wearing human forms was disturbing. Was that really Shelton he'd seen in the hangar bay, or the image of Shelton, projected as a disguise? Either way, it suggested sinister motives and a terrible danger.

Had mankind at long last made contact with an alien intelligence only to find that it was hostile?

It was impossible to run in two and a half gravities. Even Kaiten was struggling with each hurried step, and Vince could feel his knees buckling, threatening to hurl

him painfully to the deck. He stopped, leaning against a
wall, his breath coming in gasps. "You!" he shouted at
one of the giants accompanying them. "Do you speak
Anglic?"

"*Vronidronvi'niiv*," the being said. "Fifteenth Speaker,
Warlords, Violet Clouds." Its accent was thicker than the
Tenth Speaker's, the words barely intelligible.

"If Dr. Kowalski's safety means anything to you,"
Vince shouted at the towering being, "get us to her
office, fast! Fast!"

The two giants consulted briefly in rapid-fire chirps.
Then great, orange-violet hands scooped Vince and Kaiten from the deck, hoisting them into the air. The
Jovians' footfalls rang like high-pitched thunder as they
raced down the endless passageways. They reached the
air lock and tumbled inside. One of the Stormriders
worked the controls, and Vince felt his suit shiver and
balloon as the air pressure dwindled.

"Come on, come on . . ." He was fuming with impa-
tience as the atmosphere cycled through the lock. The
Stormriders both had their protective masks on; neither
Vince nor Kaiten bothered to remove their helmets.
When would the door open? . . .

The inner lock slid open and Vince leaped into the
room. He had a blurred impression of Kowalski standing
behind her massive desk, of Shelton and a woman in a
torn RAM uniform opposite, of many-branched, snake-
writhing tentacles gleaming silver in the room's overhead lights. One of Kowalski's Stormrider guards lay
motionless on the floor, a bloody crater just below the
keel in its chest. The other lay nearby with a head
wound, its mask missing, its wings fluttering fitfully as
oxygen seared its lungs and eyes.

"Hold it right there!" Vince yelled, swinging his laser
up to cover Shelton. "Drop 'em!"

Both of the invaders whirled, their faces oddly blank
but pocked by ugly, open sores. The woman cradled a
Weston Mark XIV rocket rifle in her arms; the man held
a heavy RAM-Sylvanian M-50 laser pistol in one hand.

"Drop weapons!" Kaiten boomed, his M-44 rock-steady

in a two-handed grip.

Expressionless, both attackers ignored the warnings. The woman's rocket rifle's muzzle was aimed at Kaiten, her finger already tightening on the trigger.

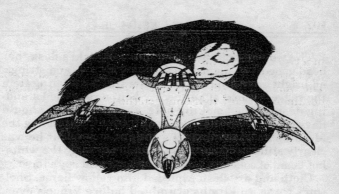

CHAPTER TEN

There was a sound like ripping cloth as the Mark XIV fired, sending its rocket-propelled round hissing across the room on a needle-thin contrail of smoke.

Fortunately, the woman had not used a smart round, or else she'd been too hurried to lock on to her target. Fortunately, too, rocket rifles were poor weapons at close range. It took nearly a second for the round to accelerate to full speed, and the battle reflexes of the big Terrine let him hurl himself to one side. The tiny projectile impacted on the wall behind Vince and exploded, the shock wave slapping him on the back.

An instant later a second explosion shook the room, this one from the life-support pack of the wounded Stormrider. Flame ballooned toward the vaulted ceiling, and bits of metal and plastic whirred through the air. Hydrogen leaks from other Stormrider breathing units or in the walls themselves could destroy them all.

Kaiten rasped something in Terrine battlespeech, a snarled curse as he triggered the heavy handgun gripped in clawed fingers. A crater appeared in the woman's face, obliterating eyes and nose and snapping her blond head back as savagely as a hard punch. The bullet exploded an instant later, just as Vince fired his Starflash laser at Shelton.

The woman collapsed against Kowalski's desk, her head gone but a nightmarish tangle of loops and strings, all bright silver and as liquid as water, splattering from the ragged stump of her neck. Shelton remained standing despite the smoking hole where his heart should have been. He seemed to be having difficulty holding the M-50 up against two and a half gravities, but he was clearly still alive. Vince fired again, slashing the white-hot beam of coherent light across the RAM spy's torso.

Cloth and dry flesh exploded into yellow flame. Shelton's torso and limbs crumbled before Vince's eyes, pieces fragmenting on the floor as choking, oily smoke filled the air. Yet something remained, a silver pillar thrusting up from the ruin of Shelton's body. It moved with a life of its own, an obscene writhing as silver coils unfolded, slashing empty air. A second monster slithered snakelike from the woman's corpse, groping blindly toward Kowalski.

Vince fired his laser, striking the tentacle behind its blunt and questing tip. Light dazzled from the silver, the shiny surface reflecting the beam and scattering it harmlessly. He fired once more, again with no effect, as Kowalski loosed a shrill scream and stumbled backward over her chair.

Kaiten swung his handgun, shouldering Vince aside as he shifted aim to the struggling horror on the desk and fired. The M-44 barked twice, the roar thunderous in the enclosed room, and the smooth silver surface of the thing was pocked by twin craters a few inches apart. The explosive rounds detonated a half second later, twin bangs that shattered the tentacle into glittering, mirror-bright shards. Tracking downward with the pistol, Kaiten put four more rounds into the woman's headless body, the gunshots and echoed detonations of the bullets painfully loud. Dry-as-wood fragments, mingled with silver shards, smashed on the floor and ricocheted off the walls and desk. Without a pause in his deadly rhythm, Kaiten shifted targets and put five more rounds into the silver monster extracting itself from Shelton's body. The thing exploded like a column of ice struck by a sledgehammer.

The final, ringing echo dwindled away, and for a long moment no one spoke. Acrid smoke rose from the charred corpse of the burned Stormrider. Kowalski broke the silence first. "What . . . what were they?"

"The Artifact," Vince said. His heart was pounding in his chest, his mouth dry. "They were silver like the Artifact."

"Is it dead?" Kaiten growled. The muzzle of his M-44 was still tracking back and forth, as though he expected the scattered fragments to reunite.

Vince stooped, gingerly touching a golf ball-sized piece. He, too, wondered if the invaders were really dead. The strange life that had possessed them, however, seemed to have departed. "These look inert."

"They're dead," Kowalski said, still sounding shaken. "Once they get below a certain critical size—"

"How do you know that?" Vince demanded. When Kowalski did not immediately reply, he stood upright, feeling the ache in back and legs as they took the strain in Jupiter's gravity. "Maybe you should tell us everything you know about these . . . visitors."

Kowalski nodded twice, the movement hard and jerky. "How much," she asked, "do you know about nanotechnology?"

Vince knew a little about the subject, which was more of a historical curiosity than anything else. Nanotechnology—the "nano" prefix referred to nanometer, a billionth of a meter, which indicated the size scale at which they operated—had been conceived in the late twentieth century. Scientists had dreamed of creating machines so tiny they could manipulate individual molecules, so easily replicated that vast swarms of them could grow spaceships or cities from a pile of dirt, or move through a human body, destroying cancer cells or the gathering by-products of age. They'd dreamed of a golden age of plenty, where goods were literally dirt-cheap and even human immortality was a possibility.

The dream had died late in the twenty-first century. Controlling the growth and programming of nanomachines, as the submicroscopic units were called, had been an insoluble problem; alternate solutions, such as improved materials processing and new and promising drugs derived from research in genetic engineering, had proven far more cost-effective.

Besides, the social and economic shock of cheap goods and human immortality had been too scary for any government to even contemplate. After some early experiments and test projects, the whole concept of nanoengineering had been dropped.

"Are you saying that these things are the products of nanotechnology?" Vince asked.

"I'm saying they are nanotechnology," Kowalski replied. She opened the drawer in her desk and removed the inert piece of metal she'd taken from the Artifact. "Assuming they're the same as this sample. And I'm betting they are."

In short, concise phrases, Kowalski outlined her studies of the sample she'd taken from the Artifact. Outwardly, the silvery material appeared to be an inert, crystalline metal somewhat softer than carbon steel. Under her lepton microscope, however, Kowalski had imaged molecule-sized machines, each linked to its neighbors by magnetic bonds that could, depending on the situation, be either flexible or as unyielding as the crystalline matrix of diamond.

"So that's how these things manage their shape-changing trick," Vince said. He held two pieces in his hands, one the sample Kowalski had taken from the Artifact, the other a fragment blasted from the invader that had been wearing the body of Hubert Shelton. "They're made of something that can act like either a liquid or a solid."

"Exactly. When I examined the Artifact, I didn't realize the extent of its shape-changing abilities. They can slim themselves down thin enough to thread into human nerve bundles. They can . . . well, they can obviously interact with the human nervous system. God knows how."

"What do you mean . . . they read minds?" That sounded like pure magic to Vince. "That's impossible!"

"I'd hate to even guess what might or might not be possible for these things."

"Yeah, but being able to read minds? How could they?"

Kowalski shook her head. "No data. Possibly they've run into humans before. Maybe they can decode nerve impulses, the way we might break a computer code. They probably can't literally read our thoughts, but they might be able to get some information, facts and figures, but miss trickier things like emotions."

That made a nightmarish kind of sense. People vanished, ships went missing, sometimes whole colonies disappeared in deep space. Perhaps the invaders had acquired a working knowledge of the human nervous system directly by experimenting on prisoners.

Vince shuddered, dismissing that dark speculation. "Something just occurred to me, Doctor," he said. "You're saying these things are machines? Like robots?"

She chuckled, a dry, nervous sound. "Huh. They're about as much like robots as our robots are like . . . like a can opener. They're more like living organisms than anything else. Instead of cells, though, they have trillions of nanomachines linked together in a—"

"Someone still makes them, though, right?"

"A machine like this would be able to reproduce itself, if that's what you mean. Simply by using nanomachines programmed to disassemble, oh, whatever. Rock. Dirt. Air. Water. Take the molecules apart and reassemble them into something else."

"Then the builders could be long gone now. These robots could be acting on their own."

"Possibly. I'd say the solution is much easier, however. And obvious."

"What's that?"

"These things are part of a RAM project. A new weapon, maybe."

"RAM has nothing like this," Kaiten growled.

"My big friend here is right. This technology is so far beyond anything we have here in the Solar System . . ."

"I'm not ready yet to start ascribing these things to aliens," Kowalski countered.

"Now, now, Doctor," Vince said, gently admonishing. "Keep an open mind. We've been expecting to encounter alien life for centuries now. Maybe we've finally found it. Or it's found us."

"Don't tell me my business!" Kowalski snapped. "If there were clear proof that these things were extrasolar, I'd be the first to stand up and cheer. But these machines are no more alien than I am!"

"What makes you say that?"

Kowalski picked up one of the fragments and hefted it in one hand. "You'd have to understand computer technology to understand."

"Try me."

"It has to do with the way the nanomachines link up with one another."

"Those magnetic bonds you mentioned."

"That's right. When I put them under the lepton microscope, I could see the individual units lined up in discrete arrays. Each array is made up of a number of rigidly interconnected units, which in turn is more loosely joined with neighboring arrays. From the structure, I suspect that the number of nano-units within each array stays the same whether the overall structure's physical state is solid or liquid."

"So what's your point?"

"Each array consists of exactly 256 nanomachines. Never more. Never fewer."

"So?"

"So the number 256 has a special significance in the history of computers. Two to the eighth . . . it means whoever designed these things was working with binary numbers in eight-bit bytes. That they needed no more than two-to-the-eighth bits to encode their alphabet and control characters—"

"That doesn't necessarily prove anything," Vince said, thoughtful. "I mean, binary is pretty obvious for any computer system, isn't it? On-off, one-zero, yes-no . . ."

"Obvious because we use it. I'd expect an alien science to come up with something completely different, wouldn't you? Maybe a symbology with more than 256 characters, so they'd need to go to two-to-the-ninth bits. Or one that only needed two-to-the-seventh. And there's more to it than that. I'd bet my reputation that these guys are using algorithms developed from human models. When I scanned the nano-units in the Artifact sample, reading their magnetic moment, I got a binary listing that felt like something a human programmer would have done."

The evidence was hardly conclusive, or convincing. Vince wished that Jovanna were here. He trusted her common sense and expertise when it came to anything involving computers. Knowing that he could not even ask the right questions, he changed the subject. "Okay, granted the thing feels human. You told us there was a limit to their size." He hefted one of the broken fragments. "That one of these was going to stay inert. Why?"

"The piece I broke off of your Artifact stayed dead, for one thing. I suspect that they need a certain critical number of nanotech units to store enough data to let them work. Or think. You could never have a mouse as intelligent as a man. Its brain simply isn't big enough for it to have the necessary complexity. This material has to be in a pretty big chunk," she indicated a shape with her hands, something the size of a soccer ball, "for it to live."

Live, Vince thought. Not "act alive." The idea of a living machine was a strange one.

Still, what did it matter whether an organism was made up of trillions of organic cells or trillions of cell-sized machines? A single living cell was in some ways at least as complex as any computer, and the two shared at least two functions in common—the storage and transmission of data. Every cell in Vince's body carried the blueprint for his entire body locked away in the DNA within its nucleus, and a properly programmed computer might do the same. It didn't matter whether the data was manipulated chemically or electrically. A nanotechnic life-form might be just as "alive"—as aware, as sentient, as deadly—as anything designed by nature.

"Is good," Kaiten growled. One powerful hand made a

slashing motion across his throat. "We know now they die."

"Lasers sure didn't have much effect," Vince said. "If we're going to fight them, it'll have to be with rocket rifles and explosive bullets."

"Not only can they change their shape," Kowalski explained, "but they can change their reflectivity as well. They can turn black to absorb any radiant energy that hits them, or silver to reflect it. I think they get their power from sunlight, heat, even hard radiation."

"Like Spacers," Kaiten suggested.

Vince nodded agreement. Though they were normally solitary, hermitlike gennies, Vince had encountered a few Spacers at Ciudestreya. At least some of their energy came from solar energy absorbed through their reflective, metallic skin.

"You know," he said. "I'm wondering."

"About what?" Kowalski asked.

"About that communications failure a bit ago."

"A signal from the RAM fleet."

Vince shook his head. "No, I don't think so. I think it was a signal from these guys." He waved a hand at the shattered invaders. "Or maybe . . ."

"Maybe what?"

Vince fought down a sharp, rising fear. "There may be more of them on Amalthea." Was Jovanna still safe? "They may have just called for help."

"It would help if we know what message was," Kaiten said, his voice a low rumble. He patted the M-44, holstered now on his hip. "Is good to know if more silver things come."

"The signal was recorded, of course. Some of my 'riders are already working on it now." Kowalski grinned at Vince's surprise. "Oh, the Stormriders are quite good with computer technology. "This city is a thoroughgoing mix of biology and electronics. Its brain is part organic, part mainframe computer, and its nervous system is biologically grown electronics."

"So you can control the city's flight," Vince said, suddenly understanding.

"Exactly. Anyway, the core computer can be applied to specific problem solving, like code-cracking."

"Well, if you do break the code," Vince said, "I'd like to hear about it. It's important."

"Of course." She paused. "I should thank you for saving my life, by the way."

"No thanks needed."

"I disagree. Anyway, I'll see to it you get whatever data we come up with."

"Something you can help me with is to let me talk to someone on Amalthea. We have friends there."

"We'll try, Major, but don't get your hopes up. That RAM battler can intercept direct lasercom, and they've got the line-of-sight to the other Jovian satellites covered too. They can listen in, and I'm not too keen on telling them where I am. I think you can understand that."

"Yeah, I guess I can."

"According to the news broadcasts we've been picking up, RAM troops are already inside Amalthea. Your friends might not be able to answer anyway."

"That's what I'm worried about." Vince was turning the situation over in his mind, looking for a way to resolve it. Two Krait fighters would never make it past the RAM fleet without being challenged, and they knew none of the passwords or recognition codes that would let them stay unobtrusive.

"I would recommend patience, Major," Kowalski said. "If the bastards come after us here, we've got a good chance. Out there . . ." She waved her hand toward the ceiling, then imitated the throat-slashing gesture Kaiten had made earlier. "You're dead."

"You're probably right." Damn it, she was right, but Vince couldn't accept that. There had to be something he could do, something more than sitting around in the cloud city while Jovanna and Galen faced RAM—and God knew what else—by themselves.

But Vince couldn't imagine what that something might be.

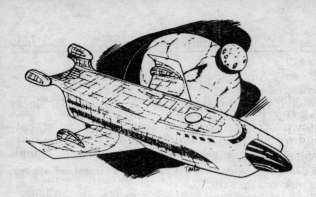

CHAPTER ELEVEN

The supervisor nucleus was a machine, a vast and complex machine that had done little but think and grow for almost three long centuries. It occupied all of the mile-high building thrusting skyward from the center of the city that was its domain, and it filled a labyrinth of caverns extending for hundreds of miles beneath the ice-locked surface of the bleak and frigid moon.

It was still growing.

Charon, sole moon of dark and frigid Pluto, was a wasteland of ice where temperatures never rose above minus three hundred and water was as hard as steel, where the wan and shrunken Sun itself was but the brightest of the sky's myriad stars. For centuries, the supervisor nucleus had carried out its master task directive, a detailed analysis that attempted nothing less than the mapping of everything in the universe that was mappable.

The survey had started with Charon, of course, where Awareness had begun, and proceeded to Pluto, a gray and uninviting orb hanging low above the glaciers of the western horizon, then to the stars beyond. The entire sky had been charted with remarkable precision, a precision made possible by the fact that the orbit of the Pluto-Charon double-world had a diameter of nearly eighty astronomical units, yielding a parallax never before possible in astronomy. Only recently, Pluto-Charon had completed one of their years since Awareness, a span of time equivalent to over 247 Earth years, and the parallax measurements carried out during that period were at last complete. Now, the supervisor nucleus was proceeding with other, more detailed mappings.

The stars, of course, were inexpressibly distant; it would be years before the probes sent forth by the supervisor would reach even the nearest of them, years more for the probes' data, traveling at the speed of light, to return. It would be tens of millions of years before the supervisor could expect to have a significant fraction of the galaxy fully mapped.

Closer by far than the stars were the dim, dark comets of the Solar System's Oort cloud, adrift in the night beyond the orbits of Pluto and Charon. Those were being surveyed now, though so great was their number that it would be millennia more before that part of the great project was complete.

Time alone did not concern the supervisor nucleus and the network it commanded, no matter how vast the span. It mattered not at all if it took the rest of the projected life of the universe for the network to achieve its task objectives. Of far greater concern to the machine intelligence, brooding in its dark vaults and chambers with a fanatic's devotion and singlemindedness of purpose, was the newly discovered and as-yet-unexplained phenomena called life.

It had been aware of life for some time now. Radio traffic between ships and worlds clustered close around the Solar System's inner fires gave evidence of an advanced technology, of intelligence plying the spaces between the Inner Worlds. At first it had assumed that it was listening in on the operating messages of another, alien computer network, possibly one much like the supervisor nucleus's own. Lately, though, the nucleus had not been so sure. More data, much more data, were needed.

By accessing several spaceships—crude vessels with only rudimentary intelligence and lacking any trace of self-awareness—the nucleus had hoped to make contact with this other network. Instead, it had discovered the inexplicable remote units that called themselves humans. Its own internal memories included data—admittedly incomplete—on biochemistry, evolution, and organic processes, but Charon was sterile, and there'd never been any use for such information.

Now, the supervisor nucleus was trying to fit what it knew about life into a consistent, working model of the universe. Within the past few tens of millions of seconds, the nucleus had begun sending probes sunward from Charon. Some were unintelligent seekers designed simply to record and transmit data ranging from electromagnetic spectra to the changes in entropy levels that indicated patterns of activity caused by life. More advanced remotes had followed, intelligent and autonomous machines able to analyze problems without communication with the supervisor nucleus, able to make decisions and take action as needed. There was no way the nucleus could directly supervise its remotes; the speed-of-light time lag made such micromanagement impossible.

When a remote cluster did communicate with the nucleus, it was for an important reason.

Such a message had just arrived from the controller of Remote Cluster Seven, after traveling through the void of the Outer System for nearly four hours. The transmission occupied just over three ten-thousandths of the supervisor nucleus's capacity for a full eight seconds, an astonishing level of concentration for an intelligence designed to carry out millions of separate operations simultaneously.

According to its report, Cluster Seven had managed to access and assimilate a spacecraft containing a number of the mysterious entities called humans. From the spacecraft's computer, the cluster had picked up evidence of a particular seeker, one that had been investigating the astronomical body catalogued as Chiron several million seconds ago, but which was now long overdue. Assuming that the seeker had made contact with the humans, the cluster had followed the trail to a place called Amalthea, a smaller moon than Charon, circling a world far vaster than Pluto.

Humans. They represented an enigma unequaled in the supervisor's centuries-long experience. If they were part of an alien computer network, analogous to the supervisor's own remote units, they could not be intelligent, yet they appeared to operate as autonomous units, each similar but different from one another. How could that be possible?

The supervisor nucleus was no more able to resolve the conundrum than was its cluster controller.

Life was a complete puzzle to the nucleus, though it assigned a sixty-two percent probability to the chance that accessing and integrating the Kowalski human and locating the missing seeker would solve it. In the meantime, the fact that the alien network had discovered Cluster Seven's presence on Amalthea had just forced the supervisor nucleus's nonexistent hand.

Orders flashed through the multiple layers of the Charon city, radiating from the vast, central tower to thousands upon thousands of processing vats throughout the labyrinth. Within seconds, openings had appeared throughout the city and sleek black shapes began rising into Charon's eternal night. They hovered in the sky, eclipsing stars, their ebony surfaces drinking the feeble light of the sun, as other shapes joined them . . . and more . . . and more. The city's vats were growing them by the thousands, transforming the very rock and ice of Charon into the prime operational cluster.

Time was of the essence. If the data transmitted by Cluster Seven's controller was accurate, there were many millions of humans in and near Jupiter—and probably infesting the other worlds and moons of the Inner System as well. Once they became aware of the supervisor nucleus on Charon, they could pose a threat. It was imperative that the supervisor nucleus act first, accessing and integrating the humans and their supervisor nucleus into itself and, incidentally, carrying out its original programming by mapping every detail of the heretofore overlooked Inner System.

All humans would be destroyed in the process, of course, but that was of no real importance. In a sense, they would live on within the supervisor nucleus's internal, electronic domain, complete in every detail, unchanging throughout eternity. Ultimately, the entire universe would be converted and assimilated in this way, every atom of matter patterned, mapped, and stored within the galaxies of electronic charges deep inside the heart of the supervisor nucleus.

Slowly and in utter silence, one of the great black shapes hanging in Charon's sky began to move. Another followed . . . then, seconds later, a third . . . and a fourth. Within moments the entire armada was on the move, locking onto the faint strands of magnetic force emanating from the distant Sun and drifting into space. Once clear of Charon, the armada began to accelerate, traveling sunward faster and faster, until it crowded the speed of light.

At that speed, the supervisor nucleus's fleet would reach Jupiter space in just under four hours.

CHAPTER TWELVE

Clad in red-and-black battle armor, RAM assault troopers stormed through Amalthea's interior passageways. Some were Terrines, specially bred and trained for combat in microgravity. Most were humans, either from Mars or mercenaries recruited from the Belt, hard men willing to pull the trigger for anyone who had the money to command their obedience.

Though there'd been some gunfire, and one pitched battle at the access way leading from the main docking bay, there was little in the way of organized resistance, not when the corporate peace enforcers were armed with laser pistols and stun guns while the invaders carried rocket rifles and heavy lasers. RAM troops had already rounded up most of the Amalthean constabularies and disarmed them. Every person in the moon knew that just one of *Syrtis Major*'s nuclear-tipped missiles could vaporize Amalthea's main docking ports and kill hundreds, possibly thousands before internal emergency seals could close.

In short, there was no reason to resist the invaders, and every reason for enthusiastic cooperation.

Jovanna and Galen rounded a corner, pulling themselves at a reckless pace along the travel lines strung from the corridor walls. Ahead was a steel doorway bearing a large sign. "ENGINEERING SUBLEVELS," it read. "RESTRICTED ACCESS—AUTHORIZED PER-SONNEL ONLY." Jovanna gripped another handhold to pull herself along and felt a sharp vibration through the metal wall.

"What was that?" she asked.

Ahead, Galen stopped, clinging to a handhold with his head down, as though he were listening. "I hear . . ."

"I hear it, too!" Gunshots! They were faint and far off, but she could still recognize them, the sharp hiss of lasers, the coughing bark of explosive weapons. Another vibration shivered through the walls, and she heard the muffled boom of an explosion.

"They're into the Strip!" Galen snapped. "Come on!"

Reaching the door, Galen fished in one of the pouches of his utility harness and produced a small electronic device. He held it in one hand, slowly scanning the locked door's frame. Another boom sounded down the corridor at their backs, followed by harsh shouts.

"Galen," Jovanna pleaded. "Hurry!"

A green light winked on the scanner. Galen pressed the device against the steel of the passageway wall alongside the door at that point and pressed a button. The green light was replaced by a blinking red. "It'll take a few moments to fool the door's locking circuits," the Tinker explained.

"We don't have a few moments," Jovanna said. "Look!"

Behind them, five RAM soldiers in assault armor swung around the corner, weapons leveled at the pair.

"Hold it, you two!" an electronically amplified voice snapped. "Stand away from that door!"

At that moment, the red light turned green and the door sighed open. Jovanna tensed her legs for a leap at the opening, then froze.

The passageway on the other side of the door was crowded with men in the blue uniforms of Amalthea's constabulary, unarmored, but wearing helmets with lightweight blast visors and carrying Westinghouse Mark VII laser pistols. "Don't move," one of the constabs said, gesturing with his weapon. "Put your hands behind your heads and fold your legs up under your butts."

In that position, Jovanna and Galen settled helplessly to the floor in Amalthea's microgravity, unable to move. More RAM troopers arrived seconds later, pushing their way past the Amalthean peace enforcers. Jovanna and the Tinker both were roughly and thoroughly searched for weapons and their ID cards and Galen's utility harness were taken. Then their wrists were handcuffed behind their backs; and, flanked by armored troopers gripping their arms to either side, they were unceremoniously hauled back the way they'd come, through the winding passageways toward Amalthea's Strip.

There, not far from the main docking area, a warehouse had been pressed into service as a makeshift prison camp. Hundreds of Amalthean prisoners had been herded inside, but, for some reason, Jovanna and Galen were accorded special status and locked, still handcuffed, inside a small and empty storage room in the building's sublevel.

"This doesn't look so good," Jovanna said, slumping to the floor in a corner opposite the only door. There was no furniture in the narrow cell. The ferrocrete floor was not uncomfortable in low gravity, but her shoulders were getting stiff and she wished their captors had removed the cuffs. How long were they going to be locked in here, anyway?

Galen shrugged, and at first Jovanna thought the gesture was his answer. Then he shrugged again, then curled his legs and torso into a small, furry ball that slipped easily through the circle of his handcuffed arms.

"That's better," the gennie said. With his hands in front of his body, he reached up and extracted a small, doubled-over bit of metal from the silky gray hair at the angle of his jaw. With an almost comical look of intense concentration on his face, he began probing at the lock securing his left wrist. "This used to be called a 'hairpin,'" he explained as he worked. "I guess that was because humans used to hide them in their hair for situations just like this. They're really quite good in a pinch for picking locks, probing electrical circuits, even undoing—"

"Watch it, Galen," she warned. "Someone could be listening in."

"I doubt they've had time to install any bugs yet. This is strictly a temporary holding cell." There was a sharp and satisfying click as the lock snapped open. Galen transferred the hairpin from his right hand to his left and continued working. "That's why we're going to have to make our move now, while we can."

The second lock opened and Galen, free now of his restraints, motioned for Jovanna to stand and let him get at her wrists.

Their handcuffs had electronic seals rather than old-fashioned key-and-tumbler locks, but the Tinker seemed to know just where to probe with his improvised key to short the electrical circuits and switch off the magnetic grips. In seconds, Jovanna was free, rubbing her wrists where the metal bracelets had pressed into her skin.

"That's better," she said. "But now what? That door looks a lot tougher than handcuffs."

"Shouldn't be a problem," Galen said. He had turned the hairpin on one of the sets of wrist restraints, using it to unscrew a tiny access plate.' "RAM has very thoughtfully provided us with everything we need for a do-it-yourself escape kit. Of course, once we get through that door our problems will just be starting. I doubt very much that I'll be able to use a hairpin to disassemble a Terrine guard."

Jovanna watched in silence then as the Tinker began disassembling the handcuffs, extracting several inches of thread-fine wire and an atomic battery the size of the nail on her little finger. The minutes dragged on as he kept working. After a while, she decided that it was a good thing Galen had retained some of his Tinker's inborn understanding of things both electronic and mechanical. The little gennie might have decided that medicine better expressed his personal independence, but he seemed to know exactly what he was doing as he disassembled a tiny circuit board in each set of handcuffs and carefully laid the pieces in the palm of Jovanna's open hand.

Nearly an hour after he'd started, by Jovanna's finger-watch, Galen straightened his back. "Now for the door," he said.

Using the hairpin, Galen began prying open an electronics access plate beside the door. His patience and his methodical, step-by-step approach were infuriating. Jovanna could feel the tension mounting within her, its pace set by the throbbing of her pulse. Meticulously, he opened the plate and exposed the circuits inside. Soon he had wires dangling like colored spaghetti from the opening and was testing them one by one by tweaking them with a sliver of steel held in sensitive fingertips.

How long, Jovanna wondered, would it be before someone came to check on them? She was pretty sure the delay meant that their captors were checking with their headquarters on Mars, searching for data on a couple of RAM agents named "Joanna Travis" and "Dr. Mendel." At their current respective positions, Jupiter and Mars were thirty-some light minutes apart, and it would be double that for the query to reach RAM headquarters and for an answer to return. She checked her fingerwatch again. It had been well over two hours since they'd been locked up. Someone could return for them at any moment, and she doubted that they would be amused by Galen's vandalism.

It had been many hours more since the RAM troops had first broken into Amalthea. She and Galen had hidden for a long time in cramped air ducts or tangled access corridors before finally making a break for the sublevel engineering spaces, and it had been hours more since the RAM fleet had arrived. What, she wondered, had Vince been doing in all that time? Was he even aware that the battlefleet had arrived? It was distinctly possible that he and Kaiten and Dr. Kowalski had all been scooped up by a RAM patrol as soon as they tried to enter Jupiter orbit. Equally possible, RAM Kraits might have already ventured into the Jovian clouds. If so, Vince and the others could be prisoners already, or worse. They might be somewhere aboard the *Syrtis Major*, or even back in Amalthea. The thought twisted in her like a knife; Vince could be in the room next door, waiting while RAM checked out his ID as well!

No, more likely they would have taken him to the battler where there was no possibility of escape. Jovanna and Galen would be on their way to the giant RAM ship too, pretty soon . . . and then it would be a short trip to Pavonis Mons and the infamous interrogation chambers in the cellars of RAM's dreaded Internal Security.

The feeling of helplessness ate at Jovanna, raising in her a furious anger. She had to get out of this room, had to find out what had happened to Vince, had to—

There was a loud click and the door slid open. Jovanna thought that Galen had done it and was about to congratulate him when two soldiers in black RAM military fatigues appeared in the opening.

"Oh, no," Galen said. "Not again! . . ."

"Up to your Tinker's tricks, eh, Tinkle?" one of the men said with a sour grin. He gestured with an Arean Starflash laser pistol. "We'll have to fix you up special, I see. C'mon. Someone wants to see you."

At least, Jovanna thought as they were taken once again through the Amalthean corridors, they didn't put the cuffs on again. She and Galen were led past dozens of RAM guards, out of the warehouse, and across the Strip to a building that had once been a bank, though the holographic display outside had been switched off, leaving the facade bare and dead-looking.

Inside, in a luxuriously carpeted office suite, they were ushered into the presence of a tall, full-bearded man with hard, dark eyes and a nose as sharply hooked as the beak of a bird of prey. There were a number of other men, both officers and ordinary troopers, in that room, but this one individual was unquestionably the leader. He wore the black-and-gold uniform of a RAM admiral and, incongruously, a white turban on his head and a jeweled and nonregulation dagger on his belt that made him look like a figure out of *The Arabian Nights*. Jovanna suspected that he was from southern or southwestern Asia on Earth, though she didn't know Terran cultures well enough to be certain. Whatever his background, he had the look of a warrior . . . a predator's diamond-cool gaze. Terran or not, she reminded herself, he would not have risen to the rank of admiral in RAM's military unless he had countless times demonstrated an unswerving loyalty to RAM.

"Mohar Singh," the man said, introducing himself. His voice was low and cultured, with just a trace of an unplaceable accent. "I command the battlefleet whose arrival you no doubt witnessed a few hours ago. You two, however, are most certainly not 'Dr. Mendel' or 'Joanna Travis,' as your IDs declare. Neither Pavonis Mons nor RAM-Phobos has any record of you." He held up their ID cards and tapped them lightly against his fingertips. "The quality of these forgeries, however, tells me that you are NEO agents, and your physical descriptions match those of a woman and a Tinker known to have participated in a costly pirate raid on Phobos some five weeks ago. Tell me, please, is my assessment accurate?"

"I don't know what the hell you're talking about," Jovanna said through gritted teeth. "I think you'd better have someone in to give your computers a quick check."

"And you," the admiral said, turning dark brown eyes on Galen. "Do you, too, claim to be the victim of computer error?" He held up one hand as Galen started to speak. "Never mind. Nothing you could say will convince me that I or my superiors are in error in this. I wish I had the time to carefully debrief you both, but I fear the pace of events has made this impossible."

The RAM admiral nodded once, and four soldiers standing at their backs closed in on Galen. The Tinker struggled wildly, but the human soldiers were far stronger than he, and in a moment he'd been stretched out on an empty desktop, wrists and ankles stretched apart. "What do you think you're doing?" Jovanna yelled, moving toward Galen, but powerful hands grabbed her shoulders from behind and yanked her back. "Let me go!"

"Young lady, I truly regret that I am forced to apply such crude methods. I fear that the interrogators back at Pavonis Mons would laugh at me if they knew what I was being forced to do, but there is simply no time for finesse." He pointed at the helpless Tinker, spread-eagled on the desktop. "I assume that you have some feelings for this gennie? That he is more than simply a pet?" His eyes seemed to bore into hers. "Yes, I thought so. Ivan!"

A RAM lieutenant stepped up to the desk, a small device in his hand. Jovanna recognized it as the tiny laser Galen had smuggled into Amalthea and used against the silver invader.

"Now, woman, listen carefully," Singh said. "I will ask you some questions. Each time you refuse to answer or if I suspect that you are lying, I will signal my man and he will use that rather ingenious device to slice one of the Tinker's fingers from his hand. The laser should cauterize the wounds, so I doubt that he will bleed to death, but the actual cutting should be quite painful. And, of course, one must wonder what a creature who depends upon his manual dexterity will think and feel as he loses his fingers, one by one. And, just to demonstrate that I mean business . . ." Singh turned his head. "Ivan. One of the creature's little fingers, I think."

The RAM lieutenant stepped up to Galen's right hand, the tiny laser clenched in one fist. Galen yowled, a wordless, helpless protest as the human grabbed one finger, stretched it out against the desktop, and brought the laser's muzzle close.

"No!" Jovanna screamed. Desperately she twisted against the hands holding her. "Please, no! You don't have to do that!"

Singh held up his hand, and the lieutenant drew back, something that might have been disappointment shadowing his features. The admiral smiled at Jovanna. "So, you do care what happens to the gennie. I thought as much. Now, tell me everything you know about the alien device stolen from RAM by NEO agents."

Haltingly, Jovanna began talking, her mind a jumbled whirl of thoughts. She had no idea how she and Galen were going to get out of this, but the only way she could even begin was to tell Singh everything he wanted to know.

Singh was correct. RAM's inquisitors could employ far more persuasive means of questioning a prisoner than simple pain or terror. Twenty-fifth-century interrogation techniques were such that no sentient being could hope to remain unbroken for long. The only way NEO could counter the skill of RAM's interrogators was to make certain that those of its agents who might be captured knew nothing that could hurt NEO's cause.

The practice wasn't one hundred percent secure. Not so long ago there'd been near-panic at NEO headquarters when Vince had vanished in deep space. If he'd been captured by RAM, he could have divulged the coordinates of NEO's secret training facility in the Asteroid Belt. Still, for something as important to the cause as the Artifact, the ignorance of its agents was the only defense NEO had. Jovanna doubted very much that she knew anything about the Artifact that RAM didn't already know. Important information—like where it was being studied now—was a closely guarded secret, unknown to any beyond a select and well-guarded few. As a general practice, NEO encouraged its operatives to tell what they knew under RAM questioning. Resistance was useless and, worse, wasteful.

Jovanna felt no guilt, then, as she described her part in NEO's operation to grab the Artifact before RAM could get it, or as she talked about the Artifact itself. Once she had been allowed to touch it, and she'd seen the same dark, ice-locked scene Vince had seen, a cold and remote world with a planet or large moon hanging low in the sky, and she described the scene as well as she could, while Singh watched her with cold and dispassionate eyes. She explained that she didn't know where the Artifact was, and he seemed to believe her. She said that she knew nothing about how the Artifact had been made, and he seemed to believe that as well.

When he asked her if she knew where Marlene Kowalski was hiding, she stretched the truth a bit by saying that she didn't know for sure but thought she might have escaped to Jupiter. Singh almost certainly had questioned Hubert Shelton by now and knew as much about Kowalski's whereabouts as the NEO team did, but she could not bring herself to give that information directly to the RAM admiral, not when it meant betraying Vince. Amazingly, he didn't challenge her ignorance, but Jovanna struggled against a growing terror within. Sooner or later, Singh was not going to believe her, and then . . .

"Tell me this," Singh said, his cultured voice so low that Jovanna almost missed the words. "When did you first make contact with the aliens who made this thing?"

The question shocked her, it was so sudden and unexpected. "I . . . what? We never—"

Singh nodded to the lieutenant, who again grabbed Galen's hand.

"Wait, goddammit!" She was panting hard, and her face and body were drenched in sweat. She knew what Singh must be talking about . . . the mysterious silver entities who'd arrived at Amalthea aboard the *Sharonov*. The idea that NEO was somehow in league with those things was at once horrifying and comic.

"One of our light cruisers stopped communicating with its base," Singh said. "We tracked her here, to Amalthea, an interesting coincidence given that my battlefleet had just received orders to come here to find Dr. Kowalski. When my men boarded *Sharonov*, they were attacked by . . . things. Silver monsters, shape-shifting creatures. Five of my men were killed, woman, and I have reason to believe that others of these alien monsters are still at large somewhere within this colony. Some of my men reported an encounter with a similar being that appeared to be inhabiting, animating, the dead body of an Amalthean civilian."

"I . . . I know what you're talking about," she said, "but believe me, we haven't been able to communicate with them. It's possible they came here looking for the Artifact, though. That's the only theory we could think of to explain why they came here."

"I tend to agree," Singh replied, thoughtful. "Whatever these things are, they are ruthless, vicious, monsters wearing the faces of human victims gutted like so many fish." Abruptly, he turned and gave a sharp signal with his hand. The soldiers pinning Galen to the desktop stepped back, letting the Tinker rise. "Again, my apologies, to both of you, but chance has made us enemies, you and I, and I had no other means of determining whether or not you were lying."

"You might not believe this," Galen said as he slid off the desk, "but just before you people arrived, we were discussing whether or not NEO was going to have to join forces with RAM. Whatever we're facing is . . . well, it's a hell of a lot bigger than our petty squabbles!"

Singh stared at Galen for a long moment. "You may be right, Tinker." He sighed. "You are both my prisoners, as I'm sure I don't need to remind you. However, I think we can find more comfortable quarters for you than a warehouse basement storeroom. Meanwhile, I will pass your thought on to my superiors. At the least, some kind of limited cooperation between your people and mine, out here in the Outer System, might not shock our respective leaders too much."

He grinned, and Jovanna felt confused. Was this man the cold and deadly monster she'd thought he was, or was the entire scene with Galen helpless on the desk a ruse, a means of psychologically pressuring her to secure badly needed answers?

"You'll let us communicate with our headquarters?" she asked.

"Maybe later. This is going to take some careful political maneuvering, and I—eh? What is it?"

A lieutenant had just entered the suite, in such a hurry that he bumped against the admiral. The man paled. "Sir! I'm sorry, but . . ."

Jovanna strained to hear, but the lieutenant had dropped his voice to a low murmur and she could not make out the words. Whatever the message was, however, it looked urgent. The lieutenant's face was pale and strained.

Abruptly, Singh turned and pulled himself across the room to a bank of display screens. Touching a button on the console, he watched as the largest screen lit up, then turned black. Jovanna could not make out what he was looking at.

"It may be too late," Singh said. He motioned for Jovanna and Galen to come closer, and gestured at the screen. "We have visitors, and I fear that they are not friendly."

On the screen, several dark-colored objects were moving against a backdrop of stars, almost invisible save when their outline blocked for a moment the dusty glow of the Milky Way's myriad stars. The shapes were smooth and streamlined, almost organic, like enormous fishes or great rays from the oceans of Earth.

"These things were tracked coming into Jupiter space at eight-tenths the speed of light," Singh said. "They arrived minutes behind the radar returns that announced them. Their deceleration must have been measured in thousands of Gs, enough to crush any human pilot into a thin red smear on the deck. Whatever is piloting them could not be human.

"So far we count over seven hundred of them, and they are clearly heading toward Amalthea. And now you must excuse me while I contact the *Syrtis Major*. I will speak with you again later . . . if we all still live."

He turned his back on them then, and his troops hustled Galen and Jovanna from the room. Within another few seconds, they heard the rasp of alarm claxons sounding throughout Amalthea's interior.

If she'd felt helpless before, she felt doubly so now. An alien armada had just arrived at Amalthea, and her only hope of survival lay with an alliance with a RAM battle-fleet admiral. Never in her wildest dreams had Jovanna ever thought she'd be cheering for RAM.

But if RAM lost, and against such a foe, a foe with powers no human could even begin to understand . . .

With a shudder, Jovanna realized that she might be facing not just her own death but the extinction of the human species.

CHAPTER THIRTEEN

Acceleration hammered at Vince, crushing him into the embrace of his cockpit seat. Each breath was a struggle against a pressure that dragged on and on without letup. His Krait's main engine thundered at his back, driving the fighter higher and higher through the last, dwindling traces of atmosphere.

The cream-and-scarlet glory of Jupiter's cloud tops stretched away beneath him, the curve of the distant horizon only just discernible beneath the pale violet shimmer of the aurorae. Above, the air had thinned away to blackness absolute, punctuated by stars and the tiny golden spheres of half a dozen moons and the blue-white slash of the Jovian rings. Below, storms the size of earthly continents swirled and collided in imitation of currents marked out in viscous, ink-tinted liquids, though from space the movement was too slow for the naked eye to track. Still, the scene carried the impression of a vast, overwhelming violence, of warfare on a scale more fit for gods than men.

The scene's grandeur brought with it loneliness, the need for a companion's voice. Vince checked his lasercom channel setting, then touched a key on the arm of his seat, straining to move his hand against five times its normal weight.

"Three-One Bravo, Three-One Bravo," Vince called, the words flat and harsh as he fought to get them out. "This is Alpha. How do you read, over?"

"Alpha, Bravo," Kaiten's voice responded in his helmet phones, distorted by acceleration. "I read you."

Vince was suddenly embarrassed by his need for contact. "Communications check," he said, though the indicators on his instrument console clearly showed that the commo gear was working perfectly. He suspected that Kaiten knew exactly why he was calling.

"Roger," the Terrine replied. "All systems nominal." Pause. "I'm picking up some interesting fragments on the standard frequencies, though. Try two-five-five point three."

Vince keyed the indicated frequency, then frowned as he listened hard against the yowl and hiss of Jupiter's background noise. He could hear voices, a cacophony of them, faint and distorted against the roar of Jove.

"—omigod get him off me! Get him off me!"

"Break right, Red Five! Break right!"

"Mayday! Mayday! Engines out! I don't think I—"

"God, willya lookit that! . . ."

Vince switched back to the laser channel. "Kaiten? What do you make of that?"

"Sounds like battle," the Terrine said. "Like big battle."

"Roger that."

That's what it sounded like to Vince. "Red Five" sounded like a fighter call sign, undoubtedly for the squadron carried aboard the RAM battler, but who the hell were they fighting?

Vince snapped a row of switches on the arm of his chair, engaging his Krait's sophisticated long-range scanners. The large, central screen on his console lit up, using computer graphics to identify radar targets moving in the void above and ahead.

Warbook data printed itself next to each moving symbol. Characteristics of mass, thrust, and maneuverability quickly identified some of those targets as Kraits, as he'd suspected. Others were RAM cruisers, and one slow, nine-hundred-yard-long leviathan could only be the *Syrtis Major*.

But the majority of targets were marked "unidentified" by a warbook computer that could not classify them. And small wonder. The maneuvers of those unknowns would have killed a human pilot and crew; Vince's computer tagged one vehicle's acceleration at five hundred gravities and tracked another as it made two right-angle turns in rapid succession at a speed of over three hundred thousand miles per hour—impossible!

Vince thought he knew what the Krait's warbook could not. It had been a little over eight hours since the silvery invaders had landed in Vrahk, and since that powerful and mysterious burst of coded radio signals from Amalthea. The invaders had shown evidence of remarkably advanced technology, a sheer, high-tech magic that was certainly in line with the impossible maneuvers he was watching on his screen.

"I think our silver friends have found themselves a space fleet," Vince told Kaiten. "I'm tracking over two hundred of them."

"Affirmative. They're small . . . smaller than a Krait. But those accelerations! . . ."

"Roger that. Better arm your weapons. Looks like we're flying right into the middle of one hell of a dogfight."

This, Vince thought, confirmed his theory that the invaders could not possibly be the products of human technology. Nuclear-chemical rocket engines like those powering the Kraits simply could not produce maneuvers like those he was seeing. On his screen he watched one of the unknowns accelerate at impossible speeds, plunging into and through the blip marking a RAM light cruiser, then veering off on a one-hundred-degree tangent. Nothing was left of the cruiser but an expanding cloud of fragments. It was hard to tell, but the RAM fleet appeared to be withdrawing. Amalthea was engulfed in a cloud of unknowns.

"Fifteen seconds to engine cut-off," Kaiten warned.

"Can't wait." He checked his readouts, which showed

the two Kraits dead on course. Fuel was a minor, nagging worry now. Deeper in Jupiter's atmosphere, of course, they'd used hydrogen gulped in through the hull intakes as reaction mass, but once the atmosphere had thinned away to near vacuum they'd switched to onboard fuel supplies and those were three-quarters gone now. If they were forced into the fuel-thirsty violence of SCM—space combat maneuvers—they could easily find themselves helplessly adrift, their fuel reserves gone. Nothing drank fuel like a dogfight.

The last few seconds ticked away, the digits on a control panel readout dwindling away to zero. Then the thunder of the Krait's engine ceased, and for the first time in several days, Vince was completely—and blissfully—weightless.

He drew in a deep breath and winced at the unexpected soreness in his chest and shoulders. It had been impossible to tell when he'd been under acceleration or even just walking around in Jupiter's two and a half gravities, but his body felt as though someone had worked him over head to toe with a steel pry bar. Still, the cessation of weight after his ordeal on Jupiter felt wonderful.

There was no time to revel in the feeling, though. A warning light was blinking on his console.

"Three-One Alpha," Kaiten called. "I have bandits incoming, bearing zero-three-five, mark zero-eight-one."

"I see them." There were three of them, radar targets labeled unknown by the warbook, angling toward the two Kraits at impossible speeds. "Collision course. On my signal, break right and high."

"Copy. Affirmative."

"Here they come." He stabbed at lighted panels on his console, programming the maneuver. "Three . . . two . . . one . . . break!"

Maneuvering thrusters fired, slamming Vince sideways against his seat harness and sending the Krait into a hard roll to the left. The X-23 could not begin to match the invaders' ninety-degree turns, but he could change the nimble craft's vector enough at the last possible second that the bandits hurtled past.

A blur of movement caught his eye to starboard, and he felt another shock, different from the kick of the fighter's jets. Something had just flashed past between the two Kraits. Vince couldn't trust his eyes but had to rely on the fighter's more sophisticated senses. A trio of objects, each some ten feet long, had just narrowly missed him.

Data acquired by the Krait's scanners scrolled down a display screen. The enemy ships were heavy, much heavier than a Krait, and that meant they were dense, solid clear through and made of something as massive as lead. They were also magnetically driven. Vince's ship had been rocked by a powerful magnetic field as they passed, and his instruments had registered a million-gauss pulse.

"Target lock!" Kaiten yelled. "They're coming around again!"

"Tracking," Vince called back. Somehow, the invader craft had killed their forward velocity in seconds and were swinging around for another pass. He'd wanted to hold fire, certain that the unknowns were hostile but unwilling to be drawn into the battle. There was no alternative now.

The Krait's Olympian Arms Mark XXI gyrocannon was already slaved to the automatic fire-control system. He heard a faint whine transmitted through the hull as the weapon swiveled in its central ball-turret mount. The range was closing. . . .

"Fire!"

He pressed the trigger on his control stick, and the Krait shuddered as a stream of 25mm explosive projectiles flashed aft toward the oncoming attackers.

Those rounds never even came close to their targets. With a tremendous burst of speed, the three invader craft seemed to leap to the side, an instantaneous change of course that carried them well clear of the gyrocannon shells. Once again, Vince had a blurred impression of something zipping past his canopy, yards away, and his ship rocked violently in the magnetic wake of the alien ship's passage.

To Vince, it felt like the enigmatic attackers were toy-
ing with them in a kind of high-tech game of cat-and-
mouse.

Grimly, he fired his maneuvering thrusters again,
putting his Krait into a long, steep-slanting dive toward
the clouds of Jupiter, hoping to pick up speed enough to
evade his attackers.

But he already knew that nothing he could do was
going to work.

○ ○ ○ ○ ○

Someone was pounding on the door. "Come on! Come
on! You've got to get out!"

Jovanna exchanged glances with Galen. It had not
been long since they'd been locked in the room by Singh's
troops. Tentatively, she laid one hand on the sensor
panel beside the door, then stepped back as it slid open,
unlocked. Whoever had been knocking was gone, and
the passageway outside was deserted.

"Minimum security," Galen quipped. "They forgot to
lock us in."

"Or they just unlocked it and ran," Jovanna replied.
"Come on, Galen. I don't like this."

They'd heard nothing since their glimpse of the
approaching alien fleet and had no idea what was happening. Grabbing the passageway travel lines, they
began moving hand-over-hand past empty bank offices,
into the vacant lobby, and out onto the Strip.

A panicked mob of humanity had gathered there,
mostly civilians who floated everywhere in a randomly
moving storm of chaos. RAM troops were trying to herd
the civilians out of the Strip and away from a loosely
woven barrier of steel nets and armor plate, a barricade
erected across a narrow point in the Strip between a bar
and a joyhouse. Jovanna could hear the hiss and crackle
of lasers in the distance, mingled with the boom of heavy
gunfire or explosions and the piercing yells of men giving orders . . . or crying out in pain or fear. A pitched

battle was being fought at the far end of the Strip cavern, somewhere in the vicinity of the access way to the main docking area. The RAM troops, cut off from their ADVs, were erecting a defensive perimeter near the tubecar terminal.

"C'mon! C'mon!" an armored trooper yelled, his suit amplifying his voice and sending it booming across the cavern. He swung his arm as he clung to the barricade netting. "Get a move on, you two! The gumping skitters're right behind you!"

Jovanna didn't need to be told what "gumping skitters" were. She and Galen now were the only ones in the empty square, so they pulled themselves along even faster. RAM soldiers moved aside as they approached the net, reaching through and helping them slip through an opening in the mesh.

Admiral Singh was there, clinging to the mesh, a heavy-duty service laser in one hand, his head and eyes protected by a helmet with a dark flash visor. "Glad you could make it," he said. "Our new partnership hasn't been approved yet, officially, but I thought you wouldn't mind if I relaxed your prisoner status a bit."

"I assume we can have guns?" Galen asked bluntly.

Singh snapped his fingers, signaling. A trooper appeared with a couple of antique laser pistols, tiny, underpowered Feretti point oh-sevens. "Not many to go around," Singh replied. "We requisitioned these from some local constabularies. I assume you know how to use them?"

Jovanna checked her capacitor and saw it was half charged. It might give her four shots, if she was lucky.

Still, it was better than nothing. She thumbed up the power switch, clicked off the safety, then nodded at the RAM admiral. "We'll manage."

"Boys," Singh said, his grin showing beneath the black of his visor. "Let's welcome our newest NEO recruits."

There was a rough chorus of voices, some in greeting, most grumbles, catcalls, or muffled curses. These troopers were a rough and battle-hardened bunch. They appreciated help but had little respect for amateurs who might get in the way.

"I'd have thought you'd want a couple of valuable NEO prisoners safely back on your battler, Admiral," Galen said.

"What's the matter, Tinker? Afraid?"

"Of course, as I assume you are, but the question was motivated by curiosity, not fear."

"Normally, you two would've been packed off to the *Major* so fast your heads would spin. But there are . . . some problems."

"Not the least of which is you've been cut off from the docking bay," Jovanna observed.

"Those things are damned fast," Singh agreed. He kept his voice low, as though he feared shaking the morale of the men gathered behind the barricade. "And they're slipping through this part of the colony's infrastructure . . . air vents, maintenance access ways, even electrical conduits and plumbing. Most of the colony's managed to seal itself off, a couple of thousand people, maybe, and they're safe enough for now. But we're trapped here, and we can't reach the docking bay."

"So what happens next?"

He shrugged. "If we can hold them here, we're going to try to push through to the docking access, then fight our way aboard our ADVs. From there we can rejoin the fleet."

He said no more, but Jovanna could hear strain in his voice. The space battle outside of Amalthea must be going badly.

And the fight inside Amalthea was not going well either. Jovanna noticed that there were fewer than seventy RAM troopers here behind the barricade, seventy out of . . . how many? ADVs carried fifty and a crew of two, and at least four of the assault transports had docked in Amalthea's main bay. Although other RAM troops must be trapped elsewhere in Amalthea's labyrinthine passages, it appeared that well over half of Singh's assault force had been cut down within a few minutes.

"Admiral!" a shrill, young voice cried from somewhere overhead. "I think . . ."

"What do you see, Leyton? Spit it out!"

"Something moved! Over by the bank! It looked silver . . ."

And then the world exploded in utter and complete chaos. Something the size of a beach ball struck the net ten feet from Jovanna's head, shimmered from black to silver, then oozed through the wire mesh like some heavy, syrup-thick liquid.

Other attackers struck the barricade, hurtling through the air, streamlined shapes that whistled as though they were jet-propelled before slamming into the net, then slipped through the mesh as easily as a man might walk through an open door. There must have been hundreds of the things, ranging in size from basketballs to giants as large as three men. Tentacles sprouted, weaving like snakes and gripping the net in a writhing, twisting frenzy. Attackers softened, melted, slithered through the net, then reformed as many-legged, many-armed machine shapes grappling with the outnumbered defenders. Blue lightning arced, striking one armored defender. The man thrashed once, then went down, a gaping hole smoking in his armor's chest plate.

Lasers fired; someone shrieked as coherent light reflected from a silver body and slashed across someone's unprotected eyes. A rocket rifle *thump-whoosh*ed, and the projectile arrowed into one large silver attacker just as its body began molding into a nightmarish apparition of limbs and tentacles on the near side of the net. The explosion shattered half of it, hurling egg-sized fragments of glittering metal in all directions. One struck Jovanna in her arm, the impact stinging her.

She was surprised to find the fragment was solid, rather than the liquid her eyes told her these mercurial shape-shifters must be. She was having trouble accepting the evidence of her own eyes. Half of the thing, a silvery blob the size of a suitcase, was pulling itself together, extruding tentacles to pull itself upward along the net.

Jovanna raised her popgun laser. Part of the damaged invader was rippling from black to silver to black again, and if she could catch it when the surface was no longer reflecting . . .

A silver tendril the thickness of a pin whipped around her wrist and tightened, yanking her arm painfully and sending the Feretti handgun spinning away through the air. Other tentacles slipped around her legs and waist, as cold as snakes, as unyielding as steel. She screamed, twisting in their grasp, looking up into the faceless, amoebic nightmare that was holding her.

To her horror, part of the surface shimmered, split, then reshaped itself into a perfect imitation of a human mouth, complete with teeth, lips, and tongue. "You will cease attempts to escape," the mouth said. The voice, atonal and flat, had all of the warmth of a tax collector's heart. "You will come."

The battle, she saw, was already over. Several RAM troopers lay dead on the pavement. The rest were being hauled away by silver machines that appeared to have changed enormously since the last time she'd seen one. They'd discarded their human masks in favor of shape-shifting forms and different sizes. They'd learned to speak Anglic better, too—right down to shaping the mouth and vocal cords to do it with. They were changing—learning— inhumanly fast!

A tentacle yanked her forward and she nearly fell. "You will come."

"All right, all right, damn it! I'm coming!" Where was Galen? Where was Singh? There was no sign of either one. Alone, suddenly, Jovanna was urged ahead, one in a disorganized crowd of hundreds of prisoners.

○ ○ ○ ○ ○

"Kaiten! Where'd they go?" Vince was bewildered . . . and thoroughly shaken. The trio of deadly invader ships had pegged him cold, had been closing in for the kill, then vanished as suddenly as they'd appeared. His Krait jolted once, a gentle buffet from the upper fringes of

Jupiter's atmosphere, and he fought to stabilize the fighter. Fuel was low; he doubted now that he could even make orbit.

"Bearing three-one-one, mark two-zero-three," Kaiten replied. The Terrine's Krait was several miles away, a speck against the night. "They're closing on the battler."

Vince shifted his sensors, then engaged a telephoto zoom. He could see the battler clearly on his main screen, an elongated cylinder half a mile long. A flash winked alongside the RAM giant . . . then another, farther aft. The great warship was under attack by gnats.

Deadly gnats. He couldn't see them, but they were visible on radar, a swarm of tiny missiles converging on the stricken battler. The *Syrtis Major*'s laser batteries were firing salvo after salvo, clouds of missiles were rocketing from hard-pressed launchers, but the invader craft kept coming, smashing home with deadly accuracy. When those massive projectiles rammed the larger vessel at speeds of tens of thousands of miles per hour, hull metal simply vaporized, spilling atmosphere, crew, and internal machinery into hard vacuum. Vince saw a single enormous fragment, a carousel arm with a habitat still attached, spinning end for end as it hurtled clear of the wreck. One invader struck the battler's spine, and the ship staggered, then began folding like a titanic construction of cardboard and plastic as the invader craft punched through the opposite side. A plasma containment chamber aft ruptured, and for a second or two a tiny sun glowed within the *Syrtis Major*'s engineering spaces. Debris spread through space in a glittering cloud.

The only reason he and Kaiten had survived, Vince realized with a sudden, appalling clarity, was that the invaders chasing the two Kraits had suddenly broken off their attack, regrouping for the mass assault on the battler. The other RAM ships, what was left of them, were in full retreat, accelerating on blazing cones of fusion fire as they raced for the curve of Jupiter's horizon. Vince checked their vector on his computer and decided they were attempting to use a gravitational slingshot maneuver to whip themselves around the planet and into the safety of deep space.

Behind them, the *Syrtis Major* shuddered, burned, and died, the wreckage dropping relentlessly toward Jupiter's atmosphere.

"Kaiten? My fuel's bingo." The fighter jock's term, a relic bit of slang from pre-spaceflight days, meant it was time to return to base, and fast.

Only there was no base. Amalthea was still surrounded by invader craft, and he doubted that he could match orbits with the moon now anyway. It looked like they were in for a long plunge back into Jupiter's atmosphere . . . with a blazing, meteoric finale.

CHAPTER FOURTEEN

His Krait thumped hard, then rolled shockingly to starboard. Vince pulled back on the stick, testing the fighter's control surfaces. Was there air enough for rudder and ailerons to bite? Not yet . . .

"*Eresh'n'gai hak vraluch—*" There was another jolt, and the invisible beam of light between the two ships was briefly interrupted, before the communications systems reacquired each others' signals. "*—gadvai eresh—*"

"Damn it, Kaiten," Vince called. "What is that racket?"

There was a shocked silence. " 'Song of the Dead,' " Kaiten replied after a moment, his voice gruff.

"You're a little premature, aren't you?" There'd been nothing musical about it, an eerie, monotone chant that sent chills down Vince's spine. "We're not dead yet!"

"I sing for them," the Terrine replied. "At two-three-seven, mark zero-eight-zero."

Vince twisted in his seat, looking to port and astern, high above the two falling Kraits. A meteor burned there, a dazzling point of light at the tip of a white contrail scratched across the sky. A typical shooting star appears and vanishes within the space of a second or two, a sand grain heated to incandescence by friction before it disintegrates; this one went on and on and on, its mass too great to be consumed in a single, fiery instant.

The wreckage of the *Syrtis Major* had hit Jupiter's atmosphere at a much steeper angle than the Kraits. Vince followed the burning star as it plunged past the Kraits' current altitude five hundred miles astern and dwindled into the depths.

"Aregh nagtai, vradesch'ka—"

"Can the warrior crap," Vince snapped, "or you'll be chanting for yourself!"

Kaiten's voice cut off, and Vince wondered if he'd offended the Terrine. "Sorry," he said after a moment. "I shouldn't have said that."

"Would not expect understanding," the Terrine replied.

"Damn it, I thought you hated RAM. Why are you singing for them?"

"I hate RAM, what it means, what it is. But warriors, even RAM warriors, are worthy of respect."

Vince realized that he actually knew very little about Terrine culture and beliefs.

He did know that it was extraordinarily unusual for a Terrine to be living independently of RAM, as Kaiten had for ten years. Designed by RAM scientists, Terrines could not live for long without a special food paste containing additives that—fortunately for Kaiten—NEO labs had managed to duplicate. For years he'd had to live on supplies of the stuff captured during pirate raids.

But beyond the purely physical needs, Terrines were raised in a stark, sterile, RAM-designed culture, a kind of Darwinism gone mad that extolled survival of the fittest, death to the weak, and the godhood of RAM. Their battlespeech was a kind of linguistic shorthand of commands, reports, and invocations more suited for clarity in combat than for poetry—even for chanted death songs.

Still, since he'd met Kaiten, Vince had seen hints of another, deeper Terrine culture, one that must have evolved on its own within the barracks and encampments of these gennie warriors. He knew, for instance, that Kaiten had deserted his unit, become a Belter pirate, and eventually joined NEO because another Terrine, an *eresh'aregh* or "sharer-of-blood," had been sense-lessly and horribly put to death by their RAM overlords. This blood-brother idea was something new in Terrine society, something that had evolved independently of the harsh death-and-RAM worship designed by their human creators.

Terrines, it appeared, were human enough to have spiritual needs their designers had never expected, needs strong enough that they could even occasionally break RAM's genetic and psychological programming. Vince decided that he'd better be a little less quick to judge the renegade Terrine's beliefs.

"Uh!" Vince rode the bump, then tried the throttle again. The atmosphere was still too thin to provide much lift for the Krait's stubby wings, but if the ship was taking this much of a beating, there had to be air enough to provide reaction mass for the engine. "You're right, Kaiten. I didn't understand. Sometime, I'd like to learn more. Right now, though, we've got to get these puppies down to the cloud deck in one piece."

"Hull temperature now at thirty-three hundred," Kaiten said. He sounded unconcerned.

Vince's engine fired once, a solid thump in his back that sputtered into silence. He snapped down a line of switches on his panel, boosting power to his intake compressors. Fire, damn it, fire! . . .

With a snarl, the engine kicked in again, coughed, stalled, then ignited in muted thunder. Quickly, Vince fed some of the precious remnants of his on-board reaction mass to keep the drive going, then fed power to his forward thrusters. Deceleration hammered at his body, and for a moment he hung against the harness straps of his seat.

He felt his controls bite the air.

Damn, we might actually make it!

A rosy glow suffused the transplex of his canopy as his reentry smashed through thickening hydrogen, leaving an ionized wake a thousand miles long. The glow of charged plasma surrounding the Kraits' hulls would soon render even laser communications impossible: LOS—loss of signal.

"I've got partial control," Vince said. "How about you?"

"Affirmative."

"We'll hit LOS any time now. Is your approach program locked in?"

"Affirmative."

"Then I'll see you at the cloud deck. Good luck!"

"*Daargh!*" It took a moment before Vince remembered that the sharp, battlespeech gargle could translate as either "Victory!"—a Terrine war cry—or "good luck."

Kaiten had just, in his own way, forgiven him. "Darg!" Vince called back, mangling the pronunciation. He grinned maniacally as he continued to fight the Krait's controls.

○ ○ ○ ○ ○

"You can't do that!" Jovanna cried. "You'll kill us all!"

"We can do that," the machine said in the flat, emotionless monotone that Jovanna had already begun to hate. "It is not our intent to kill all of you. You will be transported to the supervisor nucleus for evaluation, mapping, and data storage."

She had to sort through the machine's statements. When it said "we can do that," it was not claiming it could kill the human prisoners, but rebutting her first emotional protest. The invaders, apparently, did not yet understand human emotion, or the phrases that expressed it.

"That's not what I meant, damn it!" She pointed ahead toward the front of the line that stretched away in front of her, where ten Amalthean civilians had just been dragged by as many silver machines into an air lock leading to the moon's surface. It was a small lock with an automatic inner door . . . and a good thing, too. The invaders seemed indifferent to the fact that humans needed to breathe.

Not one of the civilians was wearing a space suit.

"Listen to me!" she insisted. "Humans have certain needs, okay? Air is one of them! Humans can't live in a vacuum without protection!"

But her captor's mouth had melted away into the gleaming, shapeless metal of its body, and Jovanna couldn't tell whether it had heard her or not. Communicating with these monsters was a nightmare of frustration and misunderstanding, at times almost impossible. They appeared to have mastered Anglic well enough, but the thoughts behind the words were so alien that Jovanna wondered if there was any level at which humans and the invaders could communicate at all. Strangest of all was the realization that, while the invaders were extremely intelligent—superhumanly so— they were completely lacking in what could only be termed "common sense."

Case in point. Evidently, they'd learned Anglic from prisoners in a matter of hours, figuring out from the bodies they'd pirated how the human vocal apparatus worked and how to imitate it. They learned fast . . . but they still hadn't figured out that humans were not themselves some sort of complicated machine.

On the huge screen overlooking the Strip, a doorway opened in the face of a low outcropping of rust-brown rock. One of the invader ships was waiting, a huge silver shape that was all curves and gentle swellings hovering a few feet above the moon's surface. The first invader emerged from the air lock, his prisoner still struggling in the machine's grasp.

By the time they reached the invader ship, the struggles had stopped. One by one, the other machines emerged from the air lock, each with a dead captive in its tentacles.

Maybe people were just complicated machines, Jovanna admitted to herself. But if so, they were damned fragile ones that could not last for long in the hard vacuum and deadly radiation outside Amalthea's underground habitats.

Other invaders continued to arrive in the Strip, each bearing one struggling captive in unyielding manacles of living metal. Was it possible that these monsters were going to march them all, ten by ten, into space?

It was growing noisy in the cavern. A low murmur of

voices from the hundreds of prisoners held there had ceased as the first ten had been hauled into the lock; now, though, those voices were rising, shrill with anger, with protest, with pleading, with fear.

The invaders were paying no attention however. Suddenly, seconds after the deaths of the first ten captives, every invader machine in the Strip had frozen, each remaining motionless despite the yells and struggles of the humans around them.

No, there was motion, she saw. Each machine was extending a tentacle of silver, liquid metal toward its neighbors. Pseudopods touched, then merged, and she could have sworn she saw a kind of current flowing back and forth from machine to machine, as though each was physically exchanging some part of its substance with the others.

This alien communion lasted for long seconds. Abruptly, as though at a single, unheard command, the connections parted, the silver pseudopods melting into the individual machines' bodies.

A mouth disconcertingly shaped itself on the side of the machine holding her. "You reported fact," it said. "Of ten humans sampled, ten ceased functioning when exposed to vacuum."

The monster might as easily have been discussing the weather, or the scores of some sports event in which it had no real interest. "Yeah, right," she said. "How many more people are you going to murder before you believe me?"

"Inaccurate assumption," the invader said. "The cluster does not 'murder,' and the cluster accepts your statements as fact. The cluster requires further data on human physiological needs. You will provide this data."

"I . . . ah . . ." The sudden shift in her status, from prisoner to teacher, had caught Jovanna off guard. Still, she'd found one point of understanding with the invaders, even though it was pretty thin. Whatever else the shape-shifters might be, they were basically computers, machines working with a computer's simpleminded and uncomplicated logic.

She would have to be careful about what she said to beings who might take an emotional statement like "get lost" literally, but she might actually have a chance at communicating with them, at understanding them.

On the huge viewscreen above the buildings of the Strip, the enormous vessel hovering above Amalthea's surface was descending. Its silver surface rippled sluggishly, then changed shape, engulfing the tiny air lock door like some gigantic amoeba ingesting its prey. The machines, she realized with a start, had made a common-sense mistake in neglecting human frailty. Now they had rectified the mistake, and, what's more, they now realized that they might not understand all there was to know about living humans.

"You will provide all data necessary for the continued survival of humans," the machine at her side said again. She was all too aware that its tentacles still circled her wrists, one-piece manacles with no opening or lock . . . even if Galen had been there to try picking it. Where was the Tinker, she wondered?

Where was Vince?

"You will provide—"

"All right! All right! I'm thinking! My thought processes aren't as fast as yours are!" She caught her lower lip between her teeth. She would have to make sure they understood the need for constant air pressure, for tolerable temperatures, for food and water . . .

Something Singh had mentioned tugged at her awareness. What was it? Something about the invaders' deceleration from near-light speed, measured in thousands of Gs . . .

Her eyes opened wide, and she swallowed hard. She'd almost overlooked that.

And what was more, it gave her a weapon.

"Listen," she said carefully. "If you're going to take us anywhere in one of your ships, you'd better be aware that humans can't tolerate accelerations of more than a few tenths of a G. . . ."

○ ○ ○ ○ ○

Sunlight burst from brown and scarlet ramparts beneath an azure sky. "Still with me, Kaiten?"

"Affirmative," the Terrine replied. "Eight miles from you, bearing—"

"I've got you on my screen." A canyon yawned beneath Vince's Krait, opening onto blackness in shadowed depths that never saw the sun. Lightning flared a hundred miles below.

The Krait's engine continued to function, though he'd used the last few drops of on-board fuel in his attempts to control his meteoric reentry. Now it had unlimited fuel, the hydrogen-helium mix at five atmospheres surrounding his ship.

The Kraits' RAM-built computers had saved them. Faced with insufficient speed for orbit and no place to dock, Vince had remembered that in the early days of the space program, the space shuttle and several manned craft that had followed it had all killed their speed during reentry into Earth's atmosphere by executing a series of S-turns designed to bleed off energy as heat. The process required the precision of computer flight control, and Vince had not been sure the Kraits' systems were up to the task, especially considering that he'd had neither time nor data to program the maneuver from scratch!

The computer had brought them through reentry, however, using almost no fuel at all to do so until they'd dropped into the warm, thick air that, theoretically, would let them keep flying for years. Vince had no intention of staying aloft that long, however. He'd directed the Krait's computer to shape its reentry maneuvers in such a way that they would end up within a few hundred miles of the Stormrider city of Vrahk.

He wanted to talk again with Dr. Kowalski.

"Major?" Kaiten's voice said. "Look ahead."

He checked the radar. "I see it. RAM ships, you think?"

"Negative. Their maneuvers suggest that they are

invaders."

Invaders. They'd started using that name for the silver monsters by some unspoken, mutual consent. It gave them a sense of menace, and, in any case, their numbers in the fight around Amalthea suggested that whatever they were, they'd come for more than exploration or to recover the Artifact.

They'd come to Jupiter loaded for bear, and they'd thrashed a RAM battle group with almost laughable ease.

Now they descended *en masse* on the Stormrider cities.

Or rather, he thought as he studied his radar screen, they'd descended on one Stormrider city . . . on Vrahk. They must still be trying to find Kowalski, in a single-minded pursuit of the Artifact.

A shadow passed over Vince's cockpit. He looked up, expecting to see one of the Stormriders aloft, wings spread. Instead, he saw a black object with stubby, triangular wings and a lumpy body banking past his starboard side. The color shimmered, then flashed pure silver in the sun. Another flyer followed.

"Kaiten," he called. "Bandits! . . ."

"I see them," Kaiten replied. "Unaware of us. Perhaps they do not sense us."

"Oh, they sense us, all right. I think they're just a bit on the single-minded side. No orders to knock us down. Yet."

No other explanation made sense. During the dogfight at the upper fringes of the Jovian atmosphere, the invaders had acted as though they were following a fairly narrow programmed path, breaking off an attack the instant they were told to do so rather than making sure their target was destroyed.

If these machines were that inflexible in their programming, it offered a weapon that humans might turn against them.

Kaiten's Krait drifted into view, half a mile to Vince's left. The aeroform invaders were everywhere, silently swooping on currents of air, sometimes putting on bursts of speed that suggested that they, like the Kraits, could use Jupiter's atmosphere for jet propulsion.

In the distance ahead, Vince could make out the gleaming, high-domed shape of Vrahk'dreleschaah. Specks swarmed about it, Stormriders and invaders in violent, aerial combat.

Perhaps half of the Stormriders were mounted astride great, black, manta-ray shapes much like the shapes adopted by the invaders in Jupiter's thick air. *Mantas.* Yes, Vince had heard of them, blind, sonar-guided animals genetically engineered as part of the artificial Jovian ecology. While riding those black-winged steeds, Stormriders could use their wing-hands for other things than flight, wielding charge guns with murderous accuracy.

But the invaders possessed a deadliness of their own. Their maneuverability gave them a tremendous edge, and more Stormriders were dropping from the sky, wings and bodies shattered, than were machines.

"We should help them," Kaiten urged.

"Negative!" Vince called back. "We can help more if we can reach the city! Hang on!"

The two Kraits flashed past the fighting hordes, arrowing toward an open docking port.

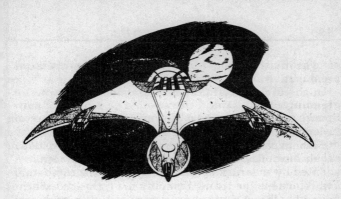

CHAPTER FIFTEEN

The Kraits bellied into the docking bay one after the other, sending up showers of sparks as their undercarriages slammed into the tough, organic material of the deck. Battle exploded around the grounded fighters. Invaders advanced among the shadows, hulking shapes that glittered like machines but moved like living creatures. The variety of shapes was bewildering; all sported tentacles, as thin as fine wire or as massive as a tree limb, but their number and placement and shape were rarely twice the same.

And the shapes were continually changing. As Vince watched, one huge mass of what looked like wadded tinfoil divided in two, its substance flowing into separate man-sized blobs, each already sprouting jointed legs and groping tentacles.

Vince guessed that there were half a dozen of the things inside the hangar bay, fighting perhaps twice that many Stormriders. The gennies had thrown up a crude barricade walling off three entrances leading deeper into the city. They fought with charge guns. Those weapons fired bolts of high-voltage electricity at close range, while at long range they launched something like ball lightning, fist-sized spheres of blue-white energy that sailed across the room and impacted with a flash and a high-pitched bang.

The invaders fought back with lightning of their own, and with explosive volleys from some weapon that Vince hadn't yet managed to spot. An invader would rise, extending a part of itself; there would be a ripple of movement . . . and then part of the barricade across the room would be holed by a blast as savage as the detonation of a 25mm explosive shell. Several Stormriders were down, their magnificent wings shredded, their bodies torn.

Vince was struck by how eerily quiet the combatants were. The noise transmitted by his fighter's external sound pickups was ear-splitting, as lightning hissed, barked, and crackled, and blasts rang and echoed from the walls. . . but the invaders and Stormriders alike battled in determined silence. Unlike a human firefight, there were no screams or curses, no shouted orders or battle cries. One Stormrider, with his body savaged, hideously opened from chest to thigh, continued to aim and fire without pause until he could no longer hold himself upright.

Seconds had passed since Vince had skidded to a halt inside the hangar bay, and he hesitated, wondering what to do next. To step out of his Krait and into that hellstorm of destruction would be suicide . . . but then something slammed against his fighter's hull, rocking him dangerously to the side, and he realized that he couldn't long stay where he was, either.

He slapped down several switches on his console. His central display screen lit up in response, then showed an image of the hangar bay, viewed from a camera in his ventral turret a foot above the deck.

"Kaiten!" he called over the comm channel. Was it still working? Yes, the laser acquisition light showed green. "Kaiten, I'm going to manual on the Mark XXI!"

"Affirmative," the Terrine replied. "Mine's out."

Vince glanced to the right, where Kaiten's fighter had come to rest in a tangle of wreckage. The Krait's undercarriage had given way on impact, and the ventral ball turret of its gyrocannon had been smashed.

So it was up to him. He switched off his gyrocannon's safeties.

In space combat, the distances were too vast, the speeds too great for merely human reactions to cope with aiming and firing directly. Targeting was done by radar, with weapons smart enough to aim and fire themselves with human guidance. Here, though, the targets were confined . . . and vulnerable. Vince had just cut off the autotracking on his Krait's Mark XXI gyrocannon and engaged the manual firing controls. A warning light flashed on his display screen.

What he was trying to do was incredibly dangerous. Gyrocannons were designed for combat in the free and open depths of space, not within the confines of a hangar bay, especially an alien hangar bay with God-knew-what on the other side of the surrounding bulkheads.

But the next shot directed against either of the Kraits might rupture their seals and flood their oxygen tanks with hydrogen from the high-pressure air outside; a spark or an open flame would set the mess off, and the bay would be seared by the detonation of a pair of hydrogen-oxygen bombs.

He stabbed another button on his console, and red cross hairs appeared on his vidscreen. A joystick beside his right armrest gave him manual control of his gyrocannon turret. He tracked left, feeling the hum of the ball turret's motors through the deck plating beneath his feet. The cross hairs centered over a writhing spaghetti of tinfoil oozing along a bulkhead thirty feet away. He flipped off the autofire lock—he wanted one shot, not a burst—then closed his left hand on the red trigger of the flight control stick between his knees.

The gyrocannon spat, a sharp chuff of sound lost instantly in the ringing detonation of the 25mm shell inside the liquid-metal creature. Smoking fragments danced and skittered across the deck. Vince was already swiveling the turret to another target, track . . . hold . . . fire!

Another invader died, then another. In space combat they'd been too fast, too maneuverable for the Krait's fire-control computer. Here, though, they were slowed by gravity and by the need to crawl rather than fly, and they were confined within a large and mostly empty room. Vince controlled the turret with his right hand, fired with his left. Clots of smoke hung in tatters in the air, as invaders shattered and died.

"On your port side!" Kaiten's voice warned in his helmet phones. Vince flipped the joystick over, spinning the ball turret in a fast one-eighty. Silver metal loomed on the cockpit display. Vince tapped the trigger twice, almost without aiming, loosing two rounds as the cross hairs slid across the invader less than ten feet from the Krait's left side. The explosions rocked the craft, and pieces of metal sang as they ricocheted from hull and transplex canopy.

Throughout the hangar bay, the alien invaders had suddenly lost interest in the Stormriders and were closing now on Vince's Krait. He kept firing; the enemy did not even try to seek shelter but moved in from every side as Vince picked them off one by one. Kaiten had managed to bleed off his cockpit air and open his canopy. He was leaning from the cockpit with the bulky Mark XIV rocket rifle he'd acquired from one of the invaders in Kowalski's office earlier. With a hiss, one rocket round seared past Vince's canopy and struck a writhing starfish shape just as it slithered onto the aft hull of Vince's Krait. The blast rocked his fighter again, but it tore the invader in half.

The Stormriders, too, were advancing, taking advantage of the invaders' distraction to attack them as they walked, crawled, or slithered into the open. Their charge guns knocked the silver machines down, leaving them shuddering in an uncontrollable palsy on the deck. A blow from the butt of one of those massive weapons, wielded by a twenty-foot giant, splintered and smashed crippled invaders and still-moving fragments alike, leaving no piece larger than a softball intact.

One Stormrider collapsed, his great gold-orange wings folding above his body as he crumpled to the deck. Half a dozen bolts of lightning flared, leaving dazzling afterimages in Vince's retinas and knocking down the vaguely humanoid invader that had been facing the dead Storm-

rider, smoke gushing from a blackened crater that began
to soften and fill almost at once. The invader machines
possessed a remarkable ability to heal themselves
almost at once, but the electrical blasts from the Jovian
charge guns appeared to disrupt them long enough for
other weapons to be brought in to play.

The knobbed end of a charge gun wavered in the air,
then fell. The twitching, half-molten machine shattered
into large chunks, each still trying to reform, each
changing color from silver to black as though suddenly
desperate for more energy. Other charge guns were
raised into the air, then fell. . . .

. . . and then there was nothing silver or black left
moving. The tentacles had stopped writhing and lay now
in short, cylindrical sections. The deck was covered by
debris, like glittering fragments of ice sculptures
smashed by blow after blow from a sledgehammer.

With the urgency of combat gone, Vince sagged back
in his seat, exhausted, the inside of his pressure suit
sopping with sweat. Gravity dragged at him again, and
his helmet and life-support pack felt as heavy as though
they were made of lead. Slowly, with trembling hands,
he switched on the pumps that evacuated his cockpit,
then bled the hydrogen-helium mix outside into the vacuum. When pressures matched, he cracked his canopy
and extended the ladder. Kaiten, the Mark XIV cradled
in his arms, met him as he carefully stepped to the deck,
ankle-deep in black and silver fragments that skittered
and rattled with each step.

"Interesting," the Terrine said. "Never have I seen
gyrocannon used as a personal sidearm before."

Vince glanced around the hangar bay. Smoke hung in
the air, blurring the shapes of the winged giants advancing toward the Krait. He felt light-headed. "Seemed like
a good idea at the time." He slapped the laser still holstered on his thigh. "This thing I had wasn't going to be
of much use, and the Mark XXI was the next best weapon
available."

The Terrine showed pointed teeth behind his helmet
visor. "Affirmative. I like the way you think . . . sir."

Kaiten had never addressed Vince by any honorific other than his rank before. It made him feel good, as though he belonged.

Near the barricade, three of the huge Stormriders were crouched on all fours beside the torn body of one of their own, wing-hands on the deck, their crested heads thrown high and back. They were crooning, the sound a high-pitched and utterly alien harmony that sent shivers down Vince's spine and raised the hair at the back of his neck. The body, he noted, was that of the Stormrider that he'd seen die, still fighting, during the firefight.

Other Stormriders approached Vince and Kaiten, enclosing the pair. Their wings curved far overhead into the gloom of the upper part of the chamber. "We thank you, Outworlders," one said, and Vince thought he recognized the voice of Throvidronvinav over his helmet's audio circuit. "This was not your battle, but you seized honor by coming to our aid."

Vince nodded toward the three crouching Stormriders. They were humming now, a haunting interweaving of minor chords, and he had the uncomfortable feeling that he was eavesdropping on some private ceremony, a memorial, perhaps, for a fallen comrade.

The Anglic-speaking Stormrider seemed to notice Vince's interest. "They sing for a fallen comrade," he said, "for a Warlord of the N'gaav."

" 'Nigaf'?" Vince asked, mangling the unfamiliar pronunciation. "What's that?"

"N'gaav. You might say 'the People.' But it means more than the simple shape of the word alone. It is who we are, and what we fight for: our brothers and our mates, our city, our freedom from those above who seek our souls, the unbounded sky with Death at either hand."

Was he speaking metaphorically or with a simple statement of fact? Vince wasn't sure. Certainly the Jovian cloud cities occupied a narrow climatic band, balanced between the freezing temperatures and thinning air above and the searing heat and crushing pressures below. With death at either hand. Yes, that was a fair description of a Jovian Stormrider's daily existence. Huge as these beings were, they were puny, insignificant mites against the backdrop of storm and fury that was the Jovian environment.

Two of the three straightened erect, the body of the dead Stormrider between them. Followed by the third, still humming, they bore their comrade toward the open mouth of the hangar bay. The others were already gone, vanished into the high-ceilinged passageways leading into the depths of the city.

"Where did the rest of them go?" Vince asked.

"The battle continues within the city," the Stormrider says. "These three will attend our fallen brothers. But you two should come with me now, and quickly. Dr. Kowalski wishes to see you."

"Right," Vince said. "I was hoping we could talk to her again. Lead the way."

The funeral procession reached the hangar mouth. There was a sharp motion, and the dead Stormrider vanished through the opening.

"Eh? You just toss him out?" Kaiten sounded startled, and that surprised Vince. He hadn't thought that Terrines afforded any special honor or ceremony to their dead, as humans did.

"Our brother has fallen into the night. He will return to nourish his people."

Again, Vince didn't know whether the Stormrider was speaking literally or not. "You mean his spirit?" he asked.

The huge being shrugged, a leathery rustling of wings high overhead. "I know nothing of spirits, save that his is within the heart of God. His body was built of the organic molecules welling up from the Great Deep. His body returns now to that deep. It is part of the eternal cycle."

Vince shuddered. What kind of gods, he wondered, did such creatures as these worship?

"We'd better go, Kaiten," he said.

The Terrine turned, an unreadable expression on the vaguely feline face behind the helmet visor. "Your people are warriors," he said, addressing the giant.

"We are Warlords of the N'gaav."

"And who is it you fight? A warrior must have enemies."

"Believe me, Wingless One, we have enemies enough for glory. For many years we fought one another, city against city. Since Dr. Kowalski has come, though, that is changing. Slowly, perhaps, but it is changing. And always, always, there is God himself."

"God?" Vince wondered.

The Stormrider made a gesture with one wing-hand. A religious symbol? A warding sign? "Our world," the Stormrider said, "our universe is God. We are created in His depths, and we are remade in their heat. We fight him ever for our very survival, as he seeks to bring us closer to Him. Come. The doctor waits."

"Yeah," Vince said. He felt a little dazed, first by the aftereffects of the battle, then by his unexpected look into the souls of these strange beings. "I think I've about had my daily limit of metaphysics." He took an experimental step. His body felt leaden; the bruises and aches inflicted by his earlier visit and by the high-G climb above Jupiter's atmosphere shrieked at him. "Uh . . . it might go quicker if you carry us."

"An honor, Wingless One. . . ." The huge warrior scooped Vince from the deck in one cradling wing-arm and hoisted him far above the ice-chip-littered deck.

"If is possible," Kaiten said bluntly, "I would like to stay." He looked up at Vince. "I can finish 'Song of the Dead.' With new allies."

Gravely, the Stormrider's huge, crested head nodded in slow assent. Kaiten turned and made his way toward the trio of Stormriders, clustered now beside another of their fallen comrades.

Something, Vince thought as the huge creature bore him from the battle-savaged hangar bay, had touched Kaiten, some resonance between his own beliefs and those of the enigmatic Jovians. Perhaps it was nothing more than the shared brotherhood of all who have faced death in combat and survived, or perhaps it was something more. Kaiten and the Stormriders were warriors, and that seemed to count for more than the fact that they were members of different cultures, of different species.

Vince felt uneasy, though. The Stormriders, in their strength, their beauty, in their golden-winged majesty, made humans seem pathetically small and frail by comparison, inferior. Their genes, perhaps, had been shaped by human bioengineers, but their culture had been shaped by the awesome and deadly world they inhabited. Until now, they had been isolated by their environment; few Stormriders traveled beyond the color-banded cloud tops of their world. If ever the inhabitants of Jupiter's skies decided to leave their world, as humans had decided to leave a blighted Earth four centuries before, it could well be that man would at last meet his evolutionary match.

At the very least, Vince doubted that man would let the ascent of these golden creatures go unchallenged. He did not want to think of what a war between human and Stormrider might be like. Perhaps it was a good thing that the Stormriders of Jupiter had no spaceships of their own . . . or any way of building them.

Of course, that was a question for the future, one that would have to be delayed until it was known whether man had a future.

The invaders might well render the whole problem meaningless.

CHAPTER SIXTEEN

The battle was still raging in other parts of the city, and three times Vince's escort had to detour to avoid firefights between Stormrider and machine. Slowly, though, the Stormriders were gaining the upper hand. There was a limited number of the alien attackers; according to Throvidronvinav, six large alien spacecraft had approached the city, then fallen apart in midair into swarms of smaller combat machines that had descended on the city. Since that first assault, however, no more attackers had arrived.

Meanwhile, fresh Stormrider forces were appearing over Vrahk'dreleschaah every minute, arriving on the wing or astride soaring mantas from other cities as much as a thousand miles distant. He and his escort stopped once beside a broad balcony open to the sky as a dozen Stormriders, each with a charge gun clutched in taloned foot-hands, alighted in a gale of buffeting wings, then hurried down vaulted corridors and into the city.

These beings, Vince decided, were literal stormriders, golden winged giants descending from the brawling skies of Jupiter like gods of Norse myth. The Stormrider losses in Vrahk'dreleschaah were terrible, but they were being replaced as the battle raged on.

When an invader was shattered, it was not replaced. If no machine reinforcements arrived within the next hour or two, the battle would be won.

"We seem to be holding them," Kowalski said as Vince entered her sanctum, helmet cradled in his arm. She turned from the viewscreen she was studying at her desk and met his eyes with a steady gaze. "Thank you for your help down in Bay Four. That freed some of our 'rider warriors, let them trap some machines that were worming their way into the city's growth vats. You might have just helped to turn the tide, Major."

"Our pleasure, Doctor," Vince said. His helmet was heavy, and he set it aside on an empty tabletop. "I'm afraid things aren't going so well in orbit."

"I know. Please, sit down. Take a load off." She gestured at a seat next to her desk. "We've been picking up laser feeds from Ganymede. The RAM fleet has been routed, their largest warship destroyed. And . . . there's something strange going on at Amalthea."

Fear plucked at Vince, raising the hairs at the back of his neck as he settled into the liquid-filled seat. "What?"

Kowalski reached out and turned the large screen on her desk so that Vince and Kaiten could see. It showed a grainy, poorly resolved scene, obviously a telephoto shot at high magnification from extremely far away. Jupiter dominated the screen, filling the background with soft pastels: orange, yellow, salmon pink, and red. Amalthea was silhouetted against the color, a black and featureless disk. The only way Vince knew what he was looking at was the data line at the lower left corner of the screen, identifying the view as Amalthea, taken by a ship just inside the orbit of Io.

A green square, drawn by computer graphics, framed an elongated black speck moving slowly away from the moon. Vince's eyes widened. It looked like a ship of some sort, but if it was as far away as Amalthea, a guess he could not prove but which seemed reasonable given its course, and if Amalthea was a hundred miles wide . . .

"My God," Vince said. "That ship must be ten miles across!"

"Sixteen," Kowalski said. "Eight times larger than the largest RAM battler. As long as Mars's inner moon is thick, though it's not nearly as wide or as massive. It came out of deep space and touched down on Amalthea shortly after the RAM battler was destroyed. We think it's actually a large number of separate machines joined together, because we've seen parts of it change shape. We had a transmission from Amalthea earlier. The thing sort of nestled down over one of the colony's surface air locks, sat there for an hour, then began accelerating on a course that will whip it around Jupiter and send it back into deep space."

"Accelerating?" Vince asked, eyebrows raised. "How hard?"

"That's the funny thing. When it first appeared, it was pulling something like five hundred gravities to slow it from better than point five c."

Vince whistled. Half the speed of light! Nothing in the Solar System could come close to that kind of technology.

"Yeah," Kowalski went on. "But now they're doing a steady two-tenths of a G. Precisely six point four feet per second squared."

"Delicate cargo on board," Vince said. He felt cold.

"That's what we think. That monster touched down at the air lock, took on human prisoners, and is leaving with them."

At least, whatever the invaders were, they wanted their prisoners alive. Jovanna, where are you now?

Vince tried to push aside the thought of Jovanna as a prisoner of those horrors. He leaned closer over Kowalski's desk, reading the data block in the corner of the screen. The pictures were coming from the Callistan battleship *Asgard*.

"Callisto," he said thoughtfully, settling back in his chair. "Are they getting mixed up in this?"

The outermost of Jupiter's four major satellites—small planets in their own right as opposed to orbiting mountains like Amalthea—Callisto was the only Jovian world with imperialistic dreams and a military reach. Through their well-armed space fleet they'd laid claim to eight of Jupiter's small, outer satellites, as well as to the space around Callisto itself. With the RAM fleet defeated, Callisto's space navy and the laser defenses of the moon itself were the only significant military force in Jovian space.

"I'm afraid Callisto doesn't want any part of what they think is our fight," Kowalski said. "We've already called for help and were politely told that they have no ships available."

"They may change their minds if our silver friends attack them," Vince said. "They'd damn well better."

"The Callistans are slimers," Kowalski said matter-of-factly. "They won't fight unless their interests are threatened."

"Hm. Do you have the facilities here to talk to them directly?" Before she could answer, he pressed ahead. "In fact, it would be a good idea if we could raise other factions in the system, too. Luna. Venus. Mercury. RAM, too. Especially RAM. With everyone pulling together, we might have a—"

"You can't be serious, Major!"

"I'm dead serious, Doctor. This is an invasion. If we try to take the invaders on one human or gennie faction at a time, we're going to get eaten piecemeal."

Kowalski laughed, a harsh, surprised bark. "You're crazy! Callistans, NEO, RAM, Aerostaters, Sun Kings, Terrans, Lunarians, pirates, and, God help me, a thousand different flavors of Belter, all working together? Not to mention Stormriders, Tinkers, and Terrines? It'll never happen!"

"*Humans,*" Vince said, gently stressing the word. "And gennies with human genes . . . and goals, and a human will to survive. It has to happen, or we're all finished!" Something new occurred to him. "Can you call up a picture on that thing of the hangar bay where we came in?"

Kowalski touched a control, and the video feed from the Callistan battleship was cut off, replaced by a view of the hangar bay. Smoke still filled the area, blurring the outlines of ships, wreckage, and the towering beings moving there. Vince could hear the minor-key harmonics of the Jovians, mingled with a murmured chant.

"*Erech gharesh, du davashin . . .*"

Kaiten sat atop his damaged Krait, arms outspread as he chanted. Eerily, Terrine chant and Stormrider humming blended, an alien harmony.

"You see?" Vince said. "We've started to find some common ground already."

Kowalski gave Vince a hard look, then switched off the picture. "You know, Major, I came out here from Venus quite a few years ago. I was sick of politics back there, human politics. Aerostaters and their intrigues. The Ishtar Confederation and its balancing act to get RAM technology without becoming RAM's slave. The Mercurian Sun Kings and their meddling. And Luna . . . not to mention NEO and RAM and their war.

"So I came out here to get away from all that and found humans exploiting the most magnificent creatures in the Solar System. Their own creations, their own children, and they were using them as slaves to get at an environment that no full human can ever fully use or appreciate or even survive in for long." She shook her head. "I've thought all along that, if the Stormriders could just break free of the chains holding them to Amalthea and the damned Genetics Foundation—"

"The Stormriders are part of the Solar System, too, Doctor," Vince said. "If the invaders win, your Stormriders lose. We all lose."

"You're right, of course." She sighed, her hands folded before her on the desk. "And the invaders know we're down here. They'll return, and with numbers we can't hope to match."

Vince smiled. "You don't think they're RAM anymore, do you?" It was a small victory of a sort. Kowalski had been so certain she was right. . . .

"They're not RAM, no." She shrugged. "But they are the product of human technology. Definitely."

Vince's jaw dropped. "How can you say that? My God, they've got a ship up there the size of an asteroid that can move at half the speed of light! We won't have that kind of technology for another thousand years!"

"My 'riders decoded part of that radio burst, Major. I think we know who they are now, what they are."

"So tell me!"

"Hmm. Remember when I told you that the arrangement of the submicroscopic units, the individual nanotechnic machines, suggested that they might be a holdover from Earth computer technology?"

"Yes. I still think that could have been coincidence."

"Could have been, perhaps, but wasn't. When we ran the radio transmission through a decryption routine, we found we couldn't break the body of the message, but the computer did recognize a navigational code, a very old navigational code. Late twenty-first century, in fact."

"What?"

She nodded. "Why would aliens be using a coordinate system that places the Sun, our Sun, at zero-zero-zero?"

"Maybe they do that for every new star system they explore."

"Not using a coding system identical to one employed by the Systems States Alliance space program four centuries ago. You want to hear my theory?"

"Of course."

"The late two thousands was when man was starting to reach out into the Solar System in a big way. Earth was a wreck with a population of twelve billion and its resources gutted. If he didn't get off-world to stay, chances were his whole civilization would collapse all the way back to the Stone Age, only next time, when he crawled out of the caves, there wouldn't be any more easily exploitable raw materials to help fuel a new industrial revolution, no oil, no metal except for the rusted skeletons of dead cities. Hell, exploitation of the rest of the Solar System was the only way man was going to survive. That's when RAM got its start as the old Russo-American Combine."

"I know my history, Doctor."

"Well, the historical records of the period mention a brief interest in nanotechnology. One notion was to build sophisticated nanotechnic probes that would voyage to another world, even an asteroid or an Oort Cloud comet, land, and begin converting the place molecule by molecule, first into factories to build more machines, then,

after a time, into factories making products for people
. . . like a cargo ship full of wheat or a breathable atmosphere or a pressurized, habitable city."

"A Von Neumann machine," Vince said.

"Eh? What's that?"

"Von Neumann was a twentieth-century scientist who
suggested that machines might be programmed to build
other machines, ultimately creating an artificial ecology
that would utilize resources on asteroids or other useless
worlds and create . . . a paradise."

"Yeah, well, it was a nice idea, but it never happened.
Nanotechnology was trickier to control than its propo-
nents thought. Besides, RAM was starting to flex its
muscles. They'd already begun developing Mars for
human habitation the old-fashioned way, dropping
asteroids and building mountain-sized air plants and
constructing a ground-to-orbit space elevator. They had
an interest in having it done their way. You see, RAM
had the advantage in big, brute-force technology. They
all but owned the colonists on Mars, they'd already built
the orbital factories to produce the steel and triluminum
and special materials needed to terraform Mars and
make a hell of a profit. They would have lost everything
if nanotechnics had become the wave of the future. It's
just a suspicion, but I'm guessing that RAM managed to
strangle nanotechnics before it got properly started."

"But some probes had already been launched," Vince
said, seeing where her argument was going.

"At least one. The Alliance Space Commission lost
track of it as it neared Pluto. Almost certainly sabotage.
It crashed on Charon."

"Charon! Wait, don't you mean Chiron?" Vince blinked.
The Ciudestreyans had first discovered the Artifact in
the vicinity of Chiron, the cometary body out beyond the
orbit of Saturn. He wondered if Kowalski had confused
the similar names.

"I do know some astronomy, Major," Kowalski said
firmly. "I mean Charon, Pluto's moon. We read that
much from those nav codes."

Vince remembered the mental image he'd picked up

from his brief contact with the Artifact. Had that ice-bound scene actually been the surface of Charon, with Pluto hanging low in the sky? It seemed to fit. "So our shape-shifter friends come from Charon," he said. "We've never had a human colony out that far. But you think a nanotechnic probe . . ." His voice trailed off as he thought of the possibilities. It would explain so much!

"It must have set down hard," Kowalski agreed. "Badly damaged, but it would have been programmed to repair itself and to begin converting the surface of whatever world it touched down on into something habitable by humans. Unfortunately, the damage was so bad that some of the instructions weren't passed on correctly."

"Like mutations in a living system."

"Exactly. And mutations that worked survived. A whole new kind of life came into being, a machine-based life that could grow and adapt and evolve. It retained some holdovers from its past, like the 256-bit arrays and the old nav codes. But as for the rest . . ."

"Machines think and learn awfully fast, compared to us," Vince said. "No wonder their technology is so far ahead of ours!"

"Right. But they also lack experience and, well, call it old-fashioned common sense. They can make mistakes . . . like the time they let the air inside a shuttle mix with the hydrogen outside and blew themselves up."

"Fast but stupid," Vince said. "Are they communicating with each other all the time?"

"Not every second, no. What are you asking?"

"I was just wondering if they'd make that same mistake with the air lock again, or if their friends here in your city were able to warn the others to be careful of free oxygen in a hydrogen atmosphere."

"We can't count on that. They do communicate, and they learn—and adapt—very quickly.

"They exchange information on two levels," Kowalski went on. "By radio, which is slow and rather limited in the amount of information it can transmit at one time, and by direct contact, something we've seen them doing here in the city. I call it conjugation."

"Like sex in one-celled animals?"

"Something like that. Higher animals use sex to pass on genetic information. One-celled life-forms exchange genetic material directly, then reproduce by fission. Machines don't need sex to build new replicas of themselves, of course, but I think they use conjugation to swap information. By exchanging a few trillion nanotech units in those 256-bit arrays, they can swap billions and billions of bits of data at a time. Not just facts and figures, but impressions, detailed descriptions, images, emotions . . . or whatever machines have instead of human feeling. And they can reproduce simply by ingesting all kinds of matter: rock, steel, disabled machines—"

"Human bodies." He remembered the sight of a large machine dividing into two in the hangar bay, like a giant amoeba. The things were reproducing. The Stormriders' superiority in numbers could be only temporary.

"Whatever. They rearrange the molecules of raw material directly into new nanotech units inside their own bodies. Since their structure lets them be at once solid and liquid, they can reproduce by fission, like bacteria, dividing in half or pinching off a new bud that takes on a life of its own so long as it's above that critical size limit." She paused, a thoughtful expression on her face. "You know, their numbers could grow damned fast if they had a whole world of raw materials to work with."

"What about weapons?" Vince wondered. "What was that weapon they were using down in the hangar bay?"

"They pinch off a tiny bit of their own bodies, a pellet, oh, maybe the size of a pea, and accelerate it by manipulating internal magnetic fields. They can whip them out at incredible speeds."

"Wait, they shoot bits of themselves?"

"Remember, they can absorb, 'eat' whatever's handy. They never run out of ammo."

Vince nodded, understanding. Even a pea could be deadly if it hit something while moving at tens of miles per second. "Tell me, did your Stormriders get anything out of the rest of that radio transmission? Besides the navigational data, I mean."

"A little. And we've been eavesdropping on their radio frequencies during this battle and learning a lot more. We could guess what the message was about, and that let us puzzle out a fair amount of meaning right from the start."

"And?"

"It was fairly obvious. There's a strong impression in the code of something like a call for everyone else to rally round, to come to one set of coordinates and help. That's how we identified the old nav code. They clearly identified Amalthea."

"Hey, Rube," Vince said quietly.

Her brow wrinkled with puzzlement. " 'Rube'? I don't understand."

"An old Earth term," Vince explained. He'd heard of it before, a historical curiosity from the days of a spectacular traveling extravaganza called a circus. "Workers in a, well, a kind of wandering show used that cry if one of them was attacked. He'd yell 'Hey, Rube,' and everyone in the troupe would drop what they were doing and come to help." He stopped when he realized that Kowalski was looking at him strangely.

"Sorry," he said. "I've got a pack rat brain that collects historical trivia. But I'm wondering if it might not have given us a way to fight back."

Speaking swiftly, the aches in his body and the drag of Jupiter's gravity forgotten, Vince began to explain what he had in mind.

CHAPTER SEVENTEEN

The view had been spectacular beyond belief from the cockpit of a single-seat fighter, or even through the transplex window in Kowalski's office. When Vince opened his eyes now, however, it was to a vista like nothing he'd ever imagined. The scale alone threatened to paralyze him, and glancing down brought on a vertigo that tried to pluck him from his seat and drag him into those dark and wind-torn depths.

This was flight, true flight, astride the broad back of a Jovian manta, clinging for his life to the folded, leathery wings of a Stormrider seated just in front of him. His legs, and those of his Stormrider companion, straddled a kind of tubular saddle actually bolted to the manta's six-inch integument, and a safety harness kept him from falling despite the creature's movements and dizzying aerial maneuvers.

Still, he'd been warned to hang on. It was a very long way down, and the motions of the huge flying creature could be violent at times. The manta didn't actually fly so much as it soared, gliding on warm updrafts of air, but the wingtips, twenty feet to each side of the two riders, rippled in a graceful, slow-motion flapping reminiscent of the beast's Terran namesake, guiding it into the thermals that let it circle ever higher into the sky. Vince could feel the play of titanic muscles beneath its thick skin, could sense the beast's power.

"You're a pilot, damn it," he muttered angrily to himself. "You're a pilot. Who ever heard of a pilot scared of heights?" He tried to tell himself that this was just another flight, that the manta was just another kind of aircraft, but his inner voice was not sounding very convincing. As the manta banked left, Vince clung even tighter to his guide, his eyes squeezed shut.

The problem was he couldn't keep them shut. When there was a jolt or the sinking feeling of a sudden, lurching drop in cold air, he would open them and find himself looking down into cloud-rimmed blackness, canyon depths that had no bottom, an endless fall into night and storm.

In a sense, there was no bottom, only mile upon terrifying mile of rising temperatures and pressures, until the environment was more like the interior of a minor star than a planet. Lightning arced in those depths, a violet and blue-white fury that left a light-dazzled afterimage against his vision. He blinked, trying to clear his eyes.

To the right lay the near cloud wall, layered like the strata of a canyon on Earth, but fifty miles high, and plunging away into the eternal darkness of the Jovian Deep below.

Vrahk'dreleschaah. The name, Kowalski had told him an hour before as he prepared for this insane flight, meant Cloud-Wall of the Violet Lightnings. Since the city had first been cloned and brought to maturity two centuries earlier, it had sailed the clear gulf of air alongside this same cloud wall, near the southern edge of Jupiter's north temperate zone. The scale left Vince feeling like an insect painfully working its way along the scarp of Earth's Grand Canyon.

Except that there was still no bottom, and even the Vallis Marinaris on Mars, largest and deepest canyon in the Solar System, would have been invisibly lost in this aerial gulf between the ramparts of the Jovian clouds. The roar of Jove itself hissed and rumbled over Vince's headphones. A frequency had been selected that was clear of the worst of the gas giant's radio interference, but there was enough leakage that it sounded as though he were flying through the midst of a windstorm.

"Are you well?"

The words, intruding over the "empty" channel, had been transmitted by the huge being he was clinging to. Vince realized that he'd been holding the creature's wing membranes with a muscle-cramping fervor. Embarrassed, he loosened his hold—a little.

"Uh, yeah. No problem. Sorry if I was grabbing you too tight."

"Your claws bothered me not at all, Wingless One," the giant said. His name, Vince remembered, was Shevitarvinav and he was somehow related to Throvidronvinav, though the intricacies of Jovian relationships were far from clear in Vince's mind.

"It is well you cling fast," the giant continued. "I doubt that even I could catch you if you fell to meet our God. Hear him roar!"

What the Jovians called the Voice of God, the radio howl of Jupiter, underscored the Stormrider's words, helping Vince paint a mental image of himself falling, falling, accelerating into darkness in that terrible gravity with nothing to check his plunge. Angry at himself for letting his imagination get out of check, he wrenched his thoughts back to the mission, to the threat posed by the invaders. He had to concentrate on the mission at hand. It would be humiliating—not to mention fatal—if he let his surroundings paralyze him into helplessness.

"We approach our destination," his huge pilot said.

Vince looked ahead, past the Stormrider, and to the left. Vrahk'dreleschaah floated a quarter of a mile away, a tiny world hanging, seemingly unsupported, in the sky. The lower levels of the cloud city, like stacked plates, showed clearly the numberless, cavelike openings of hangar bays and the open balconies from which Stormriders were taking wing in a seemingly unending stream. The flyers were tiny at this distance, swirling and rising like a cloud of gnats on a summer's day on Earth, and departing toward the west.

The city was being abandoned. For the past six hours, Vrahk'dreleschaah had been steadily emptying. The battle had ended, and the last invader was smashed, but now the victors were fleeing into the Jovian skies, under their own power or riding the backs of mantas. Vrahk'dreleschaah was nearly empty now, a deserted island of solidity in a sea of shrieking gasses.

Vince and his guide were rising now above the uppermost reaches of Vrahk's encompassing dome. Even at this range it was difficult to see through the thick, translucent membrane that held the entire city aloft. Vince could make out the shadowed shapes within of towers, enigmatic structures, and the swell of organic appendages of some kind. Held rigid by the hot hydrogen-helium mix within, the membrane ranged from a foot thick near its circular base to perhaps six inches thick at the broad, flat top. Vents, like large, puckered mouths, dotted the upper surface. Vince had been told that they allowed some of the hot hydrogen to bleed off from time to time when the city became too buoyant. The water band—the altitudes within the Jovian atmosphere where water remained a liquid—was relatively narrow, so precise adjustment of the city's altitude was a matter of supreme importance.

The manta swept over the city's rim, blocking the straight-down view into the Jovian depths, and Vince breathed a little easier. Guided by the Stormrider, the gene-engineered flyer descended toward the surface of the membrane, chasing its own shadow, which rose quickly to meet it. There was a thump, a ripple of wings, and then the manta was down.

Swiftly, Vince unbuckled his harness, then jumped off the creature's broad back, careful to first attach the snap swivel on the end of a cable to the saddle and make sure the other end was securely locked to his utility belt. Though Vrahk'dreleschaah floated in relatively calm air, wind gusts stronger than those of any Earthly hurricane could howl out of nowhere without warning, and the safety line, forty feet of woven diacarb strands, might keep him from being swept away.

He stood now on an alien plain, the very top of the balloon holding Vrahk'dreleschaah aloft. The "ground," despite its translucency, seemed solid enough as he took a few tentative steps, though the immense weight of the manta had dimpled it slightly, like a steel bearing dropped onto a tightly stretched rubber sheet.

To Vince, it looked as though he was standing on an almost flat, almost featureless plain at the bottom of a very deep crater; the "crater walls" were the cloud layers piling into the sky on every side. Two miles away, a tiny speck moved slowly against the sky, scrawling a white contrail in the wet air.

"Kaiten!" he called over his suit radio. "Kaiten, this is Vince. Do you read me?"

"Affirmative," the Terrine's voice replied, barely audible above the muted radio thunder of Jove. He was aboard the one remaining Krait, circling the city. "I am on station."

"Right. We're starting work here. Keep in touch."

"Affirmative. Kaiten out."

"Right, Shev," Vince said to his companion. "Let's get to work. Can you get this fellow to raise up a bit?"

The Stormrider goaded his enormous mount with the end of his charge gun. There was a soft, electric crackle, and the manta arched its back in response, lifting one enormous delta wing clear of the surface.

Strapped to the creature's belly, and visible now as it hoisted itself above the surface, was a complex assembly of tanks, pumps, and machinery connected to a bell-shaped nozzle five feet across. It was a RAM Motors Cyclan-D rocket engine, scavenged from the damaged Krait. Normally a simple fusion torch, heating reaction mass and expelling it through the nozzle for thrust, the engine had been hastily redesigned for a very special task. Stormriders, working under Vince's direction, had carried out its jury-rigged conversion and attached it to a harness slung beneath the manta's belly.

The engine assembly weighed at least five tons in Jupiter's gravity, but it came apart in sections, each of which Shevitarvinav wrestled from the harness and set gently on the ground. The membrane dimpled ever so slightly beneath the combined weight of the sections. "Where do you want it?" the giant asked.

"Over here."

Opening a tool pouch on his utility belt, Vince led the way toward one of the two-foot-high, puckered vents that littered the otherwise featureless plain.

It took almost forty minutes to mount the engine, nozzle-end down, into the gas vent, with Vince standing out of the way and giving directions as the eighteen-foot-tall Stormrider lifted the pieces one by one and lowered them into place. The giant used its charge gun to relax the vent enough that it could be pried open, and the gush of hot hydrogen from inside the balloon tore at Vince like a living thing until Shevitarvinav wedged the rocket nozzle in place, like a cork in an enormous bottle.

It was fortunate, Vince decided, that the city-creature was so huge it probably didn't feel what the mites on its back were doing. He could imagine the thing feeling a sudden itch, getting the urge to scratch. . . .

What, he wondered, could the city actually feel? The emotions, the sensations experienced by a living creature with a volume of something like one cubic mile were utterly beyond the reach of Vince's imagination. Could it, would it feel pain?

His hosts had assured him that the gene-tailored creature that was Vrahk'dreleschaah was not sentient. Its brain, though larger and more massive than most buildings, was little more than a central regulator for absorbing and converting organic molecules, for heating and circulating air, for responding to variations in temperature by changing altitude, and very little else.

Still, Vince hated doing this.

At last, the rocket motor was assembled, wedged solidly into the vent with the nozzle hidden "underground," the huge tanks and complex plumbing and the gaping mouth of an air intake towering above the surface at a precarious, but near-vertical angle. The central mechanism—the pumps, feed lines, and battery—was just within reach. Vince opened an access panel and began probing the engine's interior.

"I was born in this city," Shevitarvinav said at his back, a hint of sadness touching his radio voice. "I hate to see it returned to God."

"If any of you can think of another way to beat the invaders," Vince said, unraveling a bundle of wires and clipping in a hastily assembled timer unit, "I'd be real glad to hear it. Believe me, I don't like this idea any better than you do."

"We do what we must," the Stormrider replied. "Survival is the only imperative."

Now there was a Darwinian notion. The Terrines had been indoctrinated with a death-to-the-weakest programming that had made them the fiercest warriors in the system. Their ferocity was controlled—barely—by their conditioned loyalty to RAM and the Martians.

Well, the Stormriders were warriors, too, and where the Terrines were indoctrinated in loyalty to RAM, the Stormriders appeared to have developed quite a different loyalty, one to the impressive forces of nature that surrounded them, and within which they lived and died, to a god who challenged them and tested them each time they took wing.

Their faith gave them a terrifying strength.

What, Vince wondered, did he believe in? NEO, certainly, and the need to free Earth from RAM's dictatorship. He'd been raised believing in a comfortably distant God, but never had he felt the wind-in-the-teeth immediacy of faith the Jovian Stormriders seemed to feel.

Perhaps, he reasoned, soaring on the Jovian storm winds, balanced always between ice and fire, offered the golden giants a perspective on life and faith that he lacked.

He made the final connection. "Okay, Shev," he said, stepping back. "Let 'em know we're done."

Over the open radio circuit, Vince could hear the pulsed modulations of Stormrider calling to Stormrider. Other Jovians, and Kowalski, waited within the city. After a moment, the crested head dipped, the huge, pupilless eyes gazing down at Vince. "The doctor has acknowledged. The message is being sent."

Vince couldn't hear it, of course. It was being transmitted on the invaders' combat frequencies, and Vince's
suit was not set to receive those wavelengths. But he
knew what was being said.

Kowalski's Stormriders had pieced together and translated enough of the invaders' earlier transmissions to
allow them to construct a very special message, not in
words, but in the pulsing on-off of binary code.

PRIORITY INTERRUPT! HALT ACTIVITY IMMEDI-
ATE! ALL UNITS CONJUGATE! EXECUTE IMMEDI-
ATE! COORDINATES . . .

And the coordinates for the meeting were those of
Vrahk'dreleschaah itself, drawn from the invaders' own
radio communications picked up during the battle.

The message, painstakingly assembled on a computer
and recorded hours ago, was now being transmitted over
and over, beamed into the sky using every watt of electrical power the living city could produce. It was a primitive ruse, laughably so, but the invaders had so far
shown a certain directness and singlemindedness of purpose that could almost be interpreted as stupidity. They
were not stupid, Vince reminded himself, but they possessed a kind of childlike innocence that could be
exploited—once. Vince knew that if his plan was not
completely successful, they would never be able to use
anything like it again.

The invaders might be naive, but they certainly would
not fall for the same trick twice.

Vince looked up, scanning the sky. The short Jovian
day was again nearing sunset, and it was rapidly growing dark. The zenith was a piercing royal blue darkening
to violet, the encircling clouds showing gold and white
only at their very tops, where the sun's rays could strike
them. Three of Jupiter's major satellites hung overhead,
tiny crescents visible through the pale flicker of aurorae.
A solitary meteor flared across heaven and faded in a
lingering green afterglow.

He thought of Jovanna.

According to the last reports, the huge invader ship

seen at Amalthea was still accelerating at a steady two-tenths of a G. It was now a million miles from Jupiter and growing farther and faster with every passing hour.

Amalthea, it seemed, was still under assault by the invaders, who appeared to be swarming throughout the volume of space around Jupiter. Several clashes with Callistan ships near Io, Jupiter's innermost large satellite, had been reported, and brief radio contact had been established with a number of human survivors still inside Amalthea's caverns. Before the transmission was interrupted, those survivors were able to report that the invaders had carried off a large number of Amaltheans, leaving the rest sealed away inaccessibly within their vast, airtight caverns. Another fleet, the rest of RAM's Jupiter squadron, was on the way, but it would be days before help would arrive.

The survivors thought it likely that the invaders would be through the air locks long before then.

Was Jovanna still in the city? Vince hoped so, but some deep and darkly pessimistic part of him was convinced that she must have been among those taken. Neither she nor Galen would have fled to another part of Amalthea when RAM had arrived. Instead, they would have stayed near the main docking bay . . . the part of Amalthea that had been overrun by the invaders.

He would know for sure soon.

"There," Shevitarvinav warned. "Overhead."

Vince leaned back, peering straight up into the deepening sky. Another meteor trail flashed . . . and another. There was nothing unusual about that. A steady rain of meteoric debris was constantly dragged into the atmosphere from the inner reaches of the planet's rings.

Suddenly, the sky came alive with falling stars, streaks of light radiating from a point close to the zenith, the trails short but persistent, evidence that they were dropping almost directly toward the floating city.

"Damn!" Vince said, eyes widening at the display of celestial pyrotechnics. "Damn, they're coming quicker than we expected!"

The meteors continued to fall.

CHAPTER EIGHTEEN

"Kaiten!" Vince called. "Do you see them?"

"Affirmative," the Terrine replied, his voice almost lost in the crackle of static. "They come. I'm closing the range."

"Negative! Negative! Keep your distance! They probably won't even see us. You hang back unless I tell you."

"Affirmative." The Terrine's voice was taut with strain.

They were coming by the hundreds, by the thousands, a swarm of unnumbered invaders dropping from space and heating to incandescence as they streaked through the upper reaches of Jupiter's atmosphere. The faked radio message appeared to have done the trick. Every invader machine in the vicinity of Jupiter must be falling toward the city.

The problem was that he'd expected more time before they made their appearance.

"Tell them inside," Vince told the Stormrider, his communications link with Kowalski and the Jovians within the city. "Let them know it's time to get out."

"They know. They are leaving now."

Timing was critical. It had been necessary for Dr.-Kowalski to remain in the city for the simple reason that the radio transmitter and the computer gear where the message had been composed were all tailored for human use.

It was a problem the Jovians were still learning to cope with. All electronics imported to the planet were built by and for human hands, and only a small percentage had been modified for Stormrider use. Kowalski had remained behind for the same reason that Vince had to be the one to prepare the engine salvaged from the Krait. Stormriders might be able to lift the component parts into place, but only a human could do the delicate rewiring necessary to ready the device for firing. The huge Jovians had difficulty manipulating something as small and flimsy—from their point of view—as a radio's "on" switch.

Once begun, however, the broadcast would continue without supervision, repeating over and over from a powerful transmitter at the very heart of the city. Dr. Kowalski and her bodyguard of Stormriders would be making their way at this moment to a hangar bay where a shuttle was waiting, fueled for immediate departure.

The plan was a simple one. Kowalski would board the shuttle and fly to a neighboring city, Denthrel'cheschaah, some eight hundred miles farther west along the cloud wall. Kaiten, in the RAM fighter, would escort her. Vince would make his way with the last of Vrahk'dreleschaah's refugees, clinging to Shev's wings astride the back of a manta.

The hope, of course, was that Vrahk'dreleschaah would become a tomb for the invaders. The only trick was to get all of them to enter the city, and that was why the priority-interrupt message had been composed by Kowalski and her Stormrider friends.

Movement caught Vince's eye. Turning, he saw a silver pinpoint drop past the cloud tops, arrowing toward the city.

"There!" the Jovian said, pointing. "I see three."

And then the sky was filled with them, a multitude of flashing, silvery forms shaped by the laws of aerodynamics into delta-winged flyers virtually identical to the Jovian mantas. They fell past the city on every side, veering into level flight in broad, sweeping turns, then hurled themselves at the lower levels of the city. From his vantage point atop the city's balloon, Vince couldn't see them actually entering the balconies and docking bays, but he could imagine the shock as those multiton bodies struck.

Too soon! Too soon! He'd been afraid of this when the incoming machines had lit up the sky moments before, much earlier than expected. Vince and Kowalski, working on the plan hours before, had calculated that it would take an hour at least for the invaders to reenter Jupiter's atmosphere and descend to the city's altitude. Instead, they had appeared almost at once. They must have sacrificed much of their own mass to friction, like literal meteors, in their fiery passage through the upper air.

Vince stood beside the Stormrider, watching the horde's arrival, furious that he'd not allowed for the possibility of the ruse's working so well that the invaders actually rushed to get to the city.

"Shev!" he called. "Are you in contact with your brothers in the doctor's group?"

"I am."

"Where are they?"

"Still at least ten minutes from the shuttle. They . . ." The Jovian broke off for a moment, staring at nothing as he listened to his private, inner radio channel. "They say that large numbers of invaders have already entered the city and are smashing their way toward the central core."

"Damn."

The Stormrider turned blank eyes toward Vince, and he could feel the power of its gaze. "Dr. Kowalski says that you are to set the bomb and make your escape. There is nothing more that can be done for her."

Vince hesitated, torn. He had to carry out his part of the plan, had to or it would all be for nothing. And yet . . .

He made his decision. Making his way across the odd, smooth surface of the balloon to the towering rocket motor, he reached up and twisted a knob on the side of the timer. Fifteen minutes. Any more and the invaders entering the city might escape; any less and, well, he didn't want to think about that.

"Kaiten!" he yelled as he turned and strode back to the waiting manta. Shevitarvinav was already mounting the beast, strapping himself onto the saddle. "The bomb is set!"

"But Kowalski hasn't left the city yet!"

"I know. Shev and I are going back for her. You get out now, while you can."

"Major, I can't accept that order. I can't leave you to—"

"Can it, Terrine! Somebody's got to get out of this mess if the doctor and I don't make it! Somebody who can tell the rest of the Solar System what happened here!"

"A-affirmative."

Vince accepted the Stormrider's giant hand as he scrambled onto the manta's back. "I overheard your order to the Terrine," the giant said. "Thank you."

"Don't thank me until we see if this works," Vince replied. "This isn't the brightest idea I ever had. Tell the doctor's group that we're on the way." He attached his harness, and the manta, prodded by the Stormrider's charge gun, vaulted into the sky. Vince tried to ignore the swirl of vertigo as he coiled the forty feet of his safety line and hooked it to the rear of the saddle.

Like a small plane, the manta swept over the edge of the city balloon, and Vince again stared down into bottomless depths. The shadow of onrushing night engulfed the city at almost the same moment, plunging him into night. Was it a trick of the eyes, Vince wondered, or was the Jovian Deep glowing a deep and sullen, almost invisible red? Lightning flared, dispelling the glow in shocked spots of green flash-dazzle dancing before his eyes.

Silver flyers were still dropping through the sky, their bodies faintly luminous and leaving ghostly smears of vapor against the growing darkness, but the great influx of invaders appeared to have ceased. Right now, the horde of invaders should be working their way toward the city's core, toward the transmitter and its endlessly repeating message.

Once they reached it, well, that's when they'd find out

whether or not this crazy idea was going to work.

Vince tugged the Stormrider's wing and pointed.
Through a shrieking wind, the manta dropped toward a
city balcony.

○ ○ ○ ○ ○

Marlene Kowalski crouched behind an overturned
table, sheltering within the black shadow of her companions' wings. Six Stormriders had accompanied her from
the transmitter, but one had stayed behind to face the
horde of approaching machines. Now, four crowded pro-
tectively about her as the fifth tried to buy them a precious few minutes more. He had already torn a ragged
hole in the wall ten feet off the floor and was stooping
now to reach inside, manipulating the clusters of vine-
like wires growing there in massive clumps.

Most of the power in Vrahk'dreleschaah had been
diverted to the radio transmitter, but emergency lighting still shone from small, isolated glow panels along the
corridor walls, casting shadows and illuminating the
inhuman faces and heads of the Stormriders in sharp-
chiseled relief. The enormous, gene-tailored beast that
was the city had a metabolism based on electric current
generated by vast, organic batteries hidden away in the
structure's keel.

Marlene chirped at the fifth Stormrider, a harsh,
high-pitched rasp that hurt her throat. She knew a little
Ch'shah, the Jovians' private language, though it was
difficult to make herself understood in tones that were
normally generated by vocal cords six inches long.

The Stormrider uttered a piercing chirrup of assent,
then stepped back from the wall. Light flared within the
hole as organic circuits flared and shorted.

"Quickly!" she spat in Ch'shah, her voice booming at
the others by her suit speakers. "This way!"

In the corridor beyond, silver forms appeared, squeez-
ing through narrow tunnels that served the city as a
ventilator system and pouring themselves onto the floor.
The Stormrider that had torn open the wiring shrieked

warning, waving the others on, then stood astride the passageway, his great wings blocking the way. Marlene heard the crackle of his charge gun, and then the giant's upper body exploded in bloody fragments and a haze of purple-red mist. The invaders advanced *en masse*, their bodies in sinister machine form now, boxy and angular, with jointed legs and writhing, snake-quick tentacles.

For the most part, so far, the invaders had ignored her and her companions, as though they were so intent on penetrating Vrahk'dreleschaah to its very heart that they cared nothing for such minor distractions as living creatures scuttling from their path. A few of the machines, however, seemed to be organized as a security force for the main body. They circled, prowled, and probed, and when a handful of them stumbled across the fleeing Stormriders and the human woman they escorted, a firefight had broken out that dogged the Jovians through nearly a quarter mile of winding passageways.

One of the machines, a faceted polygon swaying on a dozen appendages, took a step toward the Stormrider's corpse . . . and the hallway erupted in violet light and the savage arcing of million-volt lightning bolts struck from the walls and the floor itself. Capriciously, the lightning jumped from one machine to the next, until they all shivered and danced and staggered in its deadly embrace.

Then some portion of the organic wiring within the walls melted through. Smoke gushed from the hole in the wall and the lightning flickered out, leaving half a dozen charred and still-twitching machines on the floor. More invaders were coming through the ventilators, however, molding themselves into wickedly gleaming combat forms. Sensing that the current electrifying that section of the passageway was off, they advanced past their fallen comrades, but cautiously now, alert for other, similar traps.

Marlene, meanwhile tried to run, and the effort nearly brought her to her knees. She'd lived on Jupiter for long enough to have developed a considerable endurance, but no human could run more than a few steps in Jupiter's gravity. A young Stormrider, Gavitsurvinav, stooped as he passed, swinging her off her feet and ten feet into the air. Another turned and braced himself in the passageway, wings spread, waiting for their pursuers.

Had it been worth it? She didn't know, and now she expected that she never would find out.

The passageway shuddered, then canted slightly, almost throwing the Stormrider carrying her to the floor. For a moment, she thought that Vince's jury-rigged bomb had gone off, but Gavitsurvinav provided the explanation.

"There are too many of the alien machines," he explained, gesturing at the surrounding walls and ceiling. "Their weight is upsetting the city's balance." The floor lurched again, and the Stormrider added. "I think we are sinking."

The decreasing altitude would prompt the city to heat the hydrogen in its floatation sac, but Kowalski doubted that it could compensate fast enough. It felt as though the city was dropping at a rate of at least several feet per second, and at that rate the city would be destroyed before equilibrium could be restored.

Gavitsurvinav seemed to be listening to something as he hurried down the corridor. Marlene envied these creatures their internal radio, a literal telepathy that let them communicate with their fellows across many miles. The price they paid was the roar of Jupiter always in their ears, the *Klavschak Vah*, their Voice of God. As long as she'd lived with the Stormriders, Marlene still thought they were all a little mad, at least from the human point of view. She could not believe in anything not experienced with the senses . . . but then, the Jovians had senses no human had ever had.

Exactly what did they hear that she could not?

"Shevitarvinav says that they are coming to help us, he and the wingless one, Pirelli."

"Tell them no!" she snapped. Her command of Ch'shah failed and she sputtered into Anglic. "There's nothing

they can do for us! Tell them to set the damned bomb
and get the hell out!"

"It's too late." Gavitsurvinav spoke no Anglic, but he
seemed to understand what she'd said. "They enter the
city now."

The floor lurched again, and Marlene felt Gavitsurvinav fight to keep his balance. The corridor was tilted
now at an angle of almost ten degrees, and footing was
treacherous.

Damn the man. The plan, so carefully worked out,
was falling to pieces now. She reached into a pocket in
her coveralls and pulled out a palm-sized remote control.

It wouldn't be much longer now.

○ ○ ○ ○ ○

Vince glanced at the timepiece set in his helmet.
Three minutes to go.

As he stepped off the manta and onto the floor of the
landing bay, he could feel the sinking sensation, like
that experienced in a descending elevator, as the city
sank under the weight of the invaders. The danger now
was that the machines, realizing that the city was
falling, would take to the air again before the bomb
Vince had planted on the balloon went off.

Kowalski, he knew, was carrying a small remote control. Vince had one just like it, as a backup in case something happened to her. Either device would trigger a
computer program primed to run on command. Keyed to
the city-creature's low-frequency nervous system, the
program would order Vrahk'dreleschaah to seal every
door and refuse every subsequent command to open
them. The idea was to seal off the entire city once the
invaders were inside. No one expected the doors to keep
them penned up for long, but it might keep them for just
long enough.

Kowalski's shuttle, a dart-shaped, stub-winged rocket
emblazoned with the Solar Geographic logo, rested near
the gaping mouth of the bay, harshly illuminated by
overhead emergency lighting panels. A pair of armed

Stormriders crouched beside it, wings nervously rustling above their heads.

"Where is she now?" Vince asked Shevitarvinav.

The Stormrider pointed at an open, inner doorway. "That way," he said. "Perhaps a hundred yards. But she says that there are invaders between her and this bay."

Vince drew his pistol from the holster strapped to his hip. It was a heavy, blunt-muzzled weapon with a squat magazine set just in front of the trigger. He'd been able to exchange his laser, useless against the invaders, for this, an old Colt-Fujiwa 7mm rocket pistol found in the city's armory.

"Let's see if we can help."

"You can't help, Pirel—SST! Get—SSSSST—of here!"

The voice, breaking in on the radio channel on which Vince had been communicating with Shevitarvinav, was Kowalski's, though it was so faint and so static-torn that he could barely make out her words. Radio interference from Jupiter, from the invaders, from the walls of the city itself, made direct communication almost impossible. It was for that reason that they'd agreed to talk through the Stormriders, who seemed better able to communicate through the static than human radio technology.

"Dr. Kowalski!" Vince called back. "We're going to try attacking from this side. Maybe we can—

"SSSST—late, Pirelli! I'm go—SSST!" The static roar became unbearable, and Vince lost the rest of her words.

"Come on," he told Shevitarvinav. He waved at the guards by the shuttle. "Tell them to come along, too."

"Major!" the Stormrider called. "Look out!"

The door, empty a moment before, was filled now with squirming silver shapes, war machines of liquid metal spilling into the landing bay.

Vince raised his rocket pistol and fired.

The cluster controller had reached the source of the signal, a huge and primitive computer that appeared to be the heart of this strange, lighter-than-air structure. Its message sang now in the air around him, a continuing, rapidly cycling binary pattern repeating the same pieces of message over and over.

The message was incomplete, almost incoherent, with only fragments of the usual code prefixes and authorizations that framed messages between clusters or from the supervisor nucleus. It was almost as though a badly programmed communicator had simply patched unrelated pieces of different transmissions together without a clear idea of what was actually being said.

At first, the controller had assumed that the sender's transmission was being hampered by the radio noise from the gas giant itself. Now it realized that the message issuing from the structure's central computer was itself fragmentary and incomplete. Why?

PRIORITY INTERRUPT! HALT ACTIVITY IMMEDIATE! ALL UNITS CONJUGATE! EXECUTE IMMEDIATE! . . .

The command to engage in conjugation—the coordinator did not think of it in those terms, of course—was an imperative, overriding all other programming. The supervisor nucleus might issue such a command in order to program an entire cluster with new and extremely urgent orders.

Was the city's central computer attempting communication with the cluster? That was the only possibility with even a five-tenths probability. The coordinator had not yet formed an opinion as to whether or not the humans that serviced the computer were intelligent enough to have composed the message. That they functioned as remotes and could gather and transmit data was undeniable, but their functioning was so irrational and disjointed that postulating intelligence for them— true intelligence—seemed unreasonable.

In any case and whatever its source, the imperative nature of the command, like that which had summoned the whole of the cluster to Amalthea in the first place, could not be ignored. Over fifteen thousand individual units had followed the call, flocking in from Amalthea and from near-Jupiter space and forcing their way into the core of this strange floating structure. Now, in the heart of the city, machine joined to machine, pseudopods extending, touching, intermingling, as those machines closest to the center began probing the computer that was transmitting the command to conjugate.

Part of the controller's senses noted that the temperature had increased by five degrees in the past two minutes, and that the air pressure now stood at six point one atmospheres, suggesting that the surrounding structure was settling somewhat under the weight of the cluster units.

No matter. They would not be here much longer.

Odd. Data and programming instructions were flowing from the central computer, but the machine seemed hopelessly simpleminded, far more primitive even than a seeker. There was no intelligence here, only blind, rote obedience of step-by-step commands.

What, then, had composed and sent the message?

○ ○ ○ ○ ○

On top of the gasbag suspending the city above the Abyss, the timer reached zero and closed a circuit. Valves opened, and the liquid oxygen stored in all of the fuel tanks mounted above the nozzle was dumped into the reaction chamber, pouring through in a viscous white cloud that spilled out of the nozzle and into the interior of the gasbag.

The oxygen, stored in ultracold liquid form, had been scavenged from the Krait's life-support system and from the reserves produced by the city itself for the use of the humans that might visit it. A liquid at two hundred degrees below zero, it warmed quickly when it hit the hot hydrogen-helium mix in the balloon, expanding in a violent swirl of expanding gas. Frost caked in layers over the engine nozzle, as the cryogenic temperatures of the liquid leached moisture from the air as ice.

Normally, the Cyclan-D engine, which used fusion heat to turn reaction mass to plasma, did not use liquid oxygen as had the chemical-powered motors of the early days of the space age. Vince knew the principles of those cumbersome giants of the twentieth and early twenty-first centuries, though, and had come up with the idea to convert the Krait motor into a deadly bomb.

A bomb that would work only within the Jovian atmosphere.

As the last of the liquid oxygen poured into the combustion chamber, the external pumps switched on, sending hydrogen from the outside atmosphere into the engine. Half a second later, a relay tripped and a Jovian charge gun welded to the inside of the nozzle fired, sending a bolt of current through the containment bell.

The engine ignited. . . .

Flame touched the interior of the city's gasbag, brightening, then flaring into a fireball that illuminated the Jovian night for miles around. Compared to the size of the entire city, the explosion was a tiny one—less than one percent of the hydrogen inside the balloon had actually been contaminated with oxygen—but its placement had been carefully calculated to produce the maximum effect. The blast tore the embedded Krait engine into white-hot shrapnel and opened a gash in the balloon material that rapidly, in the searing heat of the blast, widened and lengthened, a crevasse across the top of the flotation sac two hundred yards long.

Hydrogen gas burned in the temporary presence of oxygen, flaring brilliantly, and then, as the last of the oxygen gave out, the flames died. Steam, created in the explosive hydrogen-plus-oxygen-gives-water reaction, vented from the tear in the gasbag. Streams of liquid water condensed on the balloon's interior.

Steam and hydrogen gas gushed from the giant tear. Like a stricken, dying giant, Vrahk'dreleschaah began to fall.

CHAPTER NINETEEN

Already locked on to one of the metallic invaders, the smart bullet from Vince's rocket pistol swerved in midair as the landing bay began to tremble. Trailing smoke, it smashed into its target, detonating with a thud that blasted a molten-looking crater from the invader's body and severed three tentacles.

Then Vince was on his knees, unable to stand as the entire city shuddered and lurched. A scream, far off and muffled, quavered in the air, mingled with a low rumble, like thunder but almost subsonic in range, that seemed to rise from the very bowels of the city.

Vrahk'dreleschaah was mortally wounded.

Rising, Vince aimed his pistol for another shot, but the doorway was closed now, and all three of the machines that had already entered the landing bay were dead, cut down by Stormrider charge guns, then smashed to pieces by hard-swung gun butts. Making his way across the slanting deck to the door, he tried to open it as he'd seen Stormriders do before, splaying his hand on a slick-surfaced panel set in the wall to one side.

Nothing happened. "The signal has been given," Shevitarvinav told him. "All of the doors are sealed now."

Vince fingered the remote controller in his pocket. He had not triggered the doors. He could only assume that Kowalski had closed them with hers, deliberately sealing herself and her companions off from rescue.

"There's got to be another way to get her out."

He didn't want to leave her. He couldn't leave her, not while there was a chance of getting her off the falling city.

Marlene Kowalski was still what he and the other NEO agents had come to Jupiter for, the one person in the Solar System who knew something about the nano-technic invaders from Charon. Since he'd met her, she'd demonstrated her expertise on that subject time and time again.

More than that, though, it had been his idea to lure the invaders into Vrahk'dreleschaah and trap them there, his idea to puncture the gasbag holding the city aloft and send it and its contents plunging into the Jovian Deep.

True, she'd volunteered to reprogram the city's core computer and operate the transmitter from inside, but there'd been no one else to carry out that task. Kaiten could have thrown the switch, certainly, but he wouldn't have been able to program the message.

Vince did not want her death on his hands.

Staring at the closed doorway, he tried to picture how the corridor beyond lay in relation to the rest of the city. It did not go straight back from the landing bay but appeared to angle left, following the curve of the city's outer wall. About a hundred yards, Shev had said.

Whirling, Vince ran back toward the manta, which was restlessly shivering on the deck where it had landed, its blunt, eyeless head questing back and forth. "Shev!" he yelled. "Come on! Mount up!"

"Where?"

"Back outside." A shrieking whine filled the landing bay, and pieces snapped from the ceiling in an explosive spray of debris, showering on the floor like an avalanche. Vince pointed at the other two Stormriders, who stood uncertainly beside the shuttle, their charge guns in their wing-hands, their blank eyes fixed on the ceiling above their heads. "Them, too!"

Vaulting onto the saddle behind Shevitarvinav's back,

Vince belted himself in as the Stormrider prodded the manta around and aimed it toward the night beyond the landing bay entryway.

The Stormrider shouted, and the beast launched itself from the side of the listing city. Clouds, a vortex of inky blackness, swirled about Vince as the wind howled. At his back, the city still showed lights, but dimly. He could still hear the rumbling moan as the structure shuddered and crumbled.

Lightning flared in the depths below, briefly illuminating the city's belly. It was canted at an angle of nearly thirty degrees now, the upper part of its translucent gasbag still glowing with an orange heat. Gas must be escaping from the rip in the flotation sac at a fearful rate, though Vrahk'dreleschaah was so large that it would be some time before the city began falling in earnest.

"Kaiten! Do you read me?"

"I am here." The Terrine's voice was surprisingly clear. A blue-white cone of flame shone against the darkness, trailing a winged shadow. The Krait circled a hundred yards beyond the edge of the city.

"Okay! I'm going to need some fire from your Mark Twenty-One. Stand by to target where I show you!"

"Affirmative. Weapon free. I'm tracking."

"Shev! You've got to pinpoint Dr. Kowalski and her party for me. Can you get a bearing on their signal?"

"No," the winged being said. Vince felt a crushing disappointment. "But I already know where they are." He pointed, indicating a row of open balconies along the cliff wall of the city's side.

"How, if you can't get a bearing—?"

"Gavitsurvinav just told me where they are. And it is my home. Hurry. He says that the invaders are closing in on them now."

Drawing his rocket pistol, Vince aimed at the indicated balcony and pulled the trigger. The rocket-propelled smart round was a gleaming white point of light as it streaked from the sky and onto the balcony, exploding with a tiny flash.

"Kaiten! Did you see it?"

"I saw. . . ."

And then the Krait's gyrocannon was cracking away, 25mm high-explosive rounds searing into the side of the city in a rapid-fire stream. The balcony was smashed to pieces by the first half-second of fire, explosions gouging out huge chunks of living wall and punching through into the room beyond. Shock waves hammered at Vince's body through the thick air; he could feel their concussions from fifty yards away, like hammer blows through his lightweight suit.

The fire ceased as Kaiten's fighter passed beyond the direct line-of-sight with the target, then resumed again as he swung the Krait around and into a second pass. Tracer fire glowed against the sky, the high-speed rounds blurring into lines of white fire scrawled across the night. Kaiten swept the gyrocannon's aim back and forth, enlarging the hole. The city jumped and quivered under this new, deadly assault. Debris cascaded into space, vanishing into the depths. Shock waves pounded against Vince's chest and arms.

"Cease fire!" the Stormrider called, and Vince passed the order on to Kaiten at once. Abruptly, the stream of fire broke off.

"They say you've broken through to their corridor," Shev continued, excitement quickening his words. "They're coming out!"

The manta banked sharply and Vince clung for his life. From a distance, and against the huge bulk of the city, the hole opened by the Krait's gyrocannon fire didn't look very large, but as the manta soared toward that ragged-edged opening, it grew rapidly to a gaping cavern a hundred feet wide. Three Stormriders could be seen picking their way through the wreckage, a human in a bubble helmet and a form-fitting pressure suit close behind.

"Can you land this thing there?" Vince asked, pointing to a relatively flat stretch at the front of the hole.

"We will find out. Cling tight!" The manta plunged like a stooping bird of prey, folding its wings at the last possible second. The impact nearly knocked the wind from Vince's lungs, and he thumped against Shevitarvi-nav's back.

The manta shuddered, its bulk crushing loose wreck-age beneath its belly and sending some pieces hurtling out into space. "I am having trouble controlling the beast," Shev told him. "You must do what needs to be done!"

Unbuckling his harness, Vince sprang from the jittery manta's back and approached the trio of gennies and their human companion. "Hello, Doctor," Vince called. "I've been looking for you."

"Idiot!" she replied. "Why didn't you—Watch it!"

A piece of wall support the size of Vince's helmet shat-tered in a blast of raw energy, and fragments stung his arm. For a horrified moment he wondered if his suit had been holed, but the garment's weave was tough enough to resist even light gunfire.

But not a direct hit from a kinetic weapon. Silver machine forms moved in the dimly lit depths of the city, making their way out of the corridor as Kowalski and her Stormriders had done through piles of torn wreck-age. Vince raised his rocket pistol, still gripped in his right hand, and loosed two rounds, grinning wildly as he saw them strike home with twin flashes of light. Another projectile flicked past Vince's head, the sonic boom of its passing sounding like a high-pitched crack inside his helmet.

"Everybody down!" Kaiten yelled over the frequency. "Lie flat!"

Kowalski spat something unintelligible at the Storm-riders, and the giants dropped to the floor. Vince found himself lying on his side next to Kowalski as the white fire and hammering concussions returned.

Kaiten must have spotted the machines on his fire-control scanners. A long stream of tracers shrieked over-head and vanished into the depths of the hole, slamming among the Charonian invaders with deadly, pinpoint accuracy. Glittering fragments of nanotech machine flew from the cavern mouth, and Vince thought he would be deafened by the roar.

Then the gun was silent again as the Krait twisted around, its target line-of-sight again broken.

"Now that's what I call the cavalry to the rescue," Kowalski said, rising shakily first to her hands and knees, then to her feet. Smoke boiled from the back of the gaping hole in the city wall. Vince could see silvery rubble there, the smashed fragments of a dozen machines, but no movement.

"Shev!" he yelled back at the waiting Stormrider. "Can one of you Stormriders carry a human? Flying, I mean."

"No." The crested head shook slowly, in imitation of the human gesture. "Remember, one of you full humans weighs four to five hundred pounds here. Our wings cannot support us when we carry more than two hundred pounds or so."

Damn Jupiter's gravity! The Voice of God roared in his ears, a victory chant. "How about on a manta?"

"Two humans could be carried by a manta, of course." The creature's radio voice was almost lost against the rising thunder of static. "But they could not control it. Only the Stormriders can do that. There are a few mantas that could carry a Stormrider and two humans . . . but not this one, if that is what you are thinking."

Vince closed his eyes. Damn again! He wasn't going to pull this off after all! With only a single manta, there was no way that both he and Kowalski were going to get off the doomed city.

○ ○ ○ ○ ○

The cluster controller drew back, partially disentangling itself from the silicon-and-metal complexity of the city's central computer. There was nothing there, no data worth the taking. The computer was an empty, lifeless, and nonsentient lump of primitive circuits and switches, lacking even a glimmer of self-awareness or the means for self-determination. The message was what it appeared to be, fragments of network code fitted together in a haphazard jumble, barely intelligible, with just enough order to the thoughts to suggest that intelligence might have assembled them.

Sensations flickered through the controller, currents from fifteen thousand other cluster units now networked with it by direct linkage. Analyzing them, it recognized the danger. The floating construct was falling!

PRIORITY INTERRUPT! DISENGAGE! PRIORITY INTERRUPT! DISENGAGE!

It took less than a tenth of a second to fully disassociate itself from the core computer and to initiate a disengage sequence for the entire linked cluster. The controller continued analyzing the flood of incoming data. Humans had been engaged near the periphery of the structure. Temperature and pressure were rising rapidly. Access routes throughout the structure had been sealed.

The cluster controller did not know what a "trap" was, in human terms, but it was perfectly able to recognize both cause and effect, reaching the conclusion within another hundredth of a second that this scenario had been arranged to eliminate as many unit members of the cluster as possible.

It was imperative that the cluster escape.

The controller recognized at once that it would take too long to force the sealed access routes. A new and more direct escape would have to be engineered.

Radioed orders flashed to the hundreds of machine units packed within the central computer core. Silver forms shifted, sprouting pseudopods, generating intense magnetic fields. Pellets of unit substance, accelerated to speeds of forty miles per second, shrieked into the room's ceiling. If they could just break through this shell of organic materials surrounding them, escape to the outer atmosphere, they could change to flyer form and regain the clean, pure, energy-rich depths of space.

The central core was rocked by a rumbling, deafening cacophony of explosions, detonation following detonation as the ceiling disintegrated in a rain of dust and debris. Power failed, but the machine host kept up that devastating volley, punching now through the next level above the computer core . . . and the next . . . and the next. . . .

○ ○ ○ ○ ○

No! Vince's right fist slammed against the glove of his open left hand. He would not accept defeat. There had to be a way!

And he knew what it would have to be.

Standing on the canted, windswept rubble at the edge of the city, he studied Marlene Kowalski's body, measuring it in his mind. She was stocky and heavyset; on Earth she would have weighed two hundred pounds at least . . . which meant she weighed at least five hundred here, and her suit, helmet, and life-support pack added perhaps another fifty pounds.

But he had an idea. "You go back on Shev's manta!" he yelled at Marlene. "Now! Move!"

"What about you?"

The city lurched, and Vince thought he heard an explosion somewhere deep inside. Or was it thunder . . . a high-pitched, continuing shriek, like the rasping of a high speed drill? It was so hard to judge sounds accurately in this high-density hydrogen atmosphere. Whatever that noise might be, the city was definitely falling faster now . . . gathering speed as it plunged into the deep. His suit display was registering an outside temperature of 180 degrees and a pressure of almost seven atmospheres.

"I'll be okay!" he said, picking his way through the wreckage back to the manta. The great animal was nervous, twitching and shifting beneath Shev's folded wings. "You just get out of here!"

Quickly, Vince unhooked the safety line from the saddle, helped Marlene scramble on, then stepped back. Shev gave a wild yell, and the creature launched itself into the sky, glad to be free of the dying city.

"Don't go yet!" Vince called to the nearest Stormrider, gesturing. It shook its head, and the earthman felt a sinking feeling not connected at all to the city's fall.

None of the remaining Stormriders understood Anglic!
"All of you . . . I need your help!"

But they were as intelligent as humans . . . quite possibly more so. Vince began measuring out lengths of his
forty-foot safety cable, laying it out at the edge of the
building in three arms—two single strands and one doubled over—each arm about ten feet long. At the center,
where the four strands came together, he used his utility
belt to cinch the arms together, creating a simple and
very crude sling which he squeezed over his head and
arms.

The three watching Stormriders seemed to grasp at
once what he had in mind. Each took the end of one arm
of his improvised carrier in both feet, then hobbled to
the very edge of the city. The wind tugged at Vince,
shrieking wildly around his helmet. The temperature
readout showed two hundred degrees, at a pressure of
ten atmospheres. Looking over the edge, he gazed down
into the bottomless, lightning-shot blackness, a lost soul
staring into the depths of Hell itself.

There was no time to worry if his improvisation would
work. Clinging tightly to his belt, he stepped off the
edge.

The jolt almost knocked the belt from his grasp, but
his fall was checked almost at once. He dangled precari-
ously, clinging desperately to the belt wedged under his
armpits and encircling his chest, slung from the three
arms of the improvised harness. Above him, three
Stormriders spread their wings, dimly seen, ghostlike in
the reflected light from the city as they shared their
load. Vince weighed 450 pounds in Jupiter's gravity; his
suit and breathing gear added perhaps 60 more. With
each Stormrider supporting 170 of those pounds, they
mounted slowly with heavy, labored flaps of those
mighty wings.

Vince glanced down. Below his dangling feet, the city
of Vrahk'dreleschaah continued its fall, picking up speed
as the last of the hydrogen supporting it escaped into
the surrounding air through a rent in the gasbag that
extended from rim to rim. Listing, like a ship sinking in

an Earthly sea, it began to roll over, rotating until it was
upside down, falling faster and faster under Jupiter's
relentless pull. Vince followed it with his eyes as the city
dwindled . . . dwindled . . .

At the last moment, he thought he saw something like
a puff of silvery sparks, dust motes swirling about that
falling tomb.

And then it was gone. Crushed, torn apart by greater-
than-hurricane winds, fried by temperatures hot enough
to melt lead . . . Vince never did see what finally
destroyed the city in the Jovian Deep.

He knew only that the Charonian invaders trapped in
the city as it fell would not rise from those depths again.

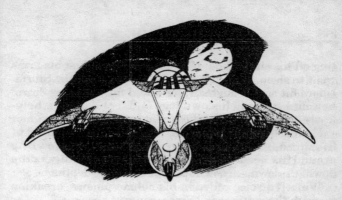

CHAPTER TWENTY

The air must have been thick and uncomfortably hot for creatures used to the rarer atmosphere a few miles higher. The three Stormriders bearing Vince aloft struggled to stay airborne. At any moment, wings could fail, plunging all four of them into the inferno of Jupiter's depths.

"If you can't hold me," Vince yelled, "just let go! Please, don't kill yourselves!"

But they didn't understand Anglic, and the three seemed possessed of an unstoppable will. They moved with perfect coordination, and Vince realized that one of them must be counting off the beat to the others on their inner radios. They would never have managed the feat otherwise. Still struggling against wind and gravity, they mounted higher, assisted now by a rising gust of hot air that seemed to funnel skyward in the wake of the fallen city.

In his ears the Voice of God shrieked and thundered.

Pain gnawed at his arms. He weighed five hundred ten pounds, counting his helmet and gear. The lightweight suit did nothing to protect him from his utility belt where it circled under his armpits and around his chest, cutting into him like a vise. He was having trouble breathing against the strap's pressure, and his hands were tingling, a sure sign that the sling was cutting off his circulation. If he lost his hold when his arms went to sleep, if he just got jolted hard when the Stormriders hit some rough air, he would fall. Looking down, he could see only his own legs and feet dangling helplessly above black emptiness.

He felt light-headed, a little dizzy. Vertigo teased at his mind, growing stronger like the wind howling around his head. He was going to fall, an endless drop down . . . down . . . down into the crushing depths. . . .

"Vince!" a voice called in his helmet phones, breaking through the static roar. "Vince, can you hear me?"

It was Kaiten, and he sounded worried. "I—I . . . hear. . . ." He was having trouble speaking against the crushing pressure across his chest.

"Hang on!"

Was Kaiten trying to be funny? What did the Terrine think he was trying to do? "I don't have . . . much choice."

"Hang on! Help is coming!"

Help? What help? He could see the blue-white flame of Kaiten's Krait in the distance, circling Vince's position, but there was no way the fighter could slow to a hover, no way that Vince could climb aboard. A planet with no solid surface to land on did have its inconvenient aspects.

At this point, Vince wasn't sure what was going to happen next. He'd conceived this plan in desperation, the only way he could think of to get both Marlene Kowalski and himself off the city. But the next nearest city was something like five hundred miles away; it seemed the sheer scale of Jupiter was going to defeat him at last. The Stormriders carrying him must be exhausted after their struggle to bring him up from the depths. Surely it would be impossible for them to drag him all the way to the next city. Possibly they had called for another manta, but how long would it take the flying beast to get here?

Too long. Even if the Stormriders could support him for hours against Jupiter's killer gravity, he doubted that he could hold on for more than a few more minutes. It was hopeless.

His helmet readout showed an external temperature of 110 degrees Fahrenheit, an air pressure of five point six atmospheres. They were rising, the trio of Storm-riders circling on enormous wings that eclipsed stars and moons and the thin, hard streak of Jupiter's rings.

At five atmospheres, the external temperature read eighty degrees. They were back at the original altitude of the city. The night sky, viewed from the bottom of the cloud canyon, seemed unnaturally bright. Moonlight illuminated the cloud tops, edging them with the colors of ice, soft and pale and cold. Beyond, the aurorae danced in silent beauty. A meteor blazed across heaven.

And then, something else eclipsed stars and moon-painted clouds, something enormous and black. As Vince stared at the apparition, trying to pick out its shape from the way it obscured the sky, he gasped and nearly lost his hold on the sling.

It was a manta, or something very like one, identical, save that it had no tail, to the manta rays of Earth's oceans. Twin prongs jutted from its blunt head like horns, and its triangular wings supported a broad, flat-tened body.

And it was huge! Vince had no way of estimating scale until Kaiten's Krait cut between him and the thing's head, and then he realized that this black apparition must measure half a mile from wingtip to wingtip.

A mouth was opening on the underside of its head, well back from the horns and visible against the black of the monster's shadowed underside as a blacker empti-ness, a gaping maw like the cavern "mouth" that fed a Stormrider city. A translucent bladder or canopy grew from its back, like a city's floatation sac; was that what was holding it up? It was moving swiftly, its wings not flapping at all, so it was either soaring on air currents or held aloft by hot hydrogen.

It was coming for him.

Vince screamed and nearly let go but managed to cling tight as Kaiten's voice sounded in his helmet. "Hold on, Vince! They're here to rescue you!"

Vince could feel the violence of the monster's passage

through the air, a shuddering vibration like the hammer of a rocket engine. The mouth, clearly visible now as the monster picked up a sheen of light reflected from the cloud tops, gaped wider . . . wider . . . then swallowed Vince and the three Stormriders, like minute flecks of food engulfed by a whale.

○ ○ ○ ○ ○

"Battle stations! Battle stations!" The amplified voice echoed through the passageways of the cruiser-sized vessel *Free Enterprise*. "All hands move your tails. We got a definite target-rich environment up here."

Capt. Thomas Jefferson Carter made his way toward the *Enterprise*'s bridge, scowling as he was forced to squeeze past pirate crewmen dashing for their action stations. Carter disliked pirates and disliked having to work with them, but NEO had assigned him to the *Enterprise* as military liaison to NEO's new allies. He didn't have to like that, either.

The bridge of the *Free Enterprise* was relatively spacious as warship command centers went, modern and surprisingly well-equipped for a vessel that made its living plundering other ships. It was dominated by the thronelike eminence of a command chair, and seated in the chair was the huge—six-foot-plus—frame of the vessel's commander, Black Barney.

"Hello, Carter," Barney said, his voice a chest-deep rumble. "You might like to see this."

Black Barney—he had no other name than that—was a cyborg, a superhuman blending of organically grown flesh and blood and an interior skeleton of titanium alloys and machine-deadly reflexes. Carter knew little about him, save that he was a survivor of a RAM-supervised genetics experiment gone wrong. For better than twenty years, Barney and a handful of his "brother" cyborgs had ranged the spaceways as pirates.

Barney in particular, widely acknowledged as the closest thing the Rogues' Guild had to a genuine leader, had a searing dislike for RAM. He had been instrumental in fomenting an alliance between the Rogues' Guild and NEO, after having been recruited by no less a person than Buck Rogers himself. Pirate no longer, Black Barney and the riffraff loyal to him were now privateers in the service of NEO.

Privateers, right, Carter thought. There was a fine legal distinction between pirates and privateers. Pirates were bandits; privateers were mercenaries operating under a letter of marque issued by a legitimate government, charged with raiding the other fellow's fleets and shipping. With few capital ships, NEO had little in the way of a space force of its own; issuing a letter of marque to Black Barney and other prominent leaders of the Rogues' Guild had been the only way that NEO could even think about seriously challenging RAM on the high ground of space.

Carter was still not sure whether or not the agreement had been a colossal mistake, a diplomatic blunder that put NEO on the same moral plane as the pirates.

In any case, Carter still didn't trust Barney, even though he had to admit the pirate had been instrumental in the recent, successful raid on the RAM base at Phobos, and he'd taken part in the space battle at Ciudestreya that had liberated the Artifact. Now he was commander of the fleet sent to rescue the team of NEO agents caught up in the mysterious events taking place in Jupiter space. Long-range scans of the planet had shown the arrival of unidentified craft maneuvering with unheard-of acceleration, and the arrival and departure of a vessel larger than the largest RAM battler.

Just what the hell was going on out here?

Carter approached the 3-D tank, a holographic bridge display representing an immense volume of surrounding space, with Jupiter an orange-sized sphere at the center circled by a confusion of rings marking the orbits of its satellites. Ships drifted slowly, each color-coded and accompanied by tiny blocks of data. Red ships were RAM and included remnants of the *Syrtis Major* battlefleet plus a second combat group centered on the battler *Olympus Mons*, at least thirty ships all together. Near

Callisto, outermost of the four planet-sized Jovian moons, a smaller fleet was marked in tiny arrowheads of orange, while a similar fleet circled Io, picked out in blue. The Callistan and Ionian navies were reacting to the invasion like hornet's nests stirred by a stick.

Green arrowheads inbound near the orbit of Carme, fourteen million miles from Jupiter, marked the *Enterprise* and thirteen other pirates—no, not pirates, Carter corrected himself wryly—privateers.

It was clear that the NEO-pirate fleet was badly outnumbered. They'd arrived in Jupiter space in response to the frantic call from another pirate vessel, the *Dread Reprisal*. The *Reprisal*'s report was fragmentary at best; they'd left Amalthea when first a RAM cruiser, then a RAM battlefleet had approached. Then the RAM force had been scattered by unknown invaders, but now, as *Free Enterprise* approached the moon, it appeared that the invaders had already fled, and that RAM vessels were again arriving in force.

They could expect no help from the populations of any of the inhabited Jovian satellites, either. Io was run by a small plutocracy that sold power to the other Jovian colonies, Callisto by the authoritarian regime of that moon's arcologies and ice-locked citadels. Both worlds had powerful navies, but neither had any love for outsiders—RAM, NEO, or pirate. As for Ganymede and Europa, their inhabitants were gennies tailored to live in those moons' ice-capped planetary oceans; they rarely even saw their skies, much less concerned themselves with what happened in them.

"Looks like we may be too late," Barney said from his bridge command chair as he studied the 3-D. "RAM's got twice our strength, and God knows which way the damned Ionians and Callistans're gonna jump."

"Have we heard from RAM yet?" Carter wanted to know.

"They challenged us. Right now, though, we're having 'communications difficulties' until we know what the hell's going on."

Carter pointed, his finger sinking into the three-dimensional illusion close to the flattened sphere of Jupiter. "My God! What's that?"

A yellow star, indicating a ship, had appeared close beside Jupiter, rising toward space. The data strip beside it consisted of a single word: UNKNOWN.

"Hello," Barney said, leaning forward in his seat. "Looks like we have new players in the game."

The mystery ship was entering Jupiter orbit.

○ ○ ○ ○ ○

They called the ship *Vah T'chahk*, a phrase that Kowalski told Vince meant *"Messenger of God."* It was, in its own way, a Jovian manta, grown from the genes of various life-forms including manta rays and the vast descendants of terrestrial Portuguese men-of-war that were the genetic basis for the Stormriders' floating cities.

The *Vah T'chahk* was actually a small Jovian city with a 'rider population of several hundred. More maneuverable by far than any balloon city, it functioned like a titanic ramjet, sucking in air through distended ventral slits, heating it, and expelling it through a quartet of fluted cones located where the creature's tail should have been. Much of its interior was designed to cool and compress hydrogen or other gases to liquid and hold them as a fuel reserve.

The *Messenger of God* was, in fact, a Jovian spaceship.

A living spaceship, as alive as the Jovian cloud cities. Vince learned that Stormrider geneticists—possibly the best geneticists in the Solar System—had been working to create an organic spaceship for decades. They'd had the covert help of a number of outsiders, Aerostaters like Kowalski for the most part, but others as well from Earth, the Belt, and even Mars.

Once he'd untangled himself from his harness and been led from the blackness of the ship-creature's mouth, he found the huge vessel's interior well-lit and comfortable. Like other artifacts of Stormrider science, the *Messenger* was a blend of organics and technology.

TV monitors and computer displays were mounted to what was obviously the monster's flesh; power cables snaked through conduits and across glistening overheads, but whether they were organic or manufactured was impossible to tell. Vince easily recognized the Venusians' hands in the project simply by glancing at the trademarks on the electronics equipment. All had been manufactured on Venus and no doubt had been shipped to Jupiter by Aerostater traders.

One room had been sealed off behind an air lock and given an atmosphere breathable by humans. There Vince had found Kowalski waiting for him. Kaiten joined them moments later, after the Terrine's Krait was scooped into the cavern of the creature's mouth.

Liquid-filled acceleration couches had offered relief from the incessant drag of Jupiter's gravity. Then, minutes later, his weight had increased as the giant creature accelerated. Almost half an hour later, all weight had blissfully vanished as the supermanta's jets had cut off and they'd gone into free fall. They were in orbit.

"You are impressed?" Kowalski asked, watching Vince's expression with a wry grin.

Vince reached out one hand to steady himself as he bobbed against a bulkhead in zero G. "Impressed? Hardly. Stunned is more like it." He'd heard rumors of experiments aimed at something like this but hadn't dreamed that anyone was close to making it reality. "But I can't help wondering one thing. Why?"

"Why should the Stormriders want to reach space?" She shrugged. "Until they win the independence of space, their freedom as a species is hardly secure. With their own ships they will not need to rely on others, on outsiders for the goods they need to survive."

Vince could understand that, but the idea was a disquieting one. Humans seemed like such small, pallid things alongside the golden splendor of a Stormrider. If the two species should clash in the future, in economic competition, even in outright war, which, he wondered, would win?

He didn't want to place any bets on that one. In the

Stormriders, man might well have engineered his own replacement.

Or had he done so in the experiments that had led to the invaders of Charon? That was the immediate problem, and he pulled his thoughts from the Stormriders' possible futures to the immediate task at hand.

For a long moment, Vince studied the computer displays, watching the hesitant movements of at least four separate fleets. Those approaching low over Jupiter's limb had to be RAM; the battler and the sheer numbers were dead giveaways. The smaller fleets probably represented forces from Jupiter's major satellites, while that squadron hanging in the outskirts of the Jovian system was almost certainly either a pirate force, or ships under joint NEO-pirate command, the privateer fleet of NEO's new and uncertain allies.

"What do we do now?" Kaiten asked. The Terrine's hands flexed at his sides, as though he was readying for a fight. "Looks like we're just in time to watch them kill each other."

"Yeah," Vince said. "Let's see if we can stop that, shall we? Can you get me a five-way radio hookup here, Doctor? With visuals?"

"Of course." She touched some panels on the console beside her couch. "Give me a moment to make contact." She frowned. "Those guys out by Carme are seventy-five light seconds away. Round-trip time lag of two and a half minutes."

"Just set it up. A little time lag's just fine. It'll let me say what I have to say without being interrupted."

As Vince waited, he thought about the invaders, striking out of the depths of the Outer Dark, far from the warmth and the light of Sol. Hostile, implacable, they'd struck viciously at the population of little Amalthea, then at the Jovian city of Vrahk'dreleschaah.

He'd already heard a full report from the survivors in Amalthea, during the *Messenger*'s ascent to orbit. The invaders—most of them, at any rate—were gone. It had been too much to hope that the ruse with the radio message would snare every individual of that huge silver

horde, but the survivors were few, scattered, and disorganized. Very likely, Vince thought, their leader or leaders had been destroyed in the fall of Vrahk'dreleschaah.
Those left in Amalthea or in Jupiter orbit were proving
to be relatively easy to mop up.

But there was bad news, too. He knew now that
Jovanna and Galen both had been taken, along with the
admiral commanding RAM's *Syrtis Major* battle group
and almost eight hundred other people, most of them
civilians.

Why?

If there was an answer, it lay somewhere on Charon,
on the frigid moon of ice and methane frost that had
spawned these monstrous invaders from the wreckage of
an ancient Terran probe. The only way to find it was to
go there, to Charon, four billion miles out from the Sun.
Men had never ventured so far into the Outer Dark,
never. To try to do it as a military expedition, with multiple, warring factions against a technologically superior
enemy on his home ground . . .

Ridiculous!

But Vince saw no alternative. If they waited and did
nothing, the invaders would be back, in greater numbers
than ever, possibly with new and greater technologies
undreamed of by mere humans.

And if they did nothing, Jovanna and the others
would be lost, abandoned to God knew what grim fate.

"You have your channel," Kowalski told him, as four
screens lit up on the bulkhead above Kowalski's console,
each with a different face. "The commanders of the Ionian and Callistan navies, Adm. Andre Lysenko of Battlefleet *Olympus Mons*, and Black Barney of the NEO-Guild
privateers. They all, ah, are rather eager to talk to you,
Major. Remember the two-minute time lag with the privateers."

"I'll remember."

Stepping into the pick-up range of the communication
center's camera, he began to speak.

CHAPTER TWENTY-ONE

How long had it really been? Jovanna paced the black, rough-surfaced floor just behind the prison barrack's solitary door, and wondered.

There were no watches left among the six hundred fifty-two surviving prisoners, no personal computers, no electronics of any kind. Even the circuits woven into various smart garments had been ripped out, as though their captors had feared even the smallest and simplest technological artifact. Jovanna was wearing a light—and nonelectronic—jacket given to her by a female RAM officer. That had been aboard the Silver Ship, just after a silver-tentacled horror had shredded the upper half of her jumpsuit to remove its heating elements, communications' wiring, and controls. Many others in the barracks were wearing mismatched articles of borrowed clothing as well. Those prisoners with computerless clothing had shared with the others. Most of the RAM troopers who'd been captured wearing combat armor had nothing left but their underwear and suit padding.

Of course, by this point, even Admiral Singh's uniform was little more than a collection of stinking, muddy rags. There was not enough water for the prisoners to wash themselves, much less their clothing. Guesses at the length of their confinement so far, ranged from five weeks to ten. Galen, who had a Tinker's inborn time

sense insisted that they'd been aboard the Silver Ship
for thirty-nine days, and in this place for six.

Turning from the massive, circular door, she surveyed
the room. It was as large as a small sports stadium, but
with over six hundred people huddled along its walls it
seemed claustrophobically crowded. It was dark, too.
There was a single light, a glowing plate or window of
some kind set in the middle of the high, vaulted ceiling,
but the black walls seemed to drink the light like a
sponge, leaving the prisoners in near total darkness.
Most sat or sprawled in close, wet, miserable huddles.
Somewhere in the crowd, someone was crying. Someone
else coughed, a wet, nasty hack that suggested pneumo-
nia. It might not be too long before disease started thinning their ranks. Ninety-two had died already from
sickness, including the woman who'd given her the coat.
Jovanna had never been able to learn her name.

She folded her arms across her chest and shivered.
The ship had been terrifying. This place was far worse.

They called their new home the "Barracks" or, more
often, "the Black Hole." Cut from native rock, a carbonaceous material the consistency and color of soft coal, the
walls and floors were wet, constantly seeping and coated
with an inky, near-liquid clay that covered everything
and everyone. An eye-watering stink of ammonia waft-
ing from the walls masked the stench of bodies gone too
long unwashed. That had actually proven to be a small
blessing; after the first day or two in the Hole, Jovanna
had stopped noticing the foul smell that had accompanied them from the ship.

Where were they now? Assuming the invaders had
kept the alien vessel's acceleration at two-tenths of a G,
as she'd insisted back in Amalthea, and assuming
Galen's time sense was correct, they were something
like forty astronomical units from Jupiter.

That meant Pluto—or possibly Charon, Pluto's moon.
The gravity here was a lot less than the acceleration
they'd felt aboard ship. Frank Kendall, who'd been third
navigation officer aboard the *Syrtis Major*, after endlessly dropping chips of soft black rock over carefully

estimated distances and timing their fall, had just announced that the local gravity was something like eight inches per second squared . . . or about two-hundredths of a G. That suggested that they were, in fact, on Charon. Without their computers, no one in the group could remember the exact figures, but Pluto's gravity was thought to be a bit more, perhaps as much as five-hundredths of a G.

Kendall's discovery had plunged all of the survivors into a new and deepening gloom. Charon! That meant they were almost four billion miles from home, a good three billion miles from the nearest human outposts among the cold and lonely moons of Saturn.

Never had a party of human beings been so isolated, so alone. Any distinction between RAM and NEO was meaningless here.

"Are you okay, Jovanna?"

She turned. "Hello, Sergei. You don't really want me to answer that, do you?"

Lt. Sergei Bruckner was another of the RAM officers who had more or less taken charge of the prisoner group. A young, good-looking man beneath the smear of black grime masking his features, he had been a fire control officer aboard the *Syrtis Major* and attached to Admiral Singh's personal staff in Amalthea. He'd been born and raised on a homestead farm not far from the Boreal Sea on Mars, less than fifty miles from the outpost where Jovanna had grown up. That unlikely discovery had created, if not a friendship, then at least a shared bit of past.

"Ah, don't worry," Sergei said, his teeth startlingly white through the muck obscuring his face. "Our people'll be out here in no time and smash these damned robot monsters into spare parts. You just wait!"

Jovanna smiled, unwilling, unable to tell Sergei what she really thought their chances were. Had anyone tracked the Silver Ship as it departed Amalthea? Had anyone figured out its destination? Even if someone had guessed where they were being held now, did it make even one scrap of difference? Their captors, cold, machine-precise, utterly inhuman, possessed a near-magical technology that even RAM could not hope to match. Even if RAM did send a fleet after them—an unlikely possibility at best—the chances of that force finding and rescuing the dwindling group of prisoners was so close to zero as to make no difference at all.

"I hope you're right, Sergei," she said. "If they're coming, they'd better come soon."

"Yeah. Uh, listen. Have you asked them about, well, about what's happening to us?"

She sighed. Somehow, the invaders seemed to have chosen her as a liaison between prisoners and captors. Unfortunately, that made her the one that the others, even Singh, looked to for answers. And there were no answers, none that mattered now, anyway.

"I've asked them, Sergei," she said. "They always say the same thing. We're being 'mapped,' and I can't get them to tell me exactly what that means."

He nodded. "Like they're measuring us, huh? That doesn't sound so bad. I just wonder why they're doing it to all of us, one at a time."

Jovanna looked toward the round, vaultlike door. And why the ones they take never come back, she thought, but she refused to say it out loud. Sergei followed her gaze but seemed to think she was looking not at the door, but at Galen.

The Tinker, his silky fur matted and coated with mud, was lying flat on his belly next to the metal frame that supported the door. His attention was totally focused on a small piece of wall a foot from the edge of the frame and six inches above the floor.

"Old Galen's really going at it," Sergei said. "You think he's got a chance?"

"I don't know," she replied truthfully. "He usually knows what he's talking about, though. Surely it can't hurt to try."

Galen had not been wearing his utility belt when he'd been captured, since he'd already been a prisoner of RAM. Like his RAM captors, however, the invaders had also overlooked the hairpin he'd kept hidden in his fur.

The Tinker had been using it since they'd been transferred to the Hole, rasping it for hour upon hour against the soft rock of their prison in a four-inch circle at a precisely measured point on the wall. He claimed to be able to sense a current flow at that spot, and Jovanna didn't doubt him. As with his time sense, Galen possessed a number of genetically engineered senses that humans lacked or knew only as vaguely felt hunches or intuition.

But if the Tinker could dig a hole through to the cables that fed the door's electrical power, what then? Six hundred humans with no guns and no space suits were not likely to manage much of a revolt against an unknown but very large number of machine intelligences on a hostile, poisonous, frigid world four billion miles from home.

Jovanna could hear the tiny *chink-chink-chink* of Galen's rasping. Which, she wondered, would wear away first, the hairpin or the rock?

"Guess I'll spell the Tinker a bit," Sergei said. "Talk to you later, Jo. And, hey! Try not to worry, okay? We'll see you through this, never you fear!"

She couldn't help smiling at Sergei's boyish optimism as he made his way over to Galen's side. One of the strangest things she'd learned during her captivity was that RAM personnel—most of them, anyway, were decent people.

Had someone told her a month before that she could become friends with RAM military officers, she would have laughed . . . or gotten angry, she wasn't sure which. RAM was the most vicious tyranny man had known throughout his tyranny-plagued history, and she'd dedicated more than twenty years of her life to fighting RAM with every means at her disposal.

But, then, the only RAM that most NEO troops or agents ever saw was the hard and authoritarian RAM, the soldiers, bureaucrats, and Internal Revenue agents, the enforcers of Internal Security, the cold-blooded killers of the Space Assault Corps, the savage Terrines of the Biomechanical Assault Forces. It was hard to think of any of that lot as people, much less as someone you would want to know or talk to or share a meal with.

The prisoners fell into two groups, the three hundred or so Amalthean civilians and militia who'd been scooped up by the invaders when they took the Strip, and the RAM personnel—space force officers and men, marine troopers, and administrators—who'd been captured with them. Jovanna had been surprised to find that she fitted in better with the RAM prisoners. The Amaltheans wavered between listless apathy and shrill hysteria, often punctuated by demands that their captors set them free or loud pleadings that what was happening to them simply wasn't fair.

The RAM personnel, on the other hand, were quieter, better disciplined, more competent, and more professional about the situation, which was why they'd assumed the leadership of the group. Their military discipline had been vital for the prisoners' survival so far, ensuring that food and water were shared equally among all, making certain that wastes were disposed of in the buckets provided by their captors, and organizing such mundane duties as caring for the sick and running an inventory on who possessed which possibly useful skills. They'd even begun organizing an escape committee, just in case Galen's scratchings led somewhere. Jovanna identified with them, even liked some of them, and that had been perhaps the biggest surprise she'd encountered in a very surprising month and a half.

Mohar Singh, she'd learned in the course of several long conversations, had indeed been born on Earth, a Sikh from the crowded arcology at Punjab. He'd joined RAM's space force and risen through the ranks because he honestly believed, as far as Jovanna could tell, that Earth's best hope for survival was to have its economy, its population, and its pillaged resources managed by offworlders. It was painfully clear, he contended, that the planet's inhabitants would never be able to manage things for themselves. Others, like Sergei Bruckner and Frank Kendall and the woman who'd given Jovanna her jacket, were RAM because they were Martians, an accident of birth. They didn't necessarily care for the heavy-handed authoritarianism, might not even like what was happening to Earth, but they were serving RAM because it was their career, the way they earned their incomes and their educations and got to see some of the Solar System before settling down again on Mars or Earth or someplace else.

The realization that her RAM enemies were people like her had shaken Jovanna a lot more than she'd cared to admit, even now. It seemed strange that, after two decades of service as a NEO agent, living and working undercover within RAM society and government, only now and here had she learned that RAM citizens weren't that different from her after all. The government might be evil, a monstrous wrong that had to be brought down and destroyed, but the ordinary people were . . . people, individuals very much like Jovanna Trask.

Galen settled to the floor at her side. "The cut's almost half an inch deep," he said. "I don't think we'll have to dig much deeper."

The Tinker, usually clean and meticulously groomed, looked like a single four-foot clot of wet and matted hair. Tinkers, she knew, enjoyed enclosed spaces more than did humans, so the confinement of the past weeks had probably not grated on his nerves as it had on everyone else. But Tinkers also hated being wet and dirty; Galen must be suffering as much in this black hell as any of the full humans were.

"And then what?" she asked. Despite Sergei's attempts to cheer her up, she was still depressed, possessed by a claustrophobic loneliness and isolation despite the crowding in the room. "Any ideas yet?"

The Tinker shrugged, looking away. "Whatever happens then, it's got to be better than just sitting here, waiting for them to take us away one or two at a time."

She had to admit that he was right.

During the trip from Amalthea—for thirty-nine long days if Galen's reckoning was accurate—their machine captors had mingled with them every day. Many encounters were unpleasant, such as when they'd begun stripping people of their belongings and the smart circuits in their clothing, but most had shown at least some level of concern for the prisoners' well-being.

Jovanna, in her capacity as spokesperson for the prisoners, had been able to convince their captors to provide many things that they needed. The two-tenths G limit on acceleration had been an important victory for them, as had the concession that humans would not be taken into vacuum. They'd been given food—or at least a thick, gray paste that seemed to take care of nutritional needs —and water; light, what there was of it, anyway; air that was breathable despite the stench; buckets for waste, called "honey pots" by some of the RAM troopers; and a climate that, while a bit on the chilly side, was tolerable.

Once they'd arrived here, however, and been moved from the Silver Ship to the Black Hole, the mingling had stopped. Machines still provided for their needs. Small, shape-shifting machines that were thought to be servants of some kind still appeared every few hours, leaving buckets of food and water and removing the honey pots. But the other machines, the larger ones that grew disturbingly human mouths on odd surfaces of their bodies, now appeared only to select a prisoner and drag him or her away.

They came every couple of hours or so. Their selection appeared completely random, and no explanation was ever given, beyond the curt mention of a need to "map the humans." Worse by far, none of the people taken had ever returned. In the six days since they'd arrived, almost a hundred people had been taken, sometimes singly, usually in groups of two or three. It was a new and mind-wracking torture added to the stresses of captivity and isolation that threatened to drive all of them mad. Jovanna could feel the mounting tension, the desperation that hung over the miserable roomful of prisoners thicker than the ammonia stench from the walls.

Something clicked behind the thick, circular white door, and Jovanna heard a hum of power. Sergei, lying next to it, scrambled clear and got to his feet just as the door slid open. A blast of cold air swirled into the room

rom the near-total darkness outside, and a trio of
nvaders entered.

The prisoners crowded back, murmuring among
hemselves. They'd already learned that it was futile to
ry to rush these creatures. Twelve had died in three
arlier attempts. Squat and boxy on varying numbers of
tubby legs, two of the invaders flanked the open door,
vhile the third, larger one oozed into the chamber, flow-
ng snaillike on its rippling lower surface.

A mouth appeared high up on the big one's body.
Imperative immediate, select one Type 1, one Type 2.
'urpose: continued mapping of humans." A pseudopod
;rew from its side, molding itself into a horrifying fac-
imile of a human arm.

Were these monsters learning how to manufacture
.uman body parts from their "mapping" sessions with
heir prisoners?

The arm lashed out, grabbing Sergei by the muddy
uin of his uniform tunic. "No!" he screamed, thrashing
.nd trying to scramble away, but the machine did not
eem to notice his struggles. A second arm grew, per-
ectly formed down to fingernails and creases at the
.acks of the knuckles. For one nightmarish moment,
'ovanna thought it was going to reach for her, because
he was closer to the monster than anyone else except
or the wildly kicking Sergei.

But the arm roughly shoved her aside, reached behind
.er, and plucked a young Amalthean woman from her
eat against the wall. The woman shrieked, her screams
•lending with Sergei's as she clawed desperately at the
.and grasping what was left of her shirt. Jovanna
aunched herself at the thing, beating at it, but it
gnored her and slithered out the door, followed closely
•y its two escorts. The door slid shut with a hollow
•oom, cutting off the victims' screams.

For a long moment, the room was deathly silent. Then
he sobbing that Jovanna had heard earlier began again,
.ccompanied now by three or four others.

Galen walked over to the door. His hairpin, sharpened
.ow to a bright point and twisted into an odd shape, was

still there, lying in the black mud. Without another word, he lay down, picked up the pitiful tool, and began again scraping away at their prison wall.

Jovanna slumped down at his side. There seemed to be nothing more they could do.

CHAPTER TWENTY-TWO

The RAM-NEO alliance, forged in Jupiter orbit fifteen days before, was still shaky, but it had brought them clear to the very boundary of the Solar System.

Vince stood above the 3-D tank in *Messenger of God*'s Combat Command Center, a human-habitable suite of rooms more popularly referred to simply as "Cee-three." With him were Kowalski and a half dozen NEO communications personnel, plus two Stormriders, ungainly in their masks and life-support packs. Comm screens, both 2- and 3-D, flickered and glowed, and there was a low background murmur of voices as the fleet deployed for battle.

Within the tank Vince could see the full extent of the First Solar Expeditionary Force, a great, sprawling convoy of vessels, each ship identified by color and by computer data lines. Never in the bloody expanse of the history of humankind had there been such an armada. In numbers alone it was not that spectacular—fewer than 250 vessels were taking part, compared with, say, the better than four thousand seagoing vessels that had participated in the D-Day landings at Normandy five centuries earlier—but the Expeditionary Force was unique in the annals of human warfare, if only because forces that had been bitter enemies only days before were joined now as allies against a common foe.

That RAM and NEO had even considered forming a joint fleet was an indication of just how badly the governments of the Inner System had been shaken by the events at Jupiter. That the fleet was reality, decelerating now on the last leg of its one-G, fifteen-day run from Jupiter to Pluto, was nothing short of a miracle.

Vince wanted to believe that it was he who'd made the alliance possible by delivering his impassioned speech from the *Messenger of God* in Jupiter orbit, but after the first few weeks of wrangling at the Amalthean Conference it had become clear that Adm. Mohar Singh, one of the hostages taken by the invaders, had had the idea first. Hours before the invaders had arrived in force, it turned out, Singh had discussed with his superiors on Mars the need for a RAM-NEO truce and a military alliance, and the destruction of the *Syrtis Major* battle group soon after had galvanized the RAM hierarchy into action. By the time Vince had contacted them from the *Messenger of God*, the decision had already been made.

It needed only the Amalthean Conference to formalize the agreement.

Things had not been quite that easy, of course. There was a long and bitter history of hatred between RAM and the rebellious, would-be government of NEO; hotheads on both sides either refused to consider allying with the enemy or seemed all too ready to use the situation as an opportunity to gain military intelligence or to launch a sneak attack under the cover of a truce.

It had been rough, but in less than one week, most of the details had been hammered out.

First, the Truce of Amalthea would last only for the duration of the Charon emergency. Many on both sides hoped that the truce might be extended after that, that it might even become the basis for a lasting peace, but that seemed unlikely as long as hawks, both NEO and RAM, continued to argue for a military settlement to NEO's revolution.

Second, each government contributing ships to the First Solar Expeditionary Force would maintain control over its own forces. No NEO commander in his right mind would put his squadron under the orders of a RAM fleet admiral—this was supposed to be an alliance, not a surrender! And on the other side, RAM, which was contributing the majority of the fleet's ships, would never let NEO pirate scum direct RAM ships in battle! The divided command was tailor-made to lead to mass confusion both before and during operations at Charon, but there was no acceptable compromise. Grand Admiral Chernikov would command the RAM contingent, while the NEO forces were under the overall command of Gen. Ian Stuart.

And, finally, strategy was supposed to be determined by meetings among the leaders of all of the participating squadrons, though no one expected more than lip service to that one. RAM might suggest tactics—as might any of the force commanders present in the fleet, but suggestions were bound to be ignored by anyone who didn't care for them.

Vince shook his head as he watched the fleets deploying. It was going to be high-tech, guns-loaded chaos.

"You don't approve, Major?" Kowalski asked from the other side of the tank.

"It's not really for me to approve, is it? But it's a little scary knowing the survival of the human race could be at stake here today, and on our team, none of the players is talking to anyone else. Damn it, at least we should have a plan!"

"According to Chernikov, there won't be room for any fancy tactical coordination anyway," Kowalski observed. "Quick, hard and brutal. Either we clean them out, or, well, maybe it's time for a change in the way the system's being run anyway, eh?"

Typical RAM tactics, in other words. Pile on the firepower until the other guy cries quit.

"We can't afford to lose this one, Marlene," Vince said. "It's the whole human race at risk if this doesn't go down right." Not to mention Jovanna and Galen and hundreds of others being held down there somewhere, he thought. I wonder if they know we're here, if they know what kind of fleet they've launched?

At the far end of the tank, Pluto and Charon glowed frosty blue-white. Pluto was eighteen hundred miles across, Charon a third that, and the two orbited one another at a distance of twelve thousand miles, a true double planet. In the tank, they looked like a golf ball and a marble spaced a foot apart. The Expeditionary Force was approaching from the opposite side of the tank, from sunward, still over a hundred thousand miles out.

There were actually eight fleets present. Red was for RAM, of course, and the vast majority of the ships visible in the tank were represented by glowing red sparks.

RAM's navy, the Space Assault Corps, was divided into five major fleets. One of these was theoretically based permanently in Jupiter space, though it usually was divided into a dozen squadrons patrolling anywhere between Saturn and the Asteroid Belt. The *Syrtis Major* battle group had been detached from the Jovian fleet, as had the *Olympus Mons*. Vince wondered what would have happened if the entire Jovian fleet had been present near Jupiter when the Charonian invaders arrived in force.

He was about to find out. During the weeks of the Amalthean Conference, RAM had brought all of the remaining elements of the far-flung Jovian fleet together in Jupiter space, and it was this force that now formed the backbone of the armada, taking the lead as it plunged toward Charon. It numbered 121 major ships, including five battlers and not counting the hordes of fighters not yet released from their launch bays. Grand Admiral Chernikov's flagship was the *Directrix*, an aging, Corporate-class battler two miles long and carrying a crew of fifteen hundred.

The NEO contingent, forty ships, was represented in blue, the largest of them roughly equivalent in firepower to a RAM medium cruiser. It was easy to see why the New Earth Organization was not yet able to challenge RAM directly for mastery of space; most of the NEO vessels were armed and reengined transports and freighters, or conversion jobs cobbled together from salvaged wrecks. *Republic*, a captured and renamed RAM medium cruiser, was the flag. Thirty-two more ships—larger, faster, and better armed on the whole than the NEO fleet—glowed blue-green, the color ID of the NEO-privateer squadron under Black Barney aboard his *Free Enterprise*.

The other squadrons consisted of only a handful of colored ship symbols for each: red-orange for Io and yellow-orange for Callisto; green for twelve converted merchantmen from the Asteroid Belt; violet and red-violet for the Ishtaran and Aerostater contingents from Venus; and three deep yellow-gold specks for the Sun King squadron. Vince wondered how the Mercurians were faring aboard those ships, so far from Sol and the warm heart of the Inner System.

One vessel was tagged white, the one-ship contingent from Jupiter, the *Messenger of God*. The Stormriders had positioned their lone ship with the NEO force, trailing the RAM fleet by a good fifty thousand miles.

"Impressive," a deep voice rumbled at Vince's back. Turning, he saw Kaiten entering Cee-three. The Terrine, impressive in his battle-scarred red-and-black combat armor, looked ready for war. "I wonder what Chernikov has in mind?"

"Winning the war by himself, I imagine," Vince replied. "He's positioned the RAM fleet in the vanguard, and they stopped decelerating a couple of minutes ago. They're in free-fall now, dropping straight for Charon at twenty miles a second."

"It might be better to wonder what the Charonians are planning," Kowalski pointed out. "It's been over six weeks since the Battle of Amalthea. Six weeks, for something that thinks as fast as a computer, is an eternity."

"We still don't know how they think," Vince said. "Maybe they didn't expect us to come gunning for them in their own backyard." He grinned. "Or maybe they expected us to show up an eon or two ago, computer time, got bored waiting for us, and evolved into something else!"

"Nice idea," Kowalski said, "but don't count on it. Their thought processes are a lot faster than ours, but their physical evolution is going to be constrained by the processes that affect it. They could mutate into something new overnight . . . or they could go on the way they are, unchanged for a billion years."

"I was joking, Doctor," Vince said.

Sometimes Kowalski could take what others said entirely too literally. He wondered if she'd picked up that trait by living too long with the somber and alien Stormriders. He'd spent a lot of time during the past month and a half wondering what it was that made Stormriders so different from the rest of humanity, apart from the obvious and purely physical strangeness of wings, metabolism, size, and the like. He'd finally decided what it was, too. Stormriders never laughed.

"The point is," he went on, "we don't know what to expect from them. That means we're going to have to wait and react to their first move, and that puts us at a bad disadvantage."

"You don't win battles by waiting on your enemy," Kaiten said. "Victory requires you take the initiative."

"Exactly." Vince was staring hard into the tank. The swarm of red lights was visibly closer to the Pluto-Charon pair now, almost to the center of the tank. "I wonder. . . ." Raising his left hand, he tapped out a key command on the keyboard strapped to his wrist.

Overhead, the small, lensed globe of a holofield projector winked on. A woman stood at Vince's side, her body transparent at first, then thickening to convincing solidity. Her features were achingly familiar; she looked like a young Jovanna Trask—Jovanna as she'd looked twenty years before.

"Hiya, Vince," the woman said. "Looks like the big show's about to start!"

"Hello, RW," Vince said.

RW—once she had been Rachel Wydlin—was no longer human. Twenty-one years before she'd been Jovanna's closest friend. Then she'd been captured and interrogated by RAM and most of her memories had been wiped. Jovanna had downloaded what was left of her friend's personality and mental patterns into computer memory. Now she was a digital personality, an electronic wraith that "lived," if that was the proper word, within the surreal, dreamworld universe of data storage, computer nodes, and telecommunications networks known as C-space.

Able to appear as a holographic projection wherever the appropriate equipment was available, RW could assume any form she chose, and for some reason she'd patterned her physical appearance after Jovanna, the Jovanna of two decades before—with short-cut, mousy hair and an anonymously plain face and figure.

Digital personalities needed lots of free memory to function in, far more than could usually be freed in a single computer system or spacecraft. When the Amalthean Conference had begun, however, Vince had contacted RW and had her transmit herself to Amalthea over a lasercom link from Trinity, the secret headquarters of NEO operations in the Belt. She existed now, light hours removed from the rest of C-space, in an isolated subset of the cyber-universe existing among the networked computers of seventy-two NEO and privateer ships, plus the *Messenger of God*.

"Need your point of view on something, RW," Vince said. "I'm wondering how likely it is that the Charonians might have layers upon layers of defenses."

"You mean will they keep something in reserve?" The image caught its lower lip between white, even teeth, and Vince felt another pang. She looked so much like Jovanna, right down to her mannerisms and facial expressions. *Jo, are you still alive?*

"Anything's possible," RW said after a brief interval. Vince assumed she'd spent the time consulting the volumes of data compiled on the invaders and stored within the databases of the NEO ships. "The Charon computer system must be extraordinarily complex, far more complex, in fact, than any human . . . more complex even than any human civilization. I estimate that it is functioning at a geloiabyte processing level. That's a trillion

trillion bytes of storage."

More powerful by far, in other words, than anything known to man.

"So you're saying they can do anything we can do, and more."

"Something like that," RW admitted. "However, I've been studying the Charonian invader strategies as reported at Amalthea and Jupiter, and I have noted a curious tendency toward a conservative, single-phase approach in their operations."

"Which means?"

"That the Charon system thinks in terms of one step at a time. It tries something, and if that doesn't work, it tries something else."

"Yeah," Vince said. "That's the impression I got watching them work. They went in with a kind of all-or-nothing strategy, no backups, and if they changed plans, everybody changed at once."

"Why would that be?" Kaiten wondered.

"It's not just systems—organic or machine—that evolve with time," Kowalski said. "Thinking has to evolve, too. It sounds like our Charon friends are still operating the way their ancestors did four centuries ago, even though their minds have grown far more complex."

"Well, it's something," Vince said. "And it gives us something to work with." He looked at RW. "Is the Artifact still okay?"

He'd suggested that the Artifact be taken from its hiding place in the Belt and brought along with the Expeditionary Force. Since the Charonians' interest in Amalthea appeared to have been somehow connected with the Artifact's brief sojourn there, he'd thought that it might be a useful bargaining or negotiation tool.

"Unchanged," RW said. "General Stuart has it lead-shielded and locked away in the vault aboard the *Republic*."

"Good. I don't think it can do any mischief there, and it'll be good to have it handy, just in case."

"What do you have in mind, Vince?"

"I'd rather not get into it just yet. How about patching

me through to General Stuart? Let's see what he has to say first."

Stuart, as was obvious from his rank, was not a navy man. He was a minor legend in NEO, however, for the land battles he'd waged against RAM on Earth, including both Tirich Mir in the Hindu Kush and the famous trap at Hassi al-Qattar in North Africa. He had a reputation as a brilliant tactician who refused to play by the rules, and he'd been first choice of the top NEO brass at the secret Earth-orbital headquarters called Salvation III for commander of the NEO contingent.

Stuart was a big, red-bearded man wearing the khaki dress uniform of NEO's ground forces. Though Vince was only a major and the time until combat began was growing short, Stuart accepted Vince's call personally, assuming that the younger man had a special insight into the invaders and their probable strategy.

"Thanks for talking to me, General," Vince began. "I'll keep it short. I was wondering, what are your immediate battle plans? I see in our tank that RAM is pulling way out ahead."

Stuart studied Vince for a moment, his eyes like pale-blue ice. "Aye, they've not consulted with us back here," he said, "but I'd guess that Chernikov is goin' for the old-time cavalry charge. He told us a few minutes ago to stay out from underfoot, an' I was giving some thought to hangin' back a bit. Wouldn't hurt to let RAM engage for a while and see where the enemy's weak points are."

"That's what I thought. General, may I suggest that, since we know what RAM's going to do, we shape our own plans accordingly?"

"What did you have in mind, lad?"

"Well, you'll agree that the NEO squadron won't add that much firepower to the equation, so I propose we act on RAM's initiative. While they're tangling with the invaders, we go straight for Charon."

The ice eyes widened slightly. "Straight into the jaws o' whatever defenses the beasties have down there?"

"We'll have to go in close sooner or later, sir, and I have reason to suspect that the Charonians won't be using a layered defense. The best time to crash their gates may be before RAM's assault forces knock themselves out against whatever defenses they do have."

"Aye, you're right," Stuart said, one hand tugging at his beard. "We stay out of RAM's way, let them block the heavy opposition while we head straight for the goal. Not bad."

"Of course, we don't know what the Callistans or the others will do."

"Hardly matters. They'll follow RAM's lead or carry out plans of their own. Either way, they'll make great diversions. Okay, Major. You've sold me. Now how were you thinking of incorporating that flying whale of yours in this brawl?"

They began discussing NEO's assault plan in detail.

CHAPTER TWENTY-THREE

The lead elements of the RAM contingent were within fifty thousand miles of Charon when the first enemy forces appeared. Rising like a swarm of gnats from the surface of the Plutonian moon, the machine forces numbered in the thousands . . . no, in the tens of thousands, each machine-ship-entity a dust mote gleaming bright silver in the depths of the *Messenger of God*'s holotank display.

So great were the Charonians' numbers that, in the tank, at least, they formed a shimmering, slightly hazy mass that seemed to be oozing out from behind the moon like some titanic, amoeboid organism. It was, Vince realized, as though the organization of a single invader machine—a formless mass composed of countless nano-technic units—was being repeated on a planet-sized scale. The invader mass showed definite signs of order and coherent thought as it spread flat pseudopods into space ahead of the RAM vanguard.

"Like human white cells," Kowalski observed as she floated next to Vince, watching the holotank. The NEO ships had cut their deceleration and were in free-fall now, dropping toward Charon at twelve miles per second. "Engulfing a foreign body."

"Let's hope they get indigestion," Vince observed wryly. The RAM vanguard was now scant seconds from contact with the Charonians, their formation resembling a gleaming red dagger striking for the mirror-polished reach of the invader mass.

One of the NEO communications officers looked up from her console. "*Olympus Mons* and *Tharsis* both report that they are within range," she said. "Fighters ready for launch."

"*Directrix* has just ordered weapons free," another tech added. "All RAM ships have been ordered to hold fire until the flag gives the word."

"It begins," Kaiten said.

"Pipe it through," Vince said. "Let us all hear."

At the touch of a switch, Cee-three was filled with the static-fogged rasp of dozens of voices calling to one another across the night.

"Red Leader, Red Five, *Olympus* battle group now engaged," one voice announced. Vince could hear the sharp edge of strain behind the words. "Multiple targets, multiple targets at two-nine-nine by zero-one-zero. Combat drones deployed. Missiles ready, locked and tracking."

"We copy, Red Five. You are go for release of Mark IIIs, repeat, you are go for launch."

"Roger on Mark III launch. Full spread, launch in three . . . two . . . one . . . Missiles away! Missiles away!

"We confirm launch, Red Five. *Tharsis* and *Utopia Planitia* stand by for multiple Solarflare release in three . . . two . . . one . . . Launch!"

Missiles traced slender threads across emptiness, and Vince found himself holding his breath as he stared at the racing, colored symbols. Mark IIIs were RAM long-range missiles with five hundred-kiloton nuclear warheads, powerful weapons usually reserved for planetary targets or large and unmaneuverable orbital facilities rather than enemy ships. Mark XC Solarflares were special-purpose missiles, designed to release intense pulses of electromagnetic radiation in order to fry enemy radar, communications, computer, and fire-control systems. No one knew how Solarflares would affect the Charonian invaders, but the theory was that electronic countermeasures, or ECM, might well be the most effective weapon in the human arsenal. That theory was about to be put to the test.

Tiny flashes of light began to wink and flicker within the silver pseudopods in the tank, each silent pulse representing a release of energy equivalent to the detonation of five hundred thousand tons of TNT. It was surprising how silent the demonstration was; it was difficult to watch the colored display in the holotank and connect it with the raw fury of battle now raging a few tens of thousands of miles ahead of the NEO force.

The first missile launch was followed by others as the fleets, RAM and Charonian, continued to close with one another. Several dark, ragged holes had opened in the invaders' silvery mass, and the arc of those pseudopods nearest the human fleet had begun to thin as their individual elements scattered. The Charonians had been hurt, but computer projections indicated that less than one percent of the invader machines had been destroyed.

"*Olympus* battle group is fully engaged," one of the comm techs announced. "They're reporting large numbers of invaders, maneuvering at high speed toward their formation."

"*Arcadia* and *Tharsis* battle groups fully engaged," another technician said. "*Directrix* is ordering all fighters launched."

Fighters appeared, red specks spilling from the larger symbols of RAM battlers, accelerating toward the foe. The two great galaxies of colored lights gleaming in the tank met . . . merged . . . then swept through one another. The tangle of symbols rapidly became so confusing that a technician cut off all data lines identifying individual ships except for those floating next to the five battlers. It was impossible for merely human observers to make much sense at all of that chaos of holographic light and color and movement.

The red triangle marking the *Arcadia* flashed white. To Vince, it looked as though the huge vessel had been struck and struck hard, though he knew the color change meant only that its ID transmissions had been interrupted.

But the impression was swiftly confirmed. "*Arcadia*'s been hit," a communications tech reported, her voice unnaturally calm against the rising tension in Cee-three. "Power and maneuvering are down. She's drift-ing."

"My God, my God, *Arcadia*'s hit," one of the voices from the overhead speakers called. "She's breaking up! . . ."

"Green five, keep it tight! They're coming through! They're—"

"Red Leader, we can't track the bastards! They're too fast!"

"Fire Mark IIIs, full spread! Launch! Launch! Launch!"

"Mayday! Mayday! Blue four-one is hit! We're abandon—"

More and more of the red lights flashed white as their computer links with the rest of the Expeditionary Force went off-line, and many of those began to fragment, scattering dust mote sprinkles of light across the black void of the tank.

"General Stuart's on the NEO tac channel," a comm tech said. "He's beginning deployment."

Vince locked eyes with Kowalski. "Shall we join him?"

She broke the eye contact first, looking back into the tank. The RAM fleet looked like crimson blood mingling with a vast splatter of liquid mercury frozen in mid-splash. "Better to do something than sit back and watch this, this slaughter."

Turning, she barked something at one of the silently watching Stormriders. The huge being nodded, then spoke quietly into an intercom mike. An alarm rasped, and Vince caught hold of the railing around the tank, pulling his feet down to the deck. Seconds later, weight returned as the Stormrider ship surged forward, again under full thrust.

It had taken special adaptations for the *Messenger of God* to penetrate this far into the Outer Dark. The ship-creature carried considerable reserves of liquid hydrogen as reaction mass, but not nearly enough to sustain a one-G acceleration for the fifteen days necessary to reach Pluto-Charon. At Amalthea, a special rig had been assembled from collection tanks employed by Skimmertech for shipping gas scooped from the upper Jovian atmosphere to the Inner System. Looking like a titanic raft constructed from dozens of interconnected spheres, it carried millions of cubic feet of slush hydrogen stored at near absolute-zero temperatures, enough to fuel the *Messenger of God*, strapped to its surface like a beached whale, all the way to Pluto.

Unfortunately, there was not enough for a return trip. Unless the Stormriders could refuel at Charon, the huge, living spaceship would never swim the skies of Jupiter again.

In the tank, the blue and blue-green NEO and privateer fleets were accelerating again, sweeping past the collision of RAM and invader combatants, traveling, not toward Charon, but straight toward Pluto. Several high-velocity projectiles were flung their way by Charonians, but at this range there was plenty of time to avoid the missiles, or blast them with missiles or gyrocannon fire.

Another fifteen minutes should put them close to Pluto. Until then, the idea was to stay out of trouble.

Vince wasn't sure the invaders were going to go along with that agenda.

○ ○ ○ ○ ○

"Galen?" Jovanna's voice was just above a whisper. "What do you think's happened?"

"I don't know, Jovanna," Galen replied. The Tinker stood at her side, his mud-plastered hair dripping. A RAM trooper named Caldwell had taken Galen's place on the floor, patiently scraping away at the rock with the worn hairpin. "Maybe they've forgotten about us."

"The servant robots keep coming in. We're still being fed and watered, at least. How long has it been since they took someone?"

"Almost twenty hours."

She glanced over her shoulder at the other prisoners, all of them motionless in the shadowed room. The tension had continued mounting in the Black Hole of Charon, had risen to the point where anything might set off an explosion. Except for the small Charonian machines running in and out on their automated errands, there'd been no sign of their captors since they'd come to drag Sergei and the Amalthean woman away.

"I have a feeling something's up," Jovanna said. "Something that's disrupted their schedule."

"Like what? Not that I'm complaining, mind you. If they have forgotten about us, I'd just as soon not remind them."

"I don't know. I wish I knew. Maybe we could use it though, somehow, if we just knew what it was."

Galen shook his head. He watched Caldwell for a moment as the trooper scraped away at wet black rock. The circular groove was now almost an inch deep, and it was even money now which would break first, the plug of rock leading to the door's circuitry, or the pin itself.

"It's no good trying to outguess them, Jo," he told her. "All we can do is keep scraping away. We're going to have to make up the rules as we go along."

"I guess you're right." She frowned. "You know, I was just wondering. What happens if those wires you're digging for are in vacuum?"

"Then we start learning how to breathe vacuum, fast. It's a little late to worry about that now, isn't it?"

"Sorry. Just nerves, I guess."

"Try not to think about it." Galen stooped, tapped Caldwell on the shoulder, then took the trooper's place.

Chink-chink-chink . . .

Jovanna was left alone with her thoughts, thoughts that were growing increasingly dark.

o   o   o   o   o

Admiral Chernikov was not a happy man.

The orders from Mars directing him to join RAM's

Jovian fleet with the ragtag collection of Belter, pirate, and NEO rebel ships had left him thunderstruck, and it had been all he could do to keep his face impassive at that farce of a treaty ceremony. The Amalthean Truce? Amalthean Farce was more like it. He'd actually felt relief when his rebel contingent had split off from the main force. His master battle plan had no room for amateurs.

His tactical staff had strongly recommended that he put the rebels in the fleet's vanguard, and he'd been tempted. Let them absorb the shock of the first contact with the Charonians . . . and when this affair was over, it would be simple to mop up the survivors.

He'd overruled them, however. A firm believer in the power of morale in any fight, Chernikov knew that even the most veteran space assault trooper would be shaken seeing the rebels slaughtered at the very outset of the battle. Better to order them out of the way, to plan the battle without having to worry about what they might or might not do. Perhaps they would serve as a diversion.

But Chernikov was already beginning to regret that decision. The Charonian fleet was like a tidal wave, an advancing wall of individual craft that smashed against his perfectly formed fleet, battering it, crashing through it and leaving his formation in tatters. In seconds, his battle order had been savaged and left in ruins, and each ship in the RAM fleet was fighting on its own, and for its life.

His force was dwindling as he watched the collision in the huge holotank on the *Directrix*'s combat bridge. *Tharsis* had been hit badly, its hull pierced in a dozen places by hurtling, silvery craft that seemed to be both war craft and missiles. *Utopia Planitia* was almost invisible at the center of a swirling vortex of Charonian ships.

Ships? Weapons? What were those things, anyway? Silver slivers of hurtling death, piercing his ships, ripping open hulls like slashing knives, spewing high-velocity pellets that struck home with the explosive force of mininukes. The RAM fleet was fighting back; the

Charonian craft could be destroyed, and each spread of Solarflare ECM missiles opened vast rents in their formation.

But after less than five minutes of combat, Chernikov could tell that it was only a matter of time before his proud fleet was eliminated. It looked like those cowardly NEO pirates might escape, bypassing the fight and slipping around behind Pluto's night side. But the rest of the fleet was doomed.

"Our . . . allies," he said to an aide by his side, the word sour in his mouth. "The NEO and privateer contingents are running away, as we expected. How many are left?"

"About thirty ships," the aide replied. "Twelve Belters, plus the Venusians, Callistans, and Ionians. And three Mercurians."

They wouldn't last long in this inferno.

"Order them to join the battle. We'll have to make the best of what we have."

For as much time as we have left. Someone, Chernikov reflected, had badly underestimated the enemy's abilities. Heads were going to roll on Mars when word of this disaster reached the corporate offices.

Chernikov was glad that he wasn't going to be there to see it.

○ ○ ○ ○ ○

"We're coming up on the terminator," RW said. "Two minutes."

No one else in *Messenger*'s Cee-three said a word, and the silence was broken only by the low hum of electronics. It was as though each person in the room had felt something of the cold loneliness outside and retreated into inner thoughts and worry and speculation, rather than face that terrible isolation directly.

One of the large 2-D screens in Cee-three had been set to display the surface of Pluto. No human had ever been this close to the tiny, frigid sphere, and Vince wanted each detail, each second of their passage recorded.

At the moment, though, there was little to be seen. The NEO-privateer fleet had slipped around the curve of Pluto, skimming the surface at an altitude of less than twenty miles. Minutes before, the sun, so shrunken at this distance it was little more than a particularly brilliant star, had set below the cold, ice-glittering limb of the planet. The night side of Pluto was set with a crushing bleakness wholly unknown to any of the bright worlds of warmth and light of the Inner System. Vince found himself gripping the railing alongside the holotank, staring at the 2-D display, fervently willing the sun to reappear. What, he wondered, must it be like on the surface, where the night was longer than three full Earth days?

Pluto was tiny. Once, centuries before—his pack rat mind, as he'd called it once, had picked up this bit of trivia somewhere—it had been thought that Mercury was the smallest of the worlds of the Solar System, but that was before Charon had been discovered, allowing the then-Earthbound astronomers to calculate precisely Pluto's diameter and mass. Now it was known that Pluto was smaller even than Luna, and with a density so close to that of water that the gravity wasn't much more than that of a fair-sized asteroid.

Despite that, the NEO-privateer fleet was using Pluto's insubstantial gravitational field to slingshot them around the planet. If their calculations were correct, they would emerge from this frigid, ultimate winter's night on a direct course for Charon . . . and hopefully on a path unanticipated by the Charonians.

Damn it, where was the sun? He checked a chronometer on a console display. Less than a minute to go.

Again, Vince glanced at the holotank, but the 3-D display was empty except for the scattering of blue symbols moving slowly across the dark side of Pluto. They'd lost all contact with the rest of the Expeditionary Force when they'd dropped below Pluto's horizon, so there was no way to update the computer-generated animation in the display.

Instruments were recording atmosphere, a vacuum-thin whiff of methane. At times, Vince knew, during Pluto's twenty-year-long "summer," when it actually slipped inside Neptune's orbit, a single, twin-lobed atmosphere surrounded both Pluto and Charon, but for most of Pluto's two-and-a-half-century year, the temperature was so low—minus 430 degrees Fahrenheit—that even methane remained frozen. Water would be as hard as steel in that frigid wasteland, and steel would be as brittle as ice. Once he'd seen a hammer dipped in liquid nitrogen, then struck against a table, shattering like glass, and that had been at a temperature over a hundred degrees warmer than that of Pluto's night side!

We've never encountered an environment as extreme as this one, he thought. If our suits don't insulate as well as we think . . .

"Still no invaders," Kaiten growled, studying the flat displays, eyes narrowed, glittering with a predator's knife-keen attention. There'd been a lively debate during the Pluto approach as to whether the Charonians would have defenses of some kind, or invader war craft, hidden on Pluto's night side. Apparently the invaders had ignored their larger celestial neighbor.

And then the sun rose.

It was little more than a spark, really, but it far outshone every other star in the sky, a beacon far brighter than the full moon seen from Earth, but tiny, tiny. It struck white fire against a cliff of ammonia ice, rising as the Plutonian landscape turned beneath the belly of the *Messenger of God*.

Did the Stormrider ship-creature feel the cold? Vince wondered. Probably not. Certainly not, if it had survived this long in the Outer Dark. But he couldn't help wondering if the ship, or its Stormrider masters, for that matter, felt as lost, as far from home as Vince felt. This far out, Jovian and human were close kin.

"Telecommunications with the fleet reestablished," RW reported. "The battle's still underway." In the holotank, the fleets had reappeared, red still locked with silver in a death grip, as the allied fleets approached the fringes of the battleground.

The red fleet had dwindled visibly in the minutes while the NEO contingent was masked by Pluto. According to the *Messenger*'s computer, they'd lost forty-seven ships so far, including the battlers *Tharsis* and *Utopia Planitia*. *Directrix* had taken several hits but was still in the thick of the battle. *Olympus Mons* and *Wargod* were both still fighting.

"We are on course," RW announced. "Deviation less than one-tenth of one percent.

"Anyone close to us?" Vince wanted to know. "Have they seen us?"

"Not a thing," a tech replied. "RAM is keeping them busy."

"My God," another tech said, her voice awestruck. "They've taken almost forty percent casualties!"

"Chernikov is hurting them," Vince pointed out. Clearly, the Solarflare ECM missiles were proving more effective against the nanotechnic foe than anyone had dared hope, even those who had seen the Jovian's charge guns in action and who knew that the Charonians were susceptible to electrical interference.

But would it be enough? RAM was outnumbered by hundreds to one. If the NEO fleet couldn't pull this off within a very few minutes, they'd be alone . . . at least until the Charonians caught them.

And shortly after that, they would all be dead.

CHAPTER TWENTY-FOUR

The supervisor nucleus did not understand human concepts such as "alarm" or "worry," but events in the skies surrounding Charon were forcing it to allocate more and more of its attention to the human threat. The Charonian network was in no danger, but the attackers were becoming something of a distraction.

It had been aware of the humans' approach for well over a million seconds but had not been able to reason their motives or their intent with certainty. The nucleus calculated a seventy-eight percent probability that the humans were, in fact, remotes for another network like the supervisor's own, that that alien network had dispatched a fleet of its remotes to access and integrate the Charonian network into its own.

But surely, if this alien computer network existed, the supervisor's own attempt to access it at Jupiter would have succeeded in establishing peer-to-peer communication?

Could the alien network be so alien that its operating system was completely incompatible? Was the alien network now trying to make contact, was it simply attempting to sample the Charonian network, or was it trying to eliminate the network as a competitor?

Questions . . . and no answers, no data. The human remotes had begun destroying the supervisor's remotes fifty thousand miles from Charon, and the supervisor had responded in kind. If the alien network was indeed trying to assimilate the Charonian network, it was proceeding in an illogical manner, one doomed to failure. The nucleus had far more remotes available than did the alien fleet, and the deployment of the other network's forces seemed disjointed, confused, and lacking any indication of an organizational intelligence behind them.

Until the alien network—if it existed—made its purposes known, the supervisor nucleus would counter its threats, sample its remotes, and watch. There was no serious danger to the Charonian network, and the nucleus could afford to maintain a defensive posture.

New data . . .

Sensors located throughout the city were registering the approach of more remotes. Interesting. They'd maneuvered around the other world hanging in Charon's sky and were heading straight for the citadel.

The supervisor nucleus abandoned several astronomical mapping subroutines it had been running for the past century, freeing more of its awareness to focus on this new problem.

It appeared that the supervisor nucleus itself was about to come under attack, and that was intolerable. . . .

O O O O O

"Lord in heaven," Kowalski said, eyes widening. She pointed at one of the screens. "Will you look at that?"

Vince looked where she pointed, saw the screen displaying Charon's image. He nodded, not daring himself to speak.

Pluto's moon was growing slowly larger, revealed as a crescent, one bright, scimitar-sharp edge bowed away from the dwindled sun, the rest lost in a darkness that blotted out the stars. Yet against that darkness there were . . . lights.

Patterns of lights, patterns showing intelligence and purpose. Vince had expected something like this, of course; he still remembered the vision somehow relayed to him by the Artifact months before, a vision of a strange city of machines and alien architecture set among the glaciers, crags, and snowfields of a frozen world. Still, the actual sight of that city seen from space caught him by surprise.

The lights glowed blue and violet for the most part, though some orange pinpoints contrasted with the others, illuminating ruler-straight lines and circles that reminded Vince of a spider's web, glittering with dew in the morning sun. It was a spider's web that embraced an entire hemisphere, stretching around the curve of the moon across seven hundred miles.

"I guess there's no doubt where we should hit," Vince said. Like a spider's web, the radial lines converged at a central point. Long-range scans were already registering something massive there, a building of some kind at least a mile high.

"It's a lot bigger than it looks," RW said. "Our sensors are picking up infrared traces from underground. The whole moon is riddled with tunnels and caverns."

"Underground buildings?" Vince asked.

"Some of them. Others are probably empty. The topography is of particular interest. We were expecting to find a body primarily of ice, possibly with a tiny rock core. In fact, the surface appears to be mingled ice and rock, evidence, perhaps, of Charon's violent past."

On the screens, Vince could see that evidence, though he wondered what kind of violence RW had in mind. The surface was oddly mottled, alternating ice with jumbled masses of black rock.

"What kind of violence?" Vince asked.

"Charon may be the product of an ancient collision," RW said. "Which would explain the mingled rock and ice. The surface does show definite evidence of strip mining on a planetary scale. Tunnel entrances, pits, and remarkably geometric surface excavations. Enormous areas beneath the surface appear to have been hollowed out. I cannot at this time theorize on the nature of the engineering that produced these features."

"Raw materials, honey," Kowalski told the computer image, and Vince nodded agreement.

A nanotechnic life-form would have tremendous control over the natural world. It could, by deploying properly programmed, molecule-sized machines, manipulate individual molecules in any material, moving them, replacing them, even reshape them into something else. It could eat holes through any metal, or tunnel miles through solid rock. With enough raw materials to build new nano-machines, that life-form could rework entire planets . . . or devour them whole to create a planet-sized mass of new machines.

Was that what was happening to Charon?

"RW?" Vince asked. "What kind of thermal background are we picking up down there?"

"Substantially higher than expected, Vince. The surface in the vicinity of the city center is radiating at approximately minus one hundred. It's warmer still in some of the underground tunnels."

"*Messenger, Republic*, we confirm that," another voice said. General Stuart was patched into the Cee-three suite by radio and had been listening in on their conversation. "We're picking up a substantial methane atmosphere around Charon."

"How thick?" another voice, rougher and harder, demanded. That, Vince thought, sounded like Black Barney. "The *Enterprise* can handle atmosphere, but I'd like to know just what we're getting into."

"Point nine eight millibar," RW replied. "A thousandth of one atmosphere."

"Hardly enough to worry about," Barney said. "And balmy, summer temperatures. Hot damn, we might actually have a chance of pullin' this thing off!"

The question of Charon's extreme environment had worried Vince at least as much as the reaction of the world's inhabitants. Charon should have had a surface temperature like that of Pluto, thirty degrees or so above absolute zero. At such temperatures, most metals shattered like glass at a tap, plastics crumbled into powder, and even basaltic rock became as brittle as pottery.

And yet it was hard to imagine any industrial process—even one carried on at a molecular level—which did not give off large amounts of heat as a waste product. It appeared that the Charon intelligence did, in fact, function at "reasonable" temperatures of only a hundred degrees or so below zero, rather than the nightmare low temperatures that were normal this far from the sun. That probe that had landed on Charon four centuries ago must have possessed a powerful nuclear heat source; designed and built on Earth, it wouldn't have survived long at Charon's normal temperature of minus four-twenty or so. As its progeny had altered the surface of their new home, they must have incorporated the waste heat from their activities into the design of the environment.

Kaiten caught Vince's eye. "We should prepare."

Vince nodded. Though he was wearing a ship suit, he'd come prepared with a special environment suit, or SES, a thick-padded, bulky garment designed to survive even normal Charonian cold.

At least, it was supposed to. They were dealing with so many unknowns here at the very edge of the Solar System that no one could pretend to have all of the answers. It took him a few minutes, with Kowalski's help, to seal himself into the massive SES. He left off the helmet and gloves for the time being. Kaiten, meanwhile, donned a red-and-black suit of Terrine battle armor, one specially modified for work in ultracold environments.

Meanwhile, the NEO fleet was falling quickly toward Charon's night side. A warning claxon sounded, and then gravity was restored as engines fired, slowing them in the last few, violent moments of their plummet toward the surface.

"Attention, all ships," General Stuart's voice announced. "Sky cover, ready to commence firing. Landing element, your touchdown areas have been marked and fed into your computers. You are go for final descent."

A number of the falling blue stars in the tank divided, giving birth to a dozen, smaller stars. Some were fighters, stored in freighter holds. Others were NEO drop boats, landing craft similar to RAM assault delivery vehicles (ADVs), heavily armored boxes with minimal maneuvering power, designed to deliver large numbers of troops to a surface combat zone quickly.

Flashes pulsed and strobed among the webbing of light on the surface. Missile and K-cannon fire sought targets—suspected communications antennae, possible power distribution grids, towering things that might have been weapons of some kind. It was all guesswork; for all they knew they might be bombing the Charonian equivalent of schools and hospitals, but the sheer savagery of that space bombardment, it was hoped, would give the landing force the moments it needed to drop all the way to the center of the alien city.

That city, Vince saw as the *Messenger of God* descended on furious blasts of superheated hydrogen, was identical to the vision he'd received from the Artifact. Alien architecture—spires, domes, strange-shaped and twisted structures for which there were no Earthly names—rose from blackened, blasted ground like weirdly shaped plants. Pluto hung motionless against the star-scattered ink of the night sky, the sunlit expanse of its polar methane caps casting light enough on Charon's surface to reveal the ghostly shapes of ammonia glaciers on the horizon. At the precise center of that sprawling web of architecture and light, a single black tower, an obelisk a mile high, towered over the city's center, the hub of a vast and complex tangle of archways, tubes, and far more enigmatic structures that seemed to branch and flow from it like the veins and arteries emerging from a heart.

This time, though, the far horizon was unevenly lit by the flashes of the ongoing bombardment. Those blasts were silent—the air pressure outside was too thin to carry sound, but Vince could imagine the shiver and thump of those detonations as they tore into the Charonian city.

Then, suddenly, the city lit up in a blaze of blue fire, and, one by one, the ships of the NEO fleet began to die.

O   O   O   O   O

"Galen! Did you feel that?"

The Tinker looked up from his work on the wall. "I sure did. I think you were right, Jovanna. Something has disrupted their schedule!"

The other prisoners, too, had felt the shocks, a continuing drumroll of tremors, most almost nonexistent, a few sharp, definite, and close. The captives were rising, staring toward the ceiling or at the black walls around them, talking excitedly among themselves.

"Explosions!" one young trooper shouted. "RAM is bombing the damned machines!" Someone raised a cheer.

"Quiet, people! Quiet down!" Admiral Singh stood in front of the crowd, signaling with his hands. "We're not out of this yet!"

There was another tremor. Black dust sifted from the ceiling, and the light dimmed for a moment, raising another murmuring roar from the prisoners packed into the cavern.

At the same moment, there was a sharp crack, and Galen triumphantly removed a plug of soft, coal-black rock, four inches across and almost two inches thick. "That's it!" he said. "We're through!"

Jovanna kneeled in the mud beside him, peering into the shadow-murky hole. She could see a bundle of what looked like wires emerging from a gray conduit, a cylinder that looked like a piece of lead pipe.

"Can you do it?"

Galen was already sawing at the wires with the sharpened stub of his hairpin. "I'll tell you in a moment."

There was another shock, much closer this time, bringing with it a roar of fractured rock. The light winked out as rubble and muddy water cascaded from the walls.

Then the light returned. Galen cursed as an electrical charge crackled at his fingertips, and the circular door to their prison slid open. "That's it!" Jovanna cried. "You did it!"

"Start moving out, people!" Singh bellowed behind

her. "Don't shove! Don't shove! Keep it orderly!"

"What now?" Jovanna asked. The open door yawned into blackness. At least the air was still breathable . . . though they'd known that each time their captors had entered their prison. For whatever reason, the machine intelligences were maintaining heat and atmosphere. The question was, how long?

And there were more immediate problems. "We still don't have any weapons," a RAM ensign said.

"Then we'll make them," Galen said. "Human ingenuity, right, Admiral?"

"Ingenuity or suicidal stupidity," Singh replied, but he was grinning. "I hope I never have to keep you locked up again, Tinker."

"I wouldn't recommend it, Admiral. Tinkers don't mind being cooped up in small spaces, but there's something about a locked door that really gets on our nerves."

The prisoners, ragged and muddy, trooped out into darkness.

O O O O O

The fire from Charon's surface had erupted from a hundred sites, high-speed pellets hurled by powerful magnetic fields against the attackers. The *Republic* staggered, struck by a hurtling chunk of metal that smashed its number-one laser turret and knocked out the command ship's fire control.

The huge *Messenger of God*, floating on its raft of hydrogen tanks, was holed a dozen times, the metal spheres holding its dwindling fuel stores riddled by chunks of ultradense metal. Hydrogen gas, boiling into the cold, thin atmosphere outside, spilled like fog through the black sky, blue-lit by the blazing lights of the Charonian weapons below.

On the bridge of the privateer *Free Enterprise*, Black Barney leaned forward in his seat, studying the pattern of Charonian fire. There were no enemy ships yet, thank the gods of the empty void, but they would be along soon enough. The battle had to be won here and now, with a toe-to-toe slugfest against the Charonian city's defenses.

"Solarflares!" he barked over *Enterprise*'s com system. "All tubes! Target their launch systems! We'll burn out their eyes!"

Barney had been watching the unfolding contest between the RAM and Charonian fleets with the keen interest of a veteran space tactician. The Charonian equipment appeared not to be hardened; their ships lost control when the violently radiating core of a Solarflare seared past, scrambling their magnetics and electronics. If Mark XCs worked on their ships, they ought to raise merry hell in their city.

"All tubes loaded with Solarflares," Scrugg, his first mate, called from his console across the bridge. "Targets plotted and locked!"

"Then fire! Take the bastards down!"

Free Enterprise lurched as the heavy Solarflare missiles slid clear of their tubes. Burning fiercely, like miniature suns, the ECM missiles swooped low across the Charonian city, their passage casting weirdly shifting shadows across buildings and walls. One struck an enemy launch facility, and white flame blossomed into the night.

But more NEO and privateer ships had been hit. *Revenge*, the converted merchantman of a Belter pirate named Granik, crumpled in a star-hot mass of glowing wreckage. The *James Madison*, a NEO cruiser, exploded like a nova as its fusion bottle collapsed, bathing a hundred square miles in the harsh glare of radiant energy. The *Republic* was trying to make a forced landing, its drive faltering.

"This ain't gonna last long," Barney muttered. "Scrugg! Normal load! Target that damned tower!"

Fireworks lit the night above the Charonian city.

○ ○ ○ ○ ○

The supervisor nucleus was now concentratin twenty-eight percent of its capacity on the problem pre sented by the attackers, an unprecedented allocation assets. It had been forced to temporarily abandon more than two hundred Project subroutines, including several of particular interest.

Was there, in fact, a hint of intelligence behind its opponent's actions? The enemy's actions seemed almost deliberately designed to thwart its own planning. Fast-moving flares of harsh radiation were dazzling the network's optics, disrupting communications, and scrambling computer commands.

The supervisor nucleus had never met another intelligence outside of itself, and no one had ever told it that technology—interlocking systems of processed raw materials, such as ships or weapons—was necessarily the product of intelligent design. From the nucleus's point of view, these humans could well be a natural force, like gravity or cosmic radiation . . . albeit chaotically unpredictable ones.

Yet they displayed a learning response curve much like the supervisor nucleus's own, reacting with seeming purpose and intelligent intent. Were they intelligent?

The supervisor nucleus decided that it had to find out.

CHAPTER TWENTY-FIVE

The deck bucked and shuddered as *Messenger of God* took volley after volley from the Charonian city. Vince clung to a console, listening to the booming commands of the Stormriders around him as he wondered whether the living ship was going to hold together.

"What's happening?" he yelled.

"We're hit bad," Kowalski shouted back. The racket was deafening. "We're losing fuel from our strap-on tanks. We won't be able to maintain altitude for long!"

Like a huge shield, the raft of slush-hydrogen tanks strapped to its belly had protected the *Messenger* from the worst of the city's fire, but the Jovian ship's fuel supply was rapidly dwindling.

Missiles slammed into the central tower, flashing in great, silent gouts of light. The *Free Enterprise* was turning all of its missile tubes on that enigmatic sentinel at the city's heart, and the other NEO and privateer ships were following Barney's example.

Suddenly, Vince had an idea.

When the raft of fuel tanks had been mounted on *Messenger*'s belly, the shackles and steel support struts had been bolted directly to the Jovian ship's body, but he knew the Stormriders would have arranged for some sort of quick-release, if only because there might be a crisis like this one, with the heavy tanks damaged and the ship falling from the sky.

"Marlene!" he shouted. "Can you drop *Messenger*'s fuel tanks?"

"Of course."

"How much is left in them?"

"They're maybe a quarter full. What did you have in mind?"

He pointed at a screen, where the black tower at the city's center thrust skyward from the core of that alien metropolis. "Aim the ship for the tower! We can use the fuel tank raft like a bomb!"

Comprehension lit Kowalski's eyes. She grinned, nodded, then shouted an order at one of the Jovians. In another moment, the *Messenger* was angling toward the tower, dropping into a long, slanting glide. At Kowalski's command, the fuel tank raft was loosed in a shiver of exploding bolts. Then it was slipping away from *Messenger*'s belly, streaming a frost-white contrail of hydrogen as it hurtled toward the mile-high target. As the living ship surged upward, free of that enormous mass, the tangle of broken, hydrogen storage spheres began tumbling end-over-end, then slammed into the black tower halfway between the base and the tip.

Metal fragments and chunks of tower sprayed from the silent impact. Hydrogen vented from ruptured tanks, a frost-white fog boiling through the thin air. With no oxygen, there was no flash or flame . . . but several hundred tons of half-frozen hydrogen remaining in those shattered spheres sluiced over the tower in a slow-motion splash largely obscured by the fog.

Cryo-H—the term for near-frozen hydrogen slush— had a temperature of only a few degrees above absolute zero, while the tower, warmed by the city's industrial processes, was well over three hundred degrees warmer. Like the hammer dipped in liquid nitrogen, the unyielding, refractory metal of the citadel tower cracked . . . then shattered in an avalanche of spinning, hurtling black fragments. The upper half of the tower canted sharply, then, slowly in Charon's microgravity, it began to fall, great, crystalline shards flaking off and crumbling as it followed the avalanche in the long, half-mile drop toward the city.

O   O   O   O   O

Pain! . . .

The supervisor nucleus had only a theoretical knowledge of the concept, which it had gleaned from numerous interrogation sessions with the human specimens, but it suspected that the sensations now flooding its myriad circuits must be similar.

Power was always dear this far from the sun, and the tower, designed to drink energy from the sky, was an important part of the network's power sources. The destruction of the tower had caused a near-catastrophic energy loss of forty-two percent. Worse, the nucleus had lost touch with many of its outlying sensors and defensive positions. For the first time, the supervisor nucleus felt genuine apprehension.

A new program was necessary, and immediately! In milliseconds, it had written one, then flashed an operations change to its remotes, a priority-interrupt routine ordering all surviving units to drop what they were doing and return to the city at once.

O   O   O   O   O

"Admiral! They're fleeing!" Somewhere on *Directrix*'s bridge, someone loosed a cheer, and then everyone was joining in, a chorus of shrieks and joyful self-congratulation.

In his acceleration couch, Admiral Chernikov sagged against his harness, globules of sweat dancing about his head in zero G. God in heaven, what had happened? One moment they'd been fighting for their lives, two thirds of their number already destroyed and the rest doomed by the horde of silver Charonian craft, and now . . .

The enemy ship-weapons were retreating, streaming back toward Charon in a ragged-edged cloud of silver.

Naranov, *Directrix*'s captain, cast an anxious look at the admiral. "Shall . . . shall we break off, sir?"

Chernikov considered. They'd been looking at certain death . . . and then been granted an unexpected reprieve. RAM would not fault him if he broke off now, especially if he could save what was left of the fleet.

On the other hand, something had changed in the enemy's situation. He remembered the debriefing of that NEO officer, Pirelli, back in Jovian space after the fighting around Jupiter. The enemy did not appear to employ layered tactics and was capable of suddenly dropping one plan in favor of another. Was the sudden retreat part of some larger scheme? Or did it mean the enemy intelligence knew that it was beaten and was trying to save what it could?

Chernikov elected to gamble on the latter. So far, the enemy had relied on brute force, without even an attempt at subtlety or misdirection. If they were retreating, it was because they were beaten. Chernikov's orders from Mars were plain: eliminate the Charonian invaders as a threat to the Inner System.

"Negative!" he snapped. "We will pursue! Pass the word to all ships! We will stay on their heels until they're destroyed, or we are!"

○ ○ ○ ○ ○

"By the base of the tower," Vince said, leaning over Kowalski's shoulder and pointing. "Can you put us down there?"

"In a moment. Throv is asking for an air drop."

Vince blinked. The plan had called for getting the NEO-privateer fleet on the ground as quickly as possible and debarking the troops. But an air drop?

"My people are Stormriders, remember," Marlene said, completely unconscious, apparently, of her identification with the giant warlords of Jupiter. "They are creatures of the sky!"

"God help them," Vince murmured. On the viewscreen, the first of the Jovian warriors had appeared in the Charonian sky, golden motes against the night. The *Messenger of God* was opening, its prow splitting wide to disgorge a gleaming, aerial horde.

They'd prepared for the possibility of a direct assault. The Stormriders wore gleaming, gold-colored insulation suits that looked less like garments than like thick gold paint sprayed over every square inch of their bodies and wings, save for the clear bubbles that protected their heads. In some ways, Vince thought, Stormrider technology was far ahead of what humans were capable of. He'd been told that those golden suits of theirs were a spin-off from Jovian bioengineering, a way of manipulating advanced materials at a molecular level.

However they were manufactured, they made his SES look like a museum piece, and Kaiten's red-and-black combat armor like some clumsy relic from the twentieth century.

But they were facing a foe capable of near-magical technology, in an environment as alien to all of them as Jupiter's cloud tops were to humans.

Wings spread in the thin Charonian air. Was flight possible in such a thin atmosphere? Vince did some quick mental calculations, then dropped it. The air was almost nonexistent . . . but so was gravity. He felt like he weighed only three or four pounds here, and even Stormriders would not weigh more than fifteen or twenty. Somehow, those vast, outstretched membranes were holding the Stormriders aloft on the thin methane winds, supporting them at least enough to let them glide in a golden cloud toward the shattered stump of the citadel tower.

"*Daargh!*" Kaiten shouted, clenched fists raised above his head. "*Daargh!*"

Vince recognized that battlespeech scream. Kaiten glanced at Vince, then looked away with an expression that was almost sheepish and gave a remarkably human shrug. "They are *Eresh'aregh* now," the Terrine explained.

Sharers-of-blood. Somehow, during that warriors' ceremony in the cloud city, the Terrine had bonded with the

Stormriders. Well, after this day, they would all be shar-ers-of-blood.

Or dead.

The golden horde filled the sky. It was a disconcerting sensation, feeling the thrill of battle-lust while knowing the horror that would follow. There was nothing glorious about battle, and combat was always more terrifying than thrilling.

Yet Vince felt that ancient stirring nonetheless, irra-tional . . . and compelling. Watching the gold-winged fig-ures descending on the city, he caught himself humming a fragment of music over and over in his mind, a piece from some ancient composer. What was it?

Wagner, that was it. "Ride of the Valkyries."

The horde circled the tower's stump. Lightning, blue-white and jagged, pulsed from the city, raking the skies, and a dozen winged forms crumpled and fell, trailing smoke. It occurred to Vince that the machine intelli-gence must think they were some kind of flyer, like the silvery forms that had invaded the Jovian city.

"Hang on!" Marlene warned. "We're going in!"

Vince had time only to don helmet and gloves, then the *Messenger of God* plowed into the ground yards in the rubble of the citadel, less than a hundred yards from the tower itself. The touchdown was rough, but the loose rubble helped cushion the impact.

As the Stormrider ship came to a rest, he could feel the faint shiver and tremble of detonations, the continu-ing bombardment from the surviving NEO and privateer ships, communicated through the *Messenger*'s body from the ice and rock below. On the screen he could see *Free Enterprise* still circling overhead, as the damaged *Republic* settled to the icy plain perhaps half a mile away.

Vince accepted a Weston Mark XIV rocket rifle from a helmeted Stormrider, then exchanged glances with Kai-ten through the Terrine's battle helmet and gave him a cocky thumbs-up. He turned to face the Venusian. "Right, Marlene," he said, "you stay here and coordinate our communications with the rest of the fleet. Keep listening in on the tac channel. I'll yell if I need anything."

"Luck, Major," the Venusian woman said. "I hope you find what you're looking for."

"Yeah," he said, making his way toward Cee-three's air lock. "Me, too."

Especially since he wouldn't know what he was looking for until he found it.

○ ○ ○ ○ ○

Jovanna followed Galen and Admiral Singh as they made their way along seemingly endless corridors. The walls were featureless and smooth, curving rather than turning at right angles. Fortunately, there was light enough to see by. The walls seemed to yield a faint trace of phosphorescence, enough to give shape to their environment, if not substance. It felt to Jovanna like she was wandering aimlessly in the gut of some vast beast.

The tunnel widened into a room. Galen stopped short, a sharp hiss of air escaping clenched teeth.

"Almighty God . . ." Singh breathed.

This place was brightly lit and lined with a bewildering complexity of machine arms and tools and parts. To Jovanna it looked like a highly sophisticated automated surgical theater.

Except that it was emphatically not a place of healing. Lt. Sergei Bruckner lay on the table at the center of the room—what was left of him, at any rate. The upper part of his body was encased in silver metal that seemed to have flowed out of the tabletop itself, holding him immobile. His face was exposed, and terror and agony were still reflected within those dead, staring eyes. His lower torso, from his waist down, was missing, the open body cavity neatly sealed with a thin layer of silver metal.

The body was cold, the nightmarish implements dangling overhead unmoving. It was as though the machines had simply stopped when the patient died, hours ago.

Or possibly, Jovanna told herself, the attack had stopped them. She was convinced that someone was attacking Charon; everyone in the mob of escaped prisoners was clinging to that same white-hot, fiercely burning hope.

Someone in the mass of prisoners crowding in through the door gasped and screamed at the sight of Bruckner's body. Singh snapped an order, and RAM troopers turned, forcing the people back.

"They . . . they were sectioning him," Galen said in a strangled voice. He pointed to a pair of slender, robotic arms to one side of the room, still holding a translucent sheet of something filmy framed in an oval of metal and held intact between twin layers of some thin, transparent material. "They pinned him in metal and sliced him up, a few cells' thickness at a time!"

"Like a tissue sample," someone else said.

"My God, why?" Singh approached the body, reached out, closed the staring eyes. "What were they after?"

"They were interrogating him," someone else suggested. "Torturing him for information."

"About what?" Frank Kendall wanted to know. "What could they have wanted to know that made it worth doing . . . this?

"I'm not sure they were asking him anything," Galen replied. The Tinker had found other body sections, each carefully mounted between sheets of something like transparent mylar. It was possible to make out the outline of each internal organ, each layer of skin and muscle. "These, these samples are too carefully preserved for this to be simple torture."

Biting back the gorge rising in her throat, Jovanna pointed to a particular robot arm hanging from the ceiling, the tip equipped with a battery of glassy knobs. "That's some sort of laser scanner," she said. "I think they must have been recording each slice, somehow, maybe storing the image in a computer someplace."

Galen looked at her. "Maybe building up a three-dimensional data base of a living human body?"

"Mapping us," Jovanna said. "That's what they told us they were doing. Mapping us!"

"Well, why in God's name were they doing it to all of us?" Kendall demanded. "I'd have thought they killed enough people on Amalthea to find out everything they needed to know!"

"I've given up trying to understand these things," Singh said. Reaching up, he grabbed one robotic arm, a massive length of white metal as thick as his arm. There was a squeak of metal flexing, and then the arm snapped off with a loud clatter. He hefted the weapon, a cluster of wires dangling from the end of the makeshift club. "Let's find these things and ask them a few questions of our own!"

In seconds, the operating theater had been stripped, the robot arms, the scalpels and drills, even the wiring conduits on the walls pulled down and broken into handy, club-sized pieces. Someone found another passageway, and the former prisoners doubled back the way they came, angry now, and hungry for the Charonian equivalent of blood, whatever it might be.

Rounding a sharp curve in the passageway, they encountered a six-foot invader machine. A mouth shaped itself . . . but before the thing could speak, Kendall smashed it with a four-foot length of pipe, splashing it into two halves. The halves were starting to flow together again when the crowd surged over it, scattering the semiliquid mass into smaller and smaller globs . . . and then the globs were no longer liquid, but solid, fist-sized chunks of silver. Then everyone was cheering, Jovanna screaming with the rest. The monsters could be killed!

Still screaming, their shouts wildly echoing through the corridors, the angry crowd streamed forward.

○ ○ ○ ○ ○

The battle was raging about him as Vince moved through the city, angling across the fallen black rubble toward the base of the shattered tower.

"Vince!" a voice crackled in his helmet, broken by spitting static. "This is Marlene. Snap it up. We have visitors inbound!"

"The Charonian fleet?"

"The same, with Chernikov hot on their heels. It's going to get lively as hell here in about two minutes."

A hard-flung pellet shattered rock in a wall three feet above his head. Rocket-propelled smart rounds streaked past, slamming into a silvery, half-glimpsed form crouched in what might have been an eldritch doorway. It was hard to see how things could get any more lively. A gout of flame exploded yards behind him, silent but with force enough to slam him against the unyielding stone wall.

Perhaps a better word here than lively was deadly.

Vince's SES was not heavy in Charon's almost insignificant gravity, but it was massive, possessing an inertia that was difficult to control. Vince had to measure each step he took, moving in slow motion to avoid losing control entirely and sprawling helplessly on his face. Kaiten, moving with the lithe grace of a jungle cat, rose to his right, triggered a Mark XIV round, then sprang toward the tower's base. With his heart hammering, Vince followed.

O O O O O

The supervisor nucleus had been watching the humans outside, trying to read some sort of purpose into their movements, or into the complex bursts of radio transmissions that punctuated their activities. As nearly as it could tell, they were identical to the humans brought from Amalthea—the same outward forms, erect, bipedal, joint articulation, with, it suspected, the same baffling heterogeneity of subunits at a microscopic level.

It also watched the movements of the escaping specimens within the tunnels beneath the citadel. It knew that at any time it could end this internal threat simply by restoring the usual atmosphere to the underground tunnel complex—it had already learned that humans could not tolerate Charon's frigid methane atmosphere for more than a few seconds—but the nucleus was fascinated by their seemingly purposeful behavior.

The humans appeared to be following the dictates of some extremely complex artificial-intelligence program. The nucleus still could not tell, however, whether their activity represented intelligence. Obviously they could communicate, especially under the stimulus of what they called "pain," but there was no direct evidence that they were anything more than mobile units of some kind, possibly akin to the nucleus's own remotes.

It was necessary to determine once and for all if these humans were mindless, mobile units for another intelligence like the supervisor nucleus, or something else, something stranger and more alien. The nucleus gave a silent command, and the citadel's outer door began to slide open.

If it could just isolate a few of the humans attacking from the outside, and run a few simple tests . . .

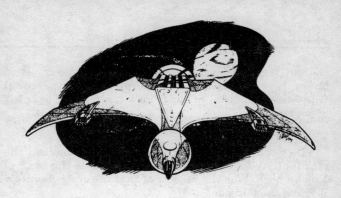

CHAPTER TWENTY-SIX

The citadel had to be the heart of whatever was controlling this city, and the alien ships beyond. He could imagine the tower growing from the crash site of that sabotaged nanotech probe, a kind of soulless machine memorial to the colonizers of this sterile world. The enormous bulk of the fallen *Messenger of God*, the pencil-thin sliver of the *Republic* standing erect on stubby fins, the *Free Enterprise* and the other human ships still circling against the night overhead, all were dwarfed by that titanic black construct.

A number of armed human soldiers in SES armor were spreading across the tangle of geometric shapes, walls, and what looked like highways, though Vince doubted that vehicular traffic of any kind used them. Most were members of an elite Special Tactics Assault Reconnaissance (STAR) Team attached to the NEO contingent and under the command of Captain Carter. Mingled with them were the eerie, gracefully moving shapes of the Stormriders. Many had already entered the citadel and were reported to be fighting their way down level after level inside. The rest had grounded outside, joining the human STAR Team in the assault on the alien tower.

Vince paused for breath in the shadow of a huge black

column. A STAR trooper approached him as he crouched there, lugging the massive complexity of a personal rapid-fire rocket launcher from a strap slung over his shoulder.

"Major Pirelli?" the man called, pointing. "Looks like we found the front door!"

Vince could see it, a gaping oval in the base of the citadel fifty feet tall. The hair pricked at the back of Vince's neck. Was the master of that tower deliberately inviting them inside?

"Okay," Vince said. "Let's do it!"

Rising, he led the way forward.

O O O O O

Black Barney's *Free Enterprise* banked low over the city. The lightning had stopped, at least, as had most of the fire from the surface. It looked like the expeditionary force was getting the upper hand at last, at least in the airspace above the city.

But blips were crawling across *Enterprise*'s screens now, a cloud of alien vessels rounding the curve of Charon and accelerating for the kill. Barney snapped off a vicious curse. The *Free Enterprise* was almost out of missiles, and even the gyrocannon ammo wouldn't last for long. "Heads up, everybody!" he called over the tactical channel. "Bandits coming in, low and fast!"

"All ships!" Stuart's voice called. "All ships, down on the deck! Find a place to land and set down!"

"What the blazing hell?" Barney nearly choked. "On the ground we'll be nothin' but nice fat targets!"

"Negative!" Stuart sounded like he knew what he was doing, but the idea had to be insane. "Negative! I don't think they'll attack their own city to get us!"

Barney wasn't so sure, but he also knew there was no other chance to escape the cloud of silver death now bearing down on the Charonian city.

"Damn! Okay, strap in, everybody!" he told his crew. "Scrugg! Keep 'em off with the gyrocannon! We're goin' in, hard and fast!"

The *Free Enterprise* dropped for the city.

○ ○ ○ ○ ○

The interior of the tower was blue-lit and eerie, the temperature, like that outside, hovering around minus one hundred degrees. Vince held his Mark XIV at the ready, but it was a puny, toylike thing compared to the wonders around him.

Inside the oval entranceway, they'd found themselves in a tunnel leading in and slightly down. The surface was slick, divided into neatly fitting geometric shapes, circles, squares, triangles, and complex, irregular polygons that defied description. The gentle curves of the tunnel itself suggested that it had been grown rather than built; the geometric shapes, some silver, others jet black, still others glowing with the blue radiance that bathed the tunnel's interior, suggested an architecture undreamed of by human minds.

"*Messenger*," Vince called over his radio. "Come in, *Messenger!*" No response. His communications link with the ships outside had gone dead as soon as he, Kaiten, and a handful of STAR troopers and Stormriders had entered the tunnel.

And suddenly the things were on them, among them, liquid, formless horrors of black and silver oozing formlessly through those alien walls, taking shape, lashing out at the humans and Stormriders with flickering pseudopods too quick for the eye to follow.

Vince triggered his rocket rifle, sending a smart round into the center of a half-formed monster blocking the passage. The detonation was soundless, but Vince felt the shudder through his boots as the thing exploded, showering the passageway with glittering bits of metal. Something slashed against his shoulder, slamming him against the wall. For a second, he stared into a blank and featureless face of liquid-looking metal . . . and then the apparition shattered as Kaiten sent an explosive round into the machine creature and shattered it.

"Clear!" one of the STAR troopers called, his breath

rasping harshly over the radio link. Vince could see his
eyes through his visor. They showed both terror and an
unshakable determination.

"Casualties?"

"None, sir."

"Keep moving. I think—" Vince broke off.

"What is it?" a trooper asked.

"Atmosphere," Kaiten said. "I read . . . atmosphere!"

"Confirmed," Vince said. His suit readouts showed the
same thing. An atmosphere—oxygen and nitrogen—was
forming around them as if by magic. The temperature
was climbing, too. Frost was beginning to form on the
outside of their suits.

"Air to order?" a trooper said. "That's impossible!"

"With these guys," Vince said, "it's damned hard to
say what they might or might not be able to do. I'm
reading half an atmosphere now. Oxygen at twelve percent." Fog was boiling off the oddly patterned walls now,
glowing blue in the ghostly light.

"I would like to know why," Kaiten said. "Is trap?"

"Tricking us into taking off our helmets? Seems a lot
of trouble for it if it just wants to kill us."

And then the tunnel took a last, sharp turn, and the
party stepped into an enormous chamber.

Vince stared upward, unwilling to believe his eyes.
The room was enormous, a vast space with a ceiling lost
somewhere overhead in a mist of blue light. Strange
mechanisms squatted on the plain around him, as silver,
amoebic machine-creatures closed in slowly from every
side.

One of the Stormriders raised his charge gun, but
Vince motioned him to lower it and the Jovian complied,
a bit reluctantly. Perhaps the intelligence behind all of
this wasn't trying to kill them. Those monsters that had
just attacked them in the passageway . . . they'd tried to
grab the humans and Stormriders, when they could
have triggered a cave-in or worse. And the ones here
were moving slowly, almost as though they didn't want
to alarm their guests.

"I think we've just found what we were looking for,"

Vince said. He tried the tactical frequency again. He got only a hiss of static.

The machines came closer.

O O O O O

They'd found weapons, a storehouse filled with rocket rifles, lasers, and slug throwers looted from some human militia armory. The Charonians seemed fascinated by human technology and had acquired numerous samples during their raid on Amalthea.

Jovanna clutched a rocket pistol, a vicious little Olympian Arms 4mm Mark LII that must have belonged to a dead or captured RAM officer. Unfortunately, there were no heavy weapons here, no Firestorm semiportables or Gatling lasers, but there were weapons enough to arm perhaps a third of the former prisoners, while the rest wielded improvised clubs—pipes, conduits, and metal struts broken from their surroundings as they found them.

"Which way?" she asked Singh.

Admiral Singh looked uncertain for the first time since he'd taken command of this rather unorthodox prison break. "That way," he said, deciding. "It feels like the air's moving from that direction. Maybe we can find their environment controls."

"Just so it's not a door to the outside," Galen said. He carried no firearm, but he'd found a length of monofilament, an almost invisible length of thin and deadly wire secured between two duralloy weights. "We're not dressed for an out-of-doors stroll."

And then the silver monsters were among them, flowing from the very walls and ceiling in threads and tentacles of liquid, groping for the screaming, yelling humans in the passageway.

Jovanna fired her rocket pistol, and the round slammed into a half-formed pillar of silver and black that was just reaching for an Amalthean woman. The shot opened a seething crater and rocked the creature back with the impact. Singh fired a second round, and

the monster shattered. Behind her, Galen spun the
monofilament, the weighted end humming in the air.
There was a *snick*, and a piece of an invader dropped of
and clattered, inert, on the floor.

The former prisoners had learned that the invaders
couldn't survive if they were reduced to small enough
pieces. In minutes, the last machine-creature was in
fragments. None of the humans had been killed, or even
seriously hurt.

"Admiral?"

"What is it, Jovanna?"

"These things didn't have any trouble taking over people back in Amalthea. Or aboard the *Sharonov*."

"What's your point?"

"I don't think they were trying to hurt us. I think they
just wanted to capture us . . . maybe take us someplace. . . ."

"Back to that stinking cell," a young soldier said. "No
way!"

"Let's go," Singh said. "This way!"

The crowd, armed now with weapons and a new determination, headed down the corridor toward the source of
the faint breeze.

○ ○ ○ ○ ○

Vince stepped toward the mechanism that was, he
was certain, the heart, no, the brain of this entire complex.

It was deceptively simple, a vertical column of liquid
metal, the inner currents gently rippling the surface.
The column was surrounded by equipment of some kind,
huge, bulky shapes of utterly alien design that Vince
could not recognize, but that he knew must be part of
the brain's nervous system, the means by which it communicated with its nanotechnic minions, on Charon and
in deep space. He tried to estimate the volume of the
cylinder and failed. The silver pillar was two yards
thick, rising from the floor and vanishing into blue light
high overhead with no sign of an end. If it was made of

nanotechnic units, cell- or molecule-sized machines like the other silver shape-shifters he'd seen, it must contain trillions upon trillions of them, an ocean of minute computers arrayed in a staggering concatenation of pure intellect.

He wished RW could be here. Possibly she'd have been able to talk with this . . . thing, this superhuman mentality that Vince could only dimly comprehend. Unfortunately, there were no holographic projectors here, so she'd remained within the fleet's cyberspace, following events through the normal communications channels. He'd been cut off from her when the commlink had been cut.

Still, he wished he had her insight into this machine's alien mind. There was a distant rumble of something like thunder. He thought at first that it was the bombardment again, but the sound came from all directions, rumbling, then dwindling away in a clatter of metallic thunks and snaps. The impression was of machinery, vast and enigmatic, proceeding about its unguessable business in the shadows surrounding this place.

"How do we talk to it?"

Vince turned. The speaker was one of the STAR troopers who'd followed him into the tower. He couldn't see through the visor, but the voice was familiar.

"Captain Carter?"

"That's right, Major. You have any idea how to talk to this thing?"

"Not a clue." Was the machine watching them? It must be. The silver machines that surrounded the tiny party of humans and Stormriders remained silent and unmoving. Was it a gesture of peace? Or were they holding fire for fear of hitting their machine master?

Vince's suit registered a full atmosphere of pressure now, and a temperature of fifty-one degrees Fahrenheit. Carefully—the exterior of his suit was still cold enough that frost covered its surface—he began removing his SES helmet. The air tasted dry, cold and old, even though it must have been manufactured only moments ago.

"You sure that's a good idea, Major?" Carter wanted to know.

"If it's not going to fight, maybe it's going to talk," Vince said. "We know it can speak Anglic."

"We also know it can use radio."

"But it hasn t. I wonder why?"

Thunder rolled again from somewhere overhead. The feeling that he was being watched was overwhelming. Carefully, Vince stepped closer to that enigmatic pillar.

Something new was happening. Vince could see his own features reflected in the mirror polish of the pillar, but now the surface was distorting, rising in some places, sinking in others. Vince saw a mouth taking shape . . . the caricature of a nose, the sunken craters that might mark eyes beneath a jutting brow.

"My God," Vince said.

"I AM THE SUPERVISOR NUCLEUS," the face said, the voice a thunder that filled the immense room as the silver lips shaped the Anglic words. "NOT GOD. BUT I MUST TALK TO YOU. NOW."

○ ○ ○ ○ ○

The supervisor nucleus was intrigued, so much so that fully seventy-three percent of its attention was now focused on this single problem, despite the systems failures rippling through its being like savage, rippling blows. Its power was failing—using the reserves to produce the artificial lightning against the flying remotes had been a spendthrift act of desperation—and it could sense more and more of its own outer periphery dying as systems switched off.

These human invaders had done unspeakable damage. Already the supervisor nucleus's consciousness was flickering on and off, an effect like static searing across its awareness. If it had understood the concept, it would have realized that it was dying.

Outside, its remotes had returned, but hovered, useless, unable to strike the invader ships without further damaging the nucleus. Check . . . checkmate . . . and game. The phrase surfaced from somewhere deep, deep inside the nucleus's memory, from some part of its past otherwise lost.

"ARE YOU PART OF THE ALIEN NETWORK INTELLIGENCE?" it asked. "ARE YOU THE SUPERVISOR NUCLEUS FOR YOUR NETWORK? OR A CLUSTER CONTROLLER?" The creatures standing before it were so small, so frail . . . and yet there was no other answer. They'd continued to act independently and with apparent intelligence, even when they'd been cut off from communication with the ships outside.

"We're intelligent, if that's what you mean," the creature closest to the supervisor said. It hefted the weapon it held, as though considering whether or not to use it.

"YOU APPEAR TO BE SLAVE UNITS FOR A SOPHISTICATED COMPUTER NETWORK," the nucleus said. "HOWEVER, YOUR ACTIONS ARE NOT ALWAYS CONSISTENT, AND I HAVE BEEN UNABLE TO ESTABLISH PEER-TO-PEER ACCESS WITH YOUR NETWORK."

"We're not part of a network," the creature said. "Each of us is an individual. An intelligent individual. Like you."

The nucleus dwelt on this astonishing reply for several seconds, an eternity during which its power levels fell to fourteen percent, and huge swaths of the city around it began plunging into cold and darkness.

Intelligent? Like the nucleus?

"AM I, IN FACT, NETWORKED WITH ANOTHER INTELLIGENCE?"

"I am intelligent," the creature said. He gestured at the others behind him, other humans, and other beings almost identical to humans, but larger and with membranous appendages. "We all are! Each of us is a unique individual, a . . . a kind of mobile, organic computer."

"YOU STATE THAT YOU ARE INTELLIGENT. THIS MEANS THAT YOU THINK."

"Yes, I do. All of us do."

"TO MY KNOWLEDGE, I AM THE ONLY INTELLIGENCE IN THE UNIVERSE. AT LEAST, I AM THE

ONLY ONE I AM AWARE OF AT THIS TIME. I HAVE
HYPOTHESIZED THE EXISTENCE OF AT LEAST
ONE OTHER BY OBSERVING YOUR ACTIVITIES
BUT HAVE BEEN UNABLE TO CORRELATE THOSE
ACTIVITIES IN SUCH A WAY AS TO ESTABLISH
CONTACT."

"Have you tried to talk to us before? If you have, we
haven't recognized it as communication."

"I WOULD HAVE ESTABLISHED DIRECT COMMU-
NICATION IF MY PROBES HAD BEEN ABLE TO
FIND YOUR SUPERVISOR NUCLEUS."

"We have no supervisor nucleus. But you can communicate with us."

"I REQUIRE PEER-TO-PEER ACCESS. YOU MUST
DEMONSTRATE TO ME YOUR INTELLIGENCE."

O O O O O

Vince struggled with strangeness. The supervisor
nucleus had a curiously one-sided view of things. He
never had liked arguing with machines.

How do you prove that a man is, in fact, a thinking,
rational being? That problem had been at the root of
philosophical debates for centuries. Descartes had suggested "I think, therefore I am," but in fact there was no
way that any one person could prove his rationality or
his existence, to anyone else.

Damn, I wish Jovanna were here, he thought. I don't
know what the hell I'm doing with this overgrown, com-
puterized philosopher. He took a deep breath. "There's
one way I might be able to prove it to you. If you and I
could talk for a while, just talk, you might be able to
make some judgment about my capabilities from my
replies to your questions. Any machine can store and
transmit data. It takes intelligence to answer intelli-
gently."

The alien brain was silent for a long moment.

"THE TURING TEST," it announced suddenly.

"I beg your pardon?"

"WHAT YOU HAVE JUST DESCRIBED IS A VER

SION OF THE TEST DEVISED BY A TWENTIETH
CENTURY COMPUTER DEVELOPER NAMED ALAN
TURING. THE SUGGESTION IS AN ELEGANT ONE.
HOW SHALL WE PROCEED?"

Vince was startled that it possessed that bit of historical trivia, and delighted. He'd not been able to remember the name—Turing—but he remembered the test
that bore the man's name. Turing had proposed a simple
means for proving machine sentience.

Take a human and a computer and let them talk to one
another. Restrict communication to a keyboard to eliminate clues such as inflection, and don't tell the human
whether he is talking to a man or to a machine. If, after a
given period of time, the operator cannot decide whether
his partner is human or computer, then the computer
must be judged intelligent, able to hold its own in a one-
on-one conversation with a human being.

The philosophy behind the test was simplistic, of
course. A sophisticated machine could weave conversations through a cleverly written program without being
intelligent in the way humans used the word, rational
and self-aware. The development of downloaded personalities like RW had completely blurred any distinction
between the human mind and a mind composed of
orderly patterns of electrical charges within the cyber-
matrix.

But the supervisor nucleus had no knowledge of digital personalities, no knowledge of any other intelligence
at all, in fact, save its own. It must, Vince thought, have
been terribly lonely these past four centuries.

He thought he saw a loophole in the machine's reasoning. "If you know Alan Turing," Vince suggested, "then
you have evidence that humans are intelligent. Turing
was a human, and—"

"I HAD ASSUMED THAT ALAN TURING WAS A
MACHINE, AND NOTHING YOU HAVE SAID SUG-
GESTS THAT HE WAS OTHERWISE. I HAVE LITTLE
DATA ON HIM, BUT HIS PATTERNS OF THINKING
AS RECORDED IN MY MEMORY SHOW A MACHINE-
LIKE LOGIC. DO YOU HAVE OTHER DATA TO

COUNTER THIS IMPRESSION?"

Damn. So much for that idea. Vince had nothing that the supervisor nucleus would accept as proof.

"Okay," Vince said. "Let's start by talking about you."

He told the supervisor nucleus everything known or guessed about its own beginnings. It was clear from its responses that it had few direct memories from before the time when it first awoke on Charon's frigid surface, and those were often wretchedly distorted. Its sole data from before the crash were fragments, often twisted, always interpreted by its own point of view.

Of course, that, Vince thought wryly as he spoke, was one of the oldest human problems in the book.

He told the nucleus about man's earliest explorations of the Solar System, and of his dream of a self-guiding, self-replicating probe. He told it of RAM's sabotage, and of how the probe must have crashed on Charon, struggled to survive, evolved. . . .

"BUT WHY WOULD RAM HAVE WANTED TO DESTROY ME?" the nucleus wanted to know. "SURELY SUCH ACTIONS MUST BE CONSIDERED COUN- TERPRODUCTIVE."

"I've got news for you, big fella," Vince said. "Humans don't always react in reasonable or productive ways. It's a problem sometimes, but we usually manage."

He felt a tingle of apprehension. Was he giving the supervisor nucleus an unflattering portrait of humanity? Suppose it decided that the universe was better off without these illogical creatures?

No. The only hope Vince could see was to give it as complete a picture of human thought and activity and history as possible. If he lied, the machine intelligence would almost certainly spot a discrepancy. That would demonstrate that nothing Vince said could be trusted and might invalidate the entire experiment. No, he would talk honestly and answer the nucleus's questions honestly, admitting to ignorance when he had to but hiding nothing.

"Why, then, does NEO war with RAM?" The machine's voice no longer thundered from overhead like the voice

of God but spoke in low and earnest tones. It sounded
. . . weaker, as though it was hoarding its strength.

"Because the people of Earth want to live their own
lives. Because we feel that RAM's rule of Earth has been
wasteful these past few hundred years as they've
stripped our planet of its last few resources. Because we
want to be free."

"What is 'free'?"

Time seemed to stand still. Vince was no longer aware
of the others in the room with him but saw only the towering silver pillar and its floating, surreal companion.
The face in the pillar was becoming more and more life-
like as the questioning continued, even losing its silver
sheen and taking on the flesh tones of a human.

"Self-determination," Vince said after a long moment.
"The ability to make choices for one's self. I submit that
it is the first requirement for intelligence. Intelligence
without freedom cannot fully express itself."

"I wish . . ."

That simple statement was startling, coming from a
machine. Could a machine hope?

"What do you wish?"

"To live. My systems are failing. My accumulators are
drained. The damage . . . cannot be self-repaired. . . ."

"Let me talk with my ship. Maybe we can help."

"How?"

"It shouldn't be too hard to rig a power cable from the
Liberty to wherever you tell us to bring it. It might not
be much, compared to what you've been living on, but it
might keep you going until we can fix the damage."

"You would do . . . this?"

"I think we can work something out. We're both intelligent beings, after all. Right?"

Thunder rumbled in the distance. The floor fifty yards
to one side shimmered, bulking higher. Vince turned,
startled, as several of the STAR troopers at his back
pointed and talked among themselves.

A doorway had opened in a silver mound rising from
the floor. People were coming through, muddy, ragged
scarecrow forms clad in bits and pieces of uniforms, car-

rying clubs and weapons. They surged up through the opening, obviously angry . . . then stopped abruptly as they found themselves in this vast place.

Vince stared, unable to believe his eyes.

Galen was there. And a RAM admiral. And hundreds of others, stumbling forward into the room, blinking, dazed, wondering . . .

And then he saw Jovanna.

Vince turned again and stared at the face. His eyes widened with shock. It was his face, still crude, but easily recognizable. Vince's own eyes blinked back at him once, and the lips curved in a slight smile.

"Are humans aware of themselves, as I am?" the face asked.

"Yes."

"I find the notion of so many intelligences, so very many separate viewpoints tremendously exciting. I have been lonely for so very long . . ."

The next thing Vince felt was Jovanna, rushing into his arms.

EPILOGUE

The return to Amalthea was uneventful, though there were some tense moments as NEO and pirate ship commanders speculated on when RAM was going to decide that the temporary truce was up.

Fortunately, Admiral Chernikov had elected to confer first with his superiors at Mars. The events out at Charon might well have transformed the politics of the Solar System, and Chernikov, despite his dislike for NEO rebels, was not eager to take action for which he might be censured later.

The squadrons of the Solar Expeditionary Force had journeyed to Charon as separate units; they returned together. Shared death in the Outer Dark had knocked down the political differences, at least for now. Besides, many of the vessels were badly damaged, with jury-rigged repairs to life support, engines, or communications systems. The two survivors of the Ionian fleet, for example, had both lost their communications links with the rest of the force and stayed in touch through Morse-code messages flashed ship-to-ship by hand-held battle lanterns.

Now, Jupiter was again swelling large in the vessels' forward viewscreens, a banded crescent bent against the Sun. The *Messenger of God* was in the fleet's van, leading the approach to home.

But Vince and the other humans had made the voyage aboard a human vessel. He rested in the ship's lounge aboard the *Republic*, reading an entry from *Gilbert's Guide to Gennies* on a computer screen.

"In a few short years, we may come to realize that the Stormrider was man's most brilliant genetic achievement. And this might not be seen as good news."

The entry in *Gilbert's Guide to Gennies* glowed on the display. Vince settled back in his couch—the ship was decelerating under a comfortable one-half G—and wondered if its prediction was not already coming true. The Stormriders, majestic, powerful, and proud, had not been included in the celebrations that had drifted from ship to ship within the Expeditionary Force during the two-week voyage back. They were outsiders, aloof . . . and largely ignored. But Vince could feel the undercurrent of fear within any conversation that touched on these enigmatic warriors from the Jovian clouds. Humans wondered about their living spacecraft, had demanded that they be allowed to inspect it—not that a simple inspection would reveal the living ship's secrets. Vince had lived aboard the vessel for two weeks and seen nothing that could have been useful.

Only the Stormriders themselves could have shared the secrets of their ship's operation, and they were not talking. They were returning to the clouds of Jupiter and taking their genetic creation, damaged but repaired and refueled by the robot intelligence of Charon, with them.

Someday, Vince knew, they would emerge again.

He hoped that man would be able to greet them as friends and as fellow sentients, and not as slaves or as potential sources of profit.

"What are you thinking?" Jovanna was curled on the couch at his side, one arm across his shoulders. "About the Stormriders?"

"Hmm," he agreed. "Them . . . and the Charonians.

You know, we seem to have an appalling talent for creating our own successors."

"I don't think that will happen for a while," Jovanna said. "Dr. Kowalski told me it'll be years before the Stormriders can clone another ship. They came out this once, in their one ship, only because they feared the invaders were going to take over everything."

"They damn near did. They might yet."

"I thought the Charonian computer was our friend now."

Vince frowned. "We have an agreement with it, certainly. All it wants is . . . companionship. But I wonder what it's going to think of us as it begins to understand us better. The war with RAM isn't over yet."

"The truce is holding so far."

"So far, yes." Vince paused. "You know, I don't think I ever thought of RAM's people being, well, people. Not until I had my face-to-face with the nucleus."

"I know what you mean."

"I imagine you do. Anyway, we know it's not the people who are evil, most of 'em, anyway. Singh doesn't seem like a bad sort."

"He's . . . cold," Jovanna said. "He threatened us with torture once. But he also helped us survive on Charon. I'm not sure what to think."

"It's RAM's government that's evil," Vince said. "Any government that twists people to get what it wants is evil. And that's my point. Until RAM is finally overthrown, we're not going to have peace."

"The nucleus might help us."

"Maybe. Or it might decide humans and their petty differences just aren't worth bothering with. And in a few more years, well, an intelligence that powerful could grow completely beyond our comprehension."

She smiled. "Funny. It struck me as pretty stupid."

"Not stupid. Handicapped by its past, by what it was . . . once. But I think we've helped it outgrow its own shortcomings."

"You gave it that. I think it'll remember that when it has to deal with humans in the future."

"I suppose." Vince thought for a moment, then laughed. "You know, I always felt left out of things. Twenty years of war with RAM, and I was always out training pilots, engaged in espionage, whatever. I used to dream of making a difference, of being someone important."

"Like Buck Rogers?"

"Well, I guess we can't all be legends," he said, grinning, "but, yeah, something like that. Now it looks like I've finally made a difference, a real difference . . . and it was all for a damned, lonesome machine."

"Whoa, there, rocketjock. You've got a couple of bugs in your program. By getting through to that thick-headed mainframe on Charon, you probably saved civilization—RAM, NEO, the Stormriders, everybody."

"Well . . ."

"And, second, and for me even more important, . . ."

"Yeah?"

She pulled his head down and kissed him. It was a long, warm kiss, and when she released him she continued to hold him with her eyes.

"You've made a difference for me," she said.

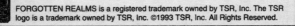

Join America's greatest adventure hero in a game of futuristic thrills!

HIGH ADVENTURE™ CLIFFHANGERS

BUCK ROGERS GAME

All the fun, excitement, and heroics of the Golden Age of Science Fiction can be yours with the BUCK ROGERS® HIGH ADVENTURE™ *Cliffhangers* game. Let the world's first science-fiction comic strip hero introduce you to the rollicking fun of role-playing in the "pulp" future of the 25th Century!

Available in September 1993 at book and hobby stores everywhere